ONCE OUR LIVES

*Life, Death, and Love in the
Middle Kingdom*

GUERNICA WORLD EDITIONS 60

ONCE OUR LIVES

*Life, Death, and Love in the
Middle Kingdom*

QIN SUN STUBIS

GUERNICA
World
EDITIONS

TORONTO—CHICAGO—BUFFALO—LANCASTER (U.K.)
2023

Guernica Editions Founder: Antonio D'Alfonso

Michael Mirolla, general editor
Sonia Di Placido, editor
Cover design: Allen Jomoc Jr.
Interior design: Jill Ronsley, suneditwrite.com

Guernica Editions Inc.
287 Templemead Drive, Hamilton (ON), Canada L8W 2W4
2250 Military Road, Tonawanda, N.Y. 14150-6000 U.S.A.
www.guernicaeditions.com

Distributors:
Independent Publishers Group (IPG)
600 North Pulaski Road, Chicago IL 60624
University of Toronto Press Distribution (UTP)
5201 Dufferin Street, Toronto (ON), Canada M3H 5T8
Gazelle Book Services, White Cross Mills
High Town, Lancaster LA1 4XS U.K.

First edition.
Printed in Canada.

Legal Deposit—First Quarter
Library of Congress Catalog Card Number: 2022949661
Library and Archives Canada Cataloguing in Publication
Title: Once our lives : life, death, and love in the middle kingdom / Qin Sun Stubis.
Names: Stubis, Qin Sun, author.
Series: Guernica world editions ; 60.
Description: Series statement: Guernica world editions ; 60
Identifiers: Canadiana (print) 20220469784 | Canadiana (ebook)
20220469865 | ISBN 9781771837965 (softcover) | ISBN 9781771837972 (EPUB)
Subjects: LCSH: Stubis, Qin Sun. | LCSH: Chinese American authors—21st
century—Biography. | LCSH: Women—China—Biography. | LCSH:
Families—China. | LCSH: Intergenerational relations—China. | LCGFT:
Autobiographies.
Classification: LCC PR6037.T917 Z46 2023 | DDC 818/.6—dc23

To my husband, Mark,
my beacon and my sunshine

To my children,
Keaton and Halley

From memory
Through tears
With love

As far as I know, everything in this book is true. The stories, as hard to believe as some of them may be, happened to me personally or were told to me by the people who lived through them. Most of what follows was shared privately, sometimes confidentially, often late at night, in bed, and in hushed whispers. By hearing these accounts repeated over the years, as family histories often are, I became convinced that the stories are real, or at least as real to their now long-silent witnesses as human beings are capable of ascertaining. Although I was far too young at the time to fully take on the roles asked of me, I became the friend, confidante, and small ally of all those who told me these tales, especially my mother. It is to her, my strength and true inspiration, that this book is dedicated.

INDEX OF CHARACTERS AND
NOTES ON THE EVENTS

The Sun Family

Ya Zhen: The matriarch of the Sun family whose simple act of generosity as a young woman appeared to have changed her fate and the fate of generations to come

An Chu: Ya Zhen's first-born son whose life and destiny she believed were destroyed before birth

Xin Feng: An Chu's youngest sister, who denounced him during the Cultural Revolution

Ping: An Chu and his wife Yan's first daughter, born in an ancient desert city along the old Silk Road during The Great Chinese Famine, which killed more than 30 million people

Qin: An Chu and Yan's second daughter, born in a splintery shack in a Shanghai shantytown

Min: An Chu and Yan's third daughter, a beautiful and intelligent girl, who, even as a toddler realized the disappointment of the Sun family for having all girls and swore to restore the family's honor by having a boy

Wen: An Chu and Yan's fourth and last daughter, who narrowly escaped the Neighborhood Family Planning Committee and was named in honor of the Cultural Revolution

The Gu Family

Yan (a.k.a. *Ai Zhu* and *Chon Mei)*: A woman with three identities who was born into a well-off family in a fishing village near Ningbo and, as her fortunes plummeted, helped her family survive a series of disasters from man-made, natural, and what appeared to be supernatural causes

Arh Chin: Yan's birth father, a first mate on an ocean-going freighter, who lived by the sea, roamed the sea, and became part of the sea

Ho De: Yan's adoptive father, a successful Shanghai businessman who loved Western culture and ideals but was ultimately—and tragically—bound by his conservative Chinese beliefs

Jin Lai: Yan's cruel adoptive mother and cousin of Yan's birth mother

Chon Gao: Yan's "brother," related to her not by birth but by Fate's whimsical hand in an opium den

Others

The Beggar: A mysterious visitor who some believed to be a wandering spirit

A Fortune Teller: Bearer of an ominous prophecy that appeared to come true

Yue Hua: An Chu's first love

Hui Jing: Yan's friend and sister actress at the Tong Yi Performing Arts Society

Pei: An Chu's ambitious best friend in the shantytown

Lao Ma: The kindly old housekeeper at Ho De's ancestral home who nursed Yan back to health after an ill-fated ocean voyage gone dangerously wrong

Arh Bun: A desperate laborer in Zhang Ye City in China's "Wild West"

Historical & Family Timeline

221 BC	Era of Imperial China begins
1839–1842	First Opium War
1856–1860	Second Opium War
1904	Ho De is born
1910	Jing Chuan is born
1912	Era of Imperial China ends; Republic of China founded by Sun Yat-sen
1912	Jin Lai is born
1914	Ya Zhen is born
1921	Chinese Communist Party secretly founded in Shanghai
1930s	Shanghai blooms and becomes known as the "Paris of the East"
1932	Yan is born near Ningbo
1934	A mysterious beggar appears at the Sun Family's residence in Shaoxing. Soon after, An Chu is born
1937	Start of Second Sino-Japanese War; the Sun family factory is bombed and destroyed
1939	With the Sun fortune destroyed, An Chu's family moves to Shanghai and he is forced into child labor
1941–1945	The Pacific War during which Arh Chin perishes
1945	Sino-Japanese War ends

1946–1949	Chinese Civil War between the Nationalists and Communists
1949	Founding of the People's Republic of China by Mao Zedong
1950	Yan Gu joins Tong Yi Performing Arts Society
1951	Jin Lai succumbs to TB
1957	An Chu and Yan answer the government's call and join thousands of other young people to resettle and build a prosperous new frontier along the old Silk Road
1958–1962	The Great Leap Forward and The Great Chinese Famine
1958	Ping is born in the ancient desert town of Zhang Ye, home to Marco Polo and Kublai Khan
1960	Qin is born in the squalor of a Shanghai shantytown
1962	Min is born and joins her sisters in the shantytown
1966	The Cultural Revolution begins
1966	Wen is born in Shanghai's French Quarter
1968–1975	An Chu is detained for "crimes" against the Cultural Revolution
1976	End of the Cultural Revolution
1982–1989	An Chu imprisoned for seven years for "crimes" *in support of* the Cultural Revolution
1989	Qin is the first of three of her parents' "four golden phoenixes" to leave China in pursuit of a better life
1999	Ya Zhen and An Chu's fates converge for the last time as the family prophecy seems to come true

A Family Myth

EVERYONE SAYS MY FATHER'S life was ruined before he was born.

When I was a little girl, my grandmother Ya Zhen used to tell me one particular story about my father every time I visited her. Soon, I memorized every word of it but without really understanding what it meant. I used to wonder if she always repeated it so she wouldn't have to talk to me. My grandmother never liked girls. As far as she was concerned, only boys had any value, and my father should have had sons instead of four worthless daughters.

I can still see myself as a little girl, walking the five long blocks to her apartment. Before I could ever finish saying "Happy Birthday, Grandmother" or "Happy New Year, Grandmother," the way my mother taught me, she interrupted and made me sit down to hear her story—the story about herself, my father, and the old beggar.

"Listen and remember," she said. "Your father would have had a good life if that beggar did not come to my door. I was too young and stupid to see bad luck coming. It's too late to change anything now, but you can learn from my fate."

When she was in a mean mood, she would say, "I bet you that beggar brought all you girls to our family," meaning me and my three sisters.

Sure, blame the beggar for everything. You always do. I sat and listened until she was done. I doubted her fantastical story and

1

couldn't wait to get out of there. But on my way back home, I always turned around a couple of times to make sure no beggar was following me.

When I grew older, I went to my father and asked if Grandmother's story was true. My father laughed. "Do you believe in spirits and ghosts? Do you think dead people can walk around, talk to you, and control you? Your grandmother is old-fashioned. She believes in a lot of strange things."

I felt silly.

Now that my father is gone and I am a grown woman, I wish I had asked him more questions. Whenever I have a painful longing to see him again, I try to replay his life in my head, seeing him the way I knew him when I was growing up. As my mind wanders back, I am startled to see the shadow of my grandmother's story creeping like a stubborn vine over my father's path as if it contains some dark truth. Then, it seems that a spell had indeed been cast over his life. I find myself haunted by the story that I have been told so many times, a story that happened so long ago when my grandmother Ya Zhen was just nineteen years old.

———

Tap. Tap. Tap. The knocking at the front door was so faint that it could have been the sea breeze gently rocking it back and forth in its thick wooden frame. But Ya Zhen knew someone was outside waiting for her. She went to the kitchen and fetched a big bowl in which she had carefully hidden some delicious fried fish, meat, and vegetables under a generous mountain of yesterday's leftover rice. Holding the bowl with one hand and her swollen belly with the other, she slowly made her way to the front door.

Of course, he was there. The old beggar nodded silently, shuffled his rag-covered feet, and stared greedily at the rice bowl, searching for any traces of the treasures buried underneath. His nostrils flared, sucking in every faint scent escaping from the bowl. In those hard times, amid foreign wars and the Great Depression, beggars were usually given some stale rice and a sympathetic look. People could not afford to give away what they did not have enough of themselves, but Ya Zhen had married into a wealthy family, and food was plentiful.

She felt a special attachment to this beggar whose daily visits had started a week before. For some reason she could not explain, she waited for his gentle knock and eager eyes and fed him herself instead of ordering the servants to take care of the matter.

Who was he? Where was he from? Where did he live? Ya Zhen did not know and never asked. But she knew he could starve to death if she did not feed him, and she pitied him. She was feeling unusually sensitive these days. Her first baby was coming, and she was scared. Women often died during childbirth in remote sea villages such as hers where doctors did not exist. Somehow, in her Buddhist mind, keeping this old man alive made her feel more secure, as if she was ensuring the future for herself and her baby.

A few weeks before, the village fortune teller had been summoned to the house and brought both good and bad news about her baby. As big and round as a banquet table, she rolled into the sitting room with a gigantic smile and a hungry-looking mouth full of shiny gold teeth.

"Show me your daughter-in-law's birth records," she said importantly, with half-closed eyes, ready to do business.

Ya Zhen's mother-in-law bowed as she presented her with a package wrapped in red satin.

The fortune teller's pudgy fingers fumbled with the soft, slippery fabric before managing to open the packet. Her eager eyes fixed instantly on the stack of silver tucked discreetly inside. She grabbed the coins, sized up the amount, and dropped them into her pocket before picking up the documents and studying them with intense concentration.

"Good, good," she kept on repeating as she nodded her round head. Her golden earrings danced with her words.

Then, she frowned, opened her eyes and mouth wide, wider, and even wider, as if she couldn't believe what she saw. "No, not good, not good at all ..."

She narrowed her eyes and mouth until they were shut tightly. She swayed slowly back and forth and, for a moment, looked as if she were in a trance. Her face showed the sufferings of a tortured soul.

Anxiety filled the room. The silence became unbearable as everyone waited nervously for her imminent, prophetic speech.

"First, the good news," she finally said. "Your daughter-in-law is very fertile and will have many grandchildren for you."

Everyone sighed with relief.

"But she is a Tiger, and it is not good to have her first baby in a Dog year. Her life is too strong, and the baby could have a hard time coming out, which can hurt the mother, or the baby, or both." Her eyes darted around her audience as she slowed her words almost to a halt, pleased to see the tension building up in the room.

"Don't worry. I can do something ... a lot, in fact, to change that. Just add another twenty pieces of silver." Her voice was firm, and her palm was open.

"Good. Now you shouldn't worry anymore. I'll take care of it," she said cheerfully as she deposited the silver into her pocket.

"The baby will be ... will be ... will be a boy, a boy! I can feel it. It's a boy!" Her face was radiant. "Oh, he is lovely! He is sensitive, caring, and hardworking. He is a Dog, you know, a lucky Dog, a boy with a lot of luck. As a matter of fact, I've never seen a baby with so much luck. That's why he will end up in your family. Watch out, though! His luck doesn't have depth. A lucky soul is always looking for opportunities. A dog can be jumpy, curious, and led away easily, so his luck can change."

The fortune teller didn't take away Ya Zhen's worries. She only added more, but the in-laws seemed to be pleased by her prophecy: A boy, a grandson, a first-born grandson!

Ya Zhen felt her baby's strong kicks inside her and worried about her own fate as she took the empty bowl back from the beggar. He wiped his greasy face on his torn sleeves and gave out a loud, satisfied burp. She stared at him. He smiled at her. His smile reminded her of a little boy's—bright, innocent, satisfied, and grateful. She felt surprised by her maternal instincts, brought out by this total stranger, a vulnerable beggar whose very life now depended on her. She started to say something to him but stopped. His smile had disappeared, leaving him with a strange, blank face. Her eyes met his, and she was startled by what she saw: For a moment, the beggar's eyes seemed like a pair of deep, dark tunnels, taking her to an unknown world. He put his hand on her belly and muttered, "He is coming. He is coming," before turning and walking away.

Ya Zhen stood watching him until he shrank to a dot in the distance. *When tomorrow comes, I hope I will be here to feed him*, she thought.

That night she gave birth, an easy birth, to a healthy baby boy whom the family named An Chu Sun. My father.

The day after she had the baby, Ya Zhen broke a cultural taboo: Instead of staying in bed for a whole month, as required by tradition, she got up, for she was eager to feed her beggar. As usual, she prepared him a special feast and waited. She went to the door several times at the slightest noise. But he was not there. He never came back. Not the next day. Not the day after. Not ever.

Sometimes, as she nursed her baby, she pondered her seven encounters with the beggar. One day, as she examined her own child, she was startled to see a familiar twinkle in her baby's eyes. She suddenly realized that she knew all along that the beggar was a wandering spirit—a *youhuen*—searching for a home. And now, that beggar's spirit was in her son!

An Chu was a first son, and first grandson, born into a prosperous family, so his birth brought joy, glory, admiration, praise, gifts, and feasts. But, even at the celebration banquet, held under a silver moon with hundreds of colorful paper lanterns, tables filled with roast ducks and suckling pigs, sea cucumbers as dark as the earth, bowls of fresh peanuts, flying firecrackers and thick stacks of lucky paper money in red envelopes, red-faced uncles shouting loudly over drinking games, and fat-faced aunts gabbling and predicting glorious things for the newest heir to the Sun name, Ya Zhen worried about her son's life path, for a beggar's existence was destined to be a struggle against poverty, hardship, and all sorts of unpredictable dark forces ...

Later in life, when the Japanese burned her family's factory, civil war destroyed the Sun fortune, and she and her son were plunged into poverty, Ya Zhen silently saw all these events as signs confirming the treacherous path of the beggar's life An Chu had yet to walk. She prayed that, one day, all the good luck the fortune teller had predicted for her boy would shield him and break the beggar's spell.

PART I

A TALE OF TWO FAMILIES

(Shanghai, 1940s to the 1950s)

Chapter I

CHARCOAL SLAVES

THE WINTER OF 1942 was cold. Eight-year-old An Chu shivered as he watched the city's usually fashionable ladies hurrying down the streets, buried under bulky fur coats, hats, and scarves to protect themselves against the Siberian wind. Old men shielded their reddened faces, little icicles clinging to their mustaches. Coolies pulled down the yellow oil-cloth curtains of their rickshaw cabins to protect their passengers. Most children were hiding inside their warm homes. But not An Chu. With only rags on his back and bare feet, he dashed through the streets of Shanghai behind a rickety wooden wheelbarrow, delivering charcoal. "Excuse me, Madam! Sorry, Mister!" he shouted as he steered his cart through crowds of pedestrians. Most people were kind enough to move out of his way. Some yelled at him after being brushed against. Some spat in his face or kicked his bony behind with their patent leather shoes. Policemen in black uniforms often drove him away with their whips.

"Get lost! Stop blocking traffic!"

"Get out of my way, you little black devil!"

"Be careful, you filthy bastard! You couldn't afford to buy me a new coat, even if you sold your mother!"

It was a time before gas stoves became popular in Shanghai. Charcoal and rice occupied equal importance in everyone's daily life, and you could find more charcoal delivery boys than milkmen out on the streets. They were poor and dirty, and people called them *xiao hei guei* ("little black devils").

An Chu learned never to argue with anyone on the street. He needed to make as many deliveries as possible and get home before his mother started to worry. He knew his mother didn't want him to become a delivery boy at such a young age, but she had no choice. His uncle—his father's only brother—owned a charcoal store and decided everything for them.

For as long as he could remember, his father worked as a charcoal presser and his mother toiled as a housecleaner so they could live for free in the attic above the store. Instead of playing with toys, An Chu packed rows and rows of charcoal cakes onto racks and bagged charcoal nuggets. Once in a while, when work was slow, he sat atop a stack of coal crates, wiped his runny nose on his blackened sleeves and closed his eyes, letting a few gauzy, half-remembered images drift in front of him like dust motes in the afternoon light. He could hear the distant song of a golden canary and felt himself dancing in the arms of a beautiful lady. As she spun, her black, shoulder-length hair flew in the air and cascaded all around him. He shook the small, golden bells tied around his wrist and heard the tinkle of his mother's laughter. The memories were so faint and impossibly idyllic, it was as if they had all occurred in his dreams. Now, he was just a very poor boy and had to earn his keep.

"Your kids eat a lot of my rice," his uncle often said. "Of course they should work in my shop!"

Ya Zhen shook her head and swallowed her pride, for she had nowhere to take her family. Her husband, once a pampered, soft-spoken young man, had never learned to deal with the ruder, more practical aspects of life. Five years before, as the new mistress of a prosperous household, she would never have imagined him toiling in front of anything, let alone a charcoal machine. Now, that was all he did.

"I'm home!"

Ya Zhen heard An Chu's little feet beating against the wooden steps. Her poor baby was home. She could stop worrying about him now, stop making up stories in her head that he was hurt somewhere out there on the dark, wicked city streets. She had reason to worry about An Chu, for she often found bruises and gashes on him. "I fell down," he often said lightly as he avoided her inquisitive eyes. "It was an accident." But she always knew there was more to it.

The attic was cold with plenty of holes for the winter wind to squeeze through and spend the night with them. Other times of the year were no better. In the summer, the place was like a dumpling steamer. It was always too hot or too cold, but at least they had a home.

She scooped a ladle of porridge into a bowl just as An Chu appeared, black as a charcoal ball. He brought with him a gust of wind that almost put out the weak glow of the candle on the tabletop.

"Why didn't you wash downstairs?"

"I want to show you my new shoes, Mom," An Chu said gleefully. "A nice lady gave them to me. She said nobody should have bare feet in this weather."

"Did you thank her?"

"Yes, I did. Oh, it feels good to have shoes!" He couldn't stop looking at his feet, moving happily and freely in the worn-out loafers that were a few sizes too large.

"Come and look at my new shoes," An Chu called to his brother and sisters, but they showed little interest.

"I'm cold, Mommy. I want to go to bed," one of the girls complained and pulled Ya Zhen's apron, while her younger son sat on the floor, sneezing, and coughing as he made paper toys out of an old newspaper. Her youngest baby kept herself warm by crying.

Ya Zhen waited until An Chu slurped down his porridge and wiped his mouth with his sleeves. Then, she rounded up all her children, sent them to bed, and blew out the candle.

All the whining, crying, talking, sneezing, and coughing gradually came to a stop. The dark room gave quiet audience to the wind as it sang through the leaky window and a hundred knotholes. Under one large, old quilt, the children snuggled against each other, sheltered, for the time being, from the winter's cruelty. Ya Zhen took one more look into the dark room before she went downstairs to help her husband wrap up the day.

Life in the Sun household could have gone on like this forever, but, one day, An Chu got up with a bad stomachache.

"Why don't you eat your breakfast?" his mother asked as he pushed away his untouched bowl of porridge. "You should have something hot before you go out into the cold."

"I'm not hungry, Mom," he said. "My stomach doesn't want me to eat."

Ya Zhen shook her head as she took away the bowl.

His younger brother stared at the bowl with hopeful eyes. "Can I have An Chu's porridge, Mother?" he begged. "I'm still very hungry."

"Of course, you can," she said, passing along the bowl. "Hurry up, though. Your uncle wants you to pack fifty bags of charcoal balls by noon for a special order."

"I want more porridge, too, Mommy."

"Me, me, me ..." her two other little ones cried out, both holding out their empty bowls.

Ya Zhen scraped her pot hard, added a bit of hot water, and divided the burnt mush evenly between her eager, hungry children.

An Chu stumbled out onto the street, pushing his loaded cart. After a couple of deliveries, his stomach started to churn. His arms began to shake, and he had a hard time maneuvering the cart. *What happened to my cart?* An Chu wondered. It felt heavier than ever before. *I need to finish my morning rounds, I have to, have to ...* He squeezed those words out between his chattering teeth as he pushed forward one step at a time. Halfway through his route, his body gave in, and he stopped to lean on the remains of an abandoned wooden wagon. *What should I do?* he wondered, but An Chu couldn't think of anything. His head was hot, and his heart was beating like a drum. He stood on a street corner for a couple of minutes, feeling cold and miserable, and decided to turn around and head home before a policeman could approach him with his whip.

Of course, his uncle was upset. Now, he had to pay some local boy to finish the deliveries. He went up the attic, kicked the door open, and dragged An Chu out of bed by the ear.

"Lazy bastard!" he screamed. "Son of a bitch! You want to be a prince and stay in bed all day?!"

"I didn't feel good. I … I threw up."

"Threw up? You ate too much! It serves you right. I'll teach you not to be so greedy next time."

Too weak to resist, An Chu let the blows fall on him until his uncle got tired of hitting him.

"If you don't want to work, don't stay here," his uncle warned, pointing his long, bony finger at him as he dashed out. "Remember, I'm the one who gave you a home."

Two streams of tears ran down An Chu's face as he struggled to his feet and went back out into the cold to finish his deliveries.

An Chu staggered along an alley, his teeth chattering and his breath hot in the frosty air. He felt a familiar twinge in his stomach as the nausea came back. He tried to hold it in but could not. So, he dragged himself to a corner where he could lean against a building. As he bent down, he spotted something red and glittering, half-hidden under a piece of crumpled paper. Was he dreaming? It was a desolate street filled with nothing but garbage. He wiped his eyes and opened them wide. Just as he was about to poke the paper, a gust of wind lifted it up into the air and blew it away. There, on the ground in front of him, was a gold ring with a sparkling red stone. An Chu knew it must be precious, for it looked just like the one on the fat finger of his uncle's wife.

"*Red stones are called rubies.*" He remembered what his mother had once told him. "*Only the rich can afford them.*"

He looked left and right to make sure that no one was around before he picked up the ring, wrapped his small hand around it, and stumbled on.

That night, as Ya Zhen shepherded her kids to bed and was about to douse the candle, An Chu called her over.

"Mom, don't blow it out."

"What, baby? You should be asleep."

"Mom, I want you to look at something."

An Chu struggled out of his bed and opened his fist under the candlelight.

"A ring!" Ya Zhen half-shouted in panic before she clapped her hand over her mouth. She turned around and checked to make sure that no one was at the stairs who could hear their voices.

She looked at An Chu questioningly with great seriousness, as if he had done something terribly wrong. "Did you steal it?" she asked in a low voice.

An Chu shook his head. "Mom, you always told me that we may be poor, but we have our dignity. We would rather be poor than be thieves," he said, reciting her teaching. Ya Zhen continued to stare at him, not sure what to think. "Where did you find the ring?" she asked, her voice shaking.

"On the street corner, when I was sick."

"You didn't take it from anyone?"

An Chu shook his head and looked back at his mother.

For a while, Ya Zhen tossed the ring from one hand to another as if it burnt her hands. She gazed hard at the ring as she tried to make some sense of the situation. Then, her face brightened.

"Buddha sent us a ring! Buddha knows our sufferings, after all!" she exulted. When she finally realized that she now owned this ring, she was happy beyond belief. "You are a blessed child, just as the fortune teller had said. You still have your luck with you! We can trade it in for a place of our own, and maybe something else as well, and soon we will leave this dirty charcoal store for good."

With the ring in her hand, her eyes closed, and a smile on her face, Ya Zhen had already planned out her family's future.

"Oh, my special boy!" Her eyes shone under the candlelight and glistened with tears as she wrapped her arms around him. Only then did she realize how hot her son's thin body felt.

"First," she said firmly in a low voice, "we need to take care of you and make you well again. Then, we will get out of here." She helped him back to bed and blew out the candle.

As her eyes adjusted to the darkness, Ya Zhen searched for the precious package of dark brown sugar she had saved for special occasions. She found it safely tucked away inside a hole in the family's worn mattress, warmed by her sleeping children. By the light of the room's one-and-only half-sized window, she opened the packet, poured a generous amount of sugar into a mug and then added hot water. The cold wind howled through the window and blew in her face as she plunged her stiff index finger into the mug, swirled it around, and popped it into her mouth. She tasted its sweetness and felt the blood racing through her finger, pain mixed with pleasure at the same time.

She brought the mug to An Chu. "Drink it. Drink it all and you'll feel better tomorrow," she said as she supported his burning back and weak neck.

He drank it down. Ya Zhen was relieved to see him drift off as she sat with him, stroking his hair.

Such a good boy.

Thanks to him, she now held the passport to her family's freedom from slavery. She got up and found her sewing basket. Standing next to the window, she quietly sewed the ring into her underwear, wiped back tears of joy, regained her composure, and went downstairs. She decided to keep everything a secret—even from her husband—until An Chu felt better.

Chapter II

LIFE IN A SHANTYTOWN

I T WAS THE SPRING of 1956, and An Chu Sun was twenty-two years old. Although of average height, he was muscular and strong. His shoulders were broad, and he was as powerful as a crane. He could lift five hundred pounds with his bare hands. With only three years of elementary school, strength was what he used to make a living and help his parents to raise six younger siblings. An Chu worked odd jobs as a laborer. Years of life on the street had taught him to be smart, sensible, and reliable. By his early twenties, he had already built a network of jobs for himself.

His home sat among clusters of broken-down shacks in a shantytown, off the hustle and bustle of a big commercial street in the old French quarter of Shanghai, which was established in 1849 after the First Opium War. The huts were built of used wood, nailed, glued, or sometimes tied together, their perilously tipping walls inset with crooked doors. Some sported windows of odd and varying sizes, scavenged from condemned houses. The doors were useful enough, but the windows seemed almost pointless. Nobody could see through the decades of dirt, cooking grease, and dust encrusting their ancient panes. However, they did provide some light and could be opened for ventilation.

All the roofs were made of thin, recycled metal sheets, easily found at construction sites, where they were used for fencing. The shantytown residents readily took advantage of this convenience, although it had consequences. Whenever it rained, it was like sitting through a percussion concert: the harder the rain, the louder the music, punctuated by the crash of thunder. Under those roofs, little boys and girls learned to have fun by hiding themselves dramatically under quilts for protection. With their fingers in their ears and their eyes half open, they waited in anticipation of each lightning flash and thunderclap until, gradually, their excitement was exhausted and they were overpowered by sleep, surrendering to the rhythm of a steady rain.

Often the metal sheets were rusty and soon developed little holes, which were discovered only during a rainstorm. The water would then drip and disappear into the dirt floor beneath. Only when the drops fell onto a bed or some other valued piece of furniture would the owner find it necessary to get up and search for pots and pans to catch the leaks. Then, it was time to find a new metal sheet and fix the roof.

Outside the crooked shacks, community life was in full swing, especially in front of the neighborhood's only water pump. You could always find a crowd there: Women came with their family chamber pots in the early hours of the day, just as the sun peeked over the horizon. Still in nightclothes, they rubbed their barely opened eyes with their sleeves and emptied the heavy pots into a cesspool. Throwing in a handful of detergent, they scrubbed the basins as hard as they could with special long bamboo brushes and rinsed them clean.

It generally took a while for the women to warm up and start their first conversations of the day. But soon, one exchange led to another, until their chatter gushed out like the water from the spigot in front of them. An eavesdropper could hear everything, from complaints to marriage advice, gossip, recipes, and even formulas for miraculous medicines.

Next came the housewives and old folks, equipped with laundry baskets, washbasins, buckets of dirty breakfast dishes, and bars of rough, brown soap. As they dug into their piles of laundry and

chipped crockery, they greeted each other, argued, and tried to figure out what everyone else had for breakfast by studying the tiniest
traces of evidence left inside the pots and rice bowls. There were
very few secrets among people living so close together. By afternoon, laundry flew like colored flags in front of every hut, giving the
entire shantytown a cheerful, celebratory feeling.

In the summertime, groups of children hung around the water
pump, as well, waiting for their chance to get close to the busy water.
They couldn't wait to dip their bare arms and legs under the cool
gushing stream or give themselves an instant shower by pouring a
bucket of water over their heads. They sloshed each other using cups
and buckets and then chased each other around, until somebody
was wrestled to the ground or got hurt. Then, they stopped, standing
dumbfounded with muddy water and sweat dripping off their cow-
licks, noses and chins into the hems of their shorts. It was time to
call off the game and sit for a while under the lazy sun, quietly recov-
ering and watching other kids' water fights. Soon, they went back to
the tap to clean themselves up, and plan some new, deadly mischief.

Since there was a severe food shortage, the slum also served
as an improvised poultry farm. Chickens and ducks roamed freely
around the grounds, pecking grass and plants, fighting over their
territories, or nibbling on random treasures accidentally dropped
by passers-by. With the help of their claws, wings, and beaks, they
kicked, scratched, fluffed, and pecked until they found themselves
a comfortable spot and dozed for hours. They would occasionally
open one eye when they were disturbed by a loud noise, just to
make sure that there was no immediate danger. If it was a false
alarm, they soon fell asleep again, succumbing to boredom. By
day, people, chickens, and ducks shared the slum grounds as one
big family. The birds knew where to find their owners, their coops,
and food. They knew exactly when to plod their way home and
disappear into their coops, which looked exactly like their owners'
huts—only in miniature.

An Chu's parents raised more chickens than most of their neighbors. They were used to supplement what little food they had for

the seven children under their shaky roof. Luckily, they had more to feed their chickens than most because An Chu's mother and father worked as vegetable vendors in the morning market. Every morning at dawn, when the roosters made their first squawks, Ya Zhen and her husband, Jing Chuan, were already on their way to work.

The front door groaned and gently swung shut until the lock clicked. An Chu laid in the dark and listened. He could hear his brother and sisters sound asleep next to him and familiar footsteps outside fading away in the distance. It was still as quiet as night, but An Chu knew that his parents had left for work. He, too, should get up and start his day. He gently withdrew his legs, one at a time, from underneath his brother's, pulled himself out of the tangled sheets, and managed to get out of bed.

He closed the door behind him. A light bulb glowing dimly above the outdoor stove swayed gently in the early morning breeze. His mother must have left it on for him. He opened the lid of a four-foot-tall earthen jar next to the stove and scooped out some water. There was nothing like a drink of cool water the first thing in the morning. It ran through him like fresh energy. Now, he was fully awake. He grabbed a towel, wrapped it around his neck and was soon out running. He had a habit of circling the shantytown a dozen times each morning to get his blood going.

The air was cool and a little damp. *Did Mom and Dad put on any jackets? The dew is always so heavy at this time of the day ... I hope they don't catch colds.* An Chu made a mental note to talk to his parents when they got home.

He had been worried about them lately, especially his father, for he had just gotten rid of a cough that lasted the entire winter. He saw his parents aging in front of his eyes: His father's back was hunched up from years of pulling a vegetable cart. He was always a slight man, and now, he looked even smaller. His mother was a big woman, twice the size of his father, but by the age of forty, a hard life had left its mark on her. Years of working in the heat and chill of an outdoor market had carved wrinkles all over her face. The back of her callus-ridden hands puffed up with frostbite every winter. He heard her cursing her own hands for bringing her aches and pains.

"You bastards, you're killing me! Killing me!" she screamed, dipping them in steaming hot water laced with hot peppers to treat her frostbite. An Chu remembered seeing purple blood running off the back of her trembling hands as she squeezed her thawing sores.

An Chu helped his parents to raise their entire family of nine. He handed his mother every penny he made. But it was not enough. A laborer's pay was next to nothing unless he worked for the government. There were more people than jobs, and a man had to know some important person in the Communist Party to get a good position. Since An Chu knew nobody like that, he had to get by with odd jobs, jobs that were either too dirty or difficult for anyone else.

An Chu thought about the places where he and his friends hoped they might find work today and happily imagined the money he would bring home to his mother.

It would be a good day, he promised himself.

An Chu finished up his last round of running and went straight to the water pump. As usual, all was quiet at this time of the day. No one was up yet. Only a stray cat guarded the tap, its body camouflaged in the darkness, invisible except for its glassy, glowing eyes. An Chu peeled off his sweaty shirt as he filled a wooden bucket. He always started his usual morning "shower" by dumping a bucket of cold water over his head, even in the winter. He then filled another bucket, grabbed a bar of laundry soap that somebody carelessly left by the pump and rubbed it hastily over his hair. He badly needed a haircut, but he didn't have the heart to ask his mother for the five cents Old Tong charged for his cheapest cut. An Chu poured a second bucket of water over his head for a quick rinse and dried himself with a threadbare hand towel. He washed his shirt with the same soap and headed home as the first rays of dawn lightened the sky, which was smeared with hopeful streaks of lucky red.

"Good morning! Morning!" He greeted the sleepy shadows of his neighbors on their way to the pump. Back home, An Chu flung his shirt and towel over the clothesline, his wet shorts dripping freely onto his feet.

He started his morning chores right away, opening the door of the chicken coop and letting the hungry birds out to search for their breakfast. He filled the giant jar next to the stove with bucket after bucket of water, so the family did not have to go to the pump every time they needed to cook, clean, or wash. He stuffed the stove with straw and twigs and struck a match. He dropped a handful of charcoal onto the flames, and black smoke began to rise. Shielding his eyes from the stinging smoke, he grabbed a broken straw fan next to the stove and started to wave it vigorously in front of the vent. As he fanned, orange flames shot upwards, hungrily licking the charcoal balls until they caught fire and began to glow. He added some more charcoal, set a large iron wok up on top, and filled it with water.

An Chu squatted next to the stove, comforted by the heat. Soon, the water boiled. He ladled some into thermos bottles to use later for tea, grabbed a dried gourd filled with rice and dumped a healthy amount into the steaming wok to make breakfast porridge.

Two of his sisters came out and took over the making of the meal. They spent a few hours each day helping to get the house in order before they headed out to their factory jobs. Unlike An Chu, they couldn't help support the family. They were working to save money for their marriage dowries.

An Chu grabbed some day-old steamed buns and pickled cabbage, waving one hand to chase away the stubborn, hungry flies and using the other to cover his food until he could wrap it in a hanky to take for lunch.

A voice boomed from the alley: "Good morning, Older Brother!"

"Mmohhning, Pei!" An Chu managed to grunt with a bun between his teeth, his wet hands struggling into his sleeves.

Pei, his friend from two doors down, loved to call him "older brother" even though they were not related in any way. At sixteen, Pei was taller than An Chu, though his hairless face made him look like a child. He had been working with An Chu ever since his mother got sick and was always anxious to make some money. An Chu liked him and gladly took another "younger brother" under his wing. Besides, he liked that Pei was always cheerful and on time.

An Chu finished chewing his bun but frowned as he examined his friend closely. "Pei, there's no shame in sleeping in your clothes. I do, too, but we don't want people to know—especially not our customers." Like a true older brother, he straightened Pei's shirt and smoothed his wrinkled collar. An Chu pulled him into the kitchen, sprinkled some water on his head, and used his hands to press down and straighten his straw-like hair. Pei stood and let him do it, obedient as a child.

"Now, we have a handsome lad," An Chu said as he picked up his lunch. "Let's get going."

"Thanks, Older Brother."

"How can you find a girlfriend someday if you always look like you've just crawled out of a chicken coop?"

Ah Chu and Pei had a good laugh. Soon they left the shantytown and headed into the city. Somewhere, there would be a job waiting for them.

Chapter III

ESCAPE FROM SHANGHAI

WORK WASN'T THE ONLY thing in An Chu's life then. Twenty-two also happened to be the age when An Chu met his first love. But penniless and threadbare as he was, the girl's family forbade him to visit her. He was heartbroken. To be poor was a curse. According to traditional Chinese courtship customs, a young man was supposed to secure his wedding promise with stacks of gold and silver coins. An Chu's sleeves carried only wind. He knew the situation was hopeless. He must have been devastated because he decided to abandon his family and friends, leave the city he loved, and set off for a place as far away as the edge of the earth.

He met her on a Sunday afternoon while they shared a park bench, his bench. He had a habit of going to the park and sitting on the same bench, his way of escaping shantytown life even for just a couple of hours.

That day, he was delayed by his mother's unexpectedly asking him to do some repair work around the hut. When he finally got permission to leave, he changed into his best set of clothes, picked up a dog-eared, fifth-grade schoolbook, rolled it up into a tube, and stuffed it into his back pocket. He also remembered to grab a pencil to practice his handwriting.

He had just dashed out of the door when he heard a voice behind him.

"Older Brother, Older Brother!"

An Chu turned around. "What is it, Pei?"

"We are starting a wrestling match. Will you come?" Pei asked.
"Every time you come, I win. When you don't, I lose. I'm not joking."

An Chu gave him a serious look. "I'm sorry, but I've got to go
somewhere."

Pei grunted. "You always disappear on Sunday afternoons."

"We work together and we play together every day except
Sunday. Isn't that enough?"

Pei never gave up easily. "PLEASE ..." He folded his hands
together under his chin and bent his legs back in an awkward position while his eyes rolled upwards exaggeratedly, as if he was about
to fall down and die.

An Chu pressed his lips together, trying hard not to laugh until
he could not hold himself any longer. They both burst out laughing.

"You don't look too bad for a dying man," An Chu said. "You
should be a movie star."

An Chu was easily persuaded about anything except Sunday
afternoons. Pei knew that, so he stopped being playful, searching for a new way to convince him to come and join the game.
"Really?"

An Chu cut him off. "I would if I could. You know that. Just
remember, walk away with your head up whether you win or lose.
I'll see you later."

He waved goodbye and walked away. He had to get going before it was too late.

An Chu hurried down the streets and small alleys and, soon,
started running. He preferred running. *I'll have more time to study
my book in my park,* he thought. He smiled. He always regretted
that he had only three years of school learning. He could have been
a businessman, sitting behind a desk in an office right now and
counting out money if only he had had more education. Or a traffic
policeman dressed in a uniform with snow-white gloves. Maybe a

teacher helping people like himself. But how could he go back to school? Who would provide money to his family? He tried to study his sisters' old textbooks instead, hoping to make up for the school-house years he could never have. It took him two years to finish a fourth-grade textbook, and now, he decided to graduate himself to the "fifth grade."

An Chu ran until he arrived at his bench. He was about to sit down when he realized that there was someone there already, a girl, a young lady to be exact, reading the *Liberation Daily* newspaper. She sat right in the center of the bench, her legs crossed. The way she tapped her foot made him feel that she had taken this bench as hers! He felt confused and didn't know what to do. He looked left and right, his eyes scouting out a different place to go.

Sensing somebody in front of her, the girl looked up and was rather amused by what she saw: The young man in front of her looked like a wild bushman! His thick black hair was quite a few inches too long. He could have been taken as a short-haired girl, except he had an equally thick dark beard. His bright eyes and perfectly sculpted lips attracted her. *He would be quite handsome, if someone only took a pair of scissors to that hairy mess*, she thought.

"If you don't mind, you can share my bench." She moved to the side, inviting him to sit down with her.

An Chu stood stiff as a log. "But this is my bench."

"Really?" She widened her eyes in surprise. "That's funny. I have a bench in this park, too. But some people took it."

"Don't be sarcastic." An Chu thought she was mocking him.

"Who is? I'm serious. I go to my bench every Sunday afternoon to read my paper. It's the one under the magnolia tree over there," she said, pointing. "But a young couple was sitting on it when I arrived."

An Chu followed her finger. He could vaguely see two shapes under an explosion of pink blossoms.

The girl gazed at the tree and sighed. "I love my bench, my tree. Look at the flowers! But—oh!—look at all the petals on the ground!" She had a sad look on her face as she thought of all the flowers that would be gone when she returned the following week. Her eyes were moist when she turned to look at him.

An Chu felt bad for the girl. "Well, I guess we have to share the bench."

He sat down next to her, leaving a large, gentlemanly gap in between them. He fished the curled-up book out of his back pocket and tried to study. So much for his solitude and special Sunday afternoon.

"You're reading a fifth-grade textbook?"

An Chu's face reddened. She was nosy, too, and now, she knew his secret.

"You have the old version. I can bring you a new one next week," she said matter-of-factly.

An Chu reminded her of a kid caught doing something embarrassing. She chuckled. "You shouldn't feel ashamed. You should be proud of yourself. By the way, I am a schoolteacher. My name is Yue Hua, 'Moon Flower'." She extended her hand to An Chu.

Moon Flower, what a beautiful name!

"My name is An Chu. Nice to meet you," An Chu murmured as he shook her hand.

If he had to share his bench with someone, at least it was with this smart, pretty, and sentimental young lady.

They spent the afternoon quietly reading together, side by side. When An Chu had questions, Yue Hua leaned over to help. By the time the sun reached the western edge of the park, the gap between them had disappeared. They had a lot to talk about and were surprised to discover how much they had in common.

When it was time to go home, Yue Hua suggested, "How about I invite you to come to my bench next week since I sat on yours today?"

He eagerly nodded even before she finished her sentence.

"I hope no one will sit on it," she said, giggling in a voice that somehow reminded An Chu of faraway, golden bells. "Then we have to sit here again."

I like this girl, An Chu thought.

An Chu was restless for the entire week. When Sunday finally
came, he rushed to her bench—two hours early—and he ended
up worrying, inventing reasons she wouldn't show up. When she
finally arrived—on time—she found him looking both pleased and
worried, bright and bleary-eyed, as if he doubted she was real. For
several weeks, An Chu repeated this sweetly anxious routine.

An Chu was in love.

Soon, crazy ideas got into his head. Their meetings in the park
were not enough for him anymore. He wanted to see her in her
home. He wanted to kiss her. He wanted to touch her. He wanted
to marry her!

One Sunday afternoon, he sat on her bench and waited for her,
as usual. He waited and waited, but she didn't show up. When the
sun started to redden, he got worried. *Is she sick?* She had never, ever,
been late before. He kept rolling and unrolling the new textbook
she had given him, and his mind raced with explanations. Still, she
did not come. After a long while, he reluctantly got up and was
about to walk away when a boy on a bike appeared.

"Are you Comrade An Chu Sun?" he asked.

An Chu grew alarmed. "How do you know my name?"

"Here is a letter for you." The boy handed him an envelope and
rode off.

He tore open the letter. It read:

> *Dear Comrade An Chu Sun,*
>
> *I can't see you anymore. I told my parents that we
> were in love. My father flew into a rage. He said he
> didn't want his daughter to marry a day laborer and
> live in a shantytown for the rest of her life.*
>
> *My mother cried and begged me to obey my father
> and threatened to kill herself. I am the only daughter
> they have. I can't disobey them and ruin their lives. I
> am so very, very sorry. Please forgive me and forget me.*
>
> *Yue Hua*

An Chu held the letter, read it again and again, and then stared at it in disbelief. What was wrong in being with a day laborer? After all, this was now Communist China where everyone was equal and workers were respected. What was wrong with living in a shanty-town? Lots of families lived there. He never thought being in love would cause any trouble.

"There must be some kind of misunderstanding," he said aloud, sounding braver than he felt. "I will talk to her parents and clear it up." His hopes of marrying Yue Hua came flooding back to him. He rushed to her apartment building and shouted her name under her window again and again. Suddenly, he was hit by something and was cold and soaking wet. He looked up. A gray-haired head poked out next to a wooden bucket. "Beggar! Bad luck!" the head shouted and spat on him. "Go back to the slum where you belong." The only warmth he got from her family was the old man's saliva on his face.

An Chu couldn't remember how he got home that night. He only knew it was very late. He spent hours sitting on his bench—the bench where they began their friendship and his first love. Now, his love was as dead and cold as the fallen petals under her beloved tree.

An Chu never told his family about his first love and how he lost her. He only hoped that his sisters would save enough for their dow-ries so someday they wouldn't face the same situation he was in now. They could leave this shantytown when they got married and move to their husbands' houses. He had always thought they were selfish not to hand over their paychecks to Mother, but he was not sure about that anymore. Actually, he wasn't sure of anything anymore.

An Chu didn't go to work the next day, or the day after. He told Pei to take over and spent his whole precious Sunday sleeping. Soon after, he left the city, vowing to get as far away as he could.

Before he left, he circled the block where Yue Hua lived ten times. He hoped that he would catch one last glimpse of her, but he never did. When he dragged his tired feet back home, Ya Zhen was at the kitchen table waiting for him. She wanted to say goodbye to her boy and have one last good look at him. She would leave for work very early the next morning and when she came back, her son would already be gone for who knew how long. He might never come back. She felt his pain as she looked at his pink, moist eyes, which kept avoiding hers. She didn't have the heart to ask him why he was so unhappy or why he had to leave his family so suddenly, right away, and why he wanted to go to such a faraway place. Whatever it was, it hit her son hard, real hard. She had never seen him so disheartened. He was always a cheerful boy, whether dressed in silk or clad in rags. The shantytown was a hundred times better than the charcoal store they had escaped from, even though she knew it was never enough for her boy, born with all the fortune teller's promises of good luck.

Let him go, a voice within her said. *He will be better off in a new place where his luck may soar. This slum is too poor and hopeless. An Chu deserves better. Maybe he will find a good woman to take care of him. He doesn't need to stay with his mother anymore.*

They spent a long time together in silence.

"Your mind is made up?" Ya Zhen finally asked.

He nodded stiffly, staring at the dirt floor.

Ya Zhen held on to her hope for one more precious moment and then surrendered it, letting it go—the last of her many lost possessions to slip away, one at a time, forever.

"Don't forget to write to me," she said. "You know I can't read … just a blind woman in front of words, but I can ask your sisters to read me your letters. I want to know everything. Promise that you'll visit when you make enough money."

He shifted his eyes slowly upward to look at his mother. All the wrinkles on her face stared back at him as she smiled. He always knew she loved him the most out of all her children. He was her oldest and her biggest helper. A hard life offered them few opportunities to sit down like this and talk things out, but they always understood and supported each other, especially at difficult times.

"I promise," he said quickly as he picked up her right hand and held it tight in his. "I promise I'll write to you and visit you."

Early the next morning, An Chu heard his parents get up and leave for work. He stayed in the dark and listened, trying to store every footstep and sound in his head. But he didn't get up. His train didn't leave until the afternoon. Today, he had the luxury of lying quietly in bed and staying there until everyone left. No good-byes, tears, or hugs from anyone. He wanted to leave by himself, like a man.

When he finally got out of bed it was already noon. He eas-ily gathered the few possessions he had and packed them up. As he searched for his missing sock, he spotted his wrinkled, ill-fated schoolbook lying face down underneath his bed. He scooped it up protectively and smoothed it with his hands. A mix of sweet and bitter feelings came back to him. *Should I take it with me?* An Chu shook his head and put it down on the bed. It was time to go. At the threshold, he turned around, took a deep breath, surveyed the dark room filled with beds and the traces of his life for the past fourteen years and closed the door.

An Chu walked fast and soon left the shantytown behind him. Striding down the street, he heard footsteps running after him. "Older brother! Older brother!"

An Chu stopped to let Pei catch up.

"I almost missed you!" Pei said, panting. "I want to see you off to the station. After all, you are my older brother."

An Chu knew it was not possible to send him back home so the two of them walked toward the station side by side in silence. It was a very long and painful trip for Pei. He wished that he could stop An Chu and this crazy nonsense. Everyone in China called Shanghai "Heaven," with more food and jobs than anywhere else on earth. Where could An Chu find a better place? Of course, Pei could make more money now that he ran An Chu's business. He always dreamed that one day he would work the way his "older brother" did. Now, he would get his wish, but he wasn't happy. He was worried about An Chu. He could not understand him. There were tons of girls in the shantytown. Couldn't he marry one of his own kind? Why did he have to have a schoolteacher as a girlfriend?

Was it worth abandoning his life and friends for some strange place where he knew no one and no one knew him?

The station was crowded with dusty, tired-looking trains, equally weary passengers, and hundreds of red flags fluttering in the breeze. Distracted by the crowd, the flapping, and his own thoughts, Pei went wherever people pushed him, and the two of them got separated. When he finally realized that An Chu was gone, he knew he would never find him again, not in that sea of people and flags.

"Older Brother, I wish you good luck," Pei whispered into the crowd. He peeled a red banner off his face, left the station, and headed for home.

An Chu stepped onto a train bound for the remote city of Zhang Ye with a thin, rolled-up cotton quilt. Inside the quilt were his only spare shirt, some socks, pants, underwear made from homespun cloth, and a hand towel. The parcel was small enough to fit under his arm. Inside the right pocket of his patched cotton coat, he had a couple of *yuan*, just enough to buy himself a few bowls of noodles and cigarettes from the noisy vendors plying their business at train stops.

Until a couple of days earlier, An Chu had never heard of Zhang Ye, a western frontier city thousands of miles away. But someone told him the government was urging ambitious young people to go there and that was good enough for An Chu. It gave him a perfect escape route, and all he wanted was to get as far away as possible.

An Chu watched his familiar city gradually slip away and turn into farm fields, gentle hills, tall mountains, forests, dry grassland, and, finally, desert. At one point, he saw a tiger resting on a rock formation, looking as comfortable and satisfied as the Heavenly Emperor on his throne. An Chu admired and envied the tiger. He was running away from his own domain to an unknown place, but he felt a sense of relief.

An Chu didn't care why the other passengers were on that train, or that he had joined thousands of enthusiastic young people recruited from the big coastal cities to help carry out the Communist Party's newest grand plan—to build a prosperous new Chinese western frontier along the ancient Silk Road.

It was 1957 and China and Russia were working hard to create a brotherly relationship. Opening businesses in towns along the border was intended to promote trade between the two countries. The Chinese government also wanted to move some of its young population from the overcrowded east coast and resettle them as pioneers in an ambitious plan to create vital new industrial and commercial centers.

Numbed by the loss of his first love, An Chu was the least enthusiastic person on the train. He didn't join any card games or talk with anyone. He just sat on his seat and chain-smoked for the entire trip. He was running away, and smoking kept him calm. No one knows what else he did during the five days and five nights it took the ancient steam locomotive to reach the middle of nowhere. He kept everything to himself. But my mother remembered him standing on the train platform, helping sleep-deprived, disoriented young women get off the train at their destination, along with the bulky, twine-wrapped remains of their city lives.

"This way, please. I'll help you down," he said as he hopped back on again and again, lent a hand to a weary someone, grabbed a bunch of bags, and then climbed down. The women generally gave him no more than a slight nod or a mumbled word of thanks before going off with their belongings. One, however—a rather small and delicate girl with a serious expression more suited to a spinster than a young woman—thanked him warmly, not only for herself but for the others whom she observed him helping. This serious little girl-woman, who looked less like an adventurous pioneer than a Communist Party secretary, then surprised him by extending her hand and bowing formally in the old Imperial manner, which amused and charmed An Chu.

"Such a well-brought-up young lady with such fine manners," he said, suppressing a smile. "You must have gotten on the train in Shanghai?"

"Yes, Brother, you are right" (it was the custom of the time for men and women to address each other as "brother" and "sister"). "I come from the Gu family on South Star Street in the Zhabei District of Shanghai."

"I am pleased to have met you, little sister. My name is An Chu, if you should ever need help again. I am also from Shanghai, but from a family and district where everyone's fortunes are self-made," An Chu replied with dancing eyes.

Yan felt An Chu was playing with her somehow, but she didn't know exactly why or how. Instead of turning shy, she did something unexpected.

"My given name is Yan," she said, not knowing why she offered it to him so easily.

"*Yan?* Hmm. So, you are a 'Swallow,' eh?" An Chu said thoughtfully. "And why have you flown so far away, little bird? Well, whatever your reason, just remember, if you ever need help, or a place to rest, 'An Chu' means Peaceful Shelter. If the little sister bird ever needs a nest in stormy times, I will do my best to help. But enough joking now. Perhaps we will meet again. Goodbye, Miss Gu … and good luck."

They parted, each slightly red-faced and feeling unexpectedly happy. That five-day train ride may have taken them to the very middle of nowhere, but it also brought their lives together.

Yan had gotten on that train for a very different reason than An Chu. She hadn't taken lavish amounts of supplies with her like some of the spoiled city kids had. She had only two pieces of modest but presentable luggage and dressed very much like a "schoolteacher" (a nickname that would stick with her for life). A pair of spectacles on the bridge of her nose and a plain but neat Western-style coat over a gray jacket and black pants showed both her middle-class openness to Western ideas, and her basic conservativeness when it came to colors. She took an instant liking to An Chu for his leadership and impressive physical strength. People's eyes opened wide as they watched him balancing five pieces of luggage at a time on his broad back. His generosity in helping strangers made a remarkable impression on Yan.

As she left her new friend and the train station, Yan looked around at the bleak, alien surroundings: the partially frozen dirt road, the gray sky, the clusters of mud huts with straw roofs, and barren fields. Donkeys slowly dragged carts filled with luggage and the stiff bodies of exhausted young ladies, while the rest of the crowd marched forward to meet their future.

Yan walked with the hardier bunch, looking around for some hint of what had brought her here. Local children giggled and skipped along with them, not for the benefit of the new arrivals, as they soon discovered, but for the donkey droppings. As soon as the animals relieved themselves, the children rushed forward with lightning speed, scooped up the steaming dung with their hands, and put it in their baskets. When they finished, they grabbed each other's baskets and looked inside eagerly to find out who got the most. They laughed crazily when they saw the newcomers turn their faces away in surprise and disgust, some holding their noses.

Yan could only imagine what her father would say if he saw this place. For anyone coming from the big city, such filth and behavior were shocking, but for a worldly, cosmopolitan gentleman like her father, who had worked so hard to protect her and bring her up like a young lady, her decision to give up her safe, comfortable life for *this* would be incomprehensible ... no, terrifying. The very thought of her father made her face flush and her heart beat heavy with guilt. He loved her so much, and she loved him more. Yet she abandoned him and her little brother for a dirt pile, donkey droppings, maybe even danger. Yan looked around, searching wildly for some reason she should be here. She began to regret her hasty actions but knew it was too late.

Is this my punishment for getting my freedom? Yan asked herself.

Yan trudged forward, pushed this way and that by the crowd. Not far away, An Chu, who had spotted her again on the road, noticed her blank stare and called her name several times, But Yan was in her own world and didn't hear him. With the memories of her now-past life still five days fresh, all she could think of was her embroidered silk quilt, feathery pillow, and especially, her soft bed.

How she wished that she could rest her tired body on it right now and drift away.

"Yan! Yan!" For a moment, she thought her father was calling her. But when she looked at the dirt road ahead of her, she knew it was not possible.

Chapter IV

YAN'S REAL FAMILY

MY MOTHER'S NAME WAS not always Yan. She wasn't born a free-flying "swallow" among all the big-city, street-smart sparrows of Shanghai. As a little girl, she lived an innocent, happy life, listening to the songs of gulls as they soared over the ocean waves.

Her village was a picturesque pile of sea shanties and large, elaborate homes with round Moon Gates, fronted by crooked docks, hand-painted fishing boats, and prosperous markets selling jellyfish, oysters, crabs, and fresh and smoked fish. Da Chi Tou did well by supplying fresh seafood to the hungry millions in the major nearby port city of Ningbo, and as a result of their good fortune, the people were able to keep up their local tradition of having large, sometimes extra-large families. In Da Chi Tou, even daughters had worth. Most women named their girls after exotic flowers or treasures from the sea. But for Yan's mother, her oyster contained one "pearl" too many. And that pearl was Yan.

Her father, Arh Chin, had a prestigious, well-paying job, working as a first mate on ocean-going freighters. He had seven children of whom Yan was the third. Her parents named her "Ai Zhu," meaning "Loving Pearl," a perfect name for a girl living by the sea (and the first of three names she would bear during her life). Yan had two brothers and four sisters. All her sisters' names contained the word "pearl."

Arh Chin loved his family and friends, although because of the nature of his job, he, like many of the men in his village, was always away at sea. To make up for his absences, he would return home with all sorts of treats and surprises and spend as much time with his children as he could.

Yan lived for the days when Papa came off the ship with his worn leather suitcase and an armful of presents, yes, always presents for her, and her brothers and sisters. And, of course, the biggest package was for her mother. His eyes glistened in the sunlight and his loud voice echoed through the harbor, along with the ship's horn: "I'm home, precious ones! I'm home!" Everyone ran to embrace him. Small Yan raced to be the first one to get to him, feel his scrubby face, and hang happily around his neck. She inhaled deeply and smelt the ocean and faraway lands.

"Papa! Papa! Papa's home!"

Papa always returned in triumph with children hanging on his neck, his back, his arms, and legs as he walked toward home.

One day, he returned on Yan's birthday and handed her a package right on the dock. Yan looked up at her mother for approval since she knew her rules about getting and opening presents only at home. But her mother didn't say anything.

"Come on, sweetie, open it here. It's okay," Papa said in his gentle, lilting voice.

Surrounded by envious brothers and sisters craning their necks, Yan opened it and soon held in her palm a pair of miniature water pails hanging on their own shoulder-pole. They looked just like the ones the village women used to fetch water from their wells.

"I bought them from a village far away, a village just like ours," he explained. "Happy birthday, my little pearl. Happy birthday."

That day, Yan skipped dreamily home next to Papa, her little hands guarding the precious water pails. Afterwards, they had a lunch of longevity noodles, steamed fresh fish in ginger and scallion sauce, and hard-boiled birthday eggs dyed in happy red. Everything was so special when Papa was home.

That was her best birthday. No more birthdays would ever be like it again.

Early one morning, Yan sat still as her little maid braided her hair. She enjoyed watching a pair of swallows building a nest under the edge of the red-tile roof of her home. They flew out again and again, carrying back all sorts of fine objects for their little house under the big one. Yan started to sing her favorite song:

> *Little swallow*
> *I adore you*
> *Every spring you return*
> *When I ask you where you're from*
> *You tell me that the spring is the most beautiful here*
> *Little swallow*
> *I want to tell you—*

"Ai Zhu!? Ai Zhu!?" Yan heard her mother calling. "Where is Ai Zhu?"

"I'm here, Mother!" she answered, but her mother didn't hear her. She sent the maid to find out what was going on. The maid came back with her mother, followed by a stranger with a familiar face.

"Do you remember my cousin, Aunt Jin Lai?"

Yan got up and bowed. "Aunt Jin Lai."

"I have good news for you. You don't need to call her Aunt Jin Lai anymore. Starting today, she is your mother. I have decided to give you to her."

The words made no sense. Yan felt a cold numbness creep into her stomach.

What does it mean Jin Lai is my mother? I have a mother already. Can people change their mothers? Yan was very confused. "I want Papa!" she cried out in desperation. "Papa, Papa, where are you?"

"You know your Papa is at sea. Even when he's home, I'm still the one in charge."

"Mother, please don't give me away," Yan begged. "I want to stay home with you. I want to wait for Papa to come."

But her mother didn't pay her any mind. She was too busy talking to Jin Lai.

"Get Ai Zhu's things all packed and ready. She'll leave at noon," she ordered the maid before she left the room.

Yan's new family resided in an impressive apartment in the British quarter of Shanghai. Few Chinese could afford to live in the foreign districts of the city, where rents were payable only in gold. Their home was directly over the world-famous Three Oceans Emporium, and the prestige of living on Nanking Road, which ran right into the Bund—the famous waterfront of this "Paris of the East"—was enormous. But Yan didn't know that. She mostly spent her time inside the family apartment, watching the sea of strange shoppers as it flowed freely under her living-room window. She didn't have brothers or sisters to play with her anymore. Her only friend now was a busy yellow canary in its brand-new bamboo cage. Yan didn't like it. She missed her swallow friends under the red-tiled roof back in Da Chi Tou and wondered how many baby birds would hatch this year. And, of course, she missed her Papa. She wanted to know if he had come home yet and what he said when he found out she had been given away.

Does he even know what happened to me?

Yan stood in front of a pair of tall windows and scrutinized every man's face as he passed by. *Papa could be here searching for me. I have to make sure he doesn't miss me!* Days went by. Months went by. But Papa didn't come looking for Yan. After a while, she still stood by the windows, but instead of searching men's faces, she looked at the families with children going by, children about her size.

These children have their real parents. Hear them laugh!

Even the bird in a cage is happy.

Yan looked up at the canary with its flapping wings and dancing feet, trying to figure out why an imprisoned bird would be cheerful. Suddenly, she felt like a prisoner herself being kept away from the real world, with this apartment as her cage. She was no better than her canary! She started to hate the things in the apartment, especially the dark, bulky mahogany furniture in the living room.

Everything reminded her that she did not belong there. Jin Lai's cold voice echoed within her: "It was my husband who wanted you. You know I am not your mother. And I know that, too. Someday, when your feathers are strong enough, you will fly back to your own family. It is a waste of my time and money to raise you." The look in her eyes made Yan shiver.

Yan did not like that woman. She never wanted to be taken away, forced to change her name to Chon Mei in accordance with the new family's tradition, and call complete strangers "Mother" and "Father." At the age of six, she was old enough to have a mind of her own, but too young to control her fate. She understood that her mother didn't give her away because they were poor, like some families did. Papa was doing well at sea, and they were very well-off. She was puzzled why Mama wanted to give her away— her!—and not her sisters, and regretted that Papa was too far away to stop her.

Yan missed meeting her father at the harbor, missed his beard, his laughter, and his love. She yearned for the day when she would be big enough to return home and surprise Papa at the harbor all by herself, to embrace him and breathe in the scents he carried home.

Yan spent her whole life wondering about her adoption but never found an answer. She once visited an elderly relative and over a cup of tea and nostalgic remembrances, the question spilled out of her: "Why did my mother give me away?"

The relative sat in a long silence before she shook her head. "I don't know. She never said why. Of course, your two mothers were very close when they were young. You know, we often traded children for friendship in the old days."

"I know that," Yan admitted. "But why me? Why not any one of my sisters?"

Although she couldn't find an explanation, it occurred to her that Yan's mother had a very difficult time giving birth to her, a three-day-and-night-long birth that almost killed her. Was it possible her birth doomed their mother-daughter relationship? An old Chinese superstition said the birth of a strong, new life force could kill an existing weak one, which often meant that the birth of a strong child could cause the death of a parent or a frail older member of the family. Did her mother think Yan threatened her own life?

Yan was slow to adjust to her new life. Even after three years in Shanghai, she refused to play her new role as some other family's daughter. She missed her Papa and her brothers and sisters so much that she plotted to run away and find her real family. She imagined finding her way back to Da Chi Tou and rejoining her real family. *If Papa is there when I get home, he will help me and convince Mother not to send me back. Papa loves me—I'm his favorite daughter.* Nothing here held her heart. The great city of Shanghai boasted every comfort and luxury on the surface of the Earth but to Yan, Shanghai was just an endless maze of strange places and strange faces. Shanghai had even turned her real family into utter strangers.

One day, as she was making plans to run away, Yan had a surprise visitor bringing shocking news that changed everything. Her older brother appeared at the door, introducing himself to the servant as a distant relative. Luckily, her "mother" was out shopping and her "father" was at work. The servant believed the young man and invited him in. As he sat at the kitchen table sipping tea, he kept staring at Yan as if he was trying to store her image in his head.

"You have grown," he finally said after the servant left the room. "We have moved to Shanghai. Our entire family. Mother and all of us children. Some rich relatives helped us. I have been working at a department store only a few blocks from here."

Yan couldn't believe her ears.

"Is Papa in Shanghai, too?"

Her brother's face changed color. "Not Papa."

"Why not? Is he at sea? What's the matter? Why isn't he in Shanghai?"

Her brother kept shaking his head, his face as pale as white candle wax. "Ai Zhu," he begged. "Please don't ask any more questions about Papa. He … he … is gone."

"What do you mean? Where?"

"He left on a job and never came back."

Yan looked at him blankly.

Her brother spelled it out: "He was lost at sea. Two years ago."

"But Papa is a great swimmer. He would never drown."

At that, her brother's head hung so low that Yan could only see his black hair. His chest heaved up and down, and he sighed before his head lifted, eyes staring into the distance.

Yan listened intently as her brother told her the last story of her dear Papa.

It was 1942, at the height of the Pacific War. Ocean commerce was paralyzed, and few boats dared to leave port because of the danger. Arh Chin spent long, uneventful days accompanying his wife on social calls. They visited the families of other stranded seamen, played Mahjong, and talked about the shipping business over tea, snacks, and smokes. They shared news and rumors they had heard, and tipped each other off about job prospects, which grew scarcer by the day. Arh Chin hated the monotonous sound of Mahjong. Only the sound of the ocean could stir his passion for life. After a while, he was ready to climb aboard any ship to get back onto the water. While he waited for work, his wife became pregnant with their seventh child and, to please her, he accompanied her every day to play the dreaded game. At least he got to visit his friends while she satisfied her cravings for pickled cabbage and dice.

Then came his lucky day. At the Mahjong table, he accidentally bumped into an old friend whom he hadn't seen for years. As they caught up over a pot of tea, the friend told Arh Chin a secret: A freighter was sailing from a nearby harbor in two days. Even better, its first mate was sick and most likely wouldn't make it. With his friend's help, Arh Chin was signed up as his replacement, and a fat bonus was promised upon his return. On the dock, before the ship sailed, he promised his wife that he would have a safe trip and be back before the baby was born.

"Take care of yourself and all our little pearls. I'll be here again before you know it," he said, patting his wife's big stomach and smiling. He waved to his family, ran up the ramp, and was gone.

Arh Chin's ship sailed to Vietnam to load up on charcoal and then set off for Brazil. Early one morning, as they steamed over an eerily blood-red sea, the Japanese boarded the ship and forced them to fly their imperial flag. A passing American submarine spotted the freighter and promptly torpedoed it, setting its center cabin on fire. Seeing the ship engulfed by flames, Arh Chin, who was known as an outstanding swimmer, jumped into the foaming sea along with some of his crewmates and was never seen again. An old swabby and a few others clung onto the ship's mast and were rescued by a passing ship only a few hours later. They lived to tell the tale.

Yan sat silent long after her brother had finished his story. The top of her head felt numb, as if someone had hit it with a hammer. Her ears made a ringing noise, so loud that she couldn't think. She wanted to throw up. But she needed to concentrate and figure out what had happened to Papa. She needed to string her brother's words together to get the story right. She played and replayed in her head what her brother had told her only a few minutes before. His words were already fading, too remote to be real. She felt confused. She could see Papa jumping into the ocean when his boat was on fire, but he was an excellent swimmer, and the sea was his friend. Surely, he was safe somewhere, on a small undiscovered island—who knows where? A quick glance at her brother's face, though, and she knew the truth. Papa was gone, the person who loved her so much. Her head sank lower than her brother's. Her family without Papa ... her brothers and sisters without gifts and laughter. Yan even felt sorry for her mother and wished she could see her. *I'm so sorry, Mom, about everything ... about Papa, about us ...*

"You cannot come and visit us," her brother said abruptly, as if he read Yan's thoughts. "You are someone else's daughter now. Mother would be very upset if she knew I came here and visited you. As far as she's concerned, she never had you." His words carried weight and his eyes were moist.

He drank down the remaining tea, got up, and walked toward the front door. Then, he stopped, as if he remembered something.

"Oh, one more thing," he said as he inserted his hand into the bag he was carrying, fished out something, and placed it in her palm. "I know you would like to have this back."

Her brother handed her the old pair of miniature wooden pails. Yan held them against her heart, speechless.

"I love you. I love you just like the rest of my brothers and sisters. Please take care of yourself," he said and walked out.

Watching him leaving, Yan wanted to cry. She wanted to scream: *Take me! Please take me with you!* But she didn't. She knew it would be useless. So, she held back her tears and stood in front of the window, watching him leave, walking further and further away until he turned into a small dot and disappeared.

Yan mourned the loss of Papa secretly, in the darkness of night, for fear that her new family, her new mother especially, would get upset and question the little loyalty she had to them. Only after they turned off the lights, when she was surrounded by nothing, nothing at all, did Yan vent her sorrow over the death of her father. She let her memory unreel freely in the darkness so she could revisit all those precious moments she had spent with Papa. Yan let the tears run down her cheeks and pour onto her pillow until they formed two deep wet patches. No one could hear her cry, and she often fell asleep this way.

Yan's life was in limbo: She had two sets of parents, yet she didn't feel like she belonged to either, especially now that her beloved Papa was gone. Her new dad was nice to her, but she spent most of her time with her new mother, Jin Lai, who hated her.

With the death of Arh Chin, Yan saw no reason to return to her real family. But she didn't see any reason to stay with her new family, either. She wanted to escape and go somewhere just so she could get out of this place, this miserable city where her mother had dumped her. She saved her pocket money and waited for her chance. Finally, one day she decided to act when Jin Lai went out shopping and she was alone with the servant.

"I'm getting a chocolate bar downstairs," Yan said, waving some money at the servant, who readily believed her. As soon as she went downstairs, she stuffed the money into her pocket, dashed out of the store, and disappeared into the crowd of shoppers and sightseers streaming down the road. It felt good to be out in the open. There was some sort of energy created by this vast crowd of people. Yan felt inspired and she walked as fast as her legs could carry her, determined finally to get away from the home where she never belonged. She took only her precious toy water pails, the pocket money she had saved for this day, and nothing else.

A few hours passed. Her legs got tired, and her stomach complained of its emptiness. Yan looked around but everything seemed to be unfamiliar. She had no idea where she was, except that it looked like a working-class neighborhood with children wearing worn-out clothes chasing groups of passing soldiers. Her eyes caught sight of a noodle stand and she stared at it hungrily. Suddenly, she became self-conscious, as if everyone were staring at her. They were. Judging from what she wore, she obviously didn't belong there.

"Would you like a bowl of my humble noodles, dear little Miss?" an elderly woman croaked through her crooked teeth as she brought a bowl of steaming noodles out to the table where Yan sat.

Yan took the bowl. She ate and ate till it was all gone. Then she did something that a lady should never have done in public: She tipped the bowl up and sucked down the last drop of soup, as if it were the most delicious food she had ever tasted.

Facing an empty noodle bowl, Yan felt compelled to give her seat up to some other hungry customer. It was time for her to leave the little noodle stand anyway and continue her flight. But where could she go? Yan had no answer to her own question. She couldn't think of a single place. Maybe she should just let her legs carry her somewhere, anywhere. As she put down the noodle money and left the table, she heard someone talking to her.

"Little Miss, are you lost?" She heard a man's voice above her. "I couldn't help noticing, but you don't look like you belong here. Tell me where you live, and I'll take you home."

Yan turned around to find a very handsome young man in an officer's uniform. And not just any uniform, but the army uniform of the Nationalist Party—the ruling party at the time. She knew this because she had once met a family friend wearing the exact same uniform.

"You are not safe here," he added authoritatively. "It is too chaotic."

It was 1944 and rumors were running wild in the city: The Communist Party had gathered its troops and was heading toward the east; Shanghai had been infiltrated by communists who were working underground among the young intellectuals and working-class citizens in preparation for the battle of liberation; the Nationalist army troops were overwhelmed and powerless. With the Japanese invasion and the continuing subjugation of key cities by countries from all over the world following the Opium War, the nation's future, if any, was dangling in the air. The national economy was in shambles. Paper money was devalued to the point that a person needed to carry a big bag of it to pay for a kilo of rice. Smart merchants started to deal only in gold and silver.

Yan was little aware of the situation since she had lived a very sheltered life. The sincere look on the officer's face struck her. Her nearness to a strange young man made her nervous. She kept twirling the end of her pigtail to keep herself calm. Prompted by the young officer, she became more aware of her surroundings. She saw kids with torn clothes come toward her. Their garments were so worn out that the patterns and colors were indistinguishable. Their dirt-smeared faces showed negligence on the part of their parents, if they had any. Their stick-thin arms reached out toward her, palms open, begging for money.

Yan tried to shift her eyes away from the dirty urchins and she saw crowds of people dashing in all directions, holding their parcels and belongings. Down the street, she saw men hitting each other, fighting about something. They knocked down a vegetable vendor's stand and sent everything flying in the air. But could she trust this young man to protect her and take her back to the home she was running away from? Where could she go if she didn't leave with him? Could she think of some place besides home he could take her? Yan shook her head.

The light began to disappear fast from the western sky and Yan felt exhausted both emotionally and physically. Fearful of the uncertainty she had brought on herself, she decided she had had enough adventure and silently acknowledged her escape attempt as a failure. She didn't look the strange young man in the eye but simply complied with his offer by jumping onto the back of his bicycle. In a barely audible voice, she told him her home address. And that was the beginning and end of their conversation.

The rest of the trip went in silence on both of their parts, covered by the din of the traffic. Yan held tightly onto his uniform while the bicycle raced along. Her mind raced with the bike. It had been half a day since she left the apartment. What had her adoptive mother been doing? Had she called the police? Would she hit her again with those bamboo chopsticks when she got back? Would she send her back to her real family? And on a scarier note, what if this young man was not taking her home? Where would he take her? Would she be in for more danger, even sold into child labor? What should she do?

Her worries ended when he stopped, as she took in the familiar sight of the famous store under her apartment. She gave the young man one first and last long look right in the eyes, silently said "Thank you," and walked home.

Jin Lai didn't hit her. She didn't even punish her. When Yan entered the apartment, all the lights were on. Both her mother and father sat like puppets in their living room, surrounded by dead silence, as if expecting the arrival of their worst fears. Waiting anxiously for her to return, they were overwhelmed with feelings of shock, disbelief, betrayal, pity, and a sense of guilt, which eventually led them to search within themselves why this had happened. The more they thought, the lower their heads hung. The silence in the room turned into a form of torture no one knew how to break.

Finally, the sound of footsteps roused them. Both pairs of tearful eyes looked toward the source, and both faces broke into smiles when they saw Yan. Her parents instantly got up and leapt toward her. They had never felt that she was so important to them.

"Our daughter! Our daughter is home!" They hugged her with a sincerity and warmth she had never felt before. "We're glad that you are back."

For some reason, they never asked her about her whereabouts that day. Her father only begged her not to go out by herself ever again without asking for their approval. "You made us terribly, terribly worried," he simply said. The servant brought the dinner they had saved for her, and then her exhausted parents retired for the night.

"Your mother was worried when you didn't return by dusk," the servant told her in a low voice as Yan hungrily devoured her dinner. "We searched the store downstairs from one end to the other. Then, your mother took out your favorite shoes and hung them on the wall to call you back."

At the time, people believed in the magic power of hanging a pair of shoes on the wall to bring a person back from wherever he or she was.

The servant also told her in secret that when her father came home after work and was told of her disappearance, he criticized his wife for being too harsh to their new daughter and blamed her for not giving Yan enough motherly affection. Yan felt comforted by her new father's understanding and decided to give up running away—for now. It was running away to nowhere anyway.

Chapter V

A Brother Bought with Gold

YAN STOOD IN FRONT of her window enjoying a splash of warm sun on a cold winter day as she watched the shoppers passing underneath her. She heard the phone ring in her parents' room, and her mother picked it up.

She was unusually cheerful and loud. "Yes, hello, how are you Madame Wong? You found one? Already pregnant? Just a student? Oh, I understand."

Yan's ears perked up. Who was Madame Wong? Pregnant student? Her curiosity drew her away from the window. Stealthily as a mouse, she hid in the corridor and listened.

"What does her family want in exchange? Gold? How much? Let me talk with my husband and call you back."

The phone conversation puzzled Yan. She wished she knew what was going on, but she knew better not to ask her father or mother because she shouldn't have eavesdropped on a grownup's conversation in the first place, especially her mother's. If Jin Lai found out, it would be a disaster. Her mother liked to grab nearby objects and hit her with them as punishment. Yan had been hit by a copper bowl, a handful of chopsticks, and even the handle of a feather duster. Once Jin Lai threw a pot at her and missed her by just a couple of inches. Another time she poured a bowl of hot porridge over her left foot, leaving her with a big scar. Yan shuddered as she thought about those times and decided not to ask about the mysterious phone call. That night, after they went to bed, she heard her parents through the wall, talking for a long time in low voices.

A few weeks later, her mother made a sudden announcement: "Get dressed. We're going to the Dragon and Phoenix Tailoring Shop this afternoon. We'll pick out some fabric for our ceremonial clothes."

At that time, adults never bothered to explain themselves to children and servants, but Yan found out what was going on soon enough.

Having failed to conceive any children of their own, her father convinced Jin Lai to adopt Yan, hoping that a child in the house would open Fortune's door and bring more of their own. That was the old Chinese wisdom people followed to help a childless couple.

Yan did not bring them luck, though, and after several more years of what seemed to be a losing battle, Jin Lai reluctantly let her husband take a second wife. Through word of mouth, they found out about a pregnant high school student. In exchange for a stack of gold coins, the girl's family struck a deal to let their daughter marry Ho De. The hope was that to outsiders, the child, hopefully a boy, would be seen as the legitimate heir to the Gu family. And their mutual understanding was that the marriage would dissolve as soon as the child was born. The only time the high school girl would ever appear with the family was at the wedding banquet in a local restaurant, attended by all the Gu relatives and friends.

At the feast, Yan was amazed at the sight of this girl, only a few years older than herself, marrying her dad. On the receiving line, she patiently waited for her turn to greet the new bride.

"Congratulations, Second Mother. Long live Second Mother."

As Yan mouthed what her adoptive mother had coached her to say, she had a close look at the bride, a beautiful girl dressed in a traditional red satin wedding gown that was loose enough to keep her physical condition hidden, but stylish enough not to arouse any suspicion or gossip. *Is she the pregnant student I have heard about?* Yan wondered. *She certainly doesn't look pregnant.* Yan knew her father had paid a lot of gold for her—her third "mother" since she was born. But she couldn't understand why her father needed to get married again and have two wives.

After the ceremony, the new bride was escorted into a black taxi and sent back home with her parents. She never set foot in her "husband's" house. Soon enough, Yan forgot all about the lavish banquet and her father's new marriage.

Seven months later, on a bright, windswept autumn afternoon, Yan and her parents were returning from a church service when their maid greeted them at the front door in a loud, panicky voice: "Master! Mistress! Madame Wong phoned so many times. She wants you to go to Second Wife's home as soon as possible."

Ho De and Jin Lai looked at each other, and instantly understood that the moment they had been waiting for had finally arrived. They immediately went back downstairs, leaving Yan with the maid. Ho De found a man leaning against a wall by his rickshaw. "Want a fare?" he asked. "I'll double the fare if you can run the whole way."

The rickshaw raced through the city streets, flying past pedestrians, trolleys, and pedicabs. "Hey! Out of my way!" the man shouted in between gasps, his face bright red, bulging veins gathering around his sweaty temples. In less than a quarter hour, Ho De and Jin Lai arrived at their destination, a nondescript house crammed between modest two-story dwellings.

"Want me to wait, mister?" the rickshaw driver volunteered. "I'd be happy to." He grinned from ear to ear as he held his double fare and generous tip.

"Please do," Ho De said, smiling. "And by the way, your load may be a bit heavier on the way back."

Madame Wong, their matchmaker, interrupted them from a second-story window: "Mister Gu, Mister Gu!" She signaled for them to come inside. Ho De and Jin Lai soon found themselves in a small living room, its blinds drawn and smelling of incense.

"So, where is the baby?" Jin Lai asked. "Is it a boy?"

"It's a boy all right," Madame Wong replied, her eyes staring at the rough wooden floor. "It was a boy."

"What do you mean 'It *was* a boy'?" Jin Lai demanded.

"Mr. and Mrs. Gu, the boy was a stillborn. He's dead!"

Ho De stood like a log, his head hung low. Jin Lai looked at her husband and then Madame Wong.

"The girl's family has asked for a humble burial fee before they terminate the marriage contract."

"They have not delivered us an heir. Now, they want a burial fee? How about paying us back the wedding expenses!" Jin Lai screeched.

Ho De took out his wallet and left five gold coins on the table before pushing his wife out the front door.

After gulping in some fresh air, Jin Lai calmed down and turned to the marriage broker. "Madame Wong, you need to find us a boy, a new-born boy tonight. I don't care what you have to do or how you do it. I want a son tonight."

"If you want a boy so quickly, you'll have to pay a lot to the family for the boy, and, of course, to me for a finder's fee, expenses, plus an express fee …"

Ho De dropped a stack of gold coins into her palm. "Consider this a deposit."

"No problem, no problem. It's always a pleasure doing business with you, Mr. Gu."

Very late that night, the phone rang. Within minutes, Madame Wong came by in a black taxi and picked them up.

Somewhere in the northern part of the city, Ho De and Jin Lai stepped out of the taxi and picked their way through a pile of rubble to a broken-down tenement. The broker knocked on a splintery door and pushed it open without waiting for an answer. No lights were on and they were greeted by the smell of old sweat and something powerfully, sickeningly sweet. Jin Lai made a face and covered her nose with her scarf.

"Light the kerosene lamp, woman," a man yelled. "We have guests."

Under the dim, flickering light, a newborn boy lay swaddled in soiled rags waiting to be sold. The baby was alert and smiled at Ho De. Ho De smiled back.

"Show me your money first before you touch my child."

Ho De saw a man lying on a bed, his stick-like arms supporting an opium pipe. He went over and dropped a stack of gold coins next to the man. The man took a coin and bit into it.

"We are not thieves. We're here to do business," Madame Wong cooed as she scooped up the baby. "Of course the coins are real. Now, give us the boy's birth certificate."

"No need. My boy is as good as your gold." The man smiled, revealing his crooked black teeth. He looked Ho De up and down and sensed he could squeeze more money out of him. "By the way, my wife would make a very good wet nurse." He grabbed Ho De's sleeve to get a reaction. "Just give me five more coins. Take them both and I'll give you my eight-year-old girl child for free."

Ho De pulled hard to free himself. He felt disgusted. "Let's get out of here."

Jin Lai pinched her nose and ran out of the house, followed by Madam Wong holding the baby, and then Ho De. They stumbled into the darkness.

Yan suddenly had a new brother. The boy was named Chon Gao, meaning "Worshipping Noble Heights."

Like Yan's new name, which had been changed from Ai Zhu ("Loving Pearl") to Chon Mei ("Worshipping Beauty"), Chon Gao's name also included the Chinese word "Chon," which had to be given to every child of this family's generation as dictated by their ancestral book of names. Although neither Chon Gao nor

Chon Mei carried any direct blood of the family, Chon Mei was at least a distant relative. Chon Gao was bought with gold to inherit the family name.

After the second wife supposedly gave birth to a boy, all the relatives were notified with a bright red card engraved with the "Double Happiness" character in gold, accompanied by an invitation to celebrate the birth. Such an event had to be orchestrated carefully to take place exactly nine months after the wedding and hide the inconvenient fact that the boy was already two months old. Baskets of boiled eggs, dyed bright red, were given out to relatives, neighbors, and friends—everyone who had an interest in the Gu family's good fortune.

"What a good-looking baby!"

"How adorable!"

"Truly noble-looking!"

Everyone praised him and coddled him, making sure never to call him a "boy" since boys were valuable and could be snatched by evil spirits. A girl was less valuable than a boy and less likely to interest any discerning demon. So, for the first year of his life, Chon Gao would be raised as a girl to fool the evil spirits. By then, he would be strong enough to live as a boy. The Gu family wasn't taking any chances with their precious heir. For his first public appearance, Chon Gao lay in the arms of his "mother," dressed in a pink silk garment and sporting two little pigtails wrapped in red silk.

Chon Gao was a lucky boy. A wet nurse was hired to take care of him. Tins of infant formula from America streamed into the house to boost his growth. His mother and father always gave him their undivided attention. He became the center of the Gu household.

Yan was twelve when Chon Gao was brought home, too young to make sense out of what was going on but old enough to know that her baby brother was not really a Gu by blood. She was more a Gu than he was—after all, her own real family surname was Gu! Nevertheless, all the relatives thought he was the true Gu heir, while she was adopted. She carried that secret burden for the rest of her life and never revealed the truth to her brother, even though he hurt her on so many occasions throughout her life.

When conflicts arose, he often pointed out: "You are not my real sister. You are just a distant relative and have no right to tell me what to do."

To a certain degree, Yan had a lot of empathy for Chon Gao, for just like her, he also had two sets of parents and would never again get to live with his real father and mother. Being twelve years older, she also felt obligated to protect him and shelter him from unnecessary suffering. After all, they were each other's only brother and sister. She pampered him, amused him, washed his diapers, fed him, witnessed his first steps and words, and told him stories.

Then came a hot, humid summer night when their parents went out overnight to play Mahjong. The air was stifling and still. No wind, not even a slight breeze, passed through the open windows. During the summer, Yan had a habit of sleeping on the top of a mahogany dresser because she liked how the dark wood kept her cool. She fell asleep quickly, lulled by the dull rhythms of the fan across the room where the servant woman slept with Yan's two-year-old brother. In a dream, Yan heard noises, people screaming, things falling, and crackling noises that sounded like firecrackers. Wait ... what was that? Yan heard the sound of a gong. It must be something urgent. She needed to find out what.

Then, someone was tapping her. She opened her eyes. It was the servant. "Miss, there's a fire outside. Should we run with the little master?"

So, it was not a dream. She jumped down and headed toward the window where the sounds of a growing commotion were pouring in. She could see the flames and smell the smoke. What should she do? Her little brother, awakened by the noise, started to cry and search for his mommy. When he couldn't find her, he became frantic and started to scream. The servant stared at Yan, waiting for directions. Yan didn't know where her parents were. For a fourteen-year-old, she was cool. "We cannot go out right now. We have no place to go. It's now midnight and it's safer here at home as long as the fire does not reach our building."

She ordered the servant to stay at the window, monitor the fire's progress, and report to her. Meanwhile, she bent down and picked up her little brother. She held him tightly on the edge of the bed. Placing his head on her heart, she rocked him gently back and forth and hummed his favorite songs. Soon he became calm and went back to sleep. Yan didn't put him down or pass him to the servant. She was ready to run to safety with him in case the fire got too close. Fortunately, it didn't. The fire was put out, and the noise eventually died away.

Hours must have passed, for she heard a rooster crow in the distance. The traffic outside started to flow, and the room was not dark anymore. Only then did she fall asleep, still tightly holding her brother.

When her parents came home and learned about the big fire and what she had done, they were very pleased. She was rewarded with praise for the first time. She also felt closer to Chon Gao now that she knew he needed her.

Chapter VI

THE WELLINGTON
CLOCK & WATCH SHOP

Yan's life with her new family was mostly confined to the apartment. At first, her parents would occasionally take her with them to dinner or a party at their relatives' or friends' houses. On such occasions, children would normally be sent to a different room to play and have dinner.

The first time Yan was taken out for such a visit, a housekeeper shepherded her straight to the kitchen. She found herself at a round table surrounded by children of all ages. Each of them sat in front of a white enamel plate with half a boiled egg, some soy sauce for dipping, and a bowl of plain rice. Yan never liked boiled eggs. She looked at her egg and then the strange faces, which stared back at her. She wanted to cry.

"Look, a spoiled brat. She will cry for her parents in exactly two seconds."

One big boy whispered a challenge to another, who picked up some rice, rolled it into a ball, and threw it at her. Yan was caught by surprise as a warm, sticky mass attached itself to her forehead. All the children broke into laughter, while Yan cried and tried to get the gooey stuff off her face and hair. She refused to sit with this group of rude children. Who cared if they happened to be her relatives? She complained and after the maid made several diplomatic trips between the kitchen and the grownups' dining room, she was granted permission to be seated with her parents.

"Now, now, stop crying," her father said as he wiped her face. Then he ordered a servant to bring a chair for his daughter. She felt a secret thrill hearing his words.

Soon, Yan was sitting on a big chair upholstered in red and gold brocade, sharing a twenty-course feast with the grownups.

"Try this." Her father blew on a spoonful of soup to make sure that it was not too hot before he fed it to Yan. "It's called Bird's Nest Soup."

Yan tasted it. It was delicious. Her father gave her a whole bowl of it, and she sucked down every drop. As she enjoyed the rare, expensive soup, she thought about the children in the other room, who would never see, much less taste, this delicacy tonight.

"You should never let a child taste chicken, let alone Bird's Nest Soup," a round-faced woman advised Ho De, as she smacked her lips and chewed on her roast duck.

The other women looked on approvingly in support.

"Children should only be given plain food so they can't tell the difference between good and bad. It's easier to raise them that way."

"Oh, really?" Yan's father felt embarrassed by his relatives' comments. He didn't want them to get the impression that he didn't know how to raise a child, but he also didn't know how to refuse his one and only daughter.

"You have spoiled her," his wife shouted at him in a taxi on the way back home. "Who would feed a child Bird's Nest Soup? What will all our relatives say about us as parents?"

Then she poked Yan hard. "Why do you have to be different? Why couldn't you just eat your egg and rice like the rest of your cousins? Answer me! Answer me now!"

Yan couldn't because there was no right answer. She also wondered why grownups always had to spoil the little fun she had.

Now, whenever they took her out, Yan wouldn't stay at her children's table. Her parents felt embarrassed by her behavior and stopped taking her to social engagements. This did not bother her. Yan had tasted enough grownup dishes. She preferred staying home. In fact, whenever her parents went out at night or weekends, she felt relieved. She could spend time with her servant, sharing a chocolate bar with her, cracking and devouring peanuts together until their stomachs would not take any more, listening to some strange old folktales, or whatever she felt like doing. It was a rare time of freedom, and she savored it. When she was tired, she could fall asleep on the servant's bed. The servant's room became Yan's favorite part of the apartment.

"You act like a servant, rather than the daughter of a high-class family," her mother complained.

Yan ignored her. She was not interested in class distinctions. She did what made her happy, although often at the cost of some physical punishment from her mother. Her father would never punish her. She liked him more from the beginning.

Her adoptive father's name was Ho De. He was a very attractive man, tall even by the Western standards of the time, with big, attentive eyes set under a pair of dark, handsome eyebrows. His face was a reflective mirror of his inner self: easy-going, honest, and hard-working.

Ho De was the general manager of a clock and watch shop owned by his cousin in the heart of Shanghai's most prestigious shopping district. In fact, several of his cousins pretty much monopolized the time machine business in Shanghai. They owned shops variously named the Atlantic Clock Company, Wellington Clock & Watch Shop, Pacific Watches, Inc., Hendry Chronologers, Big Shanghai Clock & Time Emporium, and many more in the British and French occupied territories. Ho De was perfect for the job, born into a well-to-do conservative business family. One of his other relatives owned the famous Three Oceans Emporium. Well-educated through years of private tutoring, Ho De was a master of Chinese calligraphy and poetry. The truth was that he preferred art to business. But above all, he was a good, obedient son who followed instructions and made few choices of his own.

Once, a friend of Ho De's father came to visit and was appalled to find the young master at home daydreaming, practicing ink strokes on a silk scroll. "Young men of his age should be at sea or learning a trade," he said to Ho De's father. "Good handwriting won't help him support a family someday. He needs to see the world to learn about the world."

"My son is too gentle to travel on the ocean. He gets seasick."

"How about a railroad job? My friend needs a bookkeeper on his train. I can recommend him."

Ho De spent the next few years on a passenger train chugging around the country. He learned how to keep accounts and daydream at the same time, all while bouncing up and down in a private railway compartment. His parents finally saved him from a perpetually shaky career by arranging for him to become an apprentice in a relative's clock shop.

"Your cousin needs someone to help him at the store," his mother said to him, one day while he was home. "Why don't you work there so I can see you more often?"

To Ho De, his mother's words were more a command than a suggestion, and he obeyed. A couple of years later, impressed by his diligence, honesty, and his ability to learn, his cousin appointed him manager of the Wellington Clock & Watch Shop—much to the envy of all his relatives. He continued to obey everything his parents told him to do. That included, of course, who to marry. Even for a young man of the time, it took total trust in his parents to tie the knot for life with a woman whom he had never seen or met. In China, marriage was the biggest gamble in life.

As the general manager at Wellington, Ho De was put in charge of purchasing, accounting, and customer service. Like most of the upper- and middle-class Chinese at the time, his customers and merchants were heavily influenced by Western culture. In turn, Ho De's thinking and lifestyle were also exposed to Western influences. Every morning, he wore a suit and tie, a spiffy white shirt, and black patent leather shoes, complemented by a pair of gold-framed spectacles and a gentlemanly black lacquer walking stick.

Wellington was his pride. The store was doing extremely well under his management. His customers loved him because he understood their needs and fashion tastes. Ho De knew exactly what to order for each upcoming season. The merchandise flew off the shelves as quickly as it was stocked. At the peak of his career there, Wellington had a pair of grandfather clocks in solid sterling silver, standing five feet tall in the display window. They turned into an instant attraction, and people from all over the city went there just to admire the clocks.

Ho De's foreign business friends were mainly from Switzerland and America. They brought him business. They brought him friendship. They also brought him a new religion—Christianity. He and his whole family were eventually converted from Buddhism to Christianity.

Chapter VII

RADIO DAYS

Ho De's fondness for foreign things brought him another new taste from a world he had never known before. Like other educated Chinese who were beginning to appreciate Western culture as much as their own, he got caught up in the craze for technology that was sweeping the country. When radio came to Shanghai, he was as excited as a child tasting candy for the first time. He dressed Yan up and took her out to a special store so she could hear what he described to her as "a talking and singing box." What happened there made him regret taking her, for Yan wanted that "talking and singing box" so much that she would not leave the store unless he bought it for her.

At that time, a radio was the size of a clothing trunk, a big machine in a big, wooden frame. It came with an equally big price tag. Yan had never asked Ho De for anything before. Now she did, and it was the most expensive novelty in town. Ho De could afford the radio, but he couldn't give a child anything just because she asked for it. What if her next wish was the moon? His Chinese frame of mind would not allow him to buy the radio for her, even though she begged, cried, and made a spectacle of herself. It was very embarrassing, and Ho De didn't know how to get her out of the store.

She moped for a few days, but Ho De would not give in. It seemed like the issue was a standoff, but, just then, a dangerous flu hit the city. Little Yan got horribly sick. Fever and congestion left her bedridden with no appetite for anything. Ho De pampered her with the best of everything, feeding her slow-simmered black-bone chicken soup with bitter herbs and bringing in expensive, black-suited Western doctors with round eyes, round monocles, and bags full of mysterious instruments of obscure purpose. Somehow, though, she just wouldn't get better.

One day after work, Ho De came to her bed. Looking at her feverish thin face and hollow cheeks, he gently said, "I wish there was something in this world that could make you well again."

Quick as a wink, a small and weak, yet hopeful voice replied, "I would get well tomorrow, if you would buy me that 'talking and singing box'."

Ho De shook his head as he patted her on the shoulder.

The next day, Yan awoke to strange voices and noises, and the servant rushed in. "Miss, Miss, there's a big delivery for you, and your mother's not home."

"What is it?"

"I don't know. It's in a huge box. Your mother's going to be mad about the mess they're making."

When they finally opened the giant box, Yan leapt to her feet. The talking and singing box! She couldn't believe her eyes.

"Daddy bought it for me! Now, I'll get better!" She jumped up and down until she got weak and almost fell off the bed.

The servant was scared by Yan's sudden burst of energy. "Calm down, Miss. You should lie in bed. No more jumping. You'll get me in trouble if anything happens to you."

But Yan didn't hear her words. She managed to get back on her feet and went straight to the big shiny box, which was as high as her shoulder and planted herself in front of it. *You are one strange-looking miracle,* Yan thought. She slid her hands over the cool wooden surface, wondering what to do next. Then, she noticed a row of ivory knobs and some square buttons and remembered from the store to twist and push a few of them. She placed her ear on the box as it vibrated to life. Startlingly loud music and voices started to pour out. Yan was pleased and so, it seemed, was the magnificent, monstrous radio, with its glowing eyes and grinning mouth full of ivory teeth. The servant forgot all about getting Yan back to her bed and they both sat on the floor listening side by side with their mouths open. They didn't even hear Yan's mother when she came home.

"What's going ON?!" Jin Lai shrieked.

The servant regained her senses. "Master has sent Miss a 'talking and singing box,' Ma'am."

"Don't talk nonsense! Stop this right now! And why aren't you making dinner?"

The servant hurried out of the room, leaving Yan and Jin Lai staring at each other. Judging by her expression, Jin Lai wasn't pleased by this unbelievable indulgence of Ho De's.

Yan didn't get well as fast as she promised. But her illness was made more bearable by spending time with her radio, listening to her favorite shows, especially Shanghai operas. She loved their mellow tunes, poetic lyrics, and dramatic themes. In her imagination, she saw all the dazzling costumes, elaborate hand gestures, and acrobatic movements she heard about so many times when Ho De and Jin Lai came back from the theater. A whole new world opened up to her. As the years went on, she could imitate the singing styles of some of the most famous actresses, and she memorized several popular operas from beginning to end.

Radio eventually led her to acting school and an acting career, which made Ho De regret ever giving her the radio. He was a conservative man who believed in raising a girl to be proper and well-behaved so that she would one day become a lady. At the time, acting on the stage wasn't considered acceptable for a young woman from a good family. It was all right to love opera, for he, too, was a fan. But acting in public was a different matter. It was an issue that would later divide father and daughter.

For now, though, radio was the first trophy Yan ever won in her life. She felt like a princess, secure in the belief that her father would give her anything she wanted. Later on, she proudly told her children that her father got her one of the first radios in Shanghai. The "talking and singing box" never lost its charm for her. Throughout her life, in good times or bad, in health and sickness, the radio was her constant companion. As she became more dependent on radio, it became more and more accessible, until it was transistorized, and, finally, was small enough to fit in her pocket or under her pillow.

Chapter VIII

Educating a Daughter—
the Old-fashioned Way

Because of the radio, the relationship between father and daughter was strengthened. Ho De and Yan listened to operas together. They shared laughter and applause, as well as sympathy for doomed lovers and praise for heroes and their endeavors. Most of all, they found a channel to communicate and connect with each other. The more Ho De spent time with his daughter, the more he was surprised by her intelligence and sensitivity. *She needs to be educated*, he thought. And yet he was not willing to send his daughter to a school, to be seated shoulder to shoulder with boys in the same room, to voice her opinions in public, and to be heard by everyone.

However, times were changing fast. Yan's feet weren't bound the old-fashioned way, as they were for her mothers and grandmothers. She could walk as fast as a man if she wanted to, though she would be criticized for not being elegant and ladylike. If her parents permitted it, she could go to school and become the first woman in her family to read and write. Foreign missionaries were opening more and more schools to serve girls just like her. She could even sit face to face with a doctor, instead of sitting behind a curtain and extending her arm through it to have her pulse felt. Ho De didn't object to these social changes. But he opposed the idea of sending his daughter to school, as more and more upper- and middle-class families were doing. To him, young girls should be kept private, delicate, and domestic. Girls were too vulnerable to be exposed to strangers and should always be protected. There had to be another way besides sending Yan to school. Then, he realized the answer to his dilemma: He would do the job himself.

One day, before he returned home, Ho De went out of his way to a stationery store and bought some pencils, a large pink eraser, a writing brush, a stack of rice paper, and some notebooks. He had everything gift-wrapped in a fancy silk box. When he finally turned the key and opened the front door, he could barely contain his excitement.

"Where is Yan?" he asked his wife.

"You know where she is," she grunted. "Always in her room with her radio."

Jin Lai turned her head toward the kitchen and trumpeted an order: "The Master is home. Come and get his coat!"

Ho De didn't wait for the servant to appear. He went straight past his wife toward Yan's room.

Jin Lai's heart sank when she realized that the gift box wasn't for her. She wished that her husband would not spoil Yan the way he did, feeding her "Bird's Nest Soup," buying her a radio … and now what? That box surely contained another one of his indulgences. No wonder Yan liked him more than her. Why wouldn't she? But Ho De never learned to be a proper parent.

Without my strict supervision, heaven knows what kind of girl she will turn out to be, she thought.

The more Ho De spoiled her, the harder she had to discipline that child. It would have been much easier just to stop her husband from spoiling Yan with his little treats, but Jin Lai's upbringing only allowed her to obey Ho De and not to contradict him. In a family, a husband ruled. She shook her head.

"Yan!" Ho De called, as he gently pushed her door open.

Soft, melancholy music wafted around his ears, and with it, the sad song of a lonely young heroine burying fallen flower petals in the classic tragedy, *Dream of the Red Chamber*. Yan was leaning against her window like a statue. She stared at the dim lights in the distance as tears streamed down her cheeks and made two wet spots on the front of her blouse.

Ho De walked quietly to the radio and turned it off. Only then did Yan notice his presence.

"Dad," she breathed in a barely audible voice.

"You have listened to this song too many times," Ho De said gently, trying to give her some fatherly advice. "*Dream of the Red Chamber* is good literature, but too sad for a sensitive girl like you."

Yan flushed as Ho De stared at her puffy, red eyes.

"You are a smart young lady," Ho De went on, trying to gloss over her embarrassment. "I've decided to tutor you myself, and soon, you'll be the first girl in our family to read and write."

"What? What did you say, Dad?" Yan couldn't believe what she had just heard. She blinked her eyes again and again to make sure she was not dreaming.

"I've decided to teach you to read and write," he repeated a word at a time, still wondering whether he had made the right decision.

"Really?" Yan's face brightened up.

"Yes," Ho De promised.

"Thank you, Dad! Thank you!" she said, as her eyes welled up with tears again, this time with happiness and gratitude.

"It's my pleasure, daughter. I should have done it sooner." Ho De was pleased that Yan embraced his idea with such enthusiasm.

He then presented Yan with the gift box and told her that he would teach her Chinese, mathematics, and calligraphy.

He did not know it, but Ho De was fulfilling his daughter's secret wish. Yan had always wanted to go to school, although she never said so. Sometimes, she wished she was a boy, since she believed boys could do anything they wanted. She knew that all her boy cousins attended school, while most of her girl cousins stayed home learning knitting and embroidery. Now, she could do schoolwork at home! Soon, she would be able to read books and newspapers, put her most secret feelings on paper, and write down songs from radio broadcasts … imagine that!

As she untied the gift wrapping, and took out the pencils, writing brush, and notebooks one at a time, she could see herself filling the paper with words, her own words. *I will work hard and make Dad proud. I will read and write from morning till night if that will help make me a good student.* Yan was determined to impress Ho De. Her eagerness drove her to absorb every bit of new knowledge, like a dry sponge dropped into a bucket of water.

Home schooling went well. As his confidence in her grew, Ho De even allowed her to cross the street to the Wellington Clock Shop by herself when he was too busy to come home on time. He would teach her in the manager's office so she would not miss her lessons. Back home, she never stopped reading and practicing her calligraphy. She did all her homework and was eager to get more. Between her radio, homework, and the arrival of her brother, life was getting more satisfying. Still, there was still a hollow feeling in her heart that could never be filled by anything other than her real family. She missed them and could never find an answer as to why she was given away. Instead of letting her feelings subside, her obsession to find both her real family and the truth grew stronger over time. Since she couldn't ask Ho De and Jin Lai, she suppressed her feelings and put her energy into learning and becoming somebody.

After only one year of home schooling, Yan reached the third grade. Ho De was very proud of her, both as her teacher and as her parent. To celebrate, he took her to his store and presented her with a dozen gold watches of the latest European design. He asked her to pick any one of the twelve to keep. Looking over the parade of gleaming, ticking watches, Yan felt at a loss. She was not drawn to any one of them. What really caught her attention was a slim, three-inch-long object inlaid with ivory. On it was an image of a crouching lion with the exotic word "Cyma" engraved on its tail. On the other side, inscribed in stainless steel, it proclaimed, "On time, all the time."

She shyly avoided the eyes around her, pointed her index finger toward the object with the lion on it and hesitated. "What is this, Dad?"

It was a pocketknife. For every dozen gold watches the store bought, there was a bonus knife in the package for promotional purposes. And that was what she wanted. She liked the lion. She liked its smooth touch and the practicality of its being a knife.

"Are you sure you want this knife and not a watch?" Ho De wanted to make sure that his daughter was happy.

Yan nodded with glee.

"When you do well the next time, will you let Dad buy you a watch?"

"Yes, father."

Yan was very happy that day. On the way back home, her fingers clasped her father's big, firm hand tightly while with the other hand she held her trophy knife against her heart. She could see her tears twinkling on her lashes as she blinked her eyes. *I'll always treasure this moment and take care of this knife*, she thought. And she did, for she never lost the knife, or sold it during hard times. Yan kept it with her throughout her life. It even traveled to the western frontier with her.

Yan's life became more settled and enjoyable with home schooling, occasional outings with her dad as rewards for her academic achievements, and her favorite companion, the radio. She grew fonder of her little baby brother and learned to cook and take care of all the household chores whenever the maids and serving ladies left. This happened more and more often since none of them stayed long. They were either fired by her ill-tempered mother or ran away after a few days of backbreaking labor. Instead of changing her ways, her mother only became pickier and less compromising after each servant was fired. She was always angry and thought they were stupid or lazy—or both. Somehow, no maid could ever follow her commands quickly enough. She never liked any of them anyway, but she could not live without their help, for she could not, and would not, do any housework herself.

Without servants, life would have come to a halt. Fortunately, Yan always intervened. Being a good observer and a quick learner, she was able to perform most chores early in life. She found herself cooking and washing dishes and clothes for the family, but it never seemed to please her mother, who reacted to her doing more by making more and more cutting remarks.

"You were born to be a servant."

"You must have been a servant in your last lifetime."

"When did you learn that? I would never want to do that!"

Her mother screamed in horror one day when she saw Yan's bloody hands after she had gutted a fish and scooped out its stomach.

"Mother," little Yan innocently replied. "I'm making your favorite fish dish for dinner tonight."

Her mother waved her arms and stamped her feet. "If you do everything, what's left for you to say to the servants when you have a family?"

Those were the typical rebukes Yan would get for helping out when the servants ran off. She was even beaten a couple of times by her mother for having spiced the food with a little too much salt or breaking a plate. Housework was not rewarding for her.

Chapter IX

TREASURE ... AND PIRATES ON THE CHINA SEA

THOUGH SHE WOULD BE hard-pressed to say exactly when she first noticed it, Yan began to feel an air of brooding hanging over the family. There were secretive murmurs behind locked doors. There were unfamiliar relatives who came to call. There were firm handshakes and serious faces that made her wonder.

Sure enough, one day, her parents summoned her. *It must be serious,* Yan said to herself, when her eyes met her parents' as she entered the living room. Her father and mother were sitting on two exquisitely carved, extra-large mahogany armchairs with such straight, high backs that they made even her father, who was a very tall man, seem small. There were four such chairs in the living room and a matching tea table in between each pair. Yan knew that her parents reserved such formal settings exclusively for serious events.

Are they going to give me back to my own family?

Has something gone horribly wrong?

Have I done anything bad?

Yan kept guessing.

Her father motioned for her to come closer, and she walked gingerly toward them with little steps, hoping she would not be reprimanded. His first words told her it wasn't anything like that, but as the conversation went on, her anxiety grew.

Having been carved into foreign concessions, Shanghai was then subject to the rules and laws of several different nations. To maintain international peace, each of these small "foreign countries" within the city coexisted and respected each other, creating a safe haven for foreign businessmen and rich Chinese families alike. Lately, however, worries plagued the city, causing chaos. Fanned by rumors that Communist Party troops were approaching and the ruling Nationalists were secretly planning a retreat to an unknown place, rich and influential foreigners were packing up the fortunes they had made in Shanghai and sending them to safer harbors.

As the city became more unstable and unpredictable, the Gu clan finally held a meeting. They decided to charter a big boat, load up the family's wealth, and ship it back to their ancestral hometown near Ningbo. Because of the size of the boat, each family was only allowed to send two members.

Ho De and Jin Lai talked long and hard about who would accompany the ten trunks they had filled with their most valuable possessions. Ho De could not leave his job, and his wife had to take care of their son who was too small and tender to go on a rough sea trip. That left Yan. Ho De worried that she was too young to travel alone, but Jin Lai pointed out that the boat would be filled with other relatives, and she would not have to handle anything herself. Ho De reluctantly agreed, and the sailing was set to take place in a week's time. He did insist on her having a guardian and arranged that, once she got to the destination, she would live with Lao Ma, the caretaker of their ancestral family estate.

At 15, Yan longed for adventure, but her feelings about going to Ningbo were mixed. She still remembered the last sea voyage she took when she left for Shanghai. She could smell and taste the bitter, salty air and remembered the fear of sailing with strangers into an ocean of uncertainty. Didn't Jin Lai grab her arm and pull her onto the boat, while she struggled to get off? No one came to the dock to see her off, not her own mother, not her older brother who always protected her, not anyone. Drowned by her own tears and emotion, she didn't remember much of the voyage and how she arrived in Shanghai. She hated the water. She hated the big steamboat. Since then, the same water had consumed her father, the man she loved more than anyone. But in her mind, Arh Chin was now also part of that water, and this trip would offer her an opportunity to be with him. Would Arh Chin be upset that she had another father? *Does it matter now? I just want to be where he is. Oh, how I miss him!*

Yan was aware of the dangers. On her radio, she heard about pirates roaming the seas and how people were kidnapped and kept on faraway uncharted islands until huge ransoms were paid. A number never came back and those family members who refused to pay the pirates sometimes received packages containing the chopped-off body parts of their unlucky relatives. It was a time when "Shanghai" lived up to its name as a verb more than a noun, and the China Sea was a war zone filled with greedy outlaws and gruesome stories. But what was the use of worrying over every possible danger? After all, not everyone who went to sea was kidnapped.

In front of her seated parents, Yan silently nodded her head and agreed to go. Ho De and Jin Lai smiled and praised her for being a dutiful and obedient daughter. They then revealed a stunning secret that at the same time pained and pleased her: They told Yan that half of the trunks contained her dowry, which they had prepared for her future, and that they loved her like a real daughter.

On the morning of her departure, a special black taxi was hired to take Yan and the trunks to the Shanghai harbor where the boat was docked. As they stopped at the pier, Yan could see laborers using thick straw ropes to tie trunks and boxes to bamboo poles, which were then lifted by two men, one at each end. They sang a rhythmic chant to synchronize their work and walked up the thin wooden planks connecting the dock to all the boats lined up at the pier.

Quite a few rich families were loading up that day. Most of the passengers were middle-aged women and young children. Many passengers wore flashy silk garments and fur coats, and shiny gems encrusted their fingers. They had to be helped up the narrow walks into the boats, which were gently rocking from side to side.

Yan was introduced to a distant aunt who would be her chap-
erone for the trip and settled down next to her as the boat pulled
slowly away from the pier. Yan waved good-bye to everyone on the
dock until they disappeared. Then she turned toward the water. The
bow waves foamed as the boat started to pick up speed, heading
along the China coastline.

The voyage proved to be the worst decision the Gu family clan
ever made. What was supposed to be a day trip became a two-week
ordeal, and when it finally came to an end, most of the family's fortune went into the pockets of pirates.

Later, they learned that danger had been present even before
the boat sailed away. Pirates were apparently monitoring the harbor's activities, searching for easy targets—boats that were loaded
with goods and women. They knew where they could find the best
pickings just by counting the number of diamond rings that went
into a boat. Whatever was in the trunks and boxes was gravy. The
boat the Gu clan had hired appeared to be their best opportunity
for the day. A pirate ship shadowed the unwary boat. When they
reached a remote section of the coast, dotted by small, uncharted
islands, several pirate ships in the area attacked and robbed Yan's
boat. The women and children aboard panicked, and the boat was
captured without a fight.

The able-bodied crew held up their hands and surrendered almost too quickly, raising questions later as to whether or not they
had any connection with the pirates. But for now, it was everyone
for him or herself.

Yan was resting in a deckchair when she heard a commotion.
Before she could open her eyes—PLOP!—a huge, fat woman fell
on top of her, knocking the wind out of her.

"Pirates! Pirates! They're climbing up onto the ship!" she
shouted, before struggling to her feet and running off. Yan looked
around: The boat was lurching violently, and the deck beneath her
feet was shaking with footsteps. She quickly woke up her dozing
aunt, who was half asleep and disoriented. They moved around aimlessly in search of a hiding place. When the aunt spotted a pile of

coal ashes, she smeared them all over Yan's face, hands, and clothes. She undid her pigtails and messed up her hair.

"You are dirty, plain, and thin as a stick—you look like an ugly little servant girl," the aunt comforted her. "No one will bother with you." But the fat under her chin trembled as she moved her lips, and Yan did not feel so sure.

With Yan safely transformed, the aunt began furiously applying ashes to herself, but halfway through, she realized it wouldn't work. She stared sadly at her spoiled brocade jacket and fur coat. Her diamond rings and gold bangles sparkled even under the grime. She realized that to look like a servant herself, she would have to get rid of all her finery and her beloved jewelry, so instead, she and Yan frantically began looking for a hiding place.

Their search ended seconds later as the bandits swarmed around them, holding knives and grinning as the women screamed. The boat was commandeered and taken to a wild island where the brigands opened and inspected all their loot. Trunks and boxes were tossed overboard to bare-chested men standing in the surf. Gold, jewels, jade, rare boxwood carvings, and the greatest treasures of cosmopolitan Shanghai soon disappeared into the island's wild thickets, never to be seen again. The passengers were all left stranded on the boat, except for one of Yan's distant cousins. She was taken by the pirates, along with her trunks and boxes, leaving her mother behind, weeping and moaning.

Later, Yan learned that the head of the outlaws wanted her cousin to be his mistress and would not release her. It took her family a fortune and months of negotiations to get her back. But after her release, her university-educated fiancé broke off their engagement when he heard a rumor that she was not a virgin anymore.

Back on the boat, the provisions stocked for what was supposed to be a day trip were quickly consumed. Everyone was living on dried salty fish and rice porridge made with sea water. The more they ate, the thirstier they got. With no fresh water and no rescue in sight, Yan felt weak and dozed by her aunt's side most of the time. She could not eat. The very smell of fish and porridge made her want to throw up. She was also scared. What were the bandits going to do with her and all the people on board? Stories of hostages being cut up and mailed home in pieces haunted her. She felt homesick and missed her parents and her little brother who was just becoming a wonderful chatterbox, eager to ask every silly question in the world. Most of all, she missed her radio with all her favorite operas. But she was glad that it wasn't there, or the pirates would surely have taken that away, too. Would she be able to get home? It didn't look that easy. They were being watched closely. They took away her favorite silver necklace and bracelet set, which she had been wearing for as long as she could remember. Did her parents, or anyone, even know that she and everyone on the boat had been kidnapped?

And if they found out, how could they ransom her, since the bandits stole all the treasure she was taking to the family estate?

Through her fear, she also felt hope. Her dear father Arh Chin's spirit would certainly overpower the bandits. He would never let his daughter be harmed by these bullies. No. He would protect her. Staring out to sea, she hoped for a miracle. Her dreamy eyes could almost see help approaching from afar—the rescue boat that was never to arrive.

Then she came down with a bad fever and spent several delirious days not knowing where she was, without food, without fresh water. Her desperate aunt used drops of rain she collected from the roof of the boat to moisten Yan's cracked lips and dry throat. Yan probably would not have lived through the ordeal except that the bandits decided to let the boat go. It was time for them to move on and find a new target.

The plundered vessel continued on its course toward Ningbo, without its treasure or Yan's cousin, occupied only by the sick, the weak, the helpless, the old, and the young. Everyone was disheartened, having lost everything except their chapped, sunburned skins.

Yan had to rest for a week at her ancestral family estate before she felt her strength coming back. Lao Ma was the gentlest woman she had ever met, attending to every tiny detail of her recovery night and day. Yan constantly asked for water. Having been deprived of it, she panicked whenever she couldn't see water, or wasn't sure whether a glass of it was real drinking water or came from the sea. A single sip provided her with relief. It took her a while to realize that she did not have to worry about water anymore, and that she was safe again.

The first thing she did when she was strong enough to get out of bed was to worship all the ancestors in her family temple and get their blessing. Yan had not set foot inside a temple since her family converted to Christianity, but this shrine contained spirits of all the Gu ancestors, and it was only appropriate that she worship them.

With Lao Ma's help, Yan lit an incense stick in front of each ancestral tablet and placed a big bunch of them in front of the Goddess of Mercy, whose carved figure soared as high as the ceiling. Then she kneeled in front of the entire congregation of figurines representing all her inherited ancestors to receive their communal blessing. On her hands and knees, Yan lowered her head all the way to the floor three times, while Lao Ma fingered her wooden prayer beads and sang a Buddhist blessing. When Yan finished bowing, she closed her eyes and folded her hands together in a praying position, remaining that way until Lao Ma finished her ritual. Then, together, they thanked all the spirits and asked them for guidance and protection.

Afterwards, Lao Ma took Yan around her family's lands and introduced her to less fortunate relatives who had been given merciful permission by Ho De Gu to work his land and harvest the crops without paying any fees. Yan was received like royalty. Baskets of the freshest produce, eggs, cured meats, and smoked fish were presented to her. Everyone called her "Little Miss" out of respect. One elderly woman with powder-white hair dropped to her knees in front of Yan and started to kiss her feet, calling her the "Savior of our humble existence." Yan was utterly at a loss, and she insisted on pulling the old lady up. She knew that what her father had done for the less fortunate relatives in their home village meant a lot to them, yet she felt uneasy accepting their gratitude on her father's behalf. Still, she was very proud of her father for his kind deeds.

The trip changed Yan's feelings about her new family. She learned about their origins and their history, and no longer felt bound to them by force. She began to feel that she had indeed become the daughter of this family, accepted by all the ancestors.

Having been given away and enduring years of criticism from her new mother, it was an unusual feeling to be surrounded by people who looked up to her and were eager to please her. She felt proud and happy. Every morning, Yan woke to Lao Ma's gentle whispers. Snuggling under a soft, homespun cotton blanket, she could hear the birds twittering and smell the bowl of honey-sweet egg custard fresh from the steamer on her nightstand even before she opened her eyes. Lao Ma was always the first thing Yan saw in the morning, bending over her bed and holding a warm, moist towel to freshen her up. Her silky white hair was perfectly combed and pinned up into a bun in the back.

As Yan enjoyed her breakfast, Lao Ma worked on her hair and brought her a fresh change of clothes. There was so much to look forward to. Yan was taken on seaside excursions, oversaw the unloading of the fishing boats, and was given the first taste when freshly smoked fish were brought—still warm—out of the curing huts. In turn, she insisted on undertaking the task of making hundreds of rice cakes during the holidays, stamping them with festive red seals and then distributing them to the grateful villagers.

Yan enjoyed life on the family estate. She loved and was loved back; she gave and was given to. Nobody ever blamed her for things she hadn't done or had done wrong. If she failed to do something right the first time, she was encouraged to try again. She began to gain confidence. Yan felt she could stay there forever and be happy in this ideal and simple country life.

Sadly, the day came all too soon when she had to say farewell to the people she had come to love. For the second time, a gigantic passenger boat puffing white steam came and took her away from the life of her dreams, carrying her back to Shanghai.

To her surprise, her family had moved to a new location in the Zhabei District in the northeastern part of the city. After a couple days of rest, Yan finally caught up with her parents on everything that had taken place while she was gone. It was then that she discovered that her family life had once again taken an unexpected turn.

Chapter X

A Topsy-turvy World

Ho De Gu was an upright man who believed in a world where everyone treated everyone else fairly. Unfortunately, his good luck and success caused jealousy among his relatives, and they began spreading rumors that Ho De was abusing his power as general manager of the Wellington Shop and putting money into his own pocket. After making the rounds, this slander reached Ho De's own ears, thanks to some kind friends who warned him to be careful and watch out for those with bad intentions.

It was hard for Ho De to hear such rumors. He had done nothing wrong and he didn't see any point in responding to lies. But an honest man who did not have a flexible tongue to defend himself could seem as guilty as a thief. He simply swallowed the insults and did nothing. Besides, he had enough problems already. Jin Lai, who had not been feeling well for some time, was diagnosed with TB, and Ho De felt guilty that he never had time to stay home and take care of her. The rumors continued, though, and, increasingly hurt and frustrated, Ho De finally decided to quit his position and retire from social life altogether even though his cousin, the owner of the shop, insisted he should ignore the rumors and stay on.

By the time Yan came back from the country, Ho De had already settled his wife and young son in a small but comfortable ground-floor apartment attached to a small mom-and-pop store, selling everyday necessities such as soy sauce, cooking wine, matches, cigarettes, and toilet paper. Using all his savings, he bought the apartment and store at an estate sale despite a rumor that the place was haunted and in a cursed location. A toothless knife-sharpener who worked on the street outside the store approached Ho De and whispered in his ear that the previous owner had died of a mysterious illness with empty pockets. But Ho De did not listen, and he detested rumors now more than ever. Besides, he was a Christian and did not believe in *feng shui* and the old superstitions. Gold watches might bring jealousy and bad luck, but what could go wrong selling matches in his own shop with no one to badmouth him? A new start was tempting and after spending hours happily imagining how he would make an easy living and spend all his time with his family, Ho De put a thick stack of gold coins into the hand of the surprised seller.

With the store now safely his, it was time to bring Yan back from the countryside. Ho De proudly showed her around his new prize, but she was shocked by the changes that had occurred in the family, the city, and the world. Her socially prominent father had fallen to the level of a lowly shop owner, her stepmother had fallen sick to a fatal disease, and the country had fallen to the Communists. The Nationalist Party, its troops, and followers, which had ruled since 1911, fled to Taiwan, and the English, French, Germans, and other foreigners who helped make Shanghai so colorful and cosmopolitan deserted the city in a panic, lucky to get out before the storied iron door of China came down once again and remained locked for decades to come. With their power secured, the Communists began confiscating all private land, homes, companies, and stores. Under the new reforms, all private property became the property of the government, the people, and the country.

Suddenly, everyone owned everything, and no one owned anything. Owners and managers of businesses and shops were now considered lucky to get jobs in their own companies. Those who were reluctant to turn their business over to the state, or resisted in any way, were sent to prison, or executed in public as criminals. For

Yan's family, it meant that their new apartment and store, bought with their life savings, would soon belong to the government. Since it was just an ordinary neighborhood store that had attracted no public complaints in the past, Ho De was allowed to stay on, tending the shop as a government employee with a small salary. The Gu family could stay in their apartment by paying rent to the state. They managed to live a simple life, meeting their basic needs. Their ancestral lands had been "nationalized" by the government and became one of the local "co-ops," soon to be turned into communes. The estate, where, just weeks ago, Yan had lived like a young princess, was seized by the poor local fieldhands who were now the proud, most prestigious members of the new order.

Yan and her family considered themselves to be fortunate when they learned about the calamities that befell their other, even richer relatives. As with many other upscale stores, Wellington Clock and Watch was taken over and closed by the government in order to eliminate services for the rich and decadent. It was wholly unnecessary, as bourgeois society had suddenly ceased to exist. The tables had turned. The poor and illiterate were made masters over the rich and educated. To have been wealthy was a sin since it was the result of exploitation. The more you owned, the more manual labor would be prescribed to clean away your sins. Ho De's cousin, the owner of Wellington, was reassigned as a janitor and paid a petty wage. His family home, a creamy yellow three-store villa situated in the French quarter, was confiscated together with their giant mahogany furniture, grand pianos, jewelry, garments, and the memories of a lifetime. To further humiliate him, the whole family, including nine of his children, was assigned to live in the servant quarters, while the rest of the villa was subdivided into many apartments for the working-class families and Communist Party members who were now, according to the nation's leader Mao Zedong, the masters of the country. Used to having a dozen maids and servants around the house, his wife was shocked to find that she was now all on her own, responsible for tending not only herself but also her husband and children. Whatever she wanted, and had always had, was there no more. Their world had been turned upside down.

Yan's eldest sister fared no better in Ningbo. She was married to the son of a famous doctor who reinvested the money he made in local farmland. By "Liberation" in 1949, he owned thousands of acres of land. He was condemned as the richest and most rotten landlord in Ningbo, someone who had exploited and taken advantage of his poor fieldhands. Public meetings were held to reveal his evil doings. All his land was confiscated and returned to the people. He was condemned to die and ordered to confess his crimes, but he refused. To the very end, he denied that he was evil and refused to kneel down in public at his own execution.

Ho De lowered his head every time these gruesome pieces of news reached his ears. He became ever more protective of his family, and the little apartment and store became his whole world. He got up early each morning, pedaling his large three-wheeled cart to fetch supplies. He was happy with this solitary routine and considered his morning rounds as his daily exercise.

By law, Ho De opened the store at nine and closed it at seven. It was always busiest during the last two hours when every family was preparing dinner and rushing out to the corner store to get soy sauce, rice wine, matches, a stack of brown toilet paper squares, or a tube of "Darkie" toothpaste, a wildly popular dentifrice sporting a blatantly racist logo of a black minstrel with a top hat and blazingly white teeth.

The end of the day was always hectic, but Yan usually managed to help out and make dinner. After the last customer left, the store closed and the family would finally have some peace. Yan served the dinner, picking out the best pieces and making a special plate for her mother to eat in bed. The next best went to her father and little brother. Yan got whatever was left.

Although Jin Lai was treated extremely well, she was getting more finicky by the day. She was always wishing for the rare, the out of season, and the unobtainable. Yan wracked her brains to find the impossible. Each time her mother craved something, Yan assured her she would get it, not knowing where she could find such a rarity or how she could pay for it.

As the sole employee of his own store, Ho De barely made enough for the family to have the bare essentials, much less luxuries. After his experience at the clock store, Ho De did not even dare to borrow a single cup of soy sauce from the store, in case the local block warden decided to step in and do an audit, which was really an excuse for extortion, anyway. You had to be very careful in this new world, even more than before.

Being a big girl of seventeen, Yan was resourceful and bold. When her mother asked for golden honey dates or Big Dam Crabs from Yang Cheng Lake, Yan silently took her order and set out to fulfill it. Leaving home, she went straight to the pawnshop to sell a piece of her own jewelry—a gold ring, a gold watch, a necklace, or an ivory brooch—some of which were longtime keepsakes she had loved dearly. Once they were in the pawnshop, she knew she would never get them back again. Clutching the money tightly to thwart pickpockets, she wandered all over the city, searching for her mother's often unobtainable wishes. Sometimes, she got lucky. Other times, she went home empty-handed and collapsed onto a chair, completely depleted of energy and hope. The next day would find her back on the streets, searching for her dying mother's little wishes.

One cold winter day, her mother woke up craving tangerines.

"How I wish I could have some tangerines!" she said to Yan in a dreamy voice as she held her untouched breakfast porridge. "I have been thinking about them all night. I even dreamed about them, their refreshing smell as I peeled them open, sweet juice running down my throat as I chewed and swallowed them." She swallowed hard, lifted her head up, and begged Yan: "Can you get me some today?"

"Yes, Mother." Yan never liked to disappoint Jin Lai.

It was a very difficult wish to fulfill, as fruits and vegetables in those days were seasonal, and quick transportation between north and south was virtually nonexistent. Fresh fruits were rare commodities during winter, especially the kinds that didn't store well.

Yan's two-day expedition finally ended when she bumped into a vendor balancing a bamboo pole on his shoulder, each end of which was secured with a cloth-covered basket. When Yan asked, "Any tangerines for sale?" as she did so many, many times with so many, many disappointments, the vendor stopped and partially uncovered one of the baskets, revealing a cache of brilliant orange fruit. Without hesitating, Yan paid him a huge sum and bought ten tangerines. She wrapped them in her scarf and skipped home as fast as she could, singing an episode from her favorite opera.

"Mother, mother," she called in a high-pitched voice. "I'm home! I got you tangerines!"

Unfortunately, this story did not end well. The taste of those tangerines did not live up to her mother's expectations. They were bitter and dry, without a trace of the sweet flavor she had dreamed about as a last pleasure before the Emperor of the Underworld came to pay her a visit. She threw one at Yan, hitting her on her head.

"You're trying to poison me!" she shouted. "You want me to die. You … you want to get rid of me!"

Yan ran out of the home, tears streaming down her face.

Her father heard the commotion and followed her outside. He sat beside her on the edge of the sidewalk, holding her hand tightly and asking her forgiveness.

"Yan, my good daughter, I am so sorry. Your mother is not herself anymore. It's the illness. Would you forgive her for my sake? Would you? Would you?"

When she saw the tears on Ho De's cheeks, she did. And life resumed in the Gu household, slowly, silently, patiently, and hopelessly. Everyone knew that it was a matter of time, for in China at that time, TB was incurable.

Chapter XI

NEW PROSPECTS IN LIFE

THROUGH HER RADIO, AS well as her work at the little store, Yan learned a lot about the new world in which she now lived. Actually, the store was the information center of the neighborhood. When people saw each other at the store, their greetings were often followed by juicy rumors and bits and pieces of neighborhood news. That was how Yan found out that the area high school was enrolling nighttime volunteers for the National Literacy Movement. Inspired by the enthusiasm of her customers and a wish to get out of the stifling atmosphere of long workdays and life with her poisonous stepmother, Yan decided to test her home education.

Wouldn't it be wonderful to do something outside this apartment, this store, and do something important? The hours were certainly fine. She could leave the house after she fed the family, took care of her stepmother, and put her brother to bed for the night. All she needed to buy was a flashlight to accompany her on her long, lonely walks to the school.

So, she went to Ho De and said, "Father, the people need to know how to read, and they need teachers. I want to sign up if it's alright with you."

Her father was silent.

"Dad," Yan wheedled. "I will still help you with the chores and take care of Mother and Chon Gao."

Ho De didn't show any sign of approval or disapproval. He was totally quiet. He didn't like the idea of a young woman walking alone after dark. But he knew Yan needed it—it was exactly the kind of intellectual stimulation she needed. She was a big girl now, eager to get out and have some experiences other than being in this boring store and suffocating apartment with a bad-tempered, terminally ill mother and baby brother twenty-four hours a day. He was torn between "yes" and "no," so he did not say a word.

Sensing her victory, Yan signed up and started teaching grownups who had never read or written a word, people whose thumbprints were their personal signatures on contracts, wedding papers and—finally—death certificates. Her enthusiasm was great and soared even higher when she was addressed with the ancient Chinese honorific, "Teacher Gu." Kind, patient, and willing to spend as much time with her students as they needed, she soon won their hearts. She was unofficially promoted by the neighborhood when customers at the store started calling her "Teacher Gu" instead of "Junior Storekeeper." In fact, she never stopped teaching from dawn until dusk, holding classes in the dim light of the tiny store while counting out bushels of mung beans or tree ear fungus. She was genuinely happy. All her chores at home—taking care of the sick and young, as well as the little store—became much more manageable since she had something to look forward to every night.

Her volunteer job made her life more meaningful, inspiring, and rewarding. Yan also made friends with other volunteers, and they all started going out after work for midnight snacks together. Their favorite hangout was a little dumpling store around the corner where they ordered bowls of steaming dumplings and noodle soup out of a large iron cauldron, sat around a banquet-sized plain wooden table, and chatted.

Amidst the cheerful noises of chopsticks and spoons against soup bowls, they talked about everything like old friends, completely open, heart to heart. Yan was always the quietest one in the group and she was an empathetic listener. But when she spoke out, her opinion was respected, and her ideas would often rise to the top when a debate grew lively.

After their brief gatherings were over, some young male colleague would often accompany Yan home, much to her father's disapproval. Ho De felt his daughter had changed. For a vulnerable young lady, she was too bold and outgoing, meddling in other people's business. She was always out with strangers and met young men without proper introductions or background checks on their families. He worried about her, her future, and her position in society. Yet he felt paralyzed, unable to make any decision, or take action. He just watched as the world around him seemed to unfold with its own will.

Soon, Yan met a very pleasant young woman much like herself. Her name was Hui Jing. Both were opera fans. Both were the quiet type.

One day, Hui Jing stopped by the store with a rolled-up poster.

"Yan, look at this!"

"What is it?" Yan asked without looking, as she filled up a bottle of soy sauce for a waiting customer.

"Have you heard of *Tong Yi Ju Se*? It's a performing arts society," she said excitedly. "They're looking for new candidates interested in studying opera, plays, and motion pictures. You don't need experience—they'll train you. Will you go with me for the audition?"

"It sounds wonderful," Yan said. "But I'm kind of scared. Do I have to sing in front of strangers?"

"I'm scared, too," Hui Jing admitted. "But the two of us will keep each other company so we won't be afraid. Will you come with me?"

Yan hesitated.

"Come on, it'll be an adventure. For all you know, they may not even want us. They may say 'Your eyebrows are too high,' 'Your nose is too big,' or something."

Hui Jing made her laugh.

Hui Jing came from a working-class family in the city. Both of her parents died when she was young. The oldest of four children in her family, she learned to be headstrong, independent, and caring. When Yan met her, she had already devoted a few years to working at a knitting factory and had been elected as the head of the Youth League. Her modest salary kept the family together, feeding and clothing her brother and two little sisters.

Hui Jing always found time to pursue her dreams and go wherever her curiosity led her. Yan admired her a lot, and, being four years younger, felt Hui Jing was the older sister she always wanted.

The adventure with the Tong Yi Performing Arts Society landed them in one more exciting activity together, where they learned with other amateurs how to act in stage plays and operas. Combined with her teaching job, Yan was out late almost every evening. Though she never earned a single *yuan* for all her effort, she was crazy about her work. She was a born actress with a natural talent for singing, and had an immense repertoire of classical opera songs, which she had mastered through her special teacher—the radio.

Soon, Yan was given the starring roles performing at the Shanghai Workers' Cultural Palace, which was locally nicknamed, "The Big Stage." Although it had a rather grandiose name, the theater was actually a former dog track in the heart of the old city. At the recommendation of her instructor at Tong Yi, Yan was sent to the Shanghai Feature Film School to further improve her performing skills.

Most people liked Yan, but some liked her so much it made her life difficult. Once, she was working as the leading lady in a new play and was assigned to a new director who wanted to date her. When she refused to go out with him and told him their relationship was only professional, she was cut from the main cast and reassigned to two minor roles as a prostitute and an old lady. This turned out to be a big mistake because Yan had a very high, young-sounding voice. She tried very hard to play the roles, but the audience burst out laughing when Yan, appearing as an old lady with powder-white hair and a wrinkled-face, spoke her first lines.

She sounded like a schoolgirl, and the director was reprimanded for this casting disaster.

Yan graduated with honors and might have made a name for herself in China's growing new movie industry, but Jin Lai's health took a turn for the worse and she became gravely ill. Instead of accepting an offer from a distinguished movie director of the time, Yan bit her lower lip and headed back home to nurse her dying mother.

Chapter XII

A Mother with TB:
Life and Death

A FEW DAYS BEFORE HER death, Jin Lai became very alert and spoke to Yan, heart to heart, like mother and daughter, for the first and last time.

Yan tiptoed into her room, carrying a breakfast tray filled with little dishes of delicate treats she had prepared: finely chopped pickled vegetables, spicy shredded pork, marinated bean curd with a dash of sesame oil, vegetable chicken and duck with dipping sauces, and lightly sautéed, crispy *bok choy*, along with a big bowl of rice porridge. The room was exceptionally bright, and she found her mother in a very good mood as the sun's warm rays fell gently on her. Yan laid the tray down next to her bed, propped Jin Lai up with several pillows and freshened her hands, face and neck with a lightly scented warm towel. Then, with the tray on her lap, Yan used a silver teaspoon to feed her mother, one little bite at a time, a little bit of this and a little bit of that. Her arm hovered in mid-air, balancing a spoonful of hope that could sustain her mother for a few more hours, a few more days, perhaps, if only she would open her mouth and swallow it.

A long hour went by, and Yan forlornly stared at her tray still full of the food she had brought. Her mother ate very little now, although she still enjoyed the formality of dining and being attended to. Yan finally withdrew her spoon and removed the tray when Jin Lai closed her eyes, and slightly but firmly shook her head, motioning that the breakfast was over.

She was tired, tired of fighting against her illness, fighting for every breath she drew. She was losing her battle, and now three meals a day became her biggest challenge in life. Every meal started out with anticipation and ended as a burden. Her whole life had become a burden. She couldn't get out of bed anymore. She couldn't brush her own hair, feed herself, or wash her own face. She could barely move her arms or legs and just lay in bed and waited. Her time was running out, and she could feel everything coming to an end. This morning, Jin Lai felt hungry and was yearning for a hearty breakfast when Yan arrived with her festive tray. Yet she didn't even have enough strength to feast on the breakfast with her eyes, let alone her stomach.

She could feel two streams of tears rolling down her cheeks, and then a soft towel gently touched her face. She opened her blurry eyes. It was Yan, her daughter for all these years, dutiful, faithful, industrious, and smart. She was a good daughter by any measure. But, what about Jin Lai herself? Was she a good mother to Yan? What did "mother" mean, really? Jin Lai searched for an answer, but her mind was blank. Was it because of her illness, or that she had never, ever, asked herself such a question and tried to learn to be a mother? She was very tired. She could feel herself slipping toward a long and endless sleep, never to wake up again. She knew, at this very minute, that her time with Yan was short and she had never been a good mother to her. She knew, as well, that she should speak now to her daughter, or her unspoken regrets would follow her to her grave.

Yan caught the sad look in her mother's eyes and got very worried. "Mother, mother, are you alright?" she gently whispered into her ear. "Do you want to say something? Is there anything, anything I can do for you? Please let me know. I want to make you feel better."

All of a sudden, Yan felt her mother's trembling arms, as thin as twigs, grabbing hers. "I am so sorry," she said in a choking voice. "I was never nice to you. I thought you knew you are not really my daughter and would go back to your own family when you grew up. So, I treated you like a stranger. I am very sorry. The fact is you are my best daughter. You did everything for me."

Her arms fell back down onto the bed. Her sudden burst of physical energy exhausted her. After a fitful spell of coughing, she closed her eyes and made an effort to breathe. Her chest rose and fell, as if she had climbed many flights of stairs.

"Please take care of your father." She hastened through her words in a barely audible voice. "He is a good man. As for your little brother, use your own judgment, for you know how we got him. When he grows up, and if he treats you nicely as a sister, you can keep him as your brother. Otherwise, he is not really your brother. I hate to leave you with all these burdens. With all the family fortune gone, I have left nothing to take care of your future. You can only go out and earn it by yourself now."

Jin Lai breathed hard through her open mouth. She summoned all her strength to finish her thoughts, her eyes fastened on Yan.

"I didn't bring any luck to your life …"

"You did, mother, you did indeed," Yan said, with a lump in her throat. "You've given me everything I have. Please rest. I want you to get better."

"But Yan, I didn't give you a happy life …"

"Please stop talking like that, mother. I beg you." Yan felt frightened by Jin Lai's words. She never expected her mother to speak to her so lovingly and apologetically, for Jin Lai was a strong-headed woman, always assertive and demanding, who reserved criticism exclusively for the people around her. And now, weak as an infant, she suddenly changed into a loving and understanding creature. Her confession moved Yan to tears. For years, Yan dreamed of all kinds of wonderful mothers to whom she could have been given. But even the most loving mothers she had imagined couldn't have spoken with more caring words and a gentler tone than Jin Lai just had. After years of administering verbal and physical abuse, Jin Lai was transformed magically into the mother Yan had long hoped for. She wanted to spend the last few minutes of her life as a good mother, an understanding and loving mother.

Mother! Kneeling besides Jin Lai's bed and holding her bony hands, Yan broke down.

"I'm sorry I've ruined the first half of your life. When I'm gone, I want you to find a decent young man and get married, a young man from a good neighborhood. Our area is too poor for gentlemen ... and I hope ... he'll bring you lots of luck and happiness for the second half of your life. You deserve the best, my dearest daughter, my daughter ..."

Her voice diminished with every spoken word. When she finished, her breathing became skin-shallow and she knew her end was very near. She asked for the priest to come and pray for her, and used the last bit of her energy to be dressed in her favorite set of clothes, which were made from pure silk. By custom, cotton and silk were the only materials allowed to dress the dead. If the dead were dressed in wool, they would turn into animals in the next cycle of life.

She died with a gauze mask of spun silk over her face to prevent the spread of germs. It was said that the last few breaths of a TB patient were extremely contagious.

Jin Lai had a Christian burial. When she died, she was only thirty-nine. Yan was nineteen and Chon Gao was seven.

After the seven weeks of mourning prescribed by custom, Yan tried to put her life in order again. Not just her life alone, but her father's, as well.

Even though Ho De knew that his wife was suffering from a fatal illness, her death was a heavy blow to him. He lost heart and couldn't pull himself together. Every morning, Ho De looked into Yan's eyes and made her promise that she would not leave him and go back to her own family.

"Please don't go," he said. "Without you, I won't have anyone or anything left to live for. I will have to end my life … I don't know how to go on anymore."

"I won't, Dad," she promised again and again. "I won't leave you."

Yet, Ho De followed her everywhere she went: the kitchen, the yard, the store, anywhere. Once a week, he shadowed her to a small flower shop nearby and waited across the street as she bought a bunch of white chrysanthemums.

After a couple of times, the old woman at the flower shop noticed it. She pulled Yan's sleeve and spoke in fear as she handed her the flowers. "Miss Comrade," she whispered to Yan, using both the old and new ways of addressing a young woman. "Watch out for that old man across the street. He's spying on you."

Yan looked across and spotted her father behind a tree with his head sticking out. "Thank you," she said. "I'll be careful." She didn't know how to explain to the kind old woman that this sad, harmless man was her own father, and that he followed her everywhere she went because he was afraid of losing her.

She walked home by herself, holding the flowers against her heart. She knew that behind her, somewhere down the street, her father was anxiously trailing her. When she got back, she walked straight to her late mother's portrait draped in black. She replaced the mourning flowers in front of the portrait every week. It became a ritual, taking down the old bunch, emptying the vase, rinsing, and refilling it. She took her time placing the fresh flowers in the vase, while feeling her father's watchful eyes behind her.

"Hello, Dad," Yan said, as he finally appeared in front of her. "Where did you go?"

"Just to get some fresh air," Ho De replied, staring at the floor. "Just to get some fresh air."

Yan did not leave Ho De, or her little brother, even though an astonishing chance arose, one day when the little shop door swung open, followed by a most unexpected visitor.

Accompanied by her son, Yan's real mother appeared to claim her daughter back. Since her stepmother—her real mother's cousin—was now gone, she didn't see any reason why Yan had to remain in their household. Yan had dreamed of this moment many, many times. But instead of being happy and rushing into her mother's arms, as she had practiced over and over in her mind, Yan was outraged by her mother's appearance and her startling offer.

"You pushed me out when I was little and didn't want to leave," Yan yelled, standing between her and the silently shaking Ho De. "You did not care what could have happened to me. You never, ever, visited me. Now, you want me to go back to you for your own selfish reasons. I am not going!" Yan could not believe the words coming out of her mouth, even as she said them. "I am not a doll that can be traded at your will. Not this time!"

After Yan said what she wanted to say to her mother, she walked out of the room with her chin up, her dignity intact ... and her heart empty. Her mother stared in disbelief, then flipped a stylish silk scarf over her shoulder, and left the dingy little shop, the rickety wooden door shutting forever with a bang.

It would be another sixteen years before mother and daughter would see each other again.

Yan was shocked by her own behavior, but Ho De was relieved, and they entered a new chapter in their lives together.

Gradually, things returned to normal in the Gu household with Ho De tending the store, Yan running the household, and Chon Gao attending the local elementary school. Yan would have gone back to teaching, but the government had ended its literacy movement and moved on to some other progressive venture. Yan spent most of her time quietly at home, much to her father's surprise, without visits from her friends, or the companionship of her radio—the only luxury left in the house.

Ho De often found her sitting lost in thought by herself. He respected her having her own private moments and understood that, like him, she was going through the grief and shock of watching a loved one leave forever. Ho De didn't know how to pull her out of her depression, any more than he did for himself. Yan's feelings were as tangled as a silk thread that had unwound improperly during boiling. After years of frustration and hope, she suddenly found—and lost—two mothers in the space of a few days. To her surprise, Jin Lai's death preoccupied her most. After so many bitter years, they finally had one rare moment when they felt like a real mother and daughter. And then it was gone, never to be repeated again, leaving her in an emotional haze, wondering if any of it had actually happened.

Yan also thought about her real father again. His was the first death that ever struck her, yet it was different. Her father was just gone, lost in the vast ocean and never coming back. She didn't see him die. She didn't see him laid out for viewing. It was like a dream. When she woke up one day, he was gone, as if he had never existed. Whenever she thought about him or missed him, she could see a vivid image of him very much alive, a handsome, enthusiastic, middle-aged, muscular man in the prime of his life. She could see his laughing eyes, his shining black hair, and his dark eyebrows. She could see a strong man who could not possibly die. She sometimes had a romantic feeling that her father was very much alive, maybe somewhere on an island. He just could not get back home again because he had amnesia, was the prisoner of an evil emperor, or was stranded far away. But now, for the first time, she witnessed a death, a real death. She watched helplessly as Jin Lai struggled for her life. She saw how life was drawn out of a young body and she lost the fight for her own breath. And she felt for the first time how everything seemed to lose importance when life ceased to exist.

Even though she had had mixed feelings toward her mother until the very end, Yan began to realize that she had become Jin Lai's closest and most dutiful companion, and that she got to know her better than anyone else she had ever known. She attended Jin Lai all by herself for three and half years. They both shared the naïve, false hope that they could somehow triumph over TB. They rode up and down together through the long battle for survival, parting ways only when one became a witness to the loss of the battle, and the other became the casualty.

Yan developed a sense of doom about her chance of ever having a mother, a mother who would love her, treasure her, and give her the soft affection that she so craved. Jin Lai's shocking confession on her deathbed still echoed within her. Yan would do anything to have turned the tables on death, to nurse her mother back to health, to see her smile again, and to have a chance of a real mother-daughter relationship. Oh, curse you, death. And curse you, unreliable hopes and wishes. They disappeared like soap bubbles when you reached out for them.

Chapter XIII

A Father's Love,
a Daughter's Rebellion

I T TOOK A WHILE before Yan could face reality again. Life had
to go on for the living. She still had her little brother, her father,
the apartment, and store to take care of. The more she worked,
the less she had time to stare at Jin Lai's portrait and think about
death. As she went about her daily chores, she recovered little by
little from the numbness of loss. She felt an urge to get out of the
apartment and work on something more meaningful, so she went
back to the Tong Yi Performing Arts Society, hoping, someday, to
continue her career.

Ho De was glad to see her get out of the stifling apartment. He
even went so far as to see her performances a few times. A proud
smile rose on his sad face every time he recalled his daughter standing at the center of the large stage, playing the heroine of *The Big
Storm*, a famous play at the time. *Yes, my daughter. Only a daughter
from the Gu family could have done so well.* But the dilemma was
clear: The Gu family was a dignified one. What would the ancestors think about her being involved with the vulgar career of acting,
which was almost on a level with prostitution?

In the old days, the poorest families would sell their daughters to performing groups to entertain the rich. Even though the

Communist Party made it clear that acting was now a respectable job because the actors and actresses worked for the government and for the entertainment and education of the masses, being on the stage meant his daughter could be seen and admired by everyone, not just by those who loved and admired her, but also by the lusting eyes of all men. His daughter could be heard by thousands over loudspeakers and even the radio. There was nothing he could do to prevent people from watching and listening to his daughter as long as she was out there performing for all to see.

Ho De wished he could consult his pastor, as he used to for private matters that were too sensitive to talk about with friends or family. A man of God had answers for everything. But the communists had closed the church and sent the pastor away, leaving Ho De with no one to talk to. He suddenly thought of something he hadn't done for years: visiting and getting advice from his ancestors in the family temple. After all, they were the very people whose honor he wished to guard. Then Ho De frowned. He remembered that the temple was not there anymore. He had learned from friends that his family shrine had been destroyed. All the sacred treasures within were gathered in the yard and burned: the books, the bamboo tablets that symbolized his ancestors, the holy incense, everything. The Goddess of Mercy statue was chopped into a pile of wooden splinters, and the local families used it as fuel to cook a few meals. Ho De had not been there to defend his ancestors.

Why hadn't he gone there earlier, packed up his ancestors, and taken them back to the apartment before it was too late? He felt heavy with guilt, knowing that he had completely ignored the temple and ancestors since his conversion to Christianity. It was depressing to imagine his ancestors' souls homeless and wandering for eternity. It was too late to help the ancestors, but he could still defend his family honor.

Ho De started to track all of Yan's movements, even if it meant that he had to pay for a baby-sitter to take care of Chon Gao after school, or pay someone to watch the little store, or go to sleep late since Yan's performances usually took place at night. He memorized all the places Yan went and the people she went out with when her performances were over. He waited patiently in the shadow of a building or a tree. That part of the city was always crowded, and no one ever paid any attention to him. The trickiest part was that he had to dash home before Yan got back so she would not know she was being followed.

Ho De did not consider his behavior undignified or ungentlemanly; he felt that, while he searched for an excuse to steer her away from performing, he would be her silent guardian to protect or save her if necessary. But he knew the danger of his game. He knew his daughter would feel offended if she knew what was going on. He also knew how much she was enjoying the freedom and independence given to her by this communist society.

Ho De also learned that his daughter went so far as to create for herself a new stage name: "Yan"—a high-flying swallow—which seemed to symbolize her wish for freedom and adventure. She was known by all her friends now as Yan, no longer his little Worshipping Beauty, Chon Mei, the name he gave her in accordance with the ancestral book. To Yan, Chon Mei was as distant as Ai Zhu, the Loving Pearl that had been so easily thrown away.

Yan was invigorated by the magic of theater life. She loved being the center of attention, getting the main roles, and knowing she was good at playing them. Every afternoon, she jumped onto the same bus to get to rehearsals at Tong Yi. Every evening, she performed on the same stage under the same spotlight. Sometimes, she wore glittering costumes with long sleeves trailing behind her and heavy make-up that felt like a mask. Other times, she simply wore the everyday clothes of a schoolteacher, a student, a little girl, a journalist, or a mother. Stage life was exciting for Yan, and she felt herself "becoming" the characters in all these roles.

When Yan arrived home each night after performing, a sense of excitement swept through the door with her. Even under the dim kitchen light, Ho De could see Yan's sparkling eyes, animated face, flushed cheeks, and painted lips. It bothered Ho De to see his well-mannered, educated daughter turning into a showgirl right in front of his eyes. Acting was something for young people from poor families, making a living by selling their looks, despite what the Communist Party of China had to say. He had to do something about it.

Ho De could just have stopped her from performing by using blunt words or locking her in her room. But he didn't. He wasn't sure what to do, because he was torn between his wish to preserve his daughter's happiness—of which she had so little—and the wish to defend his ancestors' honor. Ho De's dilemma seemed hopeless as there seemed to be no middle ground for compromise. Besides, Ho De wasn't the confrontational type. He would rather walk away from a problem, just as he had walked away from the Wellington Store and his secure life rather than dignify ridiculous rumors.

But this time, it was different. This was not something Ho De could walk away from. It was not about himself. It was about his one and only daughter, whom he loved more than anything in the world. He feared that what she wanted to pursue happened to be the worst possible choice in life. However, he also sensed that, if he took any action, an unpleasant argument was inevitable. Ho De rarely argued with anyone, let alone with Yan. As it turned out, he was right to worry. When an argument finally broke out between the two of them, it was explosive enough to change the courses of both their lives.

One day, Yan had no performances. Her little family rarely got to spend much time together anymore, and she wanted to spruce up the house and cook a decent meal they could all enjoy together. She got up early, went to the market to pick out the best items among the limited choices on the half-empty shelves, and dashed back home. She opened all the windows to air the rooms, took apart the quilts, soaked all the sheets and pillowcases in warm soapy water, dusted the rooms, washed the floors, hand-washed all the laundry, hung it out to dry, reassembled all the quilts, made the beds, and even had a few moments to darn a few socks, and patch the holes on Chon Gao's pants.

"Sit down for a few minutes," Ho De finally ordered her. "Here, have a cold drink—it's refreshing." He brought her a glass of tea with tangerine peels in it.

"Thanks, Dad." Yan drank it down while standing. "Let me finish everything before dinner. I'm getting a lot done ... I haven't done this much since Mother passed away." As she mentioned Jin Lai, their eyes met and turned moist, and Ho De hurried out of the room.

Yan returned to her work.

Finally, it was time to cook, set the table, and call the family for dinner. Yan had had a backbreaking time, trying to compress the week's chores into one day. She sat down at the table, inhaled the aroma of food and fresh air in the room, and felt relaxed. The dinner conversation soon turned to Yan's most recent successful performance, and how she came home very late, having been invited to the celebration party.

Having sipped some rice wine earlier, Ho De became talkative. "Who was that young man who kissed your hand?" he asked. "He was very good-looking, and had nice manners."

Silence fell. Ho De had slipped. The smile on his face froze, and his chopsticks hung motionless in mid-air as he saw Yan's animated expression change to puzzlement, sadness, and then, slowly to anger.

"Have I been followed? Did you hire someone to follow me, or did you do it yourself? Why, Father? Why?" Yan's voice got louder, and her face grew darker with every question. She understood why he did what he did, when he first followed her around the house and to the flower shop. But now, following her to the theater and parties, too? She would become a laughingstock: Yan, the high-flying swallow, tied to the ground by her father. She might as well forget about being a swallow if she could not break through her cage and fight for her freedom!

"You never trust me. You never want me to do anything. You just wish to lock me up in this apartment to serve you and this little store," Yan said, each accusation booming like thunder in Ho De's heart and making him shiver.

Ho De did not know what to say. He couldn't have felt worse if he had been caught red-handed and thought about denying it, but he was not good at making things up. So, he decided to be honest.

"I did it all to protect you," he said with a purple face and veins the size of earthworms around his temples. "You are my daughter. You shouldn't have been out after dark with strangers anyway. Acting is not for you. It's for the lower classes. It brings shame to the Gu family. I think it is time I told you that you should stop going to Tong Yi, right now, before it is too late, or no honest, decent man will marry you!"

Yan was now mad. She felt cornered and misunderstood. And she knew that her father was a stubborn man. Once he made a decision, it was impossible to change. Yan silently swallowed her protests, smothered what she knew would be even more lethal emotional explosions and managed to finish the rest of her dinner with her eyes cast down, her tears silently flowing into her bowl. She did not remember how she cleared the table, did the dishes, and ended up in her own room.

For the first time since Jin Lai died, Yan did not bid her father goodnight. She did not peek through the keyhole to see how her father was doing or come out of her room. She spent the rest of the night on her bed, tossing and turning. Her mind raced like a flying shadow. She needed to sort through her young, tangled, and misused life. Her heart sank as she imagined herself as a white-haired grandmother wearing a pair of horn-rimmed reading glasses and still selling soy sauce and toilet paper in this little store. She couldn't go on living a life like this. She refused to weigh herself down with the penny-ante knickknacks here. She was a swallow now, and must soar toward the sky!

For the next few days, she left home early each morning and roamed around the city, avoiding the neighborhoods near the opera society, the Big Stage, and all the places her theater friends gathered. Those familiar sights were too painful. All she wanted now was to let her legs carry her to the parts of the city she didn't know and where she wasn't known so she could plan her own flight to freedom.

One day, she appeared in front of Ho De. Looking straight ahead, she told him: "Father, I have joined our glorious national effort to develop China's Great Northwest. The government has assigned me to leave in two days."

It was now Ho De's turn to be speechless. He knew his daughter was as determined and stubborn as he. He couldn't stop her from going. He was smart enough to know that anyone who stood in the way of the government's efforts would suffer serious consequences. Ho De was paralyzed. He could not apologize to her for blocking her acting career because it was against his conscience. He just wanted to kneel in front of her, beg her not to go, and tell Yan he needed her. How could he go on living without her? How could he?

Unfortunately, he said nothing, and did nothing, to stop her.

On the recruiting form, Yan registered her name officially for the first time as "Yan Gu"—her stage name—instead of Chon Mei. The little swallow was ready for an adventure, confident that her wings were strong enough to carry her anywhere she wanted to go. No more restrictions, no more pleasing others. For the first time in her life, Yan was doing something for herself, doing something because she wanted to do it. She packed herself up, said farewell to everyone, and flew into the unknown.

PART II

TWO DESTINIES ENTWINED

(Zhang Ye City, Gansu Province, 1957)

Chapter I

Young Pioneers

I T TOOK A GOOD hour of huffing and puffing to travel from the train station to the dormitory. The winding caravan paraded with little enthusiasm down a lonely dirt path. The donkey carts moaned and groaned under the weight of piles of luggage and glassy-eyed travelers. Everyone was puzzled, disappointed, and speechless: There were no welcome signs, flags, or crowds to receive them. The local government did not send representatives to host a ceremony, thanking the thousands of young volunteers for coming. They were just there, by themselves, in an empty train station after five days and five nights of backbreaking travel, taking them ever further away from home.

They imagined themselves to be patriots who had sacrificed their own lives to benefit the nation. Many of them had left their secure, well-paying jobs to come here. Before they embarked on their journey, they were sent off as "heroes" by crowds of dancing and singing children amidst a sea of red flags. Now, they were just strangers in a strange land. The courageous travelers started to stagger, lagging behind the donkey carts, which were kicking up choking dust. Some of the pluckier New Heroes of the West managed to squeeze themselves onto the squeaking, wooden carts, while others dragged themselves forward, pulled by the prospect of a warm, soft bed, and a new place called home.

Yan kept on walking. Her stiff legs were no match for the deeply rutted dirt road. She surveyed the area, and found nothing except rough open fields that extended as far as the horizon. Actually, the road they were on was part of the fields. It existed only because uncounted numbers of people had followed each other and walked over it for hundreds, if not thousands, of years. But all the millions of footsteps were not strong enough to crush the stones and level the road. The trail was an obstacle course, packed with surprises. Yan had to pay attention to where her feet landed or suffer a twisted ankle or nasty fall.

The cunning wind was skillful at casually sweeping up dirt from the ground and blowing it right in her face. Yan felt the dry dust in her nose, mouth, and throat. She swallowed hard to get rid of it but as soon as she breathed, her throat filled up again. Her eyes watered, and her vision blurred. The dust eventually formed an opaque film on her thick glasses. She had to stop and wipe them clean before she could catch up with the others.

The first impression of her new hometown was beyond the wildest imaginings of a city girl. She felt like she had landed on an alien planet of some sort. She had never seen so much dirt in her life. Dirt settled beneath her feet. Dirt swirled in the air. The air smelt like dirt. Even the houses were the color of dirt, since they were built with a mixture of dirt and water. To Yan's amusement, people actually boasted about their homes, without shame, as "mud huts."

Dirt, dirt, everywhere. It was the only wealth and greatest natural resource for the local community, and there was not much else besides it. The locals had learned to exploit their surroundings and make the most of what they had. Inside the mud huts there were dirt floors. Their beds were made of baked dirt. The large clay beds were cool in the summer and in the winter a fire could be made underneath to keep the sleepers warm. Clay pots and containers of all possible sizes and shapes were used in every household to hold grain, water, sorghum wine, and odds and ends. The over-sized kitchen stove was made of clay, usually in the shape of a large triangle, built to fit into a corner. It devoured anything that could burn, including dried twigs, stems, and leaves left from the last harvest, along with a generous helping of dried animal dung collected by the children to help meet the household's need for fuel.

Life there was literally "down to earth," focusing only on absolute necessities. It was like winding a clock backwards for a century. There was no such thing as "garbage" or "waste." Everything was used until nothing was left. After a harvest, the grain was threshed by hand and shared by people and animals alike. The skeletal remains of the harvest were fed either to animals or into the mouth of the stove to cook the family meals. Any meager surplus was used to trade for rare commodities such as salt, sugar, matches, soap, yarn, or fabric.

Each family raised only a few sickly cattle since grain production was limited by the lack of water. It almost never rained. The only form of precipitation was the winter snow, and the only water source was the temperamental *Ruo Shui* ("Weak River").

Throughout history, when farmers had a good harvest, they prayed to Buddha and made generous offerings to him as a humble gesture of thanks, using only the very best food reaped from a hard year's work. When they did not have a good harvest, which was often the case, they somehow always managed to survive with the little they had, on top of what they had saved when they could. They were people who possessed nothing but tenacity. They were incapable of questioning the heavens or complaining when life dealt them a setback.

The chronic shortage of water left a deep imprint on the region's culture. For generations, people got by with taking only three baths during their lives: They bathed when they were born, when they got married, and when they died. Bathing became a ceremonial ritual instead of a hygienic requirement. Strange as it may have sounded to Yan and all the other city folk when they found this out, the locals took the matter seriously. Here, water was more precious than gold and was not to be taken for granted. Like all her colleagues, Yan had to go to a pump station every day with buckets and basins to fetch her daily ration of water. Once the ration card was stamped, she had no more water to use until the next day.

In the dormitories, everyone soon learned how to recycle water. In the ladies' section, each room was just large enough to fit four single beds for four young women, who called each other "sisters." Yan was the second oldest of the four, and got the title "Er Jie"— "Sister Number Two." After Yan finished her morning sponge bath, she saved the water under her bed to be used later for washing her intimate wear, socks, and handkerchiefs. In spite of such harsh conditions, she still felt certain personal habits should not be compromised. She then saved the same water to wash her chamber pot, before it was dumped into the mud, attracting clouds of bugs, birds, and the occasional stray dog looking for a drink.

By pooling their resources, the four sisters even occasionally managed to secure the luxury of a bath. Creating a bath was always a secret mission. They would bar the door, draw the curtains, and place a large shallow basin in the middle of the room. They would each pull out a precious hidden bucket of water and pour them, one by one, into the basin. And then, three of them would leave the room, leaving one lucky girl to splash, giggle and sing by herself. With the basin and a few inches of water, she felt like a princess at the most luxurious spa.

Life was very hard, and she missed her family terribly, as Yan freely admitted to her father in postcards whenever she had money for stamps. Ho De was not much of a writer, but once a month, Yan received a package of varying size and weight. She was always amazed by her father's thoughtfulness and ingenuity. He put a lot of effort into every package and turned each one into a magic box. Yan pulled out surprise after surprise, as if the package were bottomless. Knowing her situation, Ho De mostly sent food: a few dried sausages, a small bag of cured shredded pork, pickles, cookies, biscuits, and candies. Even small envelopes of sugar and salt were placed carefully in between towels, socks, thread, sewing needles, toothbrushes, and toothpaste. In Shanghai, such everyday items would be trivial, but here they were received with awe and appreciation. Though his letters contained few words, Yan knew that Ho De tried very hard to help her. After all, he and Chon Gao could barely survive themselves on his meager pay. She began looking forward to her monthly package, as much for the love it held as for the vital supplies it carried over a distance of six thousand *li*. Life in China's Wild West was harsh, but it was made even tougher by the imposition of Chinese military routine on the civilian volunteers. Men and women lived in separate row houses wired with loudspeakers that punctuated their daily routine with startling, sudden loud announcements, news, and revolutionary music. The officials in charge decided there were to be just two meals a day—a hardship for city-soft youngsters who had gotten used to enjoying rice porridge and egg breakfasts, bountiful noon meals with pork, fish, and vegetables, and evening banquets. Newcomers had to follow the customs of the locals to show respect, since they were to settle there and become part of the community. For generations, the people had eaten two meals a day—a late breakfast and dinner—to have enough food to last for the entire year. As employees of the government, the new arrivals were ordered to share the same hardships as the locals to understand their needs. Anyone caught cooking or eating extra food risked severe punishment, a cut in pay, or extra working hours.

Meals were provided only at the company canteen, and they were made in the local style: noodles, cabbage, chili peppers, and steamed buns made from coarsely ground cornmeal or barley flour were the day-to-day fare. Fish was out of the question because Zhang Ye was too far away from the water. Meat and poultry were scarce since there was barely enough grain for people, much less animals. About once a week, a few shreds of pork or chicken could be found in a vegetable dish, served with cornmeal gruel and baked oatmeal pancakes as thick as bricks, and almost as hard.

To comfort their always-growling stomachs, private stashes of food came in handy. The morsels Ho De took from his own mouth helped Yan to sneak a bite when she was tortured by hunger.

In spite of the strict rules and regulations, more and more violations occurred for cooking forbidden food. Hunger overpowered politics. When punishment failed to stop the "deviate cooking behavior," the rules were gradually eased. Soon, little charcoal stoves appeared in front of every dormitory room. Everyone spent every penny they could spare to buy whatever extra food they could get from the black market to make up for the missing meal. The local economy got quite a boost by selling food to the newcomers. The hottest topic in the dorm was where to get what special food at what cost, or who was making a secret stew with what unheard-of ingredients. In its own way, life there was getting more interesting by the day.

Chapter II

OASIS IN THE DESERT

FOR TWO THOUSAND YEARS, the tiny city of Zhang Ye sat patiently trapped in the hot, dusty, and impossibly remote corner of northwest China known as Gansu Province. By the 20th Century, it had been all but forgotten, but Zhang Ye once played a vital role in China's history. The height of its fame came in the 13th Century when it was a major stop on the ancient Silk Road, linking East and West. Marco Polo passed through Zhang Ye on his way to see the great Mongol emperor Kublai Khan, as did the uncounted numbers of spice traders, whose returns to Europe with fragrant boxes of peppercorns, anise, and cloves sparked a craze that would eventually lead to Columbus's discovery of the New World. It served as a "must" stop for every traveler on the way to Dunhuang—a major trade city and the most glittering cultural jewel in the crown of the ancient civilization along the Silk Road.

Small as it was, Zhang Ye possessed every feature of a medieval Chinese city with fortified walls, a moat, watchtowers, and even a drum tower to warn the citizens of fire or—worse—invading armies. There were only four ways in and out of the city through the four protective armored gates called, simply enough, the North Gate, South Gate, East Gate and West Gate. Above each gate stood a watchtower from which mostly bored (and occasionally terrified) guards had, for hundreds of years, warily eyed the desert for the telltale yellow clouds of dust that signaled the coming of a Mongol attack. Even in the 1950s, all the city gates still closed at sundown, and reopened only with the rising sun, cutting the city off entirely from the outside world. Sunrise and sunset marked the beginning and end of a day.

Whenever they could, farmers loaded produce, handicrafts, a few precious chickens or cuts of meat, or whatever they had to sell onto the family donkey—the most popular means of transportation. They walked across a drawbridge over the moat and entered the city through one of the gates. Then, they would set up a stand on their favorite street corner or at the Farmers' Market and try to lure customers. With the money they made that day, they could then obtain things from stores in the city before they headed back home again. It was what farmers called a "market day"—an infrequent urban adventure.

For most farmers, market days were rare. They had little to sell and a lot they needed. Often, they had to give up one precious thing in order to trade for another that was more important to them at the time. When a farmer's wife was expecting, for instance, he might have to sell his family's only pig to pay for a midwife. In this way, one pink, wiggling armful was often traded for another.

The people had become accustomed to poverty. Long ago, the city's population had dwindled as the Silk Road ceased to be the chief link between China and the outside world. With the invention of the steamboat, railroads, automobiles, and of course airplanes, camels and donkeys lost their lead roles in transportation. Adventurous travelers and business people started to use different, more efficient ways to get to their destinations. Zhang Ye City was left out. It lingered and stayed the way it had been at the height of its glory days, mournfully waiting as people from all over the world passed it by using the sea and air to reach the great cities of the east. Modernization was a fatal blow to the Silk Road and the other cities along its winding path. Without outside trade and travelers, life became locked in the past. Eventually, the tiny city of Zhang Ye fell asleep in the numbness of everlasting antiquity, shrouded by a cover of dust and lost in its own decay.

All the Chinese government's efforts to revitalize the empty and barren West counted on revitalizing its cities' historic importance in trade, and it was decided that nothing would demonstrate this more than creating a major shopping center as a trade magnet for the entire province. Thus, out of dust and dreams, was made the Zhang Ye Municipal Department Store, appearing like a mirage in the heart of the city. Trumpeted as the largest and most comprehensive trade emporium far and wide with sharp, knowledgeable employees like An Chu and Yan imported all the way from China's famous coastal cities, the store was not just a store—it was the most important part of the city.

The Municipal Department Store was an ambitious project. Located in an ancient imperial building with its own drum tower, which served as its warehouse, the department store offered the poor, blinking peasants a wealth of commercial choices not seen in six hundred years. The store boasted ten well-staffed divisions, showcasing textiles, jewelry, leather, cosmetics, housewares, foods and beverages, furniture, tools, and customer services. A novelty in the province, it generated excitement and was given a warm welcome at its grand opening. Wealthy tribal herdsmen and their families from as far away as the Gobi Desert traveled for days to get there and buy everything from needles and thread to earrings and silver teapots. Language barriers were transcended by hand gestures or a piece of paper and a pen, and these pantomime transactions ended with handshakes and smiles all around.

Yan was assigned to the Housewares Department, which employed nine people from different cities and walks of life. Yan was the youngest of them all. With two waist-length pigtails, a slim body, high spirits, and a pair of bright eyes glinting behind scholarly spectacles, she looked younger than her age. Yan was well-liked, and nicknamed "Xiao Mei" ("Little Sister") by her department, a name she hated. She did not want to be treated like the youngest, for with that came extra care, attention, advice, and help, which she did not want, especially from her manager, a single man in his early thirties whose last name was also Gu.

At first, Yan did not work well under him. She found him rigid, bossy, critical, and uncommunicative. He assigned her unreasonable amounts of work. Sometimes, she had to work a shift and a half in order to finish her job. With little food, Yan was physically exhausted by the task of unpacking and separating thousands of fragile items a day from between the layers of straw inside large wooden shipping crates. And then she had to polish the items one by one and stockpile the floor merchandise. Often, she felt dizzy and drained of energy before the day was over.

Nevertheless, she liked being a saleswoman, standing behind the counter and helping customers to pick out what they wanted. When a transaction went through, she wrote a duplicate receipt, rolled it up with the cash—the only means of payment at the time— and placed the wad in a small sack attached to a sliding clip on top of a metal "clothesline" leading to the cashier's station. When Yan gave the clasp a mighty push, the stuffed pouch glided along the string and stopped right above the cashier, who emptied it, counted the cash against the invoice, stamped the receipt, put the carbon copy of the receipt with the change back into the sack, and sent it flying back to Yan. Then, Yan counted the change before presenting it with the receipt and the purchase to the customer.

When business was slow, Yan and her colleagues had fun with the messenger sacks, passing around little treats, jokes, and messages. They had to play this game stealthily, for work regulations would not permit such childish behavior. It was risky but worth it. All the staff felt connected through this "metal spider web" close to the ceiling. It was their secret way of socializing at work and made for a bit of entertainment.

Mr. Gu always felt a little awkward managing his group, especially the group of seven women that included Yan. He was used to working with men and knew how to lead them. But women were like another species. With men, it was always, "Yes, Comrade Gu," and the task would be done. Whatever methods he used that

worked successfully with men, however, seemed to have the op-
posite effects with women. He was puzzled by how many excuses
women could produce when they did not want to obey his orders.
He learned quickly that his orders were never received with a "yes"
or "no," but aggravating, tedious reasoning and explanations that
he just did not have the time or patience to listen to. He often had
to walk away before he lost control and exploded. He comforted
himself by imagining that the women's silence when he appeared
at least showed respect, until one day, he went into the back room
looking for some order slips and overheard two women sharing the
latest hilarious story about "Grandpa" and "String Bean." Gu listened in the dark, smiling when he realized "String Bean" was a tall,
skinny worker from Nanjing and who was the only other man in
the department. Then, it dawned on him who "Grandpa" was. Gu
ran out of the room, angry and confused. The men, used to being in
charge, found themselves exiled to insignificance by nothing more
than merry peals of girlish laughter.

Mr. Gu decided to alter his management style to regain control over his department. He forced himself to approach his alien
subordinates and work with them more closely. He soon came to
a realization that they were not as strange, silly, mean, and lazy a
bunch as he had first assumed. As time went on, he learned to work
with and eventually appreciate them, even if he couldn't shake his
mortifying nickname.

It was during this period of time that he started to understand
Yan. He admired her strength and sense of independence. He noticed that Yan was the only woman in the group who didn't talk
nonstop. As small as she was, she would clench her teeth to do any
heavy task she was given without complaining, even if it would take
her a lot more time and many attempts. Gu began to feel guilty that
he had assigned her such labor-intensive work in the first place.

As they got acquainted, they learned that both of them had
been raised as Christians before religion was banned and that, in
their hearts, they were still believers. It became their little secret.
They were bound by the same beliefs, though in public he was a

Communist Party member. He vowed to protect her. And since they shared the same family name, he allowed her to call him "brother." From then on, they enjoyed a good relationship. Yan was very happy to have gained his friendship, and it greatly improved the quality of her work life.

Chapter III

WELFARE WAREHOUSE

THE DEPARTMENT STORE OCCUPIED what must have been a very important building in ancient times, for it was adjacent to a drum tower. Drums were used to warn the people of approaching danger such as fire or war, and only the ruler of the city could order their use. In keeping with both structures' importance in Zhang Ye, the building became the new center of commercial life, and the old drum tower was converted into the store's giant warehouse. An Chu was put in charge of the inventory and everything that moved in and out of the tower to the store. He was a one-man crew for the whole warehouse and the only person in the whole huge enterprise given the power to hire local workers whenever big shipments arrived.

Times were hard, and the local people were eager for work. An Chu became the center of attention and the center of many townspeople's lives. On days when there were no shipments, An Chu often found himself trailed by a group of ragged men, aimlessly begging for any job that might be coming up.

"Comrade An Chu, please, I need a job. Anything, anything will do. My wife is sick. I need money to get her some herbs."

"Big brother An Chu, I know you have a big heart. My wife is expecting our second child, and I don't have anything to feed her."

"I need a job. I have six small children at home and there is nothing to eat."

Every man that followed him had a story to tell, a tale of hardship and poverty. An Chu did have a big heart, and he took the time to listen to each one of their stories.

Although he could not save all of them, he did what he could for those who approached him. Being poor most of his life, he sympathized with these people and knew their needs well. Whenever a shipment arrived, An Chu chose a handful of "stars of the day" from the big pool of eager candidates.

"Liang, you go. Xiao Long, not you—you just worked two days ago. Let everyone have a chance. Da San! Let Da San go. His wife is due any day now ..."

One day An Chu's searching eyes fixed on a disappointed and desperate face. He looked unfamiliar. *Another hardship case when there are so many already*, he thought.

The strange man was buried under a shapeless, bulky jacket with a straw rope tied to his waist. He looked more like a scarecrow on a stick, except his toes were peeking out from his oversized shoes. He was an old man, thin and worn out, too weak to compete with this fierce group of hungry job-seekers. Only his eyes, wide and unblinking, silently begged An Chu for help, and even then, they shyly shifted away when he realized he was being examined.

"You, what is your name? You, you ..."

"Arh Bun," the old man finally managed to utter his own name out loud, quickly, like a sneeze.

As if surprised by his own courage, Arh Bun shifted his eyes again and concealed his nerves by staring at his toes instead of the crowd around him. His hands crawled into each other's sleeves.

"Arh Bun, tell me, why did you come? Do you know that the only jobs here are to lift heavy boxes?"

An Chu's questions only managed to elicit a few nods from him. But his feet did not move. Arh Bun just stared at the ground with stubborn determination.

A couple more lucky names were called. Then An Chu said more softly, "Arh Bun—you, too. Come with me."

Carrying freight from a truck to the drum tower posed a physical challenge even for an able-bodied man. An Chu stayed on the truck and lifted one giant box at a time onto the back of a man waiting below on the ground. With several hundred pounds of goods on his back, the man then climbed a set of steep stone steps up into the tower to a storage area in the deep, dark chamber. A worker had to be strong to carry round after round of freight. An Chu chose only the smallest and lightest boxes for Arh Bun. But even those were too much for him. His legs were shaky, and he could barely move forward once he was loaded up. After only the second round, he was out of breath, and was ordered to sit aside to wait until the shipment was done. Finally, the empty truck kicked up a cloud of dust and drove away. The workers chatted and waited for their pay permits, which they would take to the accounting department to turn into cash.

Everyone who worked for An Chu knew his rules. They all worked together until the job was done. The stronger people carried more, and worked more. And everyone had to do the best he could. If necessary, An Chu himself would carry boxes deemed to be too heavy for anyone in the crew. After a shipment was done, everyone was given a pay permit for the same amount. All of them—not just the strong men, but the weak men, too—needed to feed their families. An Chu always made sure of that.

As the last slips were handed out, Arh Bun got the pay permit he didn't think he would get. Not a man of words, he used his eyes to show his gratitude: a lingering look at An Chu and tears of joy. Afterwards, he wiped his eyes with the edges of his prodigious sleeves and dragged his tired feet forward, following his co-workers to the accounting department.

An Chu turned off the lights and locked up the warehouse with two giant-sized padlocks. His duties for the day were over. It was his turn to head back to the workers' barracks. Shipment arrivals often meant long hours of intense work for An Chu and days of sorting out and moving the new merchandise to the particular storage places for each department. There were slow days, too, when he had little to do. Then, he dropped off the new supplies and visited with the shop clerks at their different counters.

After a while, An Chu got to know almost everyone in the store. They all called him "Old Sun," a description well-matched by his appearance, if not his age. He had extra thick layers of wavy hair piled up high on his head, crying out for a cut, set off by an unusually dark, bushy beard that was growing willfully in several different directions. He was never concerned about how he looked or bothered by the nickname "Old Sun," even though this honor was bestowed on him at the ripe old age of twenty-three. Most men his age spent lots of time grooming themselves. An Chu was different. Dressed in his baggy blue uniform with his signature metal pocket ring holding fifty keys, An Chu seemed happy the way he was. Indeed, the shiny, jangling hoop was his only fashion accessory. Every step he took set off a cheerful chorus of rhythmically dancing and chiming keys. They kept him company in his otherwise rather lonely workplace.

Sometimes, when An Chu had finished up his tasks, he wandered into the housewares department, and chatted with his friend, Mr. Gu, or helped out if everyone was too busy to talk.

One day, to help out a sick co-worker, Yan was juggling two sales counters. There were more customers than she could handle and with little food in her stomach and the nonstop work, Yan felt dizzy. She gasped for air as she struggled to keep up with her workload.

Yan heard a voice over her shoulder: "Xiao Mei … Little Sister! Mr. Gu told me to come and help you."

She gave a quick glance in the direction of the voice while her hands kept on working—packing up a dozen glasses for a customer.

"I was wondering who 'Xiao Mei' was and it turns out it's you, Yan, the 'Swallow'!" the voice said. "Remember the train platform when we first got here? But you seem to have many names … I also heard you were 'Er Jie' (Second Oldest Sister) in your dorm." The man cheerfully went on and on, like an old friend.

Yan remembered meeting him at the station and how he helped others getting off the train when they first arrived, and then seeing him around the store. It was "Old Sun." Others were always saying good things about "Old Sun." And now, here he was, trying to help her out. Yan felt the presence of a lucky star over her. She gave a grateful nod of acknowledgement toward An Chu and playfully replied, "Forget about 'Xiao Mei.' Just call me 'Er Jie,' okay?"

She felt older already. She was secretly pleased with her own response, for she was always eager to appear more grown up.

An Chu and Yan worked well together. She did not have to run between the two counters anymore and even had a few minutes to sit down and get her strength back.

Yan liked An Chu. *What a good fellow he is,* Yan thought. *The world would be a much better place if all men were like him.*

They worked side by side until he was called away to fetch some stock items from the warehouse. Right before he left, An Chu teased her: "I'll call you 'Er Jie,' but I hope you won't regret it because everyone calls me 'Old Sun,' which means you have to be even older than me." At that, they both gave a hearty laugh.

An Chu's joking promise was kept for the remaining forty-two years of his life. From that day on, he always respectfully called her "Er Jie." Later, he found out that, despite her deceptively young looks, she was two years older than him. She was not joking with him after all.

That night, when Yan went back to the dorm, she praised "Old Sun" to her roommates for having saved her day. Da Jie, the oldest girl in their room, had never heard Yan praise a man and decided to give her some gentle words of caution: "He sounds great. From what I've heard, he always helps everyone out and does everything so well. But just remember one thing … don't ever fall in love with him because he already has a girlfriend, and she is a loose woman. She would do anything to keep him all to herself."

Yan felt nervous and embarrassed. Her face was flushed, and she could not look back at Da Jie. Though she admitted that she had lots of good feelings toward An Chu, Yan did not think she was in love. So, she calmed herself down and replied, "Don't you worry. I think I will never get married. I want to stay single all my life."

Da Jie laughed. "I was just teasing you." She saw that Yan was getting too serious.

Chapter IV

A Brush with Death

LIFE IN THE DESERT took a toll on Yan's health. For one thing, she could not get used to the food. The local diet of unprocessed grains disagreed with her stomach. Yan craved rice, something she had never lived without before she came here. How she wished to get hold of some rice, even if she had to trade, or bribe, or beg, or steal. After a few months, she became desperate. Just the idea of a bowl of plain white rice covered with pickled vegetables—something any Shanghai peasant took for granted— would make her mouth water. But that was too much to ask, for rice was nowhere to be found. Rice was not a local crop. The northern plains were too cold and dry to grow rice. And since the country was in an economic depression, no spare rice trickled northward.

Yan kept swallowing the half-bowls of indigestible millet porridge they handed out twice a day to keep herself going, but she started to have dizzy spells, cold sweats, and stomach cramps. Sometimes they were so severe that she had to curl her body into a ball and rock herself back and forth to conquer the pain. At night, she was tormented by hallucinatory dreams that startled her with wild and frightening images and bathed her in cold sweat, soaking her clothes and sheets. She often woke up and spent the rest of the night fidgeting, restless and cold, trying to figure out the meaning of the terrifying dreams she was having.

Most nights, they were about pirates and kidnappings. Sometimes, Yan saw herself surrounded by water, drowning in loneliness. Other times, she struggled in raging waters, trying to save herself by holding onto a log and trying to get to shore. She screamed as the log was smashed into small pieces by the force of gushing water. Her yells broke the still night air, frightening the creatures scurrying under her bed as they searched for a midnight snack and disturbing her roommates. Once, Yan became terrified as the water in her dream got thicker and thicker, and she realized she was stuck in a tar pit. Yan panicked, kicking with all her strength. "Help! Help me!" she screamed.

Then she heard a voice calling: "Er Jie ... Er Jie ..." The voice persisted and gradually grew louder and sterner.

"Yan Gu!"

Yan heard it this time. It was loud enough to break her eardrums. It was the dorm mother, Da Jie. She opened her eyes and found the supervisor's face only inches away from hers. In her hand was a flashlight, projecting an unsteady flood of yellow light at her.

"Yan, you got me really worried," she said. "I've been shaking you for a few minutes already. I thought you'd never wake up."

Yan sighed with relief.

"Another bad dream?" Da Jie asked as she brushed the sweat-soaked hair off Yan's face.

Yan nodded, shaking with cold. She tried to sit up and found herself all tangled up in her bedding. She must have caused quite a commotion in her sleep.

"I'm sorry, Da Jie," she apologized when she finally liberated herself from the sheets. "I'm sorry for all the noise I've been making lately."

"That's all right. You can't help it," Da Jie whispered as she picked up Yan's pillow from the ground and brushed it off. "It's not your fault."

"I'm so afraid of going to bed these days because of these bad dreams," Yan admitted as she stood up.

"I can understand it. But maybe the more you're afraid of them, the more they'll come back. We need to stop these bad dreams so you can have a good sleep once and for all." Her soft, sweet words comforted Yan.

"Thank you. I'll try."

After rearranging the bedding, Da Jie tucked Yan back into bed. With a pat on the back and some kind words, Yan managed to fall asleep. That night, she had a few hours of peaceful rest.

But nightmares still haunted her most nights, even after she told herself not to be afraid of them anymore.

One morning, Yan woke up after a terrible night of struggling in her sleep. This time, though, instead of evaporating when she opened her eyes, the nightmarish feeling lingered. She felt paralyzed and nauseous. She could not get out of bed. Her face was pale white, and the sweat beads on her forehead were the size of pearls. Numbing pain seemed to be coming from her stomach and she realized she was very ill. Her friends carried her to the only source of medical aid in this remote corner of China—a local army field hospital. A sleepy doctor, reeking of garlic, cigarettes, and last night's wine, poked her roughly with his fingers and announced with obvious annoyance that Yan had appendicitis and would need an operation right away. He stood up and shouted for Chen, who was outside fixing the transmission on the doctor's truck, to come inside. Chen, who doubled as the camp's anesthesiologist, ambled in, sized up the situation and soon reappeared holding a well-used syringe whose point was as thick as a knitting needle. He wiped his oily hands on his pants, delivered the painkiller, and went back to his other patient outside. Though he looked rough, Chen had seen much action during the war of liberation and did his job like a professional. The surgeon, however, failed in his efforts to locate her appendix.

The operating room quickly turned into a chaotic scene, accompanied by Yan's panicked screams for her father. The entire medical staff of the hospital rushed to help. Nurses managed to pin down her arms and legs. Yan could not move. She was desperate, paralyzed by the fear that she would soon die here in this strange room, without any familiar faces or family to hold her hand. She was conscious of the doctor searching inside her with her appendix nowhere to be found. Tears streamed down her thin cheeks although she could not hear herself crying. She did not know which was more overwhelming, the pain or the fear.

Could I die? Could I leave the world just like this? She wondered about her fate, and suddenly had flashbacks to her mother's death-bed scene. She lost track of reality and gasped when her eyes caught a ghostly figure in white holding a tray floating toward her.

"Your name is Yan Gu, correct?" the nurse asked, placing down her tray. She delivered the question in a muffled monotone, as if it were directed more toward herself than the patient.

Before Yan could reply, a medicated cloth was picked up with tongs and placed on the lower half of her face.

Then, everything went black.

Two days passed before Yan woke up, utterly disoriented. The room looked surreally white. Everyone around her was dressed in white. Where was she? Was this a dream? Perhaps this was where people ended up when they died. Weren't angels all dressed in white? She thought of her dead mother. "Mother?" she croaked, and searched the room for Jin Lai. But Jin Lai wasn't there. *What is this place?* She tried to move her arms and legs. They did not feel like her limbs. A wave of panic swept over her. *Maybe I'm paralyzed!*

She tried to scream, but all that came out was a low groan.

Silence.

If only someone would answer her.

"Daddy! Where are you, Daddy?"

She wanted to shout, but her voice was still too weak to be heard.

There was a row of faces in front of her, all happily sharing the news among themselves.

"She is alive! She opened her eyes!"

"She has come back!"

"She made it!"

Yan could see their lips moving, their faces animated with smiles, and their heads nodding. But no one spoke to her.

"You are all devils, devils in white! Give me back my daddy and my brother!"

Her sudden thundering exclamation startled everyone in the room. The surgeon went up to her and tried to hold her hand and calm her down. She resisted fiercely with her small strength, calling him a "devil." But the "devil" would not respond with anything other than a smile, which just made her angrier.

Having used some physical energy stimulated the awakening of all parts of her body. She felt a twinge in her stomach and before she realized what was happening, a gush of foamy, sticky white stuff came out of her mouth and splashed all over the doctor's uniform, her bed, and the floor.

Exhausted by her own emotional storm, she fell asleep as the nurses cleaned her room and changed her sheets. Yan now knew where she was and how she got there.

When she woke up again, she was calm. Surveying the blank white walls around her, she forced her memory to run backwards. She remembered that she was in severe pain when she was carried to the clinic. She still could feel the agony and fear when the doctor could not find her appendix. She recalled the sweet, sickening feeling when she lost consciousness. But she could not remember the two long days and nights when the doctors failed to wake her after the anesthesia wore off, and they had to hold their breaths and wait for a miracle.

Eventually, she was told what had taken place while she drifted between the worlds of life and death. Yan felt very fortunate to be alive. For the rest of her life, she always claimed that there was another world after life and that she had personally experienced it, although she refused to describe any details of it for fear of bad luck. She always remained a faithful Christian, despite what happened to her in life.

Yan learned later that "Old Sun" was the one who had suggested that they take her to the field hospital. He and a couple of others carried her there on a wooden board. She felt grateful to him and all those who had helped her. She sighed with relief thinking about such reliable friends. After all, friends were all she had there. Still, she wished that she wasn't thousands of miles away from home. Being away from her father and little brother was hard. Yan felt weak and helpless. She desperately needed a hug from her family to assure her that everything would be fine. Yan moved her body to touch the wall. Feeling close to something was better than nothing. The feeling of contact gave her a sense she was somewhere, and that her body and mind were still intact.

The month she spent in the hospital was long and tedious. Gradually, she was able to sit up and get out of bed without help. Energy started to seep back into her scarred body. The better food she got in the hospital helped her recover. As soon as she could take solids, she was given surprisingly good things to eat, like chicken, pork, and rice—things she had missed so much since she arrived in the northwest. She ate as much as she wanted. Her days were punctuated by three meals, but otherwise her life was monotonous. There was very little of interest beyond the two-page local newspaper or eavesdropping on the gossip in the nurses' office next door. Yan got so bored that she started thinking about giving up the good food and returning to the dorm where she belonged.

Her friends and colleagues surprised her with a couple of visits and showered her with treats, the most precious of which was a parcel from her father. Although it contained just a few words and knick-knacks, Yan felt the presence of her family. Hugging the package hard, it occurred to her that she could have died, and her family would not even have found out. Maybe the authorities would have eventually mailed her dad the ash-box? What would Ho De have done then? Yan remembered her father begging her not to leave after Jin Lai succumbed to TB, saying he could not live.

Tears welled up in her eyes. Yan wished she had never left Ho De and her little brother. At that moment, nothing else seemed to matter at all.

It was during one of her friends' visits that Yan had learned some surprising gossip: An Chu's possessive girlfriend had abruptly abandoned her love affair with him, gotten engaged to a local official, and planned to be married in a matter of months. An Chu, people whispered, had turned to stone. No one could help him because he fell silent and refused to speak to anyone.

"Poor An Chu, he shouldn't take it so hard."

"Why shouldn't he? Who would have thought she was a fox fairy put here to tease him to death?"

"Love is blind."

"Old Sun looked so strong and powerful. Who knew he was so delicate?"

Everyone had an opinion but no matter how sympathetic they were, An Chu was still suffering. His second love seemed to be full of hope and promise. In fact, his girlfriend's jealousy and eagerness to be intimate had assured him that she was madly in love with him. He was confident that, soon, they would be married and have a family. But she left him just like that, as if nothing had ever happened between the two of them.

It was a nightmare for An Chu. He had no idea who the spoiler even was. His girlfriend avoided An Chu so completely that he began to believe it would be easier for him to find a pin in the desert than to find her in this tiny city. Frustrated and forlorn, he finally found and confronted her. She just shrugged her shoulders and said that it was ridiculous of him to be so serious. Looking at him sideways out of the corners of her eyes, she denied that she was ever in love with him. Why would she marry a man like him with no social position, money, or education?

"You look good if people don't know about your background," she said, barely moving her lips. "But who wants to marry you and live in a shantytown? You've got to be kidding." She then slowly pushed her left sleeve back just enough to reveal a shiny gold watch, impatiently kicked the dirt between the two of them, and before An Chu could find the words to say anything further, turned and walked away. An Chu just stood dumbfounded until he realized that he was all alone under a darkening, gray sky. He shook his head and walked away, accompanied only by his own empty shadow.

Chapter V

A Friend in Need
Is a Friend Indeed

A LOW-GRADE FEVER KEPT YAN from being discharged from the hospital. The doctor's refusal to let her go frustrated her hopes to be reunited with all her "sisters" at the dorm. She missed them for they were her only family here, the people who knew her best and cared for her. The medical staff had healed her. Now, she needed her friends to comfort her and make her feel better.

Finally, Yan decided to outsmart the nurses. For three straight days, she managed to feign a normal body temperature by removing the thermometer from her mouth as soon as it reached the right point and only inserting it back under the tongue when she detected the presence of a nurse in the corridor. The cover-up worked. Her doctor finally granted her wish and handed her the discharge paper.

"You may leave the clinic now," he said, delivering the good news in his usual loud, bored voice. "But you can't go back to work yet. I've prescribed two weeks of bed rest. If you need more days off to recover, please let me know. Good luck with everything, Comrade Gu."

My trick worked! Yan couldn't believe her ears. She wanted to grab the doctor's hands and shake them violently to express her gratitude and celebrate her triumph. Yet she couldn't even look at him, afraid that their eyes would meet and he would sense her little deception. How could she lie to someone who had just saved her life?

"What's the matter?" The doctor was puzzled by Yan's silence. "I thought you were eager to go back to the dorm. Aren't you happy I've released you?"

"Yes, I'm happy, doctor." The words finally found their way out of Yan's mouth. "I'm very happy, and I want to thank you, thank you very much for giving me my second life."

"You shouldn't thank me. You should thank our great leader Chairman Mao. It's a great honor to serve my people. That's why we are called the People's Liberation Army." With a pat on her shoulder, the doctor was gone.

Yan stood like a baked-clay figurine, mulling over the doctor's words. For some reason, his mentioning the "People's Liberation Army" brought back the memory of the anonymous Nationalist Army officer who saved her and took her back home on his bicycle after she ran away. It happened so long ago, when she was only a child, but she could still see the uniformed officer in front of her, although his face was now blurred. He was kind-hearted, too, although he wasn't supposed to be. The Chinese Communist Party always portrayed the Nationalists as ruthless, cold, and greedy. Overwhelmed by many confusing thoughts, she wiped her eyes and started packing her things. She couldn't wait to get back to her dorm.

"Comrade Gu has been discharged. She is leaving us!"

The news spread through the little clinic in no time. Nurses stopped what they were doing and filed out to say goodbye to Yan. They called her their "miracle girl" and wanted to wish her well. When her dorm sisters arrived with the donkey cart, they found Yan surrounded by a group of white uniforms.

"Let's help our girl into her limousine!" they shouted, and everyone carried Yan onto the cart, filling her ears with cheerful wishes and laughter. As the donkey clumped away, kicking up a cloud of dust, Yan turned back and, behind the curtain of her moist lashes, saw a crowd of waving hands.

Yan looked forward to normal life again. It was a relief to go back to the dorm and be surrounded by familiar faces. But she soon found herself as much a captive as she was at the hospital. She was practically pinned down on the bed by her well-intended dorm mates. Everyone wanted to do something for her, from fetching her water and doing her laundry to trimming her nails and washing her dishes.

Yan was happy to be with her big family again. For the moment, even her daily staple of millet porridge tasted better, served up by the caring hands of a roommate. Someone from down the hall brought Yan her own transistor radio. "Take it, little sister," she said. "It receives only a couple of stations, but it will keep you company when we are gone. Just hand it back to me when you return to work." Music, news, and opera programs filled the long hours when everyone else was at work in the store and the dormitory was deserted.

One afternoon, Yan was alone as usual, accompanied only by the sunbeams that crept in through the dusty window panes. To pass the time, she turned on her radio and soon found herself mesmerized by a famous tragic opera.

It happened that An Chu came by for a visit. He had not seen Yan since he helped carry her on a stretcher to the clinic. He had been occupied by his lost love and own troubled life. Since it was a dormitory for women only and he had never been there, he had no idea where to find her room. An Chu cautiously walked along the corridor, ears open, listening for any sign of someone there. He then heard music and followed the sound.

Yan was so absorbed in the drama that she didn't hear the footsteps in the corridor even though her door was ajar. When she felt a tap on her shoulder, she jumped into the air.

"I am so very sorry. Really, I did not mean to scare you," An Chu muttered apologetically. He began nervously unwrapping a lumpy bundle covered in cloth.

"My friends brought me some apples," he said. "I thought you needed them more than anyone in the company. So, here I am ..."

Six shiny, red-cheeked apples fell into her lap. How lovely! How precious! Yan had not seen an apple since she left Shanghai. She was even more grateful that An Chu saved these rosy prizes just for her. He could have eaten them all by himself. You didn't need to be starving in the desert to be tempted by these luscious, sweet-smelling apples.

She searched for the words to thank him but felt overwhelmed by her own thoughts and feelings. After a few minutes of hesitation, she looked tenderly into his eyes and uttered just two words.

"Thank you."

She was touched by his thoughtfulness and generosity as she accepted the first present she had ever taken from a man. It was also the first time Yan and An Chu touched each other, gently, almost accidentally, like two lonely water lilies, rootless, aimless, drifting, and helpless. Theirs was not the spark of romantic love, for they were each too injured to indulge themselves in such heavenly, luxurious thoughts. They were drawn toward each other just by gravity, sympathy, and a need for comfort.

For Yan, who felt she was living a second, borrowed, life after the horror of her surgery, An Chu brought a sense of security and physical strength. He was reliable, sincere, and down to earth. If she ever needed him, he would be there for her. Between his physical power and quick, open mind, she suddenly felt that there was nothing he could not do.

An Chu also felt an unexplainable attraction to her. She was different from any of the girls he had ever known. In fact, she stood out from all the other women in the department store. She belonged to a world apart. He admired her gentle, graceful manner and elegant yet firm speech on those rare occasions when she made comments, for she was usually quiet and observant. He respected her quiet, educated air. And she offered him the possibility of female companionship without pushing him into another relationship, as had all his other lady friends. Something told him that Yan was traditional and conservative. She was not the kind of girl who would date just for fun and then leave her men behind with broken hearts. In fact, Yan seemed too shy to start a relationship. To An Chu, she appeared to be pure, fairytale-like, almost unreal.

An Chu was relieved by the feeling that Yan would never put him in the tragic situation of loving him wildly and abandoning him without explanation, leaving him feeling naked and humiliated. He had already been hurt twice. Being with Yan gave him a sense of comfort, whether it turned out to be a friendship or turned into romantic love. An Chu was content just to be with her. He was willing to take a chance, knowing that Yan would not hurt him.

They read each other right and, without saying a word, took on the responsibility of keeping the other going through the extreme physical hardships of living in the desert. He relied on her sharp wits, while she leaned on his strength and confidence. In a way, Yan and An Chu picked each other out of an instinct for survival. Each saw that his, or her, weaknesses could be compensated by the other's strengths. They needed each other—a good man and a good woman, bound together, if not by love, then by shared strength.

Chapter VI

ENGAGEMENT AND
CONSUMMATION OF A MARRIAGE

"YAN GOT ENGAGED? TELL us it's just a rumor!"
"Who is the lucky man?"
"Come on, tell us!"
"When will they be giving out the wedding candies?"

Poor Da Jie found herself cornered by a curious mob outside the dorm. Everyone knew she was the oldest one in Yan's room, the legitimate spokesperson, the "little mother," and they weren't about to let her go until all their questions were answered. Da Jie wanted to protect Yan's privacy, but she also knew that rumors were the only spices in dorm life here, and the crowd would stampede if she tried to hide anything. *An engagement is cheerful news. Why should I hide it?* she thought. So, she cleared her throat, put on a mysterious smile, and made an announcement.

"Sisters, quiet down! To answer your questions—no, I'll make you guess first." There was an instant uproar. "Okay, okay ... yes, Yan did get engaged! She got engaged to An Chu Sun, the comrade in charge of the warehouse."

More chaos, shouts, and squealing made it hard to know who to answer first.

"No, no wedding day has been set, as far as I know. Well, I'm the oldest sister … of course I know! Now, please let me go or I'll be late for work."

She squeezed through the excited crowd before more questions were asked.

The dorm was like a spy network. How did everyone find out things so quickly? She was impressed, for Yan and An Chu had only gotten engaged the day before. Their quiet promises were followed by the simple procedure of going to the City Hall, getting a marriage license and visiting the small photo studio across the street to have their picture taken side by side, both looking at the camera instead of each other. A terse statement was inscribed on the top of the picture: "Taken for engagement—1957."

They wore everyday clothes. Yan had two pigtails hung high with ribbons—she looked like a schoolgirl. Her lips were gently pressed together to conceal a smile. An Chu's untamed, black wavy hair stood up like a thicket on the top of his head—as always, he looked like he needed a haircut. His eyes shone. His back was straight and he looked pleased. The picture captured a rare moment of simple, genuine happiness between two young people.

At twenty-five, Yan was considered to be rather old for getting engaged. Most girls got married at eighteen, maybe twenty. People who knew Yan well were very surprised by the engagement, for they had often heard Yan declare she would remain single all her life. They had even teased her about sending her to be a *nigu*—a nun—if only she believed in Buddhism. Nevertheless, they were happy for her.

"Congratulations, Sister."

"Congratulations to you and An Chu."

"Happiness and long life!"

Yan was surprised at how many people stopped by, leaned over her glass countertop, and whispered the same magic words to her that day. She couldn't believe that everyone seemed to know about her secret, even though she only shared it with a handful of her closest friends. She was even more surprised when the Communist Party Secretary summoned her to his private office that afternoon.

"Comrade Yan Gu," he said as he paced around the room. "I've heard that you got engaged with An Chu Sun yesterday. Is that correct?"

Yan looked at him as she tried to figure out where he was going.

"Paper can't wrap fire. The northwest wind here is strong enough to blow everything to my ears. So *did* you?"

"Yes, Comrade Party Secretary."

"How well do you know him?"

"We've known each other for about half a year."

"Half a year? That's not very long, isn't it?" The Party Secretary had a serious look on his face, and his pointing index finger swirled around and around as if trying to dig into Yan's conscience. "That's not long enough for you to bet the rest of your life on someone. You're too young and naïve. You should have asked the Party leaders for advice."

Yan's face turned red.

"What's the matter? Embarrassed? The Party leaders are your substitute fathers in this home away from home. We protect you and care for you deeply."

Starting when did the Communist Party mind its people's private lives here? Yan wondered. *I never heard about needing its permission to get engaged.*

"Here ... I can tell you everything about An Chu Sun." The Party Secretary's voice became gentler and more persuasive. "I've got his personal file right here." He picked up a stack of crumpled paper on his desk and leafed through it. "Do you know he's from a shantytown, the poorest kind of city people? He was a wanderer and never held a steady job. We don't know what he thinks about our new socialist motherland. And do you know what he did to his last girlfriend?" His voice suddenly shifted, betraying contempt and rage. "He got her pregnant, and then dumped her! Who knows how many young women he has turned to trash and thrown out!" He was pleased by his own choice of words and Yan's shocked face. "Think again, Comrade Yan Gu. An Chu Sun is not the right man for you. He is irresponsible in every way. You should be engaged and married to a comrade with a higher social status, like a local government

official or cadre, maybe a supervisor within the department store …
at least a Communist Party member to ensure your bright revolutionary future. I can personally recommend some to you."

The Communist Party Secretary seemed to know more about
An Chu than she did! Yan was appalled. Did he dig out An Chu's
past and compile this "evidence" to convince her to break her engagement? She knew An Chu's girlfriend dumped him and not the
other way around. Everyone in the department store knew it. So,
why were they creating this twisted version of the story? Why was
the Party Secretary so interested in her affairs, anyway? She felt
disgusted that anyone was trying to turn her quiet, private matter
into a humiliating public display.

"Comrade Yan Gu," the Party Secretary went on, "one of our
Party members is very keen on you. He will bring you a bright revolutionary future here in this department store. You are still young.
It's not too late to change your mind. I'll work on An Chu Sun
should he give you any trouble."

*An Chu doesn't give me trouble. He understands me. He saved my
life. That's why we're engaged, so he can always stand behind me like a
rock. Why would anyone care if I get married? It's so ridiculous!*

But Yan didn't openly express her thoughts. She knew the Party
Secretary would get angry if she rejected his suggestions. So, she
said in a barely audible voice, "Thank you for your kind attention,
Comrade Secretary. I'll think about your wise words." Avoiding his
eyes and a handshake even though she knew he was expecting one,
she walked out of his office.

"Comrade Gu, you'll get back to me, right?" Yan heard the Party
Secretary's question echo through the dark, narrow corridor as she
hurried out. She took a deep breath after she escaped, but his words
haunted her for the rest of the day.

Anyone else who was twenty-three, muscular, handsome, caring,
and hardworking would have been considered a very eligible bachelor, but An Chu was not. As a matter of fact, most girls would never

think of getting engaged to him for one simple reason: He was penniless. An Chu could not offer Yan an engagement party or even a ritual ceremony to gain the blessings of his ancestors. No tokens of love were exchanged. There was no engagement ring, even though there were plenty of shining gold and silver bands for sale in their store's jewelry department. A friend suggested that An Chu buy a pair of matching watches—not the expensive kind, but cheap, plain ones for everyday wear—but he still couldn't afford them. Yan did not even get a kiss to remind her of the new bond between them. And she still lived in the sanctuary of the women's dormitory with her "sisters," as dictated by the customs of the time. In China, a woman and a man only lived together after they got married. But in an abstract sense and in the words on the official marriage license, Yan was not alone anymore. She finally got the strong pillar she had always wanted. It would be there for her if and when she needed it. And she was pleased.

After work that day, An Chu offered to escort her back to her dorm. Yan agreed with a nod. She walked in silence as if alone, accompanied by her conversation with the Party Secretary playing over and over in her head as it had done so many times that day already.

"How was your day?" An Chu finally broke the silence.

There was no answer.

"How was your day?" An Chu asked again.

"What?"

"How was your day? Are you alright?"

"Fine, I mean I'm fine, the day was fine. I was just thinking. It's funny that we're engaged, but I've never, ever, asked about your family and your life before, like …"

"Like what? You can ask me. We never talked about each other's families because I never thought you were interested. After all, you're engaged to me, not my family. They're more than a thousand miles away. Are you regretting getting engaged to a man with empty pockets? Do you wish my wealth could grow the way my hair does—always too much, always needing a trim? Sorry, but it doesn't."

An Chu's words loosened her up a bit.

"Of course not," Yan answered quickly. "You know I'm not money-minded. But I'm just thinking … I'm just wondering … what are your parents' names? How old are they? What do your parents do? Where does your family live? How many brothers and sisters do you have? How old are they? What do they do? What did you do before you came here …"

Yan's stream of questions only came to a stop when she ran out of breath. As she tried to regain her composure, An Chu exploded with laughter.

"What's so funny?" Yan asked with a serious face.

"You sounded like the police at the residential registry. I don't know if I can answer all your questions with one breath. I don't even remember all your questions. But I can tell you a few things about my family. First, my parents are honest, hard-working people. They are poor and live in a shantytown. The government pasted notices on our doors several times and said that they wanted to knock the whole place down. They wanted to send all the people to brand-new apartment buildings. Some of us were excited, but most didn't like the idea at all—people are comfortable with what they know. Nothing happened anyway. It's all just talk. It's not that bad there. It's like a big, big family living together. I almost wish I could take you there to see it for yourself, but with the money we're making, I doubt we'll ever get back and see each other's parents."

"It certainly doesn't look that way." Yan shook her head, and her heart relaxed a bit. She finally gathered enough courage to ask: "Did you have girlfriends before you came here?"

An Chu looked into the distance for a long time. "No," he said.

Yan wanted to ask him more questions, but she didn't know how to phrase them. She didn't know how to ask questions about things that were private. She wondered why it was so easy for the Party Secretary to say those things. They walked on in silence until they reached her dorm.

"Is everything alright?" An Chu tilted his head slightly, examining her facial expression. "You don't sound like yourself."

"Yes, I'm fine ... perhaps a little tired."

"Is there anything I should know or can help with?"

"No ... no."

An Chu waited for Yan to say something more but nothing came out.

"Well then, goodbye, Yan. See you tomorrow at the store."

"See you, An Chu."

They waved at each other and went their separate ways. Yan decided not to tell anyone, including An Chu, about what the Party Secretary had said to her in his office.

If Yan could have chosen her own fate, she probably would have remained engaged for the rest of her life without actually getting married. She was used to living with little affection or having anyone too close to her since she was forced to leave her birth family as a child. She was scared by the idea that marriage would bring a man into her life in an intimate way her parents had never explained to her. She was not ready for it. She could not imagine herself ever feeling ready to step out of the tight little cocoon she had built for herself. However, a peculiar incident changed her fate and brought a new reality into her life.

Half a year after the engagement, An Chu was ready to claim his bride. He grew fonder of Yan and finally admitted to himself that he was in love with her. He was no longer content to see her just now and then. When she was not there, he missed her presence, her high-pitched voice, pure as the ringing of a brass bell, her quiet footsteps, her shy smile. He began to find his self-control and gentlemanly feelings toward her fighting against his desire for her. His face got hot and red every time he thought about it. He dreamed of sharing a life with her. However, An Chu was perplexed by Yan's response every time he mentioned his longing for their marriage and a family. She would just lower her head, become silent for a minute or two and shift the topic to something else. She acted as if he had never brought it up and never argued with him on the subject.

Was she backing out of her promise? He wondered if her silence was a sign she did not like him anymore. But An Chu's doubts eventually gave way to a better explanation—that her reaction was caused by shyness and never having had a relationship with a man (which was partly true). Yan was as pure as a white lotus blossom and An Chu loved her virtue. But gradually he became restless and frustrated. Their relationship was not going further than a tiny engagement picture. Things were at a standstill. While Yan seemed to enjoy his company now and then, mostly in public places, she did not show any sign of wanting to explore a deeper and more intimate relationship. She preferred seeing An Chu with other people around rather than being with him alone.

"But we are paired already," he gently reminded her. "We are supposed to know more of each other. We are supposed to get married soon and live together." Sometimes, when he got exasperated, An Chu would stare at their engagement picture and mutter these words to himself. If he said them aloud, Yan would run away with a flushed face, as if he had just insulted her. It was obvious that she was not ready to take the next step and make herself his wife. But she had never actually objected to marriage, either, and that left An Chu with no explanation, or every possible explanation. He wanted her. He wanted to have a family with her.

The rest of the story is murky. According to Yan's account many years later, An Chu invited her and several of his friends to a restaurant outside the city to celebrate their six-month engagement anniversary and she gratefully accepted. Though she felt a little uneasy in the beginning since it was the first time ever they had joined their friends as a couple, they relaxed as they ate and drank, talked and laughed. Meanwhile, the time slipped away merrily and unnoticed.

Yan enjoyed herself much more than she had imagined she would. The little square dining room, plain wooden tables, and homey cooking transported them away from the worries of life in the great dusty West. They could have been back in Shanghai with a group of old friends. The dim, bare light bulb, wrapped in rising steam and smoke, made the tiny room relaxing and comfortable. Or was it because of the wine? Yan was not used to drinking. She was not a good-time girl. She was always thinking and reasoning ... but not tonight. Tonight, she felt carefree. She was entirely absorbed in the moment.

"*Ganbei!* To mud huts!"

"*Ganbei!* To our life in the west!"

"To our friendship!"

"To An Chu and Yan!" They clinked their chipped blue-and-white porcelain cups again and again until Yan's ears memorized their ringing tone. Her eyes were captured by the warm haze in the air.

It was very late when they finally left the restaurant. The cool night air felt good and it was only after they had been walking for quite a while that Yan realized they were not heading back to the dorm.

"This is the wrong way," Yan said. "Zhang Ye is over there."

No one answered, and fleeting glances were exchanged between the couples.

"Ah, we won't be able to get back home tonight," Jung Li, a friend of An Chu, explained. "The city gates close at midnight and, unfortunately, it's nearly one in the morning."

"Where did the time go?" one of the girls said, as tittering broke out among her friends.

Sensing she was somehow missing something, Yan insisted they try to get back into the city. The little group reluctantly walked back toward Zhang Ye but, as Jung Li predicted, they were stopped by the city moat and the silent city gates. Yan's tiny shouts were absorbed by the massive pile of stone and no answer—not even the echo of her own voice—came back. It was like shouting into the night sky or the ocean.

Yan's weary eyes were transfixed by the deep shadow of the city wall. All she could see was a giant pool of darkness, heavy and forbidding as Fate. Could there even be such a thing? Yan shuddered at the idea.

"Let's go," An Chu said gently extending his strong arm around her shoulder, escorting her back to the group to search for a place they could stay for the night and find shelter from the chilly, now nearly frozen air.

Yan only reluctantly accepted the idea of spending the night in a local inn and insisted that she and An Chu get separate rooms. After haggling with the hostler, they all finally settled in and the desert was quiet once again.

That night, despite her friends' reassurances, something did happen. Yan, the "Swallow," the self-proclaimed free-flying bird, lover of operas and dreamer of dreams, became a woman like any other in China, the property of a poor, honest, working-class nobody, signed, sealed, and delivered in a faceless country inn lost in the dusty, timeless desert. The "six-month anniversary" was very likely masterminded to achieve this purpose—at least according to Yan. She felt tricked into marriage.

This night marked the crucial turning point of their relationship. An Chu and Yan got married officially soon afterwards and said farewell to their single lives in the dorm. Changing rooms, however, did not change the spartan nature of their lives. Pooling what little they had, Yan and An Chu rented an empty, unfurnished room from the townspeople and settled down like any other local couple in a thatched-roof mud hut.

Their first home held only a borrowed twin bed and two suitcases belonging to Yan: the small one she had brought from Shanghai and a bigger one she had bought in the department store when she needed a private place to put things in her dorm room. Now, these two suitcases had much bigger roles to play. The larger chest (conveniently about the height of a coffee table) was placed carefully in the center of the room, and the smaller, old, dented suitcase became a bench, which squeaked and moaned every time one of them sat on it. On the center of the "table," a bright red vase made from spun glass—a wedding present from her dorm sisters—stood empty by itself. She couldn't find any flowers to put in it, for water here was too precious for plants not meant to be eaten. Yan knew why her sisters bought the vase, not because of what it was but for its color. It was red, the color of happiness, and Yan couldn't have a wedding without the blessing of lucky red.

With a few careful touches, the little room was turned into a warm, inviting, and neat little nest. Even the dirt floor was spotless and always gave out the muted scent of fresh earth. Yan and An Chu grew fond of their new home, which provided protection against the heat and the prying eyes of the local leaders. Little did they know that soon, it would also serve as a shelter against a storm that had been brewing for months and traveling for thousands of miles from its source, the ever-fertile and unpredictable mind of Mao Zedong.

Chapter VII

CHANGING POLITICAL WINDS

N O ONE EXPECTED THE winds of East Coast politics to travel all the way to the desolate, forgotten town of Zhang Ye, but they did, arriving without warning just like the local dust storms and changing everything. One day, people were working to build a new frontier for themselves and the glory of China, and the next, they were captives in endless political meetings, where the very pioneers who had volunteered to help their country found themselves implicated for unknown—and often unknowable—crimes. Power shifted from those who did the work to a few rarely seen characters. The Party Committee suddenly became a meeting organizer and the Party Secretary a glorious speechmaker. Many days, the entire store was closed down and the staff ordered to sit on cold, hard benches for eight hours straight to listen to men in thick glasses shouting slogans, warnings, and often confusing instructions. Their job was to listen, just listen, without making a sound. Role calls were made and absentees were recorded on a secret "black list." Everyone started taking the meetings seriously after those who failed to appear found their salaries cut in half.

The country was falling on hard times and the Communist Party called on all its citizens to strengthen their dedication to Chairman Mao's ideals, frugal living, and proletarian virtue.

"Petty bourgeois ideology is out!" The Party Secretary waved his arms. "If you want to seek a comfortable life, you're walking dangerously away from us, from the teachings of our beloved Chairman Mao, from the path of socialism. So, you become our enemy!" He threw his written speech aside. After all those meetings, he had memorized the words on the paper. "From now on, we expect one hundred percent attendance—no more pretending to be sick, no more aches and pains. Sickness belongs to the petty bourgeoisie! No more unnecessary eating—remember, ONLY TWO MEALS A DAY! Dorm rooms will be searched and food that is found will be confiscated! I will not tolerate anti-revolutionary behavior."

He paused, surveying the large, crowded, deadly silent room. He couldn't see anyone's faces, just a sea of motionless, black-haired heads, for no one dared to look up. He was satisfied.

"The harsh environment here," he continued, "is a perfect testing ground to find out who is a true Communist hero and who is an enemy of our country. Every time you think, speak, or act, you make a decision to become one or the other. And you don't want to become an enemy of the people."

Instead of concluding his speech and dismissing the meeting as on other days, he pointed his finger at his security chief sitting in the first row. The chief got the hint, rose, clapped his hands, and called his guards.

"Today, I want to show you what we do to our enemies."

Before anyone realized what was happening, the guards had already pulled half a dozen people out of the crowd.

"Comrade, you've made a mistake!"

"What are you doing? Don't hit me!"

"I'm not the people's enemy. I love my motherland. Please, please let me go."

"Comrade, you're hurting my arm!"

The six luckless prisoners protested and struggled frantically until their voices became hoarse and their spirits were lost. Then, with their arms bent backwards and their heads hanging low, they were paraded in front of all the dumbfounded employees before being taken away in handcuffs.

"This meeting is over!" The Party Secretary waved both of his arms and left the stage.

The crowd dispersed without a sound. People slowly dragged their heavy legs forward out of the meeting room and into the cold toward their dorms.

The struggle went on day after day. More meetings were held, and more clerks taken away. Ordinary salesmen and shy shop girls who had lived, eaten, and joked with the rest of them were revealed to be "class enemies" and "right-wing reactionaries."

After the initial shock and confusion, those left were at a loss how to react to the new political atmosphere. People were tempted to talk to each other in private, looking for answers about what was going on, but as more and more of their friends and acquaintances disappeared, so did normal life, and even friendships started to dissolve. Life became a guessing game about who had betrayed whom. No one could afford a friendship with the wrong person. To protect themselves, people withdrew into hard shells. They quickly learned not to make any comments if others were talking. People even had to worry about when, where, and to whom to nod and smile. It seemed ridiculous, but anything— simply walking away from a group, a gentle nod, or the utterance of a sound—could be interpreted as hostility to socialism. And nobody could afford that.

All the brave young people suddenly became timid and afraid. The people taken away in handcuffs were as innocent, or as guilty as themselves. Like them, they were enthusiastic, patriotic, and courageous, blessed with loud voices and free spirits. In fact, these were the very qualities for which they were praised as "young socialist pioneers" and which brought them here, so far, far away from home. How was it possible that they had turned overnight into class enemies?

Still, everyone was haunted by the same question: *Could it be my turn tomorrow?*

A frightening rumor began making the rounds that the "class enemies" led away in handcuffs had been sent to *Sandan* Farm, a labor camp, as slaves for life. Their fates were sealed. They would never be reunited with their families. This was enough to numb any young heart and dash any remaining naïve hopes. No one could make any sense out of this fearful situation. So, they gasped, sighed, adjusted to the new reality, and learned to hide their true selves. They were too frightened even to question what was happening, much less fight it.

By then, Yan found herself carrying a child. Weak with morning sickness, she was happy to stay home in bed. All she wanted was a pile of fluffy pillows to put behind her back, but she made do with a pile of coats and jackets.

Her bed was her sanctuary. With bed rest came long hours of contemplation, pondering her past, present, and future, if there was one. She let her mind wander freely wherever it chose to go. And, of course, she indulged herself in brooding over the current state of the department store, trying to make some sense out of the madness.

Yan felt a dark force spreading over the workplace, and although she could not imagine the reason for it all, she sensed the strategy of seeking random scapegoats to cause panic and hysteria. And since the workers could not trust each other, they turned even more toward their manipulators—the authorities—for answers and protection. She shuddered at her own thoughts.

Could it be possible?

Why would the people's government plot such things against its own innocent citizens?

What does the government want from us?

Maybe she was just making it up, although she had always had reservations about the new government for stripping people of their personal property and casting everyone with a different opinion as a class enemy. Maybe her views were biased because of her upper-middle class upbringing. However, there was more to it than that, and she knew it.

Meanwhile, everyone at the department store was scared and confused, ducking for cover and trying not to stand out. They would do anything to stay away from *Sandan* Farm. Ironically, to avoid being sent to the farm, people had to learn to become sheep. They learned to repeat only what the authorities said without adding any of their own opinions or even a single syllable. They learned to be meek and obedient.

Yan was angry and frustrated. "It's pathetic," she said to herself between clenched teeth. She could not, would not, turn herself into one of those meek things and be pushed and pulled around, waiting for the eventual slaughter. Neither would she be the one to stand up, question authority, and become a scapegoat. She was too smart for that. Two decades of being pushed downhill taught her to be patient, to observe and endure. So, she reasoned, why not take advantage of her physical condition by staying home full-time, staying away from everything, including the malicious meetings, during which clerks like herself were taken away in handcuffs?

It was the perfect solution to keep herself out of trouble: No one wanted to prosecute a pregnant woman who was helping produce "China's next generation." But how could Yan keep her husband away from those deadly meetings without making a public statement?

An Chu was a stubborn and courageous man who never gave in to threats and power. He would not pretend to agree with things he did not believe. Yan worried about him and was constantly haunted by the thought that An Chu might not come back home after one of those meetings. She imagined him being led away in handcuffs, leaving her and her unborn child forever. Of course, no one would dare to come to her door and deliver the bad news. By the time she realized that he would never come home again, it would be too late for her to find him. She wouldn't even be able to say goodbye to him! Her baby would never have a father. Her heart skipped every time she realized that her husband wasn't home on time. What had initially attracted her about him—his open-mindedness, his outspokenness, and his willingness to take on leadership roles on behalf of all the workers—suddenly became dangers to him, to her, and to their baby. But she could not make him otherwise. She could only shake her head and keep on worrying.

Yan consoled herself with the fact that An Chu worked alone in the warehouse, where he had only stone walls with which to share his opinions. "Stay in the warehouse," she warned him every morning before work. "Please don't visit the store anymore unless it's necessary for work. Don't trust anyone. We have a baby coming soon and cannot afford any problems."

Yan knew by An Chu's silence that he wouldn't listen to her advice; he would do what he thought was right.

"Please, for the sake of our child," she begged him.

"Don't worry," An Chu said. "Everything will be alright."

"Come straight home after work. Promise me. Tell them I need you, I'm not doing well, the baby is giving me problems … anything. Please don't go to the meetings."

An Chu readily agreed but only to please her. He was eager to get out of the house, and make it to work on time.

Yan also knew he was playing along with her because he rarely arrived home on time.

By the time he dragged his tired body home, it was always well into the night. She waited by the clock patiently, lying in bed without any lights on, feeling the dark surroundings, sensing the tiny movements inside her, and apprehensively waiting for the faintest approaching sounds of the jangling keys that dangled from An Chu's belt. Their cheerful song always arrived just ahead of her husband. Every night, half of her imagined him on his way home, walking along the dark, dirt road with his keys, while the other half tormented her with thoughts of him heavily chained, clanking his way to *Sandan* Farm. These two possibilities loomed simultaneously over her. With every tick of her little clock, her anxiety grew.

Then, the faint tinkle of faraway keys would break the night air. An Chu was coming home! They didn't send him to *Sandan* Farm! Another night of anxious waiting was over. She stretched out her hand and searched in the dark until she felt a string tied to her bed frame and pulled it. A hazy yellow light brought the little room back to life, the 15-watt light bulb swaying in the middle of the room, creating patterns and casting moving shadows on the walls. Yan was thankful for her one crude light fixture for it was a luxury to have electricity then. People outside the city wall still used kerosene lamps, candles, and kitchen fires. Yan pulled herself out of bed, set the table for her husband, and took out the warm food she had carefully concealed under the quilt on her bed. Her body kept the food warm ... or was it the other way around?

She paced around the room waiting for her husband to get closer. She could tell his mood by the way his keys danced, sometimes happy, sometimes sad, and sometimes very, very angry. Tonight, An Chu's keys sounded like dead weights. They told the story of a heavy heart. She walked to the door and opened it. An Chu was right there in front of her. His face was as dark as the night.

The little suitcase bench groaned when An Chu dropped himself onto it. Normally, he would joke about their family "throne" every time he sat on it but not tonight. Now he was silent. He picked up a pair of chopsticks, and shoveled the food into his mouth. Yan waited for him to speak. An Chu kept on eating. Yan couldn't wait any more.

"How was your day?"

"Oh, it was fine." He kept on eating.

"How was the political meeting today?"

He stopped chewing, and his chopsticks lingered in the air. He knew it was a difficult question to answer. "I wouldn't know, would I? Didn't you tell me not to go there?" An Chu wasn't good at lying. From her face, he knew she did not believe him.

"I know you went. I know you never listen to me. Your shift was over four hours ago!"

An Chu sighed. He put down his chopsticks and empty bowl. He couldn't hide everything from her. She was too smart. What should he tell her?

Yan hit him with a storm of questions.

An Chu dodged some and answered some.

The bits and pieces of news she squeezed out of him only increased her worries. The big meetings and political discussions were mainly centered around Soviet Revisionism, and those who were sympathetic to their Soviet big brother (whose friendship the pioneers came to strengthen in the first place) were now marked as rightists. An Chu thought that the Soviet Union and the People's Republic of China should be friends in spite of their political differences. Knowing that her husband always spoke his mind, Yan was worried that the Communist Party would mark him as a political rightist in his personal record. That could haunt him for the rest of his life and dog their future children's lives, as well.

Yan's worrying was not just worrying. Ten years later, An Chu came across his personal file, which had traveled thousands of miles with him all the way to the west and back to Shanghai. He glanced curiously through the stack of thin, discolored papers and saw a dark red stamp containing four Chinese characters: "An Internally-defined Rightist" was printed above the official logo of the Zhang Ye Department Store. He just shook his head, laughed, closed his file, and walked away.

An Chu was such an honest, carefree man that it never occurred to him that he should have removed that page—the only political blemish on his record. Neither did he worry about the future consequences of that dark seal. On the contrary, he found it laughable and ridiculous that anyone could accuse him of being a "rightist" just for having spoken his mind because deep within him, he knew that whatever he had said was said with good intentions and love for his country.

That night, after she squeezed what she could out of him, Yan let him have it: "I told you not to go to the meetings, and you just won't listen! Look now, I'm sure they've already marked you as a 'rightist' for the rest of your life. Your poor, unborn child has already become the descendant of a rightist!" She was so angry that she felt all her blood rush to her head and her feet became unsteady.

An Chu jumped up and grabbed her. "You shouldn't get so angry. It'll hurt our child."

"It's already hurting our child. And it'll hurt our child more if you go to *Sandan* Farm!"

"I'm not going to *Sandan* Farm. Look, I'm right here with you and our baby. I'll be more careful in the future. I promise." This time, he meant it.

Aside from the immediate danger, Yan and An Chu shared other concerns: What would happen to the department store and the bigger plan to modernize the West now that the Sino-Soviet brotherhood was breaking up? And what would eventually happen to all the idealistic young pioneers like themselves? They had come all the way here to seek a new future, filled with socialist enthusiasm to help their motherland. And on a personal level, while their adventure had "freed" them from their past, it had also cut them off from their roots. An Chu and Yan had both vowed to run away from the city of Shanghai and never return. Now, they had to discuss the impossible possibility of having to go back and resume their lives there. The question was: How to get back?

Chapter VIII

Disasters, Natural and Man-made

1958 was a drought year. As political floods washed away the familiar landscape of life for millions in the cities, in the countryside, farmlands started to dry up. As far as the eye could see, barren fields cracked with thousands of open mouths, silently, weakly begging for a drink. A few still, muddy rivers stood nearby, helplessly, too dry to offer any relief to their dependents.

Nothing grew. Farmers across the northwest lost all their crops, their only lifeline in a sea of sand. They stared hopelessly at the naked blue sky, blazing sun, and parched fields lying under a shroud of yellow dust. Desperate people started killing their livestock one by one and consuming the precious seed grain needed for next year's planting. Soon, they began eating tree bark, clay, anything to sustain themselves. Instead of farming, long, tedious hours were spent staring thirstily at the sky, searching for any wisps of moisture without which life crumbled into dust like the earth beneath them.

But no clouds came. The sky only sneered back at the farmers, accompanied by the mocking glare of the sun. Empty stomachs hurt and could not be filled. Two meals a day became one and then dwindled to any morsel small enough or soft enough to choke down.

By then, the little city of Zhang Ye was flooded with hungry people from the surrounding countryside. Famine had already reduced these farmers to walking bones, motivated to move only by a whiff of frying oil or steaming pancake. They combed through every corner of the city, searching for anything to eat: spoiled rice, dried vegetable peels, any scrap that was deemed fit for the garbage pail by the city folks. When night fell, men, women and children, too weak to leave the city and head home, curled up with other surviving family members and slept on the open streets. Many never woke up again. They drew the last breaths of their lives while dreaming of the foods they could not find.

It was hard to walk across town without encountering skeletons partially hidden under torn blankets and sheets, especially those of children and old people. Unable to feed or even clean up after the hordes of displaced, starving souls, Zhang Ye degenerated into a giant open morgue with few claiming the mortal remains of loved ones now on public display.

The city's residents were more fortunate. They escaped death because most of them were either salaried government employees or related to one. Though meager, their incomes ensured them of at least one meal a day through a monthly ration of grain or other dried foodstuffs. They ate whatever was apportioned to them: dried sweet potatoes, dates, corn meal, beans.

An Chu and Yan were getting by, although they were very hungry. An Chu was very worried about Yan and their unborn child. His wife was having a difficult pregnancy. Although she was frighteningly thin, she was nauseated by the very smell of food. Sometimes, when she felt a bit better, she would talk deliriously about the everyday home-style cooking of Shanghai: the steamed fish, fried tofu, or tender greens in roasted garlic sauce.

Looking at his wife's pale face, childlike smile and bright eyes when she recalled these dishes, An Chu felt pangs in his heart. How he wished he could go out and bring home everything Yan wanted, just one nice meal to satisfy her hunger and make her happy. He frowned and knit his eyebrows when confronted with reality, the coarse cornmeal, millet, barley, and dried hot peppers, the drought, death, and anti-revisionism, the disintegrating department store and the bleak future facing his little family.

The sense of utter helplessness irritated An Chu. When a man could not help his own family and meet their basic needs, he lost the dignity of being a man. There must be something he could do to restore his dignity and the dignity of his fellow men who were going through the same troubles.

Having attended only three years of elementary school, An Chu did not have enough education to make a speech. But he knew right from wrong. He could hear the roar of political slogans and the weak cries of dying people. He felt restless. He needed to confront reality instead of accepting it. A voice inside him urged him to speak out, to speak out on behalf of all the government employees in Zhang Ye, to confront the ugly truth of death, and to represent those too hungry to shout out. An Chu held out a naïve hope that maybe the local party committee would listen to him. Maybe his words would make them realize that it was more important to help the starving families all around them than to focus on senseless political slogans.

So, An Chu spoke out.

He spoke out several times. But no one listened to him and no one dared to support him openly, which made him appear to be foolishly wrong. He shouted. He screamed. And yet his strong, firm voice was drowned out by the endless chanting of Chairman Mao's quotations and the fierce, heated anti-revisionist slogans that seemed to be the answer to any question.

He was upset. Everyone around him seemed to be blind, blind to the naked truth. They saw having one meal a day as a challenge, a testament to brave revolutionary fervor, a glorious sacrifice reserved to be endured by the chosen few. An Chu felt he was the odd man out. He was being smothered. Eventually, he was not allowed to talk anymore for he had deviated from the main political current.

He did not realize that he was standing dangerously close to the scorching wildfire of revolutionary enthusiasm, which had begun burning violently throughout the country.

An Chu made one more attempt to speak his mind. "Why talk about Soviet Revisionism? Why not talk about people starving and dying in front of our eyes? Why don't we do something for them instead of sitting here and talking about the abstract? After all, we came all the way here to help people, not to discuss politics."

The Communist Party secretary's face turned black. No one was supposed to challenge his divine revolutionary ideology or to disobey his authority. After all, he was the highest official in the store, executing a political plan handed down from the central government in Beijing. Within minutes, An Chu was restrained and ordered to get out of the meeting room for disturbing the social order. He was banned from the meeting room for good.

"Traitor! The only reason you're not at *Sandan* Farm right now is your pregnant wife and unborn child!" he was told before he was thrown out.

Yan did not know about the commotion her husband had caused at that meeting, although she did detect a welcome change in his daily routine: An Chu returned home as soon as his workday was over. He was not going to the meetings anymore. It made her happy and brought some peace to her worried mind.

One day, An Chu gleefully brought home five kilos of fresh dates and two small fish, for which he paid a handsome price. He even cooked the fish in brown sauce just the way Yan liked. With the fish dish and a bowl of millet porridge, he served his wife a surprise dinner in bed.

At that moment, sitting on the edge of the straw mattress, enjoying the rare sight of his wife enjoying a meal and envisioning an exciting life with his unborn child, An Chu felt very content. He had everything he needed to be the happiest man in the world right there within the four earthen walls that marked his meager territory. Nothing, no outside forces, could penetrate this, no politics, no worries, no visions of dead people or beggars, just Yan and the baby and himself.

He deeply inhaled the fragrance of the fish. As he relaxed, his breath escaped and turned into a sigh. How he wished that he could see Yan eating every day the way she was now. But that was too much to ask.

When An Chu went out to dispose of the fish bones, he was almost pushed over by a dozen scurrying shadows. The moment he dumped the bones in the garbage pail, they were gone. A lightning rush of movement was followed by stillness and he felt a dozen or so intense, vigilant, yet hopeful eyes staring at him. Boys and girls, barefoot and savage, made of only a few handfuls of bones themselves, were on a mission to save their own lives. If they failed to find something for their empty stomachs, they knew it would be their turn to lie down and never wake up again.

An Chu motioned for them to wait there and went back into the house. When he came out, he was carrying the sack of dates he had bought for his pregnant wife, the only extra food he had. An Chu grabbed generous handfuls of plump dates and placed them into the palms of each child. The hungry little imps were delighted by this unexpected generosity and skipped away with their loot. In a matter of seconds they evaporated, disguised by a darkness that was getting thicker by the minute.

The episode left An Chu feeling uneasy. Questions floated through his mind and he tried to hold on to a sense of reality by tightening his grip on the rough burlap sack of dates, now down to a third of its original weight.

Where would these kids find food tomorrow?

How long could they go on like this?

How many little ones were out there scrounging for survival?

No one knew or dared to talk about how bad things might get. But An Chu could smell it. He could smell the future in the very air he was breathing. Those who had not made it through the night announced themselves silently in the rising vapors and July heat. Each morning on the way to work he saw new rag piles with protruding arms or legs, begging for the help they would never get.

As time ran out for the uncounted victims of Zhang Ye, the clock was ticking down on An Chu and his co-workers. An Chu knew better than any other employee that the store had ceased to place any new orders for goods quite a while ago and that the warehouse was almost empty.

Chapter IX

DOUBLE JEOPARDY

WILL THE DEPARTMENT STORE *close today?*
Every morning, An Chu opened his eyes with the same question. He got dressed quickly and left for work. He expected some official would appear at the warehouse to tell him the store was closed and he wanted to be there when it happened.

He dreaded the rising sun, the walk through the unnaturally quiet streets, and the long day of sitting in a dead warehouse all by himself, trying to drive away his mounting fears: When would the final day be here? What would he do if the store closed before Yan had the baby? Where could he and his family go?

Too many questions had no answers. He ended up pacing all day and heading back home with the same worries in his head. Bleak as things were, he tried to be optimistic. He wanted to keep a grip on the situation to protect his wife and unborn child. He took on each hardship with a pioneer's sense of hope. Someday everything would be better, there would be bountiful food, people would live in harmony, jobs would be plentiful, and everyone would live to see the next day because they had eaten the night before. But his hopes faded one by one in the face of the drought, starvation, and ideological warfare that like maleficent magic turned friends, neighbors, and family members into strangers—or worse.

Meanwhile, Yan was bedridden and unaware of the worsening changes going on around her. She was happy that her husband came straight home after work each day, and she was busy preparing for the arrival of their first child. Lying in bed, she knitted and sewed every conceivable item for the baby: She deconstructed the repertoire of her closet, unraveling each item she had so laboriously knitted in different seasons, different times. Out of her mufflers, skirts, blouses, and sheets came baby sweaters, booties, hats, mittens, sleepwear, baby quilts, and diapers, which proved to be a few sizes larger than were needed for a four-pound baby. She even made padded winter jackets and snow pants in the middle of July to be ready for the severe winters there.

"My baby will have everything and never suffer from the cold," she would shyly explain to An Chu as he sat on the edge of the bed silently accompanying her as she worked. He wondered whether he should fill her in on the fast-changing politics and fate of the department store.

Why make one more person worry? I should spare her this nonsense for as long as I can.

An Chu indulged Yan's devotion to their unborn child, an innocent life that was conceived in hard times. He savored this moment of peace disconnected from the outside world, absorbed by love and nothing more.

Enjoy it while you can, An Chu told himself.

It was getting increasingly difficult even for a grown man like An Chu to survive, and impossible to protect the weak and young around him. There just wasn't enough grain to live on anymore. Even the trees were stripped clean of their bark and devoured by wandering hungry mobs. When the baby was born, there would be no milk or cereal in the house. Necessities were already luxuries. If Yan did not produce enough milk, which would likely be the case with her frail health … An Chu felt frightened and could not continue his own thought.

Birth was supposed to be a time of anticipation, celebration, and joy, knowing that part of you was reborn and was a living link to generations to come. But this birth was already colored by the shadow of doubt. An Chu sighed. This was no time for nurturing. He had picked the wrong time to fulfill his fatherly responsibility, normally the most sacred mission of a man. What had he done? An Chu felt his heart tighten at the thought that he was responsible for the creation of this child, responsible for throwing a helpless being into a merciless world that had already claimed enough victims.

An Chu had every reason to worry. They could not stay in Zhang Ye if the store closed, and Shanghai, the home from which they had come, lay thousands of miles away. They would become refugees with no food, no shelter, no future.

Whatever the future held, An Chu and Yan both agreed to name the child "Ping." Depending on which Chinese characters were used to write the name, "Ping" could mean a kind of floating water plant, plain and green, yet full of life. It could thrive without a permanent home or roots. It was the perfect name for a girl whose future was uncertain. "Ping" could also be written as a boy's name to mean "peace and equality"—a hopeful omen for the family and the country. If he had a choice, An Chu wanted his first child to be a son. He was a third-generation first-born son (he, his father, and his grandfather were all first-borns), and it would glorify his ancestors to keep the family's unbroken record of having first-born sons. A boy would grow up, work side by side with him, and someday become somebody. Thinking about a boy made him smile and gave him some hope for the future.

The baby was finally born on July 7, 1958, delivered at home by a midwife after two days and two nights of difficult labor. It was very small and weighed only four pounds. And it was a girl.

Two days after Ping was born, the department store was dissolved. When An Chu handed Yan an official letter with the department store's seal on it, she mistook it as a congratulation letter for the birth of her child. When she opened it casually only to discover what was inside, she was so shocked that she had to sit down on the bed to read it through.

The letter informed her that due to the deterioration of the Sino-Russian brotherhood and the economy, her services were no longer needed. Her job had been terminated together with hundreds of others. The department store offered "encouragement" to all the young people to return to their original homes. In consideration of her physical condition, the leadership had enclosed a one-way sleeper car ticket to Shanghai.

An Chu also got his dismissal notice but without a train ticket or any good wishes, his punishment for all the public speeches he had made. He didn't care about that in itself. An Chu said what he had to say to make his conscience clear. But he worried about the precarious situation they were in. An Chu and Yan could not come up with enough money to buy another sleeping car ticket, not even a "hard seat" ticket for Shanghai. They were down to their last pennies after working so long for such meager salaries and coping with food shortages and the birth of their baby. They needed to leave as soon as possible or they would be out on the street, joining the hundreds of beggars already there with no jobs, money, or food.

Finally, they figured out a way to escape: They could trade in the sleeping car ticket for two economy seats to Shanghai, the city to which they had sworn never to return. It would take only minutes to pack up all their belongings into the two "table" and "chair" suitcases. They would have to forgo the Chinese tradition of keeping a new mother in bed for thirty days, and hope for the best with Yan's fragile physical condition and days-old baby. Getting out of Zhang Ye was a matter of life and death.

Chapter X

Exodus

WHEN AN CHU WENT to the train station to secure their lifeline to the outside world, he could not help noticing signs everywhere of a city in chaos: People lay dead or dying on the streets. Looting and theft forced citizens to shut themselves inside their homes and the streets were empty. Zhang Ye was now a ghost town in more than one sense. A foul smell hung in the air as garbage piled up in alleys and simmered in the sun along with the corpses.

Strong as he was, An Chu knew he was facing desperate people and had to take precautions. When he saw some suspicious-looking characters loitering in the street, he cut through an alley that was completely deserted except for a ragged couple resting on a doorstep. As An Chu passed them, the man suddenly drew a dagger from his boot and lunged at him. Luckily, An Chu's reflexes were fastest when he was caught off guard. He kicked high into the air and the weapon fell onto the ground with a loud clang. The kick was so powerful that the man and woman panicked and ran, not even trying to recover their knife, which to them was a precious survival tool.

With a shaky hand, An Chu picked up the dagger and hung it on his belt in case of another surprise attack. He continued walking cautiously toward the train station but the rest of his trip went smoothly, helped perhaps by the sight of his glittering trophy. He

smiled inwardly and his steps were as steady as if he was walking
with a bodyguard. He knew there were many pairs of eyes out there
watching for prey, but no one ventured forth to face him and his
new friend. Small as it was, its distinctive features—a very long,
slightly curved body and an extremely sharp triangular point—signaled to all that its carrier was a particular native breed of bandit.
Poisonous snakes never bite each other. The knife's unmistakable
features safeguarded its owner from attack.

But having escaped death once already, it patiently waited for
An Chu around the corner.

As he walked by one of the city's many scenes of despair, a
pair of eyes caught his attention among the scattered piles of dead
wrapped up in torn sheets bleached of their colors by the scorching
sun. A teenage girl was leaning against a dead woman, too weak to
get up, talk, or even whisper. She was struggling to keep her eyes
open and her lips trembled with a movement almost too slight to
be noticed.

An Chu caught those last, slight signs of life, her eyes flickering like the last burst of light from an exhausted candle before it
went out. He approached her, went down on his knees and gently brushed back her hair, which was encrusted with dust and dirt,
from her childlike face. She was so young, too young to perish. She
was like a flower bud, never given the chance to blossom. Her shallow breath, slack body, and protruding bones all told the story of a
life too hard to go on.

"Little sister," An Chu said quietly. "I'll help you."

The young girl's eyes told him that she was aware of his presence.

He quickly opened the canteen he had with him and poured
a few drops of precious water into her mouth, but she had already
lost her ability to swallow anything. The water simply dribbled out
of the corner of her mouth. Wetness dripped down his arm all the
way to the elbow.

An Chu had been a brave, strong man all his life, but for the
first time, he started to panic. He found himself repeating the same
sentence, "Little sister, stay alive, stay alive ..."

His one arm served as a pillow under her neck and shoulders, and he rocked her gently, as if trying to pump his own life and energy into her in any way he could. With his other hand, he kept dripping water over her white, parted lips in the hope of reviving her. She never responded to him in words, but her eyes communicated gratefulness and appreciation. At one point, An Chu thought she was getting better and tried to feed her one of the pancakes he had bought for the family dinner. But she could not chew or swallow. His rescue came too late. She drew her last breath in his arms.

When An Chu realized that his water canteen was dry and the girl was gone, he gave a deep sorrowful sigh. He slowly put down the canteen and reached out to close her eyes. He then lay her down next to the body on which she was resting. Before he left, An Chu placed the pancake in her soft bony hand, something he wanted her to have, even though she would never be bothered by the lack of it anymore.

Goodbye, little sister. See you in the next lifetime. I hope this pancake will bless you with all the food you need when you come back.

An Chu cast a long, silent look at her and turned to continue his long walk, his step quickened by the setting sun on the western horizon.

The next day before sunrise, An Chu managed to rent a small donkey cart from a local friend to whom he had given jobs in the past. It was just big enough to hold the family's two suitcases, which they used as seats for Yan and their five-day-old daughter. An Chu carried the dagger he captured the day before on his belt and sat next to the driver.

As the donkey cart slowly toiled along in the thick pre-dawn fog, An Chu vigilantly guarded his family against possible attacks. A couple of times he spotted shadows following them, appearing and disappearing at lightning speed. To avoid confrontations, An Chu jumped off the cart and ordered the driver to go as fast as he could, while he himself ran behind the cart, pushing with one hand, and holding the dagger in the other.

It was not until they arrived at the train station that An Chu let down the hand with the knife.

The station was packed with young people like themselves, tired, scared and blank-eyed, waiting for the next train out. Clerks and armed policemen at the station provided them with some sense of security, but most were relieved that they were finally leaving this cursed city.

Haunting reminders, however, of what they were fleeing were everywhere inside this sanctuary, for posted all over the station walls were tattered pamphlets—copies of police reports with descriptions of unidentified corpses and black and white close-up pictures of the victims' faces taken after death. There were so, so many of them, without names, without any forms of identification. The stories of their lives were condensed into a three-sentence police notice and a lifeless picture glued to a crumbling wall … the only memorial they would get. Passengers waiting for trains were surrounded by hundreds of blank faces, their open eyes frozen at the very moment their owners had embarked on a much longer journey. Some eyes conveyed shock; others seemed to be pleading for mercy, help, or just sympathy. Filled with silent outcries, the station, usually a place of excitement and anticipation, warm welcomes and fond farewells, was somber and ghostly.

Among the galleries of dead and murdered dreams, there were also posters of the most wanted bandits, armed robbers and killers. Most of them had been labeled "Dangerous!" and "Do not approach."

The message was clear: Escape or you could be the next one on the wall. Passengers glanced at the pictures, tightly grasped their possessions, and strained to hear any faint sounds of a coming train. They were ready to take flight.

For the next five days and nights, Yan, An Chu, and their newborn child were trapped in a tangle of sweaty limbs and luggage. The air in the train compartment was saturated with cigarette smoke and stale breath. The hard wood benches grew more and more unbearable, especially for Yan as the hours turned into days. Every time the train hit a rough join in the rails, it was like being hit on the backside with a hammer. Gradually, she began to predict and prepare for approaching bumps. As soon as she felt the upswing of the train, she clenched her teeth and tightened her muscles to absorb the coming shock. She never closed her eyes. The little baby cradled in her arms was always crying and it was stiflingly hot. A sickening feeling haunted her that the baby Ping was not getting enough air and would not survive the trip. Her sweat-soaked sleeves provided little comfort to the baby. Yan's arms were numb. Her body was numb. Only her mind felt alive and it was filled with worry.

It would be five days before Yan and An Chu reached Shanghai, and for five days they sat thinking what would happen once they got to the city to which neither of them ever expected to return. They had nothing waiting for them: no money, no jobs, no place to stay. They had no false hopes. Their families were not aware they were coming, and even if they were, had little to help them. The only comfort for An Chu and Yan was that the little bundle they held would be spared from bandits, beggars, and streets filled with the nameless dead.

"Ahhmm," Ping whimpered, her little fists stirring aimlessly against her tiny head. Yan tried to calm her as she held the baby up against her own sweaty chest. "Shh, my precious *Bao Bei*," she whispered into Ping's ear as she gently patted her back, no bigger than her own palm. "Mama's right here. Mama'll take care of you. Go back to sleep. When you wake up, we'll be home. Everything will be much, much better." Thinking about the future, she felt a moment of hope. But in reality, the train was only helping take them from one uncertain station in their lives to another.

The Sun sisters (L to R: Wen, Ping, Qin & Min)
Jubilee Court Lane, Shanghai, 1967.

Ping (back row left), Min (front row left), and Qin (front row right)
with two sons of a family friend. Shanghai Honglei Studio, 1964.

Yan Gu (middle row, second from left) holding Wen with Min,
Qin & Ping (front row from left to right),
and An Chu standing (back row fourth from the right).
This family photo was taken on Yan's birthmother's birthday in 1968.

Yan & An Chu's engagement photo
taken in 1957.

Ping in the shantytown,
Shanghai, 1959.

Ho De with Chon Gao in the
mid 1950s.

Yan's work ID issued in August 1960,
less than two weeks after Qin's birth.

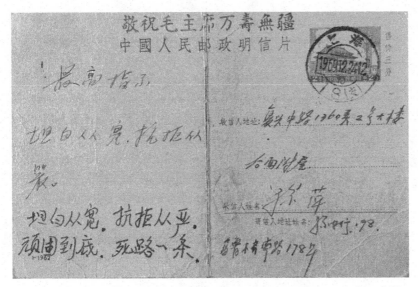

An old censored postcard dated 12/24/1969 from An Chu to Pin from jail,
including his criminal ID # 198. The Mao quotation at left,
"Confess and receive leniency, resist and receive punishment. A path to
death for those fight to the end" was added in a different handwriting.

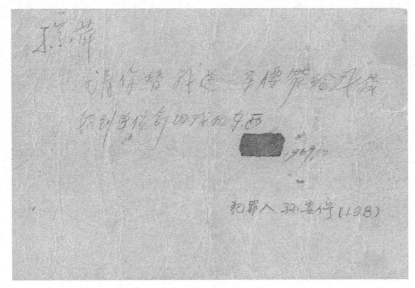

An old postcard from An Chu to Ping: "Ping Sun:
Please send me a belt. Best to go to my company and retrieve
all my belongings. Your dad, An Chu Sun (198)."
"Your dad" was blacked out, and replaced with the words: "Criminal."

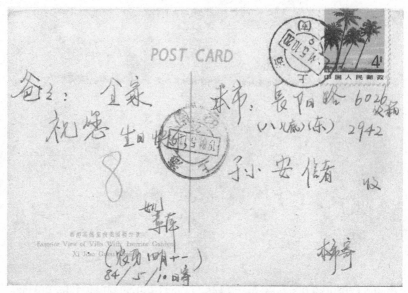

A birthday card from Qin to An Chu dated 5/10/1984,
addressed to the Shanghai Prison with An Chu's criminal ID# 2942.

An Chu's service ID issued by the Property and Land Headquarters,
Shanghai Municipal Workers' Revolution Rebel Command Center, 1969.

Yan (left) with a neighbor friend in her late teens.
Exact date unknown.

Yan at the age of 19.

The staff of the Housewares Department,
Zhang Ye Department Store, 1957.
Yan is in the front row, second from right.

Yan (right) with a friend.

Yan

Young An Chu.

An Chu in his teens.

An Chu in 1957.

Qin with An Chu at Shanghai's
Hong Chiao Airport.

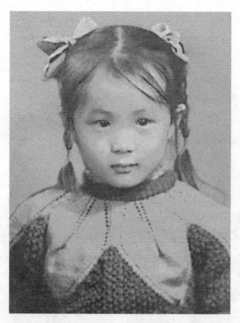

The author in 1964.

Qin's college graduation class
photo in 1982, Shanghai.
Qin, third from left, back row.

Qin as a freshman at the front gate of the
Shanghai Institute of Foreign Languages in 1978.

In 1991, Qin graduated with a Master's Degree in Communications from the University of Arizona.

Qin with her husband, Mark Stubis, in Bethesda, Maryland.

PART III

THE RETURN OF THE LOW-DOWN PRODIGALS

(Shanghai, 1958-1964)

Chapter I

A Daughter Is a
Daughter for All That

THE TRAIN MADE A sudden violent shudder, rocking sideways like a drunken sailor, shaking off its coat of dust accumulated during the slow and tedious journey. Startled by the unusual disturbance, the crowd awoke from its week-long stupor. Heads tilted and half-open weary eyes instinctively looked outside. Through the greasy semi-opaque windows, the Shanghai North Train Station came blurrily into sight. A minute later, the locomotive made one more maneuver, applied its air brakes and gave out one last, long cracked groan of relief with a huge burst of hot steam. Then, without warning, it stopped. The train lay like a giant caterpillar, depleted and motionless. Its weary passengers, enervated by the July heat and humidity, had yet to come to the realization that they had arrived at their final destination.

They were back in the city they had left only a year ago, yet few showed any enthusiasm about resuming their lives. They would have been better off staying in Shanghai with their old jobs, which they gave up in exchange for nothing but horror and humiliation. They were not looking forward to going back home and sitting down with their families for they didn't have any heroic deeds, glorious accomplishments, or found fortunes to report. Nothing except stories of hunger, death, and persecution by bosses and bandits.

An Chu waited until their car was half emptied and then let himself inhale the salty, familiar air floating his way from the open doors.

The adventure was over. No more running away. No more starvation. No more political battles. No more robbers, corpses, or ambitions of glory. A feeling of relaxation washed over him as little Ping dozed on Yan's arm like a rag doll. He let a few more minutes go by, just listening to the sounds of stumbling passengers getting off the train one at a time. They had nothing but time and nowhere to go. There was no one on the platform to greet them. They hadn't even decided on where to go once they got off the train.

An Chu looked at Yan. Yan looked back at him. Their looks said nothing and everything.

When they finally got off, Yan holding the baby and An Chu holding their suitcases, they made the only choice they could: They spent the last few *yuan* in their pocket on one of the many pedicabs waiting outside the station. Once aboard, they directed the driver to Yan's home just a couple of miles away.

It was a strategic decision, for between Yan and An Chu, they only had enough money to ride for a couple of miles, and they needed to go somewhere they could find help. At first, Yan was vehemently against the idea. She didn't want to return in such an awkward position, down and out, homeless, and helpless. She was horrified by the prospect that her father would see her in the sweat-soaked rags she had worn for a week, with a new husband and baby and nowhere else to go.

As they approached the familiar street where she lived, Yan felt her heart beating in her throat. Her hands began shaking and she could barely hold onto baby Ping. Life had played a cruel joke on

her, taking her back to the exact spot she had left only a year earlier with such strong determination never to return. Yan was so
ashamed she felt her real self disappearing, leaving only a ghost to
face her father.

It was a midsummer day, hot and humid. All the trees along the
neighborhood streets stood still, paralyzed among entrapped sunbeams and haze. Moisture hung heavy in the air, threatening to
suffocate anyone who dared to move.

All the houses had their bamboo shades down. The grownups
were taking refuge inside. Only children, mostly boys and tom-
boys, were still outside. They shed their sweat-drenched rags and
ran around in colorful, homemade shorts. Their bare skins glistened
with their own free-flowing sweat. Imitating fighting roosters, they
stood on one leg, hopping and bumping into one another amidst a
lot of yelling and cheering. The ones who fell backwards conceded
defeat and joined the audience, while the winners kept fighting until the last rooster stood alone, crowing triumphantly.

"Go, go!" the crowd on one side cheered.

"Come on, fight! Fight!" the other side yelled.

Chon Gao hit the ground with a bang just as Yan and her family arrived in their pedicab. He was so stunned to see her that for a
moment he could not get up.

For a boy of fourteen, a year was a long time to live without a
mother. After Jin Lai died, he clung tightly onto Yan as a second
mother. But she'd betrayed him. She went to a far, faraway place all
by herself without ever thinking what could happen to him. Since
then, Chon Gao had learned to get by with an elderly father four
times his age, a father who had never dirtied his hands doing any
domestic chores, even cooking and cleaning. They had yet to wash
their quilts and sheets since Yan left over a year ago. The wooden
floor had long ago lost its shine and was now coated with grease,
dust, dirt, and anything that had fallen down and was now in the
process of decaying. Dirty dishes were piled up high on the table,

patiently waiting to be reused when someone eventually, or ever, scrubbed them and put them back into the cupboard.

Chon Gao's world was now mostly on the streets with his teen-age friends, boys and girls from average working-class families trying hard to earn enough to feed themselves. Blue-collar workers often had to leave their children on their own with a chain of house keys around their necks. Chon Gao felt comfortable with these street urchins who were, in a way, as parentless as he was. They wore rags no better than those on his back. Like him, they were forced to go to school and get their twelve years of free education from the govern-ment. Except for that one chore, they had nothing but time, empty, idle time during which they were glad to see each other and found ways to entertain themselves. Street life gradually became their life.

It took Chon Gao a minute or two and a few blinks before he real-ized that Yan was really back.

Then, he sprang to his feet and raced to see her.

While Yan and her family were getting their things out of the pedicab, Ho De appeared in front of them. There he stood, shaking, filled with emotion, tears brimming behind his glasses. He ner-vously wiped his soy sauce-and-vinegar-stained hands on his apron, while his eyes shifted from Yan to the baby in her arms to the man who stood next to his daughter and then back to his beloved little girl who was little no more.

"I guess … I am a grandpa already," he murmured and nodded his head as a confirmation to himself.

Yan stood frozen as An Chu smiled, waiting to be introduced.

Ho De finally broke the silence. He extended his hands to An Chu. "And … this must be my son-in-law?"

"An Chu, Dad. His name is An Chu. And this is your grand-daughter, Ping."

Yan could not distinguish one word from the next as she introduced her new family. The heat of the July sun and her embar-rassment melted her composure.

"Welcome to my humble home. Pardon its appearance. I have had little time to attend to the apartment since Yan went away." Ho De tried to maintain his dignity, even though he was overwhelmed by the sudden appearance of his daughter and her new family.

For Yan, the reunion felt bittersweet. Her heart ached seeing how much her father had aged since she left. In just a year, he had changed from a strongly built, middle-aged man to an old man with hair white as snow. His hands were shaking. His tall frame was bent forward, and his shoulders were drooping, as if he had lost all confidence and hope in life so that he could no longer hold his head high and his shoulders could not carry any more weight. Ho De looked no better than a scarecrow after a storm. If it weren't because of Ho De's distinguished thick eyebrows (now all white), high-bridged nose, and exceptionally tall body, Yan would never have recognized him.

Seeing her father's threadbare life, a life too humble for a man with a dignified past like his, Yan wanted to cry. She wanted to embrace Ho De and weep until the whole world heard her. But her upbringing taught her to swallow her tears before they had a chance to well up in her eyes. She had to be positive in front of her father. She had to smile and tell him that everything would be fine, that she had made her way back, and come to see him first as soon as she entered the city. How would she have the heart to tell him that neither An Chu nor she had any job prospects, savings, or anywhere to settle down?

The once strong, confident, resourceful general manager she knew as her father was no more. He now barely made a living handling a convenience store and a teenage boy. Ho De's apartment was too cramped to add another family of three. Yan could not bear the thought of putting another burden on her father's sagging shoulders. And most important of all, she understood that Ho De was a conservative man. The same mindset that barred her from public education and stage life would also dissuade her from living with her family. Old Chinese tradition dictated that a married woman should live under the roof of her husband's family. A married daughter was like a bucket of water already emptied outside a house. Just as you cannot get the water back into the bucket, going back home was out of the question. It was shameful to have a married daughter at home. Yan was now officially a married woman with a child.

I must be out of my mind, Yan thought. She looked down at her sweat-soaked clothes and her pathetic little family and regretted ever coming home. *Daddy could never bear the shame of taking in a married daughter.*

She wanted to leave as soon as possible.

"Father, we just came to see you and pay our respects," Yan said suddenly. "We are on our way to my husband's family and will see you as we are settled. Goodbye." Her husband looked at her curiously but said nothing. Although they did not have a single *fen,* they hailed another pedicab and instructed the driver to take them to An Chu's family residence.

Before Yan got into the taxi, Ho De called her aside and pressed a roll of bills into her palm with such strength that she knew it would upset her father if she did not take the money.

"It's a small present for meeting my first granddaughter," he said. "Take it. I would have given you more if I could."

"Thank you, Dad."

"Come back to see me as often as you can." Ho De's voice was firm. "I would like that. An Chu seems to be a very solid and honest man. I think he'll be a good son-in-law."

At that, the pedicab heaved forward.

As Yan expected, Ho De did not extend an invitation for them to stay there, nor did he ask where they were going. She belonged to her husband's family now.

Silence accompanied Yan and An Chu as they headed to their next destination. Yan was lost in her own thoughts, shaken by the physical deterioration of her father and the ramshackle condition of his apartment. The warm old home, once so neat and pleasant, was now nothing but a squalid bachelor's refuge. Every little pleasant touch she had carefully left throughout the years had been wiped out. She almost wondered if she had ever been there at all. Only memory served as a ghostly link to her sentimental past where she now felt like a stranger.

Let the past go, Yan said to herself. *I need to concentrate on what I do now.*

What would she do now? Yan felt helpless, as if her hands and feet had been bound together. She was married and now belonged to her husband's family, whom she had yet to meet. She had a week-old baby depending upon her and a husband without any prospects. Everything considered, her future was dim. She sighed. Her eyes closed. She allowed the breeze in the pedicab to brush gently against her cheeks and dance in her hair. She needed a rest to pull herself together and be strong enough to confront whatever was to come.

An Chu and Yan had escaped from one disaster only to land in Shanghai during a famine and economic crisis caused by natural calamities and politics in the late 1950s. Grain production dwindled to a trickle as the population exploded. Millions starved.

China had few allies to help it, especially among the major financial and economic powers. China's self-isolation became even more obvious when its friendship with its big brother and one-and-only companion, the Soviet Union, withered away. The Chinese leadership would have sought international relief if not for its isolation, its belief in the ultimate correctness of its cause, and the fact that another superpower, the United States of America, was a close ally of Taiwan—the enemy of the People's Republic of China. For that, China loathed America, calling it an "imperial paper tiger" and an "enemy to socialism." What remained was a handful of socialist countries and sympathizers, which China called its "brothers." But these little brothers—Albania, Bulgaria, Cuba, North Korea, Pakistan, Hungary, Congo, Iraq and Egypt—were in no position to help giant China.

The fact of the matter was that no country could provide help, for China was too proud to ask for it. After all, the pillars of Communism were supposed to be cast from steel, strong enough to hold up the sky. China could not be in crisis. Her pride and confidence would not allow it. She was on her way to great success, establishing a brand-new social system, combining Marxism, Leninism, and Maoist Thought. She was to become the foremost and most glorious country of its kind in the history of the world.

To boost the nation's morale and overcome its economic crisis, China's top leadership called on the people to follow the principles of "self-reliance and hard struggle" and to succeed through prudence, diligence and spartan living. For the next quarter of a century, millions of Chinese people looked up to their government, faithfully followed orders, silently swallowed hardships, and waited hopefully for some miracle to happen. Yan and An Chu were just two of them.

Chapter II

Culture Shock

WITHIN HOURS, YAN, PING, and An Chu found themselves a home in Shanghai, settling down in the slum with An Chu's parents and his six brothers and sisters. Before their arrival, all eight members of the Sun family were jammed into a one-room wooden hut on whose dirt floor there was barely enough room to fit all their beds. A tin roof supported by bamboo rods hung over the edge of the shack under which sat the family kitchen made up of a charcoal stove, a picnic-style table, and a home-made wooden cupboard. To accommodate the new couple and baby Ping, a bed was temporarily squeezed into the open kitchen until An Chu could build himself a hut next door, or find somewhere else for them to live. For the time being, three generations and eleven souls nestled together under one shaky roof.

Amidst the deafening shriek of cicadas, humming mosquitoes hunting for their meals, parents calling their children to come home, clucking chickens heading back to their coops, the occasional crash of a bowl or dish, a child's crying, and a father's cursing, Yan tried to put Ping to sleep on the straw mat of their new wooden bed. An Chu sat nearby at the kitchen table, staring at the aggravatingly red sky.

His mother came and sat across from him just the way they did the night before he left Shanghai.

"It'll be a hot day again tomorrow," she said. "Just like today."

An Chu looked long and hard into the distance. "It wasn't so bad. You think nature is bad? Man is worse."

His mother stared at him with concern, prompting An Chu to return to the present.

"I'm glad to be home, Mom."

"I'm glad you are," Ya Zhen smiled. "I was afraid I'd never see you again. I wouldn't even know where to begin looking for you in that giant, empty desert."

"It's even emptier now," he said quietly. An Chu felt a chill run down his spine imagining the deserted streets of Zhang Ye, now abandoned by all but the silent crowds of the dead.

For a while they sat in silence. Then Ya Zhen glanced over at her new daughter-in-law fanning the baby. She was still in shock realizing that her son was married and had a child.

"I thought all of your good luck would have brought me a grandson instead of a granddaughter. You are the third-generation first-born son, you know, and now our luck runs out with this daughter. You named her *Ping* ... might as well have named her *Ping Chong*."

Meaning poverty.

An Chu didn't reply.

"Had you married a lucky woman, you would have had a son," Ya Zhen pressed on.

An Chu still didn't reply.

She shook her head.

"Do you know what you want to do?"

"I'd like to do many things but I have to figure out what I can do. How is Pei and his business?"

"Oh, he is a lucky boy. He made an important friend somewhere, a communist leader, so they say. He really liked Pei and got him a government job. Your friend left the shantytown and moved his whole family out of here in no time."

"Did he say where he was going?"

"No, why should he? He is an important person now," his mother said with a touch of envy.

"What happened to my business?"

"What business? You never had any business. I'm sure the people you worked for found someone else to fix their problems. Besides, life is so hard now. I doubt anyone is fixing anything these days."

An Chu felt hurt by his mother's blunt comments, but they were probably true. They put an end to the little hope he had of getting his old job back. Where could he work? He couldn't possibly find Pei now, not in a city as immense as Shanghai. And even if he did, An Chu wasn't a person who would ask for favors.

Looking around the dismal hut, he shook his head and sighed.

"I always thought you could have bought a better place with that ruby ring," An Chu said, changing the subject.

"I could have," Ya Zhen replied more loudly than he expected, "except that your uncle—"

"What did he do?"

"He is not much of a blood relative, that beast," she said as she stared at the burning sky in the distance. Her hands turned into fists. "He forced me to pay him before we left his charcoal store or he said he would call the police and say we stole his things. He claimed he had spent a lot of money on us and we were cheap, ungrateful, poor relatives. Your grandparents were too timid to say a word. Your father was their first-born son, you know. They should have come out, said something, bundled up their quilts, and left along with us, except they preferred living under his roof to going to a shantytown. They still wanted their dignity. But how about us?!"

An Chu saw tears welling up her eyes and regretted raising the subject. "It's okay, Mom. At least we got away from that rascal."

She was still indignant. "He has enough gold to choke himself and he still wanted more."

A long silence followed, during which An Chu went back to worrying about his family's future, while his mother lamented her family's past.

"I want to give you some money to start," she finally said in a barely audible voice. "Don't make a fuss about it."

She took a quick look around to make sure no one was near before she pressed a roll of paper money into his palm. "Don't tell anyone, including your father. You know how your sisters are."

"Thanks, Mother," An Chu said. "I have a family now and I know I have to find something to do soon, very soon."

I'll start looking tomorrow, he thought before he bid his mother goodnight.

Yan had a hard time adapting to her new life in the shantytown. Slum life was a culture shock to her. Her life had been spiraling down for some time, transforming her from a privileged daughter of the middle class to a shopgirl and finally, a refugee. But Yan was never exposed to the camp-style life of the truly down-and-out. Having her bed out in the open on public display was a nightmare to her. It made her feel naked.

When she first arrived, she only dared go to bed after the entire shantytown turned off its lights and fell asleep. She got up when the roosters began their first dreamy squawks. She would not allow the slightest possibility of a stranger staring at her in her sleep. Privacy was an important matter to her. Yan was brought up that way. She was taught to speak in a quiet voice, be polite, and shy away from strangers. Now her private bed was on public display twenty-four hours a day in a shantytown where anyone could stroll into anyone else's territory without permission and stay as long as they wanted.

The whole town was a big family. No one seemed to mind each other's presence and intrusions, even when they were in their night-gowns or undergarments. Every fight between a husband and wife was observed or heard by the public and then became the topic of other people's gossip and dinner conversations. Here, no one bothered to hide anything from anyone else. They couldn't, anyway.

The day after her arrival, Yan made an exploratory trip to the town pump to wash her baby clothes and diapers. A cluster of women sat among piles of laundry, enthusiastically talking about something. Seeing a stranger, they went quiet for a moment and looked her up and down with silent eyes. Without getting a greeting or word from her, they glanced at each other, as if saying, "Who does she think she is?" and quickly resumed chattering.

"Did you see Old Chan this morning?"

"No. Why?"

"Oh, you should have seen him. He had a black eye and was washing the dishes! He was so ashamed he did not lift up his head, not once!"

"Don't tell me his wife hit him again! What kind of man gets beaten by his wife?"

"What kind of woman would hit her man? She throws him out of the house almost once a week. He has to sleep in the chicken coop."

"Serves him right for marrying a woman twice his size."

"She's already given him five sons. I guess he has to pay her." At that, they burst out laughing, their soapy hands punching each other. Yan felt embarrassed. She ran back home with her half-washed laundry.

Yan decided that she did not belong in this worn-out, nosy, low-class not-much-of-a-place. She carefully avoided befriending anyone and maintained her privacy in any little way she could. When it was time to feed Ping, she did not join the new mothers outside sitting in a circle, chatting and laughing, with their babies sucking on their bare breasts. Instead, Yan ran into her in-laws' hut and nursed her baby under the privacy of a blanket. She avoided drawing water at the town's only pump during busy hours. Any conversation stayed in the general realm of "Hi."

Yan sewed a cover for her bed. Then she dragged home a stack of giant straw bags from the vegetable market. The bags had been thrown into the trash after the vegetables had been emptied out. Yan carefully picked out the undamaged ones and sewed them together to make a giant straw blanket, which she hung over the sides of the open kitchen. Now her bedroom had "walls." Nevertheless, it was still in the family kitchen where everyone came and went at all times.

Since this was the only home she had, Yan was determined to make the best of it and found multiple uses for everything around her. The giant, wooden family washbasin was placed outside the hut as a playpen for Ping, who was always neatly dressed like a baby doll, while all the other babies in the slum crawled on the ground and explored their world amidst vegetable peels, stinking garbage, and animal waste. No one worried about cleanliness here, yet almost every baby was ruddy-cheeked, seemed to be vibrant and healthy, and grew to adulthood.

When Yan and An Chu first arrived, all eleven members of the family ate together. As vegetable vendors, An Chu's parents always managed to put at least some food on the table. In lean times, they threw chopped cabbage skins into a pot of rice so everyone would have enough to eat. In good times, or when sales were exceptional, they would bring home a little fish or meat to make their children happy. In a period of famine, mealtimes should have been happy times, but Yan soon found eating at the Sun family table the most stressful parts of her day.

An Chu had one younger brother and five younger sisters, two of whom were going through the terrible teens and who just hap-pened to be in charge of the family's affairs when their parents were at work. Neither one of them liked Yan or Ping and all the extra attention they were receiving. The two sisters mocked their brother for marrying a "princess"—especially one with no money. Yan came to the Sun family without a dowry, which a bride needed to gain respect and her proper position in the husband's household. The dowry was a marriage tradition as ancient as China's five-thou-sand-year history and so embedded in the culture it could not be uprooted by Communist ideology. Of course, Yan's sisters-in-law conveniently overlooked that the Suns were too poor to throw a wedding ceremony for the new couple, an obligation of the groom's family.

The two sisters were displeased to see their brother spending most of his time on Yan and Ping, and they turned their anger on the newcomers.

At every meal, the more costly dishes were intentionally placed beyond Yan's reach. Any effort to reach out with a pair of chopsticks was met with cold and lasting stares. This simple tactic worked better than the two sisters hoped, intimidating Yan and showing their power. Yan was too proud to extend her arm across the table to serve herself what she wanted to eat. Instead, she ate the few mouthfuls of whatever was placed in her bowl and then excused herself as quickly as possible.

On a couple of occasions, when her husband or her mother-in-law placed some braised pork and fish in brown sauce in her rice bowl, Yan gratefully enjoyed the rare treat. But the two sisters quickly seasoned the meal with unappetizing words for Yan to digest with her food.

"Whatever she ate will turn into diarrhea," one said with a stone-cold voice.

"Yes! Who does she think she is?" the other continued.

"There are no princesses where we live," they growled. "So don't pretend."

"*No, no, An Chu, it's too private! People might see us!*" They imitated Yan's bedroom conversation in her high-pitched voice, punctuated by hysterical laughter.

Yan's face turned scarlet. She had to bite her lip and hold her breath to hide her distress and avoid a disastrous confrontation. She was so upset she felt her liver was bursting. She had never known people so mean.

Then and there, Yan made her decision—she was determined to start her own household.

"I'd rather have a glass of water for dinner than swallow their insults," she swore.

"Can we please move to a hut of our own?" Yan begged her husband when she could no longer hold in her feelings.

Her husband was surprised by her sudden request. "What's the matter? Isn't everything alright?"

"Of course ... yes," Yan assured him.

"My sisters aren't giving you a hard time, are they?" he asked, looking into her eyes. "They have mean streaks, you know."

She was too embarrassed to repeat the senseless assaults, so she looked down and shook her head. "I just want my own home, my own food, a little more privacy. Then, Ping can take a nap without a crowd around to wake her up."

"That's true," An Chu admitted. "I'll make us our own hut."

Chapter III

Be It Ever So Humble ...

W ITH NOTHING MORE THAN a pile of scrap wood collected from the gutters and alleys around the shantytown, An Chu was ready to build a tiny one-room hut next to his parents' shack.

Using a hammer, some nails, an ancient saw with rusty teeth, and his bare hands, An Chu soon made four crude walls, a shaky roof, a wooden bed, a table, and a couple of chairs. He and Yan became the proud owners of a home they could call their own, even if it was only a glorified mass of splinters. Yan was happy that she could finally sleep without worrying about strangers staring at her. An Chu was happy that Yan was happy. Now all they needed was a way to make money.

Every morning, Yan got up at dawn, just as the roosters started their first calls. She hurried to the market, although it was so dark she could hardly see a thing. She had to feel her way forward blindly, determinedly pushing aside the still air with every step, guided only by millions of tiny twinkling eyes, too far away to light her path.

Yan selected the best cabbage skins and gently spoiled vegetables, which had lost their sale value during their trip from the countryside and would otherwise end up in the garbage. Since her in-laws worked in the market, she soon got acquainted with a few friendly vendors who were sympathetic enough to spare her the best of the rejects before the ill-fated vegetables were sent to the city dump where the city's poor waited and scavenged for food they could not afford to buy.

A golden hue in the distance told Yan that she was getting closer. Lit by strings of bare, 15-watt light bulbs, the outdoor market was about two blocks long and crowded with several dozen vendors and their wooden stands. The dark shadows of customers, some still in their pajamas and homemade slippers, flowed around the bamboo baskets as their owners searched for the freshest green vegetables that had just arrived from the countryside. Lavender-colored eggplants, slender cucumbers, and a kind of fuzzy green squash oddly called "midnight blossoms" were lined up side by side on large, flat bamboo trays. Shanghai *bok choy*, cabbages and delicate "chicken-feather" greens spilled over long wooden boards. It was so dark that people were afraid of mistaking potatoes for radishes, scallions for wild onions, and watercress for bean shoots. So, they bent down and checked the trays carefully, making sure they were actually getting what they wanted. Meanwhile, vendors dragged large, heavy straw bags out of their carts, sliced them open with a knife, and took out more fresh produce a handful at a time, checking each piece and refilling their stands. The rejects rested in heaps next to their feet. Sometimes the vegetables were so muddy that they had to be washed in a basin before they could be sold. Others were sprayed with water to bring more money. Smart customers would insist on wet vegetables being shaken before they were weighed.

"Daughter-in-law of the Sun family, come," an old woman vendor grabbed Yan's arm. She bent down and searched under her feet until her hand touched a slightly slippery pile of roots. "Here are some radishes," she said as she tossed them into Yan's basket. "They are a bit spoiled but tender. You'll be able to make something out of them."

"Thank you," Yan said gratefully.

"Not at all. Come back tomorrow. I'm sure I'll find something else for you," she shouted before vanishing among her small crowd of customers.

The old woman's words warmed her heart. Yan walked on. She didn't bother to admire the vegetables on the stands. She knew she couldn't afford them. Her job—not as easy as you would think—was to persuade some of Shanghai's sharpest merchants to give her what they were going to throw out anyway. A few were nice enough to say yes, but many lied rather than give away their wares and said they were saving the moldy piles for a friend or relative. Others, sensing an opportunity, wanted to sell her the spoiled vegetables at a lower price. It embarrassed her that she didn't even have a few petty *fen* to pay for them, and she never learned very well how to beg. Sometimes she wandered back and forth through the market without getting anything. But under no circumstance did she ever approach her in-laws' stand. When she couldn't find enough to fill her basket, it was time to visit the city dump.

By the time the sun rose above the horizon, Yan was already home, seeing An Chu off on his daily search for work. Yan spent her day taking care of the baby and making small improvements to the house. Whenever she could, she tried to make a little money using her sewing and knitting skills. Sitting in the washbasin with her rattle, little Ping was Yan's best advertising model. Ping was always dressed cutely in neat, hand-made baby clothes and sweaters, which the slum mothers instantly wanted to have for their own daughters.

"That is a lovely sweater," one woman commented as she passed by. "My daughter's birthday is coming in a week. Will you knit me one if I give you the yarn and fifty *fen*? It's not much but it's all I can afford."

Yan was pleased. "Of course, I will."

When the woman came back to get her sweater a few days later, she brought along a friend. Yan got five bright coins and a new customer. The Sun family would have meat with their rice for the first time in a month.

Yan could finish an order in a remarkably short time, and she never charged an extra fee for a rush job. People started to like her, even though she conducted her deals in a businesslike manner with no small talk.

Yan began earning regular money crocheting scarves, knitting sweaters, and embroidering pillowcases.

During the 1950s, hand work was not well-respected in China. Only the poor and overly practical grandmothers would make their own clothes. A garment sewed by machine or sporting a label proclaimed the difference between those who could afford store-brand clothing and those who could not. As a result, Yan was paid small handfuls of change for doing a lot of skilled work. She had to keep her needle flying for long hours just to keep her family fed.

An Chu was not bringing much home even though he was out every day searching for work. Yan grew worried and frustrated. Still, she greeted her husband cheerfully every afternoon when he returned home: "You look tired. I'll bring you some tea. Where did you go today?"

"Oh, I always check out the city job agency and then some local repair shops to see if they need anyone for the day."

"How was the agency? Anything there?" She tried not to sound too concerned as she made some tea for him.

"No," he said.

With her brimming teacup suspended in mid-air, she searched for ideas to help her husband to get a job. "Did you tell them we have a baby and really need a job?"

"No."

"Did you tell them we live in a slum and don't even have a real home?"

"No."

"Did you tell them that Chairman Mao has sent us back to the city and we need a job?"

"No."

She wanted to be patient, but Yan couldn't stand hearing "no" anymore. Always *no, no,* and *no.* She rushed to her husband, dropped the cup down on the table in front of him with a splash, and looked him in the eye. "Why can't you get something? Can't you beg them or tell them you'd do anything to get a job?"

"Too many people are looking for jobs. The agency is filled with them. You should see—thousands of them! They all have excuses, newborn babies, dying parents, sick wives, starving children, no place to live, no money to buy milk, no charcoal to boil water. They haven't eaten for two days. The officials are deaf to our problems. All they say is 'No jobs today' and 'Come back tomorrow.' I'm not sure if there are any jobs anymore and I don't think they are, either. They don't care that, for lots of people, there won't be a tomorrow if they don't get jobs soon. They have their own job and that might be enough for them. What can I do? Nobody seems to understand why we left the city and then came back."

Yan was scared by the dark picture her husband painted for her. "How about the government and the Communist Party? They encouraged us to go there and then sent us back. Shouldn't they take care of us now?"

"Yan, the whole country is facing hard times right now. The government doesn't have money to help people like us. We are young. They expect us to fight for ourselves."

Yan felt physically ill. She collapsed onto the bench next to An Chu.

"What can we do now?" she finally breathed, more to herself than to him.

Yan knew that at this rate there would be many more meals of shredded cabbage and not even the tender middles but the tough outer skins mixed with a handful of coarse brown rice. She hoped they would have enough money to buy the rice.

Yan could not afford to stop working, so playing with Ping meant singing her opera tunes and telling her folktales while she sewed. She didn't care if Ping was too young to understand the love stories and tragic tales she spun along with her needle. She wanted to fill her daughter's ears with music and words while her work filled the family's bellies. She wanted her baby to learn and grow up to be somebody, so Yan worked to create an oasis of culture in this urban desert.

"Ping!" Yan caught Ping as she climbed down out of her wooden basin headfirst. "You scared me, Little Dumpling. You have escaped too many times today."

As Ping grew more independent, Yan learned to watch the baby with one eye and sew with the other.

"I want Mama."

"Do you want Mama to sing you another song?" Yan asked as she lowered Ping back into the basin.

"No, I want out!" Ping cried as she resisted, her body suspended in midair and her legs kicking. "I want Mama."

"My slippery mud eel, my sweet baby, how about staying in the tub for just one more song so Mama can finish this dress? Mama will get you white rice for dinner, just rice, no cabbage?"

Ping stopped struggling when she heard the words "white rice." She knew how hunger felt and how coarse the outer leaves of old cabbage tasted even at such a young age. She gave Yan a big smile and let herself be lowered down once again into the basin. There she patiently sat and waited for Mama's needle to stop flying, visions of steaming white joy in her tiny head.

Now that she had her own house, Yan began dreaming about school again—but not for herself. Her wish now was that Ping would be able to go someday. All her children would go. She would tell them how she wanted to get an education but could not, simply because she was a girl. She did not want her children to be punished just for being girls. A smile spread across her face when she thought how the Communist Party had ordered all children to be educated, whether they were boys or girls, from the city or the country, rich or poor, smart or average. All city children were entitled to twelve years of tuition-free education. Youngsters in rural areas got nine years of schooling.

As a woman, Yan was grateful that the Communist Party had worked to promote equality between men and women. It punished discrimination against women as severely as prostitution and opium addiction, making it a criminal offense. As a result, China was (at least in theory) a country of equal rights, where girls were respected, heard, and treated fairly.

At the family level, however, the reality was quite different. Thousands of years of Chinese history made it clear that men were more important than women. Men were physically stronger and played more important roles in family and social life. Starting at birth, boys were given more attention, better clothes and food, and more praise. Men were favored and they knew it.

The importance of the woman in a family was minimal. When a woman got married, she left her own clan and joined her husband's. Although she did not have to change her last name, her children would take her husband's family name; her own family name ended with her life. Often, a married woman wasn't even addressed by name. She was merely referred to as "the daughter-in-law of the Sun family" or "the mother of So-and-So." Gradually, no one would remember her real name. A family unlucky enough to have only daughters was a family in danger of dying out—of extinction. A woman was pressured to have sons to honor and strengthen her husband's name. A man with at least four sons was the proudest of all. His neighbors and friends would praise him with the old saying, "He has four boys to carry the four corners of his coffin," meaning his cup was full, his life was secure, and he had everything he needed for the rest of his life.

In contrast, a family with two or more daughters often became desperate and started to name their daughters Lin Di ("Bringing a Younger Brother"), Zhao Di ("Calling for a Younger Brother"), or

Yon Di ("Encouraging a Little Brother"). They used their daughters' names as ways of summoning the fates to bring them a son.

While without much value herself, a girl with such a name
would often become the family heroine when her baby brother finally arrived since she was the one who had brought him. As a
result, her status rose accordingly.

Having had a daughter and broken the Sun family's lucky streak of
first-born sons, Yan was subjected to not-so-subtle pressure to carry
on the family line.

"Did you hear? The Cheng family was giving out baskets of
lucky eggs. Their daughter-in-law just had another boy."

"How nice. Their family ancestors are so lucky to have such a
devoted daughter-in-law."

Of course, it was a woman's fault if she had daughters, just as it
was a woman's glory to have sons. Yan felt helpless. Maybe one day
she would have a son. Only then, she realized, would she be able
to gain a respectable position in the Sun family. But how could she
know what she would carry inside herself?

Life was hard and, in one way, that helped distract her from
all the ridiculous expectations, slights, and petty grudges. Yan
barely had enough time and strength to finish her daily chores
and keep her family afloat, much less worry about extending the
glory of the Suns. She just wanted to let the future take care of
itself, especially since she did not hold the key to it. In an odd way,
Yan was comforted by the depth of the abyss into which she had
fallen. Since she was sure she had already landed at the very bottom, life could not get any worse. If only she worked hard enough,
things would have to get better. What Yan underestimated was the
strength of the gravitational pull of poverty and how misfortune
usually pointed only one way—downward. Fighting fate was like
fighting a tornado—most people surrendered quickly and lost the
fire of ambition, never to be rekindled. Few possessed the type of
courage, extreme courage, to reject what life brought. Poverty only

surrendered to those with a will strong enough to unshackle the choking leash of necessity around their necks. Yan's persistence and determination would eventually pull her family up from among the dregs of society. But that would not take place until after two more decades of struggle.

Chapter IV

LIFE OF A
DOWN-AND-OUT FAMILY

PING PASSED HER FIRST birthday without celebration, much less presents. Her birthday was just a normal day. If she were a boy, she would have been treated differently.

When a boy was a month old, his father's parents gave a big banquet in his honor. He was presented to the public for the first time in a way that underscored his importance to the future of the family. Because of him, the family tree was rooted more strongly and deeply, and it was important to give this new seedling help as he started his life journey. The prosperity of the entire family tree depended on it. Guests were happy to share the special occasion and hoped the celebration would also bring good luck to their families. To ensure this, they came with extravagant gifts: gold, silver coins, paper money wrapped in red, bundles of silk, or assortments of rare fruits.

An Chu's parents did not have much, but if Ping had been a boy, they would have spent every *fen* they had or even borrowed money to make a feast, give thanks to the Goddess of Mercy, and show off their newest heir. To spread their joy, they would have given away baskets and baskets of red hard-boiled eggs to hungry friends and envious neighbors. But, no, Ping was a girl. There was nothing to celebrate. The Suns didn't even like to have her around. They did not want to see her eating and growing, a constant reminder of their bad luck.

Luckily, little Ping was too young to understand that anyone could dislike her. She returned the frowning stares of her grannies with big smiles, and giggled at her aunties' pointing fingers and pepper-hot tongues. Rather than enjoying an easy triumph, the cheerful, red-faced infant left them feeling disconcerted and annoyed.

When Ping started crawling across the dirt floor, no one picked her up except Yan. She believed even a poor child could be kept clean. But Yan wasn't there all the time and quite often when she came back from an errand or a short trip to the store, Ping was filthy. As she wiped the baby's hands, knees and face, Yan couldn't help noticing that the aunts and grannies all looked amused and victorious.

Sometimes Yan needed to be away for longer periods of time. When her husband found extra work or odd jobs that required more than one laborer, Yan accompanied him. One day, An Chu came home with exciting news. He had found a three-month assignment for two people at a quarry a few miles outside the city. Steady work was rare and they both jumped at the chance to earn a few *fen* each day, breaking rocks into gravel by hand.

At dawn, An Chu was already up, preparing his bicycle for the long day trip. There really wasn't much he could do with the ancient contraption, all rusted and squeaky, but he cared for it as much as possible. The seat was mutilated, stuffed with cotton, and topped with a homemade seat cover. Behind this, using a wooden board and some straw for a cushion, An Chu built a passenger seat. Every morning, An Chu turned the bicycle upside down and oiled the chain and crumbling brown axles where what was left of the bent and tired spokes wearily gathered. When this was done, he would spin one pedal to make the wheel turn, the chain spooling forward as smooth as silk. Only then would he stand up with a smile to soap his grease-stained hands and get ready to leave the house.

While An Chu worked on the bike, Yan prepared their breakfast and their lunches. Breakfast was simple: a bowl of watery gruel made from yesterday's leftover rice and some pickled cabbage skins. Yan used less water than usual to avoid their having to go to the bathroom before they could reach their destination.

Yan divided the leftover rice into two oblong, dented aluminum lunch boxes: a large portion for An Chu and a small portion for herself. Then she took out the leftover dishes from the night before. She stuffed most of them into An Chu's box and put just a little in her own. Sometimes, there was just enough to fill An Chu's box. To allay her own hunger, Yan placed a few pickled vegetables next to her scoop of rice. The salt, vinegar and spices of the pickles made the rice into a meal. She then wrapped the boxes carefully with a towel and placed them in a bag on the bike's handlebars.

Yan was almost ready to set out. The last and most important task she had left was to take the sleeping Ping to her in-laws'. She rolled Ping into her arm in such a gentle manner that she did not wake up.

Ping was a good baby. If she had a choice, Yan would never have left her at her in-laws'. Every day, returning after long hours of intense physical labor, Yan would put off resting and go straight to the Suns' hut to pick her up, for she knew that if she lay down on her bed, her aching bones would not let her up again.

Yan tried to be pleasant when she picked Ping up each day, but she usually got an earful of complaints from her five sisters-in-law.

"Your little dear pooped under my bed today, just like a dog."

"She peed under mine."

"She grabbed my toys," the youngest joined in. "They're not hers. She doesn't have any."

"It would be better to have a puppy," the oldest snapped. "A puppy is nice. Your baby cries for its mom all day long."

They especially disliked taking care of Ping because they were not paid for all the time they spent studiously neglecting the baby. Yan and An Chu did not have any extra money.

The sisters, however, found tricky ways to profit from the situation. They constantly left Yan with yarn to crochet scarves and sweaters, which they then sold to passersby in the street. Yan complied silently in the vain hope that they would treat her daughter better.

At daybreak, An Chu and Yan rolled their bicycle out of the hut and started the long journey toward the quarry. Yan wrapped her arms around her husband, and enjoyed the refreshing morning breeze as An Chu pedaled westward away from the dawn sky. They had to get to the quarry as early as possible to start work and squeeze in an extra hour of pay.

The work was intensely physical. An Chu rolled a huge rock into position and pounded it with a giant hammer and chisel. He had to use all his might to crack the rock. His blows were so powerful that the rock vibrated and groaned again and again before it finally shattered into large, irregular pieces. An Chu then broke them into more manageable sizes for Yan to work on.

With the help of a hammer, Yan's job was to make gravel out of the fist-sized rocks her husband had just created. Yan was good at working with small things—needlework, sewing, knitting and crocheting. She was not good with hammers. In fact, she had never picked up a hammer before. But life was forcing her to learn new things and learn them fast. She watched the other wives around her lift their hammers and let them fall singing on the dull, gray stones. But for some reason, while other wives' rocks turned quickly into gravel, Yan hit the ground more often than the rocks. Sometimes, she hit her own hand instead.

Her strenuous efforts eventually yielded a smallish pile of fine gravel at the end of the day, but not without help from her husband and at the cost of bruised hands and aching joints—more than she knew she had. Painfully aware of his wife's tiny size and physical frailty, An Chu kept a close eye on her. Whenever her rock pile got too big, he walked over and insisted he needed a break from the boring and much easier job of splitting boulders. Every swing of

An Chu's hammer magically turned granite into gravel. He made it look so simple. Yan admired her husband, and, inspired by his example, she sped up her own work, ignoring her ringing ears and the complaints of her swollen, throbbing fingers.

After an entire season of hard labor, An Chu and Yan moved on to a new business venture together.

The early morning hours now found them bicycling to the western suburbs of Shanghai, where they spent entire days wading in cold rivers and creeks looking for a certain type of reed, which locals used to wrap fragrant rice, peanuts, meat, and beans. The reeds were called *zhongye* and they grew only in the wild, often hidden in thickets along the banks of rivers. Finding them took a lot of time and patience, and more than once they failed to find their quarry, walking back to their bicycle empty-handed, cold, wet and muddy. There was nothing to be done except to pedal their way to another river and start all over again.

Sometimes nature surprised them with other, unexpected wild bounty: water celery, edible watercress, lotus roots, and duck and goose eggs, which they carefully wrapped in straw and took home for a feast. Their most joyful moments, however, came when they peered into a tangle of vegetation and spied the uniquely shaped reeds they were hunting. Time meant money and they began picking them, stacking them into neat piles, and finally bundling and stuffing them into giant cotton bags. Their bicycle was loaded until it looked like a balancing act in a circus. Only then would they set out toward home. Any reeds left behind might not be there the next time they came back for there were plenty of reed-hunters out there just like them.

An Chu and Yan happily pushed the bike and their loot all the way home. Sometimes, it took them two and half hours, but they arrived tired and happy.

They spent the next few days roaming through the neighborhood, selling their prizes and collecting a few small coins in return.

"Reeds for sale!"

"Reeds for sale!" Their cheerful duet echoed through small lanes and alleys, accompanied by the silvery sound of their bicycle bell.

When business was good, Yan had enough spare money to buy sticky rice and meat for her own *zhongzi*. They were rare treats, well worth the cost and effort of making them. More than almost any other Chinese delicacy, these ancient culinary inventions give pleasure not just while they are eaten, but for many long, delicious hours before they are served.

Zhongzi-making is an art. First, the rice must be soaked for just the right amount of time with just the right amount of water. Over-soaked rice turns into a slippery, soggy mess; under-soaked rice recalls nothing so much as the gravel Yan slaved to make.

The traditional way to make *zhongzi* is to use two or three reeds, bending them into a fat cone. Some of the soaked rice is spooned in, followed by pieces of marinated meat, dried shrimp, preserved egg yolk, peanuts, and pickles flavored with star anise or whatever else the cook had on hand, giving each *zhongzi* a unique and surprising center. The cone is completed with another spoonful of rice and the reeds folded over to seal it. The whole thing is then bound with string. When completed, a *zhongzi* resembles a dark, glossy green pyramid, appealing to the eyes.

When she finished all the wrapping, Yan lowered the *zhongzi* one by one into their largest pot, brimming with hot water, and let them slowly simmer for hours until the air was saturated with the fragrance of the reeds and everything inside. A sense of well-being and plenty came over everyone in the dark, wooden shack. Tonight, and for several nights, they would eat well, and dreams of better days seemed more real.

Chapter V

MOMENTS OF REFLECTION

WHILE WORKING IN THE countryside, An Chu developed a passion for fishing. He made instant rods out of sticks, cast his lines along rivers and creeks, and tied his tackle to nearby bushes or trees before joining his wife to scout the riverbanks. For most of the day, they searched through thickets and harvested any reeds and wild edibles they could find. When the workday was over, An Chu made his way back to his fishing gear. His heart pounded as he lifted the lines out of the water, eager to see what was waiting for him. Even in between examining the many disappointingly empty hooks, there was hope. An Chu always caught something before the day was over. Whether it was big or small, a fish, a crab or an eel, the catch of the day meant dinner that night would be a minor feast.

An Chu and Yan gradually made a life together even if it meant they had to hunt around for odd jobs and were still dirt poor. They had to start from somewhere, and they were proud of their progress. It was a period of want, and yet they were happy, roaming fields, exploring rivers, sensing the mysteries of fate, and hunting for nature's hidden bounty. They were a pair of free-spirited birds, and their bicycle served as their wings, taking them to places they wanted to go and returning them to their simple nest at the end of each day. Unlike the life they had known in the west, there were no political meetings to attend and there was no one to tell them what to do. Outside the boundaries of society, there seemed to be nothing but pure and simple life pleasures waiting for them each day. Neither had steady jobs nor income, yet Nature did not let them starve.

Unlike Yan, who liked to comb the river banks inch by inch and carefully pick whatever tiny treasures she found—a few watercress, wild celery stalks or reeds—An Chu was bold, letting his curiosity lead the way. He jumped from one place to another, poked here and there, hoping to hit it big with some spectacular find. After only fifteen minutes of such adventures, his black cotton shoes looked like muddy crabs and his pant legs were dripping with water. His eyes searched thick patches of vegetation. One day, after taking only half a dozen steps into some tall reeds, he stopped in disbelief.

"Yan, come here!"

"What for?"

"Come here right now!"

Yan hurriedly finished her own work, scooped up the pile of greens she had collected and waded toward An Chu in the cold, ankle-deep water.

"Where are you?"

"I'm here! Just walk into the reeds toward my voice."

In a maze of water weeds, Yan finally found her husband standing in front of her with an impish smile. He was coated with mud from head to toe.

"What happened to you?"

"I was wrestling with a water monster and fighting for his treasure. I'll show you in a minute." An Chu eagerly parted the thicket in front of him and showed her his surprise: A cluster of jade-green eggs miraculously appeared in front of her.

"Duck eggs!" Yan exclaimed. "What a luxury!" She put down her water celery and helped An Chu put the eggs in his blue workman's cap. "I'll make some steamed custard for Ping."

An Chu was pleased.

"I'll also make some thousand-year-old eggs and save them for the holidays."

"That's planning too far ahead. That's four months away. Isn't your father coming tomorrow? I think we should use the eggs to make something nice for him." An Chu held the cap with both hands and waited for Yan's approval.

Yan nodded gratefully.

They gathered all their booty together, wrapped it up, tied it to their bicycle, and rode home together as the sun set.

Although it boasted nothing more than a dirt floor, some crude furniture, and a leaking roof, the cramped, wooden cube that made up the newest Sun household was often a box of joy, filled with laughter and singing, the hopeful sounds of a babbling baby, and fragrant but not-quite-identifiable whiffs of roasted onions, wild greens, and An Chu's latest freshwater surprises.

By then Ho De was a regular guest at this ramshackle paradise. Every Friday, he came to share the pleasures of family, most of which he had lost when his wife died and Yan ran away. His "son" Chon Gao was turning out to be a troublesome teenager, more interested in getting into mischief with his neighborhood friends than spending time with his boring old father. Alone and with nothing else to do, Ho De buried himself in work. His life became a heavy, continuous chain of responsibilities and solemn duties, performed without any pleasure. He had little to live for and nothing to look forward to. His only occupation during the long, hollow year Yan was in the desert was self-reflection. He was angry at himself for having driven his warm, smart, and affectionate daughter away. He felt responsible for her being in peril somewhere in a barbarous place thousands of miles away—too far for a helpless old man to reach and beg her to return home. Ho De felt desperate. He would have set aside his pride and dignity to get Yan back, but he did not know where to go. It served him right to lose his own happiness. He punished himself by counting the number of days and hours since Yan left—right up until the moment she miraculously reappeared in front of his door.

That was the longest year of Ho De's life, filled with sleepless nights and nightmares that haunted him even during the day. Ho De, once a strong, decisive man, spent his days sighing, shaking his head, and mumbling to himself. After all, who else could he speak to and unload all the worries and anxieties he had inflicted on himself? Who could comfort him, talk to him, and give him strength? Yan had been the one who had done all these things. He had little, if any, contact with his relatives since he left the watch and clock business. Through rumors he learned that almost all his relatives had gotten into trouble under Mao's regime: Their businesses were taken over by the state, their lands were confiscated, and their houses handed over to the government. They had enough trouble already and could barely take care of themselves. They probably thought Ho De was the lucky one who had gotten away.

Since Yan's return, Ho De felt alive again. He was happy. The very thought of his new granddaughter made his heart sing.

It had been so long since he last handled a baby. He felt clumsy and frightened while holding Ping, yet he didn't want to put her down. Sometimes when he babysat for Ping, Ho De just stared at her, and guarded her while she slept. An eyeful of her restored meaning to his life. When he first saw her, he was horrified by her size—she seemed no bigger than a doll. At four pounds, six ounces, Ping was small enough to fit into a shoebox and until An Chu built a cradle, that is where they kept her. Ho De liked it better when Ping grew to be a toddler and could sit, stand, or wobble on her own, and he did not have to worry that some slight motion might break the baby's tender neck or twist her thin arms.

Ho De found himself visiting his daughter because he missed Ping. Then he began staying for dinner. Soon, he was visiting his daughter's house every Friday. He looked forward to the end of the week, when he closed his store, boarded a bus and headed toward his daughter's place, knowing a cozy dinner and a smiling granddaughter were waiting for him. He always brought her a treat and tickled her.

Ho De was very much aware of the poverty An Chu and Yan lived in. Their hut's bare walls and dirt floor told the story better than words. He left Yan a little cash whenever he could afford to spare it, but it was never as much as he wanted. The salary he received from selling soy sauce, vinegar, soap and sewing needles was barely enough for Chon Gao and himself. As it was, they had to skip a meal here and there just to keep things going.

Ho De felt tired from the blows life had dealt him. The memories of being the master of an estate, surrounded by his own fields and tended by his own relatives, still seemed so real that he sometimes caught himself smiling and thinking that soon he would be retiring there. But, when he realized that everything was gone, it was like losing it all over again. Ho De had to shut out thoughts of the days when he put on his favorite western suit and tie, affixed his gold eyeglasses to his nose, and strode proudly down the street with his polished walking stick toward his job at the Wellington Clock & Watch Shop.

Now his wife was dead, his clothes smelt like soy sauce and vinegar, and he struggled to keep a few pennies in his pocket. Sometimes, Ho De wondered if the things he remembered from his past life had ever really existed.

Ho De's only moments of escape came while visiting Yan and An Chu. He learned to appreciate his son-in-law and grew fond of him.

An Chu was nothing even remotely like the man Ho De had imagined would become Yan's husband—not socially, not financially, not intellectually. An Chu had only managed to finish third grade. His conversations were straightforward and matter of fact. Even in appearance, Ho De had envisioned someone a bit taller and better-groomed. Yet Ho De liked him. An Chu's inner goodness charmed him. His life had turned upside down but An Chu possessed the ability to calm him and made him forget about the outside world. His generosity and honesty impressed Ho De and warmed his frail heart. Ho De knew how An Chu always saved some of his small weekday catch for their Friday dinner in anticipation

of his coming, how An Chu tried to bring out anything and everything they had to please him, how An Chu would hold his arm in
the dark alley while accompanying him to the bus stop, only leaving
when he got on the bus. "See you next Friday, Dad," he always said
to him right before the bus door closed. "I'll catch something nice
and save it for you."

This was a son-in-law who did not have anything but was willing to give away everything he had. Ho De loved An Chu for that.

Chapter VI

A JOB ... WITH A CATCH

WHEN PING WAS FIFTEEN months old, Yan learned she was pregnant again. For the safety of the unborn child, she could no longer ride behind her husband on their bike and roam the countryside.

It was an untimely pregnancy. Neither Yan nor An Chu had a job. The coming of another child forced them to realize it was time for An Chu to look for stable work again, any work. They scouted out every possibility and after a few months, An Chu found a lead: The district House & Land Management Bureau was looking for new full-time employees. There was a catch, however: To be eligible, applicants had to agree to work in a remote bamboo forest for three full years. The bureau needed bamboo for scaffolding, and people needed jobs, so they would do just about anything to get them. Three years of back-breaking labor in a faraway jungle was not a pleasant prospect but to get a full-time job in Shanghai and make sure his little family did not starve, An Chu was willing to consider it.

After the revolution in 1949, the real estate business in China disappeared. The government took sole control of all property, and private ownership was prohibited. The establishment of so-called

224

"house and land management agencies" met the nation's needs for housing, emergency repairs, and rent collection. Since every one of China's billion people needed to live somewhere, a position in the agency was a very good opportunity.

Still, An Chu worried about being away for so long. What if the roof leaked? What about the heavy household chores that needed to be done regularly, like carrying home crates of charcoal or the family's allotted twenty-five-pound bag of rice? Yan did not even know how to ride a bike. She would have to do everything on foot while having to take care of two young children by herself. An Chu knew that even though they lived right next door, his family never helped them out. Maybe Yan would have a boy this time. His mother would be so happy that she would lend a hand. But what if it were another girl? An Chu didn't share his thoughts with Yan. He didn't want to upset her.

The young couple was tempted to snatch up this rare job opportunity, yet they hesitated, just as they would in snatching up a roasting sweet potato that had fallen into the fire even though their stomachs were empty. They talked about it for a whole week. Then, they agreed to think about it for another week, hoping something less difficult and closer to home would turn up. Finally, one night before the deadline, and with no other offers in sight, it was time to decide.

Staring at Yan's swollen stomach and with his young daughter playing at his feet, An Chu rose abruptly.

"I am going to take that job before all the openings are gone," he announced, as if in a rehearsed speech. "This is not the perfect job for us, but you will need a doctor very soon."

"But—"

Before Yan could agree or try to change his mind, An Chu was out the door.

Because of his impressive physical strength and construction experience, An Chu easily got the job. He also got the company's consent to let him work in Shanghai until Yan gave birth.

The entire Sun family waited nervously for the arrival of An Chu's second child, praying to the Goddess of Mercy, lighting incense, and hoping that this time the baby would be a boy.

It had to be a boy. An Chu's brother had just had a child and it turned out to be another worthless girl. Having too many girls meant that the family was being weighed down by *yin*—dark energy. The Sun family needed males to boost its strength and continue their proud lineage.

They got their chance three months later. Yan went into labor and was admitted to the Shanghai Number One Maternity and Childcare Hospital. After twenty-three hours of labor, fate rendered its verdict and a woman doctor presented Yan with a little bundle—me.

"Congratulations," she said. "It's a lovely little girl."

The doctor was a small, middle-aged woman who looked as if she had not slept for a month. With puffy eyelids, a complexion drained pale by overwork, and tangled, messy hair, she looked more exhausted than her patient. But her eyes were kind and so was her voice.

"You've got a very special baby. She was the only girl out of the thirteen babies born here today. See how white her skin is, almost translucent. It's obvious that since this is the Year of the Mouse, she must be from the lucky Kingdom of White Mice." She reached out her right index finger and gave the baby's face a gentle brush.

"Hundreds of babies I have brought to this world," she went on. "But your daughter is one of only two that were born so white. I would be very flattered to be her godmother and see her grow up."

Yan did not respond.

The doctor was perplexed by Yan's silence and began to wonder if Yan heard what she said.

"Comrade Gu, are you alright?"

Yan was not just physically tired; she was emotionally drained. Another daughter was a blow to all her hopes. She needed a boy to please her husband and get the troublesome Sun family off her back. Envisioning their reaction to the birth, she felt defeated.

It wasn't that she didn't want another daughter or that she preferred boys to girls—she loved Ping and knew that she would love this new white mouse baby, too. But boys—and the women who bore them—fared better in this world than girls and the luckless wretches who kept defiantly churning them out against the wishes of the ancestors. Yan knew full well that both she and her new baby would leave the hospital in a worse position than when they entered it. The hardship of being girls would always follow them. Yan's life had told her so. If she were a boy, she could have gone to school and had a very different fate. Wealth could be confiscated, but not knowledge. She could have been a teacher, a scientist, or even a doctor. She felt sorry for her daughters and felt like apologizing for not having made them boys. She had been praying for a boy every single day since the beginning of this pregnancy but still ended up having a girl. Why? Why couldn't she have boys like all the other women in this ward? Hadn't fate already cheated her enough? Did it have to deny her the smallest chance to make her life easier?

Yan realized that the doctor was still holding her baby. She looked into her puffy eyes, thanked her, and took the child. Although, in the old days, white skin was a happy sign of high birth and an easy life, Yan knew better. When An Chu was finally allowed to come in to see the baby, it took only five minutes for them to abandon any notion of using one of the many poetic, hopeful, or frilly girls' names so favored and savored in the old China. Instead, they agreed to call me by the serious-sounding name "Qin." Although in English, it looks and sounds similar to the name of the emperor Qin ("Ch'in") who first unified China and gave the infant nation its name, the character my parents picked out was anything but ambitious or noble. It was a name for a new, harder world that, like Yan, would continue to suffer the birth pains of its time. The girl whose white skin promised ease and privilege was instead named Diligence because even then her parents knew that only through struggle, patience and hard work would this poor mouse ever stand a chance to someday be someone.

My birth brought not only the sure promise of trouble, but immediate problems for my mother. Yan developed a fever and was ordered to stay in the hospital. Terrified that two-year-old Ping was at the mercy of her nasty sisters-in-law and An Chu would soon be sent away to the bamboo forest, Yan planned an escape relying on the same trick she had used before. She hid her fever by taking the thermometer out of her mouth and reinserting it when she heard the nurse coming back.

Her deception worked. She was discharged and she left for home. But as soon as she walked out the door Yan fainted. During her entire twenty-three hours of labor, An Chu had not brought her anything to eat or drink. He was unaware that the hospital did not provide any food to its patients. Or maybe it was just a man's carelessness. For months, she broke out in a cold sweat as soon as she felt the slightest twinge of hunger. She often collapsed where she stood and was almost unable to move until she had something to eat. Her fever eventually stopped, but the nasty fainting spells persisted.

Some of the old folks in the slum advised her that since it was an illness brought on by childbirth, another pregnancy was the only way to get rid of it. Yan inadvertently followed their counsel two years later when she had her third child. Miraculously, the fainting spells stopped.

Chapter VII

A "SINGLE MOTHER"

A FEW DAYS AFTER YAN gave birth to Qin, An Chu left for the bamboo forest in Jiangxi Province, five hours away by train. He worked and lived in the forest with a group of construction workers, logging bamboo trees and floating them down the river where they were pulled out and loaded onto trains destined for Shanghai. He was given six days of leave during his first two years of service—enough to get only a few glimpses of his wife and children before returning to the jungles, where the mental images of his family and city life quickly faded away like delicate black-and-white photographs, overpowered by the heat and violent green of the tropics.

Yan had to become both the man and the woman of the household. Once a month, Yan went to the accounting department of the District House and Land Management Bureau to collect An Chu's paycheck, but after the agency deducted his "living expenses," what was left was too little for Yan and her daughters to live on.

An Chu's sisters were fed up with their brother's troublesome family and stopped helping them altogether once he was out of sight. To feed herself and her children, Yan took a job sewing purses and wallets.

There was no way to call An Chu in the forest so Yan wrote him a letter telling him what had happened. It took three months for him to get the note, and, when he did, he was terribly upset and disappointed. He thought by sacrificing himself and working long, tiring hours in this sweltering hell that his family would be well-provided for. He did not know that half his pay was being deducted for the two daily cups of rice and the "rent" for the tin shack in which he and 20 other men lived without water or electricity. If he could have cut down on his expenses and lived on wild bamboo shoots to send more money home he would have, but he couldn't change the rules. He was powerless and too far away to help his family.

Life at home was worse than An Chu feared. Even with the added money from her own job, Yan was barely getting by. Every morning, she got out of the bed as soon as she heard her in-laws' squeaking door. She knew it must be four-thirty and they were leaving for the morning market. Yan searched through pitch-black room for her socks and shoes and ignored the urge to follow them. The famine had reached Shanghai, and not even a single vendor was giving out scraps any more. Yan changed and fed the baby, holding her for a few precious minutes, knowing it would be night before she would see her again. She lowered the baby gently into a comfortable bamboo cradle cushioned with a soft, clean quilt, and moved the cradle to the very center of the wooden hut in case of an earthquake. Qin was supposed to be fed and changed at noon by her brother Chon Gao, but the teenager was often too busy to stop by, and when he did, too embarrassed or disgusted to change the baby's diaper. If all went well, Yan returned late at night to find the baby's face covered with a thick glue of rice cereal and the quilted cushion swollen and heavy, serving as a giant, soaking diaper for the neglected child. Mostly, little Qin lay quietly, staring and whimpering softly after a whole day alone in the cradle.

Yan washed the soiled cushion every day so the baby would have a clean bed to start her day. Winter days were the worst. When she hung the quilt out to dry, it turned into a thick sheet of ice. Yan had to warm it on top of the family rice pot so her little baby could have a clean, if slightly sticky, quilt. At least it smelled like food on those days when the baby went hungry. Yan shook her head and sighed.

After putting the baby down, Yan got Ping up.

"Ping, Ping," Yan whispered into her daughter's ear as she held out her favorite pink sweater. "Give mama your little arm. Wake up now, my little angel."

She inserted one little arm into a sleeve, lifted Ping up slightly, slipped her own hand underneath her, and cooed, "Now, my little girl, give mama your other arm."

Ping opened her eyes, gave Yan a smile, and went back to sleep.

Yan looked at her sleepy daughter and tickled her little feet one at a time. "Wake up, sleepyhead. Please—" she pleaded. "You want Mama to make some money and buy us dinner, don't you?"

It took a few more moments before Ping responded to her mother's efforts to get her up. Pigtails were tied and breakfast porridge served before mother and daughter headed out the door. There was always one final lingering look back into the dark room where the crib lay and a moment of hesitation before the door closed with a quiet moan.

Yan held Ping's hand and walked her to a nearby state-run nursery school where kids were kept in one big room, fed home-brought lunches, and given naps in the middle of the floor on a large, worn-out quilt. Government nurseries, which only charged a small fee, were popular among working-class families, but there was a lengthy waiting list to get in. These primitive daycare centers could not cope with the baby boom of the 1950s and 60s, created by the party leadership's enthusiastic encouragement that women have more children. China had never put the infrastructure in place to care for, feed, or educate all these extra little citizens. Parents had to work and most newborns were raised by their grandparents. Yan did not have that luxury, so she felt lucky to have gotten Ping into a local nursery. As Yan dropped her off and waved goodbye, she only wished she could have brought Qin, too, but children under two were not allowed.

An hour later and a couple of miles away from her children, Yan sat with a group of women in their fifties and sixties, sewing purses and wallets in a "neighborhood processing unit"—a fancy term for a factory. She worked in a bare room with a concrete floor, benches, and a long wooden table, around which workers sat and did piece-work for the state for minimal pay.

Most of the workers were retired working-class women looking for a little extra cash. In addition to the money, they enjoyed being part of a group, gossiping all day long about minute details of the most trivial happenings around them. There were constant bursts of laughter among the bent backs, interspersed with tears, friendly slaps, and a steady stream of overlapping conversation. The old ladies all addressed each other as "sisters"—except for Yan.

When Yan first arrived, the others examined her closely with critical eyes. Yan was always neatly dressed in muted, fairly decent clothes, which hinted at a more sophisticated or intellectual side. On the other hand, the dark, shiny pigtails cascading down to her waist gave her the look of a very young girl, maybe in her late teens, they guessed.

After a few days of close observation, they relaxed and began to see Yan as a harmless, shy, and reliable co-worker. Although there was always a stream of conversation around her, Yan never joined in. Her only focus was on her work. She was respectful to all her colleagues, but Yan never talked about herself or why she was there. She just worked.

Once they became used to Yan, they started to call her "Little Girl." Sometimes, they caressed her glossy pigtails, shook their heads, and sighed. "You are such a young girl, Yan. You shouldn't be here with us, a bunch of old fools."

Their maternal instincts prompted them to protect and take care of Yan in whatever little ways they could. They brought her mugs of hot tea at lunch and let her leave early while they stayed behind to clean up. Yan gratefully accepted her co-workers' kind offers of help. She needed to get home to her children.

The years moved slowly when every minute was a struggle, and every day was a fight. Yan looked forward to when Qin turned two and could also go to nursery school. It bothered her to leave a baby in a crib all day long without being held, caressed, and pampered, with no one to change her diapers, or respond to her cries. It was torture to choose between leaving her or having her starve. Yan prayed that the baby would grow up quickly and when Qin turned one, she handed in the school application a year early. In China, a child's first birthday is considered the most important in its life, but Yan couldn't wait for Qin to turn two.

Finally, the time arrived.

It was a hot mid-July day. For the first time, Yan took a day off from work. She got up early, and scrubbed the baby clean in the family's wooden tub as Ping ate her breakfast.

"Will Qin join my nursery school today?" Ping asked with her mouth full, seeing her mother having some water fun with her baby sister.

"Come on, Qin, splash!" Yan encouraged the baby before she turned to Ping. "Yes, she will. From now on, she will be able to play with other children instead of staying in her crib all day. Will you share your friends with her in school?"

"Of course, I will." Ping promised. "And I'll tell the teachers to change her diaper, too."

"Good girl," Yan said. "You both are my good girls," she said to Qin as she looked at Ping tenderly. "Come on, let's splash some more. It's fun."

She supported the baby's back with one hand while gently hitting the water with the other. As water drops flew, Qin waved her arms and legs.

"Come on, Qin, splash Mama!"

Qin waved her arms harder and harder in and out of water as glistening droplets filled Yan's hair. She laughed hard and was surprised by the sound of her own joyful voice.

"I'm so happy today!"

She dried Qin up, and got her into the most decent outfit she could find.

"Shall we go to the nursery now?" Yan asked.

Ping couldn't wait. "Let's go, Mama! Let's go!"

Yan held Qin in one arm as she held Ping's hand. In her belly was yet another life kicking gently. Together, they headed toward Qin's new nursery.

Yan's cheeks were flushed with excitement. She wanted to tell the whole world: *Today is my daughter's second birthday and I'm sending her to a nursery!*

No more urine-soaked quilts. No more porridge-glued face. No more leaving her baby alone at home. It made her shudder to recall the time when government workers came to the slum looking for building violations. Spotting the homemade hut, they knocked on the door. When they received no answer, they began testing its safety the only way they knew—by hitting the frail walls with sledgehammers and seeing if it would fall down. Some good-hearted neighbors ran to Yan's workplace and brought her the news. By the time Yan arrived, she found her baby in her crib in the middle of the room completely buried by fallen objects. Luckily, the baby was unharmed. Whenever she thought about the incident, Yan held her baby even tighter.

The nursery interview on which Yan had pinned all her hopes turned out to be a complete disaster. After inspecting the baby, the head of the school declared that Qin was a paraplegic and would probably never be able to walk. She had never seen a child that age who could not walk ... or even sit up.

"Our school is overwhelmed as it is," she said matter-of-factly. "We can't take disabled children here."

Yan stood there, her face drained of blood. She became numb and could not feel her own body. Of course, she was not blind. She knew Qin could not sit or walk. The baby was lying alone in her crib all day with the exception of the few hours when Yan was home.

She thought the nursery school would give Qin more attention and gradually get her on her feet. But paraplegic? That was not possible! Had she ruined her baby's life?

In the end, Yan managed to pull herself together. She gathered her children and headed home with a curtain of tears over her eyes and face.

So ended my second birthday, with no nursery school, no father, no party, no gifts, no laughter, no relatives showing up to wish us well. Just a crying mother and a confused, hungry four-year-old sister in a hot, upside-down, wooden box with ugly sledgehammer marks on the outside.

The next day, Yan did not go to work. She never went back. From then on, she stayed home with Ping and me.

In spite of her growing stomach and fatigue, she was determined to get me on my feet, make me stand, walk, skip, run, and, above all, become a normal child. She quietly sold several of her precious keepsakes (among them, the last gold watch her father had given her from his beloved clock shop) in exchange for a few bottles of fish oil and calcium tablets to strengthen my bones.

Her hard work paid off, and she began to see me making progress, but at a cost. Without her job, the whole family had almost nothing to eat. There were days when she and Ping had to go to bed without dinner. She had to coax the four-year-old Ping to sleep with just two milk candies.

"Go to sleep, dear," she said. "Tomorrow we will have dinner on the table."

"But I'm not sleepy, Mama. I'm hungry."

"When you fall asleep, you won't feel hungry anymore. Trust me. Close your eyes and think about a dream you wish to have tonight, a dream that will please you."

"How about a banquet with lots of dishes?"

"What kind of dishes?"

"How about steamed fish, pork belly in brown sauce, egg custard with pork fat on top, and lots and lots of rice?"

"That sounds wonderful!"

"Can I invite Grandpa Ho De? He hasn't been here for a long time, and he loves pork belly in brown sauce."

"Sure."

"I'll pick out the best piece for him."

"That's a good girl. Now what kind of new games will you play with Grandpa? Will you take him out for a walk when I prepare the dishes? Grandpa is getting old. You have to hold his hand and walk slowly, right? Will you draw pictures for him? He loves your pictures so much that he has pasted them all over his store ..."

Yan tucked Ping in for the night while the sky was still bright to spare her an evening of suffering. Little Ping had her arms wrapped tight around her mother's neck and they talked for a long, long time. Their conversation gradually turned into a monologue as Ping's little arms slipped off and fell onto her pillow. Yan looked at her daughter: Ping was sleeping peacefully with a smile on her face. She had reached a world where food was plentiful. Today was finished. But what would happen tomorrow? What could Yan give to Ping for breakfast, and where would she get the dinner she had promised to her daughter tomorrow? These worries would haunt Yan's dreams.

Plotting and scheming in the forest, An Chu somehow managed to convince his manager to send him back to Shanghai a year early for the birth of their third child. He arrived just in time to hear the news: Yan had delivered a beautiful, dark-haired child—their third. The infant was named "Min," a warm-sounding word meaning "Intelligence." Yan and An Chu were so happy they didn't even care that she was a girl.

Chapter VIII

Last Days of the Shantytown

T HE TINY WOODEN HUT was now bustling with life. Yan enjoyed being an at-home mother for her three young daughters. The family was finally together again with An Chu working nearby. Though his wages were modest, Yan was good at stretching every penny he earned.

Yan preferred spending time with her children to doing chores and running the errands that, by necessity, occupied most of her days. Her life had always been one of haste. Now she wanted to do everything as slowly as possible, soaking in every little detail of life. Simple pleasures—hugs, giggles and kisses—were enough to make her feel rich and happy.

Every morning, she took her time making eight elaborate pigtails, two each for herself and the girls. Ping and Qin usually got "mouse tails"—long, thin, tightly braided pigtails. Min's hair was too short for "mouse tails," so she got "fireworks" with two, cute funnel-like brushes on the top of her head. Of course, all the girls got one final touch: butterfly bows. Soon pigtail-making became an important part of their day. The chores could wait.

"Mom," Ping held up an empty jar and cried out. "There's no more milk, and I think Min is hungry!" At the age of five, Ping enjoyed being a little mother, filling the baby bottle for her little sisters.

"I'm coming," Yan replied as she pulled a ribbon from between her teeth and finished the last bow on Qin's hair.

"Let's make a pot of rice and some more milk for Min," she said as she turned around and picked up a dented aluminum pot.

Poor families without the money to buy milk turned to an ancient Chinese solution—a magic formula used for hundreds of generations: Mothers added an extra cup of water to the family pot of rice. When it came to a boil, that extra cup of water bubbled into a thick layer of translucent, milky liquid. If you put that cup of rice milk into a baby bottle and added a pinch of sugar, you had yourself some infant formula. The baby got her milk and the family got their rice. Millions of Chinese babies were nourished this way until they graduated to solid foods. Ping was a rice-milk baby, and so was every one of Yan's other children, growing up without ever tasting real milk. Rice was what the rich and poor Chinese had in common: As long as a pot of rice was on the table at dinnertime, everything was fine.

After she finished her household chores, Yan did some sewing and knitting. She now had a family of five to clothe. Without a sewing machine or money, she had to plan ahead for every season. To pinch pennies, she patched socks and shoes, and lengthened sleeves of old jackets that were getting too short for her growing daughters. Yan used tricks she learned from the costume shop in her theater days. She searched through her sewing basket, and dug out matching ribbons and bows, which she stitched onto the upper parts of sleeves of the children's worn-out clothes. Her daughters' blouses and old jackets suddenly became new again. In the Sun household, necessity was the mother of fashion.

Only when a piece of clothing became completely unwearable would Yan make something new, though she often could not even afford to buy material. She shook her head as she gently washed socks full of holes, or torn underwear that was beyond repair. She had to wait until she could save a few *fen* here and there and then go to a fabric store to find leftover bits from the cutting area. Scraps of fabric were pieced together like a jigsaw puzzle and sewed to make sleeves, mittens, or little underpants for her girls. Yan was a magician who could turn old clothes into new ones or an adult sweater into children's scarves and hats. She could transform an ancient outfit forgotten at the bottom of a drawer into a trio of identical jumpers for Ping, Qin and Min.

With material in such short supply, nothing could be wasted. When old clothes and sheets could not be patched anymore, Yan salvaged the fabric to make soles for their cotton shoes.

She usually chose a sunny day to work on this labor-intensive task. First, a clean wooden board was laid out under the sun, and then a small pot of water was placed on the stove. When it came to a boil, a flour-water mixture was poured in and stirred until it turned into a mass of thick, hot glue. Now, Yan was ready to proceed to the real action: One layer of fabric was followed by one layer of glue. After each strip of fabric was applied, she smoothed it with her palm to get rid of air bubbles that were trapped underneath. Layer after layer was added until she ran out of fabric. Then she had to wait for the sun to do the rest of the work, hardening the material. It was time for her to clean her hands and the pot, and spend time with her girls.

By nightfall, Yan peeled the thick, stiff fabric off the wood. She traced shoe shapes on it with small ones squeezed in between big ones to get maximum use of the precious material. After cutting them out with a sharp knife, all the soles were stacked in a pile and Yan began finishing them. She took a piece of thick, coarse thread she had waxed smooth by rubbing it hundreds of times against an old candle and ran it through the soles over and over until the stitching was so close it became part of the fabric itself. She then attached the soles to the sewn cotton bodies of the shoes. Yan had to force hundreds of stitches back and forth through every stack of fabric board to make each shoe.

Hand-made cotton shoes took a long time to make and wore out quickly. And since they were made from fabric and flour, they were not waterproof. To help them last, An Chu trimmed rubber from broken bicycle tires and nailed an extra layer of protection onto the bottoms. At the time, it was a popular way for farmers and the city's poor to be able to afford shoes. And with three daughters and a husband, Yan had to make a lot of them.

Despite her busy life, Yan always made time for her father. Ho De's life had gotten simpler since Chon Gao graduated from high school and, knowing a lot about trouble, joined the Police Academy. Ho De now lived alone. Although he took care of the store, he stopped taking care of himself. He did not want to be bothered with starting the stove, cooking a hot meal for one, or even changing his clothes. His hair got whiter. His back bent lower, though he was not even sixty. Knowing that he would never do it himself, Yan came to clean his apartment, do his wash, and draw him a bath. She wanted to take care of him, despite her own hard life. It made her happy that Ho De came to have dinner with them once a week. He seemed to come back to life playing with his three granddaughters. He brought them gifts of fresh sugarcane to suck on, oranges to hold and smell, and walnuts to crack and share. He tickled them until they squealed and hugged them tenderly. After all the noisy fun, which was nearly enough to bring the wooden hut down in splinters, the family sat down for a hot meal. It was the only hot meal Ho De had until his next visit the following Friday. What he ate in between, no one knew. But all the neighbors later recalled that he never lit his stove.

The last time he visited, everything seemed to unfold in a normal way. Ho De came, ate, stayed until seven or eight at night, and was accompanied to the bus stop by An Chu. When he got home, he went out as he always did with two thermos bottles to buy hot water for himself. A neighbor recognized Ho De walking unsteadily in the dark and offered to carry the bottles for him.

"Are you alright, Grandfather?" he asked respectfully as he took the bottles.

Ho De collapsed before he could respond and never woke up again.

Grandpa Ho De's shocking death was my earliest memory. I woke up in the middle of the night and called to my mother to turn on the light so I could go to the bathroom. Mother was always worried I would wet the bed, and had tied the light switch to a long string attached to her bed frame so we could go quickly if the need arose. That night, I called, and called, and called. I was getting desperate when the light finally came on. Instead of my mother, I saw the motionless face of my grandmother glowing in the dim light. Why was my father's mother here? She never came to our house. And where was my mom? For the first time in my life, I had the feeling of being awake in a dream. Everything seemed unreal. Then, I started to search for my father, but he was not there, either. By that time, I had forgotten why I had called my mother in the first place. All I knew was that since that weird night, Grandpa Ho De never came to visit again.

The next morning, Mother and Father finally came home. There were no smiles on their faces when they saw us. Mother's swollen eyelids told me she had cried a lot and something awful had happened. When I went over to her and hugged her leg, I looked up and saw tears flowing down her face. Her body was shaking, as if she were laughing, but the sounds she made were strange and terrible. I was scared and held her tight as the quaking went on and on.

A few unsettling days later, Mother took out our best clothes and told us that we were going to visit Grandpa Ho De.

I was too young to understand that the fancy house we arrived at was a funeral home. I saw him lying in an oblong wooden box with a red satin blanket covering him up to his chest. He looked very peaceful, just like someone who was asleep. Mother held baby Min and wept. I never saw her cry so much. I tried to comfort her, but nothing I did seemed to make any difference.

Finally, Mother pulled herself together and instructed Ping and me to bow and bid farewell to Grandpa Ho De.

"Grandpa loved you very much," she said. "Now it's time you should say 'goodbye' to him."

I could not understand Mother's intention or why we were there in the first place, but I didn't like the sound of her request and the feeling of everything else going on around me. I refused to bow, saying, "Grandpa is sleeping. I'll wait for him to wake up and then I will play with him."

At my reply, Mother broke down again. She wrapped her arms around me and squeezed me so tightly that I could barely breathe. Her tears wet my face and alarmed me. I did not understand that people would die, and Grandpa Ho De would never wake up again or play with me.

Later in life, Mother recounted many times the story of Ho De's burial service. It was a sad scene, with only her, my dad, Uncle Chon Gao, Ping, baby Min, and me gathered around him to bid him an eternal farewell. No other relatives came. No one from my father's family came.

My mother took Ho De's death very hard. She borrowed a tremendous amount of money to buy him a decent coffin, a final change of clothes, a red silk quilt, and a burial plot. She put his Bible on his chest before the coffin lid was closed, and he was lowered into the ground.

Of the four parents Yan had, Ho De was the third who had left her. He had loved her, taught her, and given her a treasured dowry of aristocratic Chinese manners, pride, and dignity, which Yan carried all her life even during hard times. Through his teachings, Ho De's legacy lived on far beyond his years through Yan's life and the lives of her children.

When Yan and An Chu went to clean out Ho De's run-down, bare apartment, there was nothing of value left. A few splintered chairs, third-hand knick-knacks, and three dirty rice bowls in the sink were apparently Yan's entire sad inheritance. It was no wonder she fainted when she found the money. Millions of dollars in cash were stuffed into the mattress and wooden posts of the bed he had slept on. There was so much money they would have needed half a dozen wheelbarrows to cart it away. Ho De had literally been lying on a secret fortune.

And, like most astonishing secrets, it was, of course, too good to be true. The 1,000-yuan notes, decorated beautifully with blue thread, red numbers, and embossed gold seals, boasted Dr. Sun Yat-sen's portrait and signature—proud shadows of the old order, the days of the nationalist republic before the communists rose to power. Why had so much money been hidden away for so long, without anyone's knowledge? Yan had her own explanation: She believed it had been secreted away by her late adoptive mother, Jin Lai. Why she chose to keep paper currency, rather than gold or silver, no one would ever know. The heartbreak of it all was that the beautiful piles of money were completely worthless. Still, An Chu and Yan decided to use it to give Ho De a royal send-off. Taking the treasure to the house's traditional, private courtyard, they carefully stacked the thick wads of money in a pyramid reaching as high as Yan's waist and set fire to it. As Yan watched the bright sparks and yellow-rimmed, glowing ashes rise into the air, she was startled by a visual echo the colors recalled in her mind, summoning back the glinting of the beautiful, golden watches so beloved by her father so long ago. All those golden timepieces, Yan thought, as well as the golden times they had spent together, were now gone, literally gone up in smoke.

Life went on in the small wooden hut, but without Ho De, it would never be the same. In the absence of Grandpa's treats, hugs, jokes, and laughter, the children learned to keep him alive in their memories. Through their mother's stories, they understood that Grandpa Ho De was a learned man, an expert calligrapher, and a lover of books. So, they picked up books and started their own calligraphy lessons. Grandpa Ho De's tales were their childhood favorites, and they told them to each other over and over. Most of all, they loved to snuggle together under Grandpa's old black-and-white bathrobe until it became threadbare. Ho De was forever their best and only Grandfather. Years later, even when they had trouble remembering him clearly, they could still feel his warm presence under the skeleton of his robe.

Part IV

Rapids of Life,
Where Are You Taking Us?

(Shanghai, 1965 to 1975)

Chapter I

OUR NEW HOME

"Have you heard the news?"

"What?"

"The government wants to tear down our huts!"

"My hut!?"

"All our huts."

"Are you sure?"

"Old Li knows some important people in the city. He said that, if we don't leave, Liberation Army soldiers will come with their guns and drive us out!"

"It's not possible!"

"Where can we go?"

Just as Yan finally started to feel settled in the shantytown she now called home, rumors began that the whole village would be demolished. Its wretched living conditions violated many of the new public health regulations and the Communist government's vision of a new utopia. It had to go, although no one had thought through where all these people would actually live.

People panicked about the possible destruction of their homes and the poor but close-knit community they had painstakingly built. They had worked hard to create these crude huts, which, along with their broken furniture and dented cooking pots, were filled with their lives' most precious memories. Despite the squalor, the shantytown was home, and the thought of living somewhere else made them feel scared and lost. Most people hoped against hope that the rumors would go away and started to believe they might be left alone until, one day, uniformed men appeared with buckets of glue and brushes as big as spatulas, and started to post evacuation notices over their front doors. Families that ignored the notices or didn't know how to read came home from work and found everything they owned in the street, and their front doors nailed shut. Even if they couldn't understand the large Chinese characters written in bloody red, shouting, "DANGER! STAY OUT!" they knew that their homes were doomed and their lives were about to change.

Instead of creating order, as the authorities had hoped, tearing down the shantytown caused more chaos. People ran around aimlessly, not knowing what to do. Communities, neighbors, and friends disappeared along with the help, advice, and comfort they provided. Piles of broken things were scattered everywhere, people were shouting, children crying, and chickens running about loose, looking for familiar landmarks in the rubble. People began worrying about being robbed of the little they had by others who had lost everything. Families whose huts were still standing bundled up their treasures and disassembled their furniture, ready to flee when the sledgehammers started pounding on their walls.

Although I was only five at the time, I sensed something was going on. I saw neighbors moving out furniture, folding quilts, packing clothes, and loading their belongings onto waiting wagons and wheelbarrows. All the noise and activity attracted me. I wanted to go outside, stand in the middle of the action, and participate in the excitement. I wanted to find out where all my friends were going. Maybe I could play with them one more time before they were put on top of their wagons and disappeared with their parents. But Mother wouldn't let me get out. Instead, she ordered me and my sisters to stay inside our boring hut all day long. She even closed our front door so we couldn't see what was going on!

"It's too dusty outside," she said plainly as if nothing was happening. "Please stay inside with Mama."

What do you mean dusty? Our floor is made of dust! I protested in my head.

The hut was dark, just like on a rainy day. And so, I did what I always did on rainy days: I started playing the "peeking" game. Spying on the rest of the world was my favorite thing to do when I got bored. Our house was built with badly joined wooden planks filled with gaps and slits. One of my great entertainments as a child was to experience the living kaleidoscope of the outside world through long, skinny lenses. Some of the strategically located secret windows served me well over the years and taught me a lot about the life Mother had tried to hide from me. Once I crouched in a corner and watched in horror as my best friend's parents tore each other's clothes and cursed at each other until her father had enough, knocked her mother down, and walked away.

For now, I lay contentedly on my stomach and looked through a knot hole, watching our neighbors running with household objects. I saw dust swirling and babies screaming. I saw a curious rooster that was wondering what was going on stride right into the middle of the crowd, where someone stepped on it. The bird squawked, its face scarlet red, and its combs shaking with nervousness. Abandoning its ill-advised curiosity, the injured bird flapped its wings, and flew off to hide from careless human feet. In all the hubbub, no one even noticed the rooster. Maybe Mother was smart after all. Maybe she did not want me to suffer the same fate.

We did not stay in the shantytown long enough to see its last dying days. As an employee of the House and Land Management Agency, my father was offered new living space in the city. Eager to get out of the chaos, my parents jumped at the chance.

I remember leaving our home on a fine spring day. A pleasant sea breeze, just slightly cool, sweetened the usual pungent smells of the neighborhood, and I inhaled it all deeply to help me remember the only place I had ever lived. I said goodbye to the upside-down wooden box in which I had grown up, and then we all held hands and walked out of the slum into a new, completely different world.

Tall, beautiful buildings were lined up along the avenues and side streets, so many that they disappeared into the horizon in both directions. After the low shacks and open sky of the shantytown, I was dazed by the size and depth of the city, wondering if it would suck me in and turn me into a small dot like all the other people. Where we came from almost nothing grew, but here I saw rows upon rows of giant trees along the streets. Their new, tender leaves made my heart sing. The world was more beautiful than I had ever remembered, and its air was sweet and friendly.

We must have been a sight. We neared our new home pushing a bicycle piled ten feet high with junk, dragging packages, a broom, cooking pots, and a funny-looking device someone told us we would need in the big city: a toilet-plunger. Holding a precious slip of paper with the address of our new home, my mother was nervous, rushing us through the streets and herding us along like ragged little ducklings. She paid no attention to anything except for the street signs, and her concentration paid off. Before we knew it, we were standing in front of a massive pair of iron gates.

At the time, gated neighborhoods were practically nonexistent. The communist ideal was the equality of all people, abolishment of class differences, and the distribution of wealth. The stiff formality of the wrought-iron entrance awed Ping and me into instant silence and froze our childish enthusiasm. We hid behind Mother as a middle-aged man slowly waddled out of his sentry box, examining us up and down.

"You can't pass through here. This is for residents and visitors only," he announced in an official voice. He waved his hands from side to side, as if to block us from entering.

He obviously thought we were strangers who didn't belong there, judging from our modest clothes.

"We don't want to pass through." Mother replied. "We are moving in."

The man looked confused. "You? Moving in?"

After a few inquiries, Mother showed him the address and the key, and he let us enter.

"I'm not sure if the place is fit to live in," he warned us before waving us on.

We looked at each other. We didn't quite get what he meant.

Little did I know that my family and I had just moved into the most elite neighborhood in Shanghai. Like Park Avenue in New York City, or the Champs-Elysees in Paris, it was a place for the rich and powerful—retired members of the Chinese politburo, an ex-mayor, high-ranking army officers, and a few cast-off mistresses left stranded by the city's great industrialists when they vanished following the founding of the People's Republic of China. These great and faded ladies were the last reminders of the past glories of the pre-communist era, the elite of Shanghai's fabled high society, where women wore silk and diamonds, commanded small armies of maids and servants, and whose delicate, expensively shod feet never touched the ground. They were tolerated, perhaps because they had lost so much, or perhaps as curiosities—like some harmless fossils in a local museum.

By some strange luck, not only were we moving into the prestigious French Quarter, but into one of its most elegant streets. Old-timers in the area still called it "Jubilee Court," although after the revolution the new leaders quickly renamed it with the more proletarian-sounding "New Healthy Gardens." Maybe they thought that by changing its decadent name, they could change its decadent character and transform it into a perfect breeding ground for good, strong, young communist citizens. Unfortunately, the opulent, private lane remained defiantly haughty and imperial—at least outwardly—with luxurious, fairytale-like Spanish colonial villas on each side. They were designed to look like castles, and their roofs were made of beautiful orange-red tiles whose colors reminded me of ripe persimmons.

Only two families lived in each house, occupying one of the two, huge main floors and having separate entrances. At that time, most people were lucky to have a 15 x 15 room to live in, and they usually shared a bathroom and kitchen with five, or ten, other families. Of course, that would still be a step up for the Suns, who had never had a bathroom or kitchen, and managed with a chamber pot under their beds and a wood stove for cooking and warmth.

Here, in front of every villa, was a spacious garden enclosed by a seven-foot-high black bamboo fence. Spilling teasingly over the tops, tall plants and ornamental trees danced and competed to be the most beautiful and graceful. French pines, magnolias, loquats, figs, wild roses, and trumpet vines rested comfortably along with their owners in a paradise lost by the French in 1949 and discovered by the new Chinese ruling class. At the end of the lane, four Western-style six-story apartment buildings stood, forming a circle. These buildings towered over the villas, competing to be the center of attention.

Some things had changed since the French left, although the new residents didn't realize it. A giant boiler room, the size of a two-car garage, used to supply heat to all the residents in the lane, but had been abandoned long ago. Nestled between the last villa and the first apartment building, it looked functional, but a closer look through the dust-covered glass windows at the top of the door revealed the gigantic skeleton of what appeared to be a very ancient coal-eating mechanism sleeping under a blanket of dust. The new residents never seemed to miss the heating in the wintertime, or wonder why the apartments were equipped with stone-cold radiators under every window. Having heat in an apartment was an unheard-of luxury in the early Communist years. In fact, in the late 1960s, almost no one had heat in the winter—not in private homes, not in offices, not in schools, not even in hospitals. People learned to live with the cold or keep it at a respectable distance with quilted door protectors, hot-water bottles, and thick winter clothes both indoors and out. Frostbitten fingers and toes were everyday affairs and considered common winter annoyances, comparable to mosquito bites in the summer. With lots and lots of hot tea, steaming soup, rubbing of hands, and stamping of feet, people managed to make it without help through the winter to the warmth of spring.

On the other side of the lane from the obsolete boiler room, crammed into a narrow gap between the garden of one villa and the side of an apartment building, sat a miniature castle, the size of a large dollhouse. It had the same stucco exterior and tile roof as those of the grander villas and looked very sturdy. A giant sycamore tree snuggled against the tiny house, reminding me of a very small person with a comically oversized umbrella. This was our new home.

Seeing it for the first time, we were both awed and excited. Mother inserted a shiny new key into the lock of a wooden door leading to a modest inner courtyard that matched the size of the house. While she was doing this, Ping and I struggled up on our tiptoes to get a peek through the black bamboo fence.

"Let me see."

"No, let me see."

"Mom, Ping won't let me look," I screamed.

"Qin is blocking me, Mother," Ping protested back.

We had so much fun pushing each other and preventing the other from getting the first glance that neither of us could gain an advantage.

Finally, Mother pushed open the door and we leapt into the yard.

We were utterly disappointed by what we saw: There was absolutely nothing in the tiny yard except a concrete patio, which lay uninvitingly in front of a very small house. What really caught my attention was the sheer wall of the apartment building next door, which towered above us like a dark force. I looked upward through the iron slats of the fire escapes until my neck ached. The height of this six-story building boggled my imagination.

"When I grow up, Mother," I declared, my right index finger pointing upward, "I will live up there."

At that moment, I meant it. I had such a longing to be standing all the way up there, the highest point I had ever seen in my life. But it made my mother panic. We were neither rich nor famous. My declaration would make my family a laughingstock if anyone heard it. Mother muffled my mouth with her hand before I could cause any trouble and pushed me into the little house.

"Little children shouldn't talk nonsense," she scolded.

Our home used to be the bath house for the maids and chauffeurs of the four apartment buildings. Under a thick layer of dust, we could see that the now one-room house had a floor half made of concrete and the other half made of mosaic tile. The concrete section was the men's shower room and the daintier, more decorative mosaic section had served the women. Severed pipelines along the rust-stained walls told of previous shower locations and vanished drains, although I only learned what they were years later, for I had never seen a shower before.

Alone on the floor sat a porcelain fixture. I could not tell from its odd shape and size what it was or why it was not taken away like the rest of the objects in that room. But I immediately saw that Mother was delighted by the sight of it.

"A toilet!" she gasped. "Our own! What a luxury!"

We could not understand her excitement, but Ping and I grew curious.

"What is it?"

"What did you call it, Mother?"

She patiently explained its workings to us as she excavated it from under dust and spider webs, scrubbed it inside and out, then depressed its little handle. I saw water gush down into the big bowl, swirl around, and then magically disappear along with the dirt and dust, all the while making a pleasant gurgling noise. I felt I was witnessing a magic trick. I kept on wondering where the dirty water went and how the fresh water appeared. I did learn from Mother that this magic bathroom device was a western invention, and that we did not need a chamber pot anymore. Our new toilet would always be clean and fresh, unlike our smelly, old wooden chamber pot, which we only emptied out once a day.

The marvelous toilet occupied our attention for the rest of the day. We flushed it again and again, watching the water swirl down and disappear while Mother dusted, swept, and scrubbed the floor on her knees. Between this gleaming porcelain fixture and the luxury of so much clean, solid space, our hearts were sold on the new house. I forgot all about the tall buildings next to us. This was a palace compared to the wooden box and dirt floor we left behind. It was more than my parents had dared to hope for. It would be the place I called home for the next twenty-five years.

Chapter II

Days of Innocence

THE NEW HOUSE WAS a welcome change in our lives, especially Mother's. With our own water tap, toilet, and yard, and no one to share any of these luxuries, she finally got the privacy for which she dreamed so long. For us, however, privacy was a shock. All of a sudden, the hundreds of friends who stopped by, played with us, and sometimes fought with us, disappeared. Instead of the clamor and din of the slum, we discovered a new sound: silence.

Once the fascination with all the many novelties wore off, boredom set in. Since our lane was private, no one ever unexpectedly appeared at our door. In fact, we rarely even saw anyone walking in the lane. Mother granted us permission to stroll there but warned us not to go beyond the sentry gates. We took advantage of Mother's offer and wandered around, exploring outside the big villas' expansive gardens, gathering flowers that stuck their heads out from underneath fences, picking strange berries and seeds, or simply skipping back and forth down the street until we were exhausted.

Soon we discovered that we were not the only working-class family in the neighborhood. The original garages had been transformed into apartments, and in each garage, an entire household was temporarily parked. They were less fortunate than us, with no private bathroom fixtures, one public water tap, and a well to serve some twenty apartments. Nevertheless, they at least gave the feeling of one big community, which reminded me of the shantytown where everyone was part of everyone else's lives. We watched from a distance as they shared food, played cards, and wandered in and out of each other's homes. Ping and I wanted to make friends with the children there, but to our disappointment, when we peered into their enclave and our eyes met theirs, they just pulled each other's sleeves, turned, and walked away. We came to the realization that they did not want to make any outside friends.

At the end of the lane, past the sentry box, was a spacious, fenced-in public garden. This little park offered a view of *Huai Hai* Road, the famous shopping street known in the French colonial days as "Avenue Joffre." Ping and I would often take Min to the garden and play together under a giant magnolia tree. When the blossoms peaked, we industriously gathered stacks of colossal pink petals from the ground, placed assorted seeds and wild flowers in them, and played "family dinner party." We played hide-and-seek in the bushes, exploring the limits of our world, but our eyes wandered even further. We wanted to know what lay beyond the fence where we admired the endless flow of people strolling by and holding bags, boxes, and packages. Tickled by the sights and our own curiosity, we started to toy with naughty ideas like leaving the park and walking out among strangers.

One day, we did it. I remember my heart pounding in my throat as we slipped out of the gate. Ping held baby Min while I looped my arm through hers. I did not enjoy freedom as much as I had thought I would. Worry steered my mechanical steps.

Does Ping know where we're going? I wondered, afraid to know the actual truth.

We walked for a few minutes before a strange woman approached us. She was about Mother's age, perhaps a little bit older.

"Hi, little girls," she said, sizing us up. "Don't you all remember me? I'm a friend of your parents."

Her eyes were filled with smiles and her mouth with teeth.

I turned back to see if she was addressing someone else behind us, but there was no one there.

"Your mother has sent me here to find you," she said as she patted me on the head. "She is waiting for you at the North Train Station."

What?

Now I was really puzzled. Mother was doing laundry at home. We had sneaked out. She did not even know we were out wandering on our own. So how could she have sent someone here to take us to the train station? Mother said trains were for families with money traveling to faraway places. Was this woman lying? Why? Why did she want to take us to faraway places?

But she looked like a good person, well-dressed, and with a kind, gentle face. *Maybe she really knows our parents …*

I was so confused that I thought aloud: "Mother is home doing laundry, Ping. She doesn't even know where we are."

Ping and I looked at each other, and we suddenly came to a revelation: It was a trap.

We turned around and ran as fast as we could. We did not stop and never looked behind us until we slipped back inside the gate.

Mother was kneading dough and steaming buns when we returned. She wiped her floury hands on her apron and listened patiently as we breathlessly poured out the story of our narrow escape.

"That is why I don't want you to go out on your own. The time will come when I'll let you do so. First, you have to grow up a bit more," she commented matter-of-factly without any criticism, handing us each a steamed bun.

That summer soon slipped by and it was time for Ping to go to school. To prepare Ping for the first grade, Mother had been home schooling us an hour a day. She made me her pupil, as well, much against my will. Two years younger than Ping, I was not an eager student and dreaded that endless hour each day. I was glad when summer was finally over and Ping went off to school.

Ping was a good student. She always got perfect scores in math and spelling, which pleased mother very much.

"I will be a good student, too, when I go to school," I vowed. "But I'm just not ready yet."

Mother laughed.

I did not like that summer for another reason, as well. A very bad flu hit the city. To combat the chance of our getting it, Mother turned to an old Chinese trick to ward off the disease: Day and night she boiled a mixture of herbs and vinegar, filling our small home with sour steam that hurt our lungs and made tears run down our faces. If I'd had a choice, I would gladly have risked getting sick rather than be suffocated by acid. To make matters worse, every night at the dinner table, Mother dispensed to each of us, as a precautionary measure, two cloves of raw pickled garlic. I had always run to be the first at the table when supper was ready, but now I stopped. Instead, I used every excuse to be the last. The very smell of garlic and vinegar made me sick. I even started to have second thoughts about the sweet and sour foods I used to love. There were nights I sat frozen at the table and refused to eat anything until mother suspended her rule, and let me eat my dinner without those cursed garlic cloves. Only then would I wipe away my tears with the backs of my hands and enjoy my dinner with victorious glee.

To strengthen us against sickness, Mother poured packets of herbal medicine into a stockpot and made us special teas. I willingly accepted the cool, sweet concoctions until one day, I looked into the bottom of my cup and found among the dregs, beetle shells, cicada skins, and some other unidentifiable bugs. No more tea for me. With this new rebellion, Mother exhausted all her measures to guard me against the flu.

Some bad germs got me eventually. I became weak as a rag doll, boiled limp by fever and chilled by cold sweats. After three days, my father placed his firm hands under my armpits, lifted me into the air and flipped me onto his shoulder. I got a ride to the local hospital where I was kept under observation after getting a painful penicillin shot. I did not have the energy to put up a fight and lay on a gurney most of the day while my blood work was being analyzed. When darkness fell, I was taken home on my father's shoulders.

That night, Mother isolated me in one bed while the rest of the family squeezed into the other. For a whole week, my father gave me a daily "horseback ride" to get my shots, and Mother simmered hot broth and porridge to get me back on my feet.

Autumn brought chilly winds and dark, thick clouds. The elderly started to complain about their aching elbows and knees. Besides the change in weather, I also noticed some other differences.

One day, workers stopped us from entering the park on Avenue Joffre where we played for the entire summer. When we returned the next day, our hearts sank: Our garden had been closed off and filled with a gigantic public display.

We managed to squeeze through a narrow gap to assess the damage. Right in the center, facing the big commercial street, someone had staked a huge oblong poster shouting a giant slogan, each word the size of a banquet table.

"Long Live the Solidarity of All Our Countrymen!" Ping slowly uttered the words.

"What does it mean?" I asked. "Are there too many people fighting in our country?"

I was very confused and guilt-laden, remembering how mother made us hold each other's hands after she broke up our arguments, as if I had contributed to the country's lack of solidarity.

We looked down and around and found all our wildflowers and weeds were gone. The soil had been carefully combed. Six red flags had been erected on each side of the poster. They were so blazingly red they made my eyes tear. I had to look away from them, but I could not close my ears to stop their powerful fluttering noises. I could not shut out a wind that was strong enough to change the country.

Little did I know that we were feeling the headwinds of a revolutionary storm that would last for the next ten years. It was so powerful that it swept over and affected most of the Chinese people before it was over.

Chapter III

LIFE BEHIND THE IRON CURTAIN

FOR A SIX-YEAR-OLD GIRL, 1966 was anything but boring. Something new was happening all the time.

Every few days, new copies of Chairman Mao's latest quotation appeared in red ink on the front pages of every newspaper, accompanied by a giant portrait of the great leader, taking up half a page. Radio broadcasters passionately read his newest thoughts over and over again for the entire day. On those special days, there was no national or local news, just Mao's words. When I listened long enough, I memorized his speeches but without understanding much. Mother said that even grownups couldn't understand everything.

When he had something especially important to tell the people, Chairman Mao sometimes appeared on the radio himself and spoke directly to us. In order to keep track of where the country was heading, Mother kept the radio blasting all day. But that put a big strain on our poor machine, which was more a tangle of wires than a radio. (One of Father's friends had assembled it for us with old electronic parts he scavenged from a secondhand store.) Sometimes Mother had to shake it hard to get any sound out of it. A few times she had to turn it upside down or hang it out the window to make it work.

"Please, please help me," Mother often begged her radio. She was mostly very patient with it and moved it around the house for a long time until she found a place and position where it agreed to work. Then, she tuned it to the People's Central Broadcasting network, the most serious and official radio station at the time.

When Chairman Mao's distinctive voice miraculously came through the radio, Mother always got excited. "Come, children, come and listen with me." Our entire family stood by the radio and listened in awe. Chairman Mao had a very thick Hunan accent. When he spoke, Mother looked serious and knitted her eyebrows, and I wondered if she was having trouble understanding him, or if she was worried about what he was saying. Lately, she kept saying that Mao's words were "loaded with gunpowder." I nodded in agreement even though I had no idea what that meant.

Since October 1949, Mao had held the highest position of power in the country he himself had founded. He was the head of our government, our army, and our people, and he set the political course for the nation. No one ever questioned what he had to say, or what he wanted to do. His quotations were the words of a father to the sons and daughters of China. Everyone listened carefully, including my family. We were used to receiving his instructions over the radio and through the newspapers, but never as often and fervently as they came now. Sometimes, he had so much to say that newspapers had to print a "special edition" just for him.

Something was different in his tone. Chairman Mao became very critical of everything: He condemned people who held power in his socialist order but followed the path of capitalism. He used the words I couldn't understand: "capitalistic bureaucrats" and "revisionists." But I understood the severity of them because they were all "enemies of the people." Like worms, these "class enemies" had burrowed deep inside the Communist Party infrastructure and affected its health. Chairman Mao wanted to dig them out. We did not need to know how or why these people were worms. If Chairman Mao was against them, they were our enemies, too. We wanted to help our great leader stop them from corrupting our country.

Not long afterwards, Chairman Mao made history again in Tiananmen Square. He waved his powerful arms from atop the Heavenly Peace Gate and called on the working class to become masters of their own country, to stand up, rebel, and reclaim their socialist political forum. He praised the blue-collar workers, peasants, and soldiers, and assured them that he would stand by them as they had stood by him. It was obvious by now that Chairman Mao was gearing his people up for a fight, to stand up once again, and follow him in a new political revolution.

"Something big is happening right now," Mother said with her eyes glued to the front page of the *Liberation Daily*. She was splurging lately, spending a few cents every morning to buy a daily paper and find out the news. Sometimes, she bought two different papers to compare stories. "It's not that much more expensive than buying batteries for the radio," she decided.

Mother was like a weather vane. She detected storms before they actually happened. When the government started to ration rice and cooking oil, she spent every penny she had on sugar, matches and soap, predicting that all these vital necessities would soon be rationed, too. The government seemed to be eager to fulfill her prophecies and new restrictions followed almost immediately. Mother began to see Chairman Mao's new quotations as omens. A new picture was emerging, but it was too big for her to see. She was worried.

"Nothing good comes out of these political movements," Mother said to Father at the breakfast table before he left for work. "Remember our life in Zhang Ye?"

My dad slurped his watery rice and nodded.

"Ordinary people are more likely to be the victims and scapegoats. Watch yourself."

Mother was very concerned about Father and constantly worried he would get into trouble. She had every reason to be worried. Father was very popular among his co-workers. Everybody liked him, and everyone was his friend. Female colleagues often greeted him with giggles and affectionate pats on the shoulder, and men offered him cigarettes and confided in him about their private lives. He got involved in the Workers' Union, and was elected as a section leader. He willingly spent his spare time visiting co-workers with injuries and illnesses and helped needy families during the holidays.

He even got involved in resolving family disputes. Once, to stop a fight between a husband and his wife, Father slept outside their door all night long. When he came home the next morning for breakfast and Mother saw his puffy pink eyes, she was cross.

"You are not everyone's policeman," she said. "You can't sleep outside people's doors every night. Remember, you have a family, too, and the union doesn't pay you a salary!"

Father silently ate his breakfast and left for work.

Father was a stubborn man. He did what he thought was right to do. Mother's words never deterred him. Mother was well aware of that, too. "Am I talking to a wall?" she said and stamped her feet in frustration.

Father had too much hot human passion, according to Mother. She was worried that he got tangled up in too many decisions about what was right or wrong—meaning for every grateful person he helped, there was at least one who would be unhappy with his interference and might cause trouble later. Mother wanted him to stop spilling his heart and thoughts out to everyone. She wanted him to be more selective in making friends and cautious about what he said in public. But the more Mother lectured him, the more silent Father became. Finally, she gave up giving her daily monologues.

"You are one stubborn dog!"

Are dogs stubborn? I wondered. Father was born in a dog year, and Mother often ended her one-way conversation with something to do with dogs.

I could not stand my parents fighting, partly because I was afraid it could undo the solidarity of our country and make Chairman Mao angry. I did not want uniformed people to place more banners and wire more loudspeakers in our garden, and leave no room for flowers and trees. The redness of the flags hurt my eyes, and the amplified voices hurt my ears. The world around me was changing so much lately that I became fearful. So, I pulled Father toward Mother and made him apologize whenever Mother got loud, regardless of what the conflict was about. But I never really believed he was sorry because, despite all my hard work to stop it, he always managed to annoy Mother again and again.

One night, Mother found six eggs had disappeared from her storage jar. She had stood in line for many hours with her precious ration coupons and fought many elbows to buy these eggs, planning to make custard for her children. Of course, Father took them. He had sneaked them out of the house in his handkerchief and dropped them off early in the morning at the home of a co-worker whose wife had just given birth.

That night, we sat around the table and had only cabbage and rice for dinner. We ate without saying a word. No one, not even little Min, made a peep for fear that the silence would be broken by the anger in the air.

Soon after, Ping had to return all her textbooks to be replaced by Mao's quotation books and revolutionary songs. When Mother picked up those old school books for the last time, she circled her three children around her and read them out loud to us for the last time. It was a bittersweet moment for our little family and the end of formal education for our generation.

"Remember this moment, my children," she said. "Remember these lovely poems and stories. I hope we will get to read them again someday."

Like tens of thousands of other students, Ping was given a red scarf—a thin strip of bright, triangular cloth. With her scarf tied around her neck and her right arm raised in a salute, Ping officially joined the "Little Red Guards" to protect Chairman Mao and our motherland.

About this time, people all began looking the same and dressing the same. They began emulating the Great Leader, wearing "Mao jackets" in either navy blue or army green. All the Mao loyalists in the central committee wore them, and soon everyone else did, too. The unspoken fashion statement was that those who were not with Mao were against him—and against his glorious regime. No one could afford to be his enemy. Wearing Mao's clothes made everyone feel safe and close to him.

The streets were soon filled with Mao look-alikes. Old and young, men and women, soldiers and civilians, all were almost indistinguishable. Clothing stores carried only Mao jackets, white shirts and military uniforms, size 12 months and up. Mother had a hard time catching up with the style of the times. Even in the Communist motherland, it took more than an empty purse to buy the latest patriotic fashions. In the end, she illegally traded some of her ration coupons for a set of Mao jackets in ascending size order.

This new conformity spread to every part of life as old and unnecessary traditions were eliminated. Schools adopted a new time schedule called "two plus two"—two classes in the morning and two in the afternoon, instead of the normal "four plus two" schedule. Math, science, language, art, history, philosophy and geology were replaced by political science, Marxism, Maoism, and other political activities. Ping was often dismissed from school after only two morning classes because of some political event going on in the city. I was perfectly happy to have her at home. She was my best playmate, and when she was gone, I was often at a loss for something to do. Ping was good at making up games, and I was glad when she was around.

One day, Ping came home early again. She was out of breath, having run most of her way home. She was scared. Her teeth were chattering, even though the weather was warm, and it prevented her from speaking clearly.

"Sit down," Mother said as she pulled up a bamboo chair and brought Ping a glass of water. "Have a drink ... slowly! Now tell me what happened."

When Mother finally calmed Ping down and got the full story out of her, she was scared, too.

Apparently, while Ping's schoolmates were gathered in the auditorium that morning, an angry mob of Red Guards rushed in.

They smashed everything in sight, cursed, grabbed the school principal, and threw black ink all over him and his white shirt while the whole school watched, paralyzed. Then they tied the principal's hands behind his back, hit him with sticks, and left him half-conscious in front of the horrified pupils. Before the mob left, bold young men posted black and white slogans all over the campus, citing the principal as a "revisionist" and an "enemy of the people." And, on Chairman Mao's behalf, they declared Ping's elementary school a "class-struggle frontier," calling upon all the students and teachers to stand up and fight against their enemies.

Mother did not know what to make of the situation. She decided to keep Ping at home for a couple of days and keep an eye on things. But the situation did not improve. Rioting spread to factories, businesses, and even neighborhoods. A civil war had broken out, and suddenly, everyone was against everyone, clerk against manager, pupil against teacher, and son against father. Backed by Chairman Mao, an avalanche of workers, peasants, soldiers, and students fell on their inferior capitalist, class enemies: former shop owners, factory owners, bankers—anyone who had ever owned a business. "Intellectuals," who had dared to express doubts about the communists' plans for China, were rounded up. The revolution even swept away government officials who voiced their opinions.

One morning, just as Mother cleaned off the breakfast table and was getting us ready to do some writing practice, we heard an awful lot of noise outside in the street.

"Don't go outside," Mother ordered. "It's not for children."

Despite her warning, Ping and I ran outside. We watched dumbfounded as a group of red guards carried out basket after basket of perfectly polished leather shoes, shiny strings of beads, glittering dresses, and piles of leather-bound, gold-edged books from one of the villas, and set up a bonfire right in the middle of the lane.

I had never seen so many fancy things in my life. They showed off one last time by giving out brilliant sparks as they were devoured by the fire and finished their glamorous lives in a dark funnel of smoke.

Soon after, some red guards pushed a woman out of the house for public humiliation. She had on a mink jacket, a short skirt over a pair of exquisitely embroidered red silk pants, and one foot in a stiletto heel pump. She limped along crookedly with her other foot in a flat, embroidered silk slipper. Bright red lipstick had been smeared all over her face and eye makeup flowed down her cheeks with her tears. On her head was a tall, cone-shaped, paper hat covered with large black letters shouting, "Down with the capitalists!" The guards ordered her to parade around the neighborhood, banging an enamel chamber pot with a pair of sterling silver chopsticks while they chanted slogans and accusations at the condemned through a bullhorn.

"Down with the capitalists!"

"Down with class enemies!"

"See what a mistress looks like! She sucks blood from the poor! She is poisonous!"

"Long live Chairman Mao!"

"Long live the Communist Party of China!"

They hit the woman from behind with sticks. She started to walk faster, trailed by an ever-growing mob of Red Guards and curious onlookers. Ping and I watched until they marched out of our sight. Then we turned and ran back home. The smell of the burning leather lingered in the air for the rest of the day.

Later on, we heard that during their raid, the Red Guards cut up all the woman's clothes, broke her furniture, and smashed every last capitalist memory she had hidden so carefully away in that villa.

After that, Mother would not let us go out anymore. We could only play in our small yard and listen to the occasional commotion outside. We could always tell when another raid took place in the lane by the burning smell, and the tinny sound of battery-powered bullhorns. The shamed and ruined families were eventually forced out of our neighborhood, leaving more room for honorable, "real" revolutionary families.

Chapter IV

WILDFIRES OF REVOLUTION

F ANNED BY THE RISING political winds, the first sparks of the Chinese Cultural Revolution started a fire that soon engulfed the entire country. Before long, the revolution was burning out of control.

Everyone wore fiery red armbands to show their participation in the fight and their loyalty to Mao Zedong. The country seemed united in its revolutionary fervor. A careful examination of the armbands, however, revealed a multitude of symbols, names, and mottos belonging to different factions, each claiming to be Mao's most loyal soldiers. The streets were filled with members of the Ultra-Red Guard Team, Worker's Propaganda Team, Rebels, Loyal Defense Team, Red Propagandists, and Peasants' Team. You would do anything to get an armband and submerge yourself in the sea of revolution. Not wearing one would make you stand out and cause you more trouble than you could possibly imagine. Once you were targeted as an enemy of the people, your life would never be the same.

Father always seemed to be in a hurry, running in and out. Sometimes, he would not come home until after we went to bed. One day, Father rushed home with a red armband. It was marked "Rebels" and smelt of fresh ink.

Mother was displeased.

"Why did you join the Rebels? How about the Loyal Defense Team? How about not joining any group at all?"

Mother kept on asking questions without waiting for an answer.

"How about not joining any group?" she pressed on.

She remembered hearing somewhere that a member of one faction took an entire family from another group, packed them into straw bags, and sank them in a river. Since each political band claimed to be the most loyal to Chairman Mao, any other group that aspired to that honor was a threat.

Mother's voice got louder and louder. She spat out Father's full name as if she were scolding a child.

"There is too much politics going on right now. Stay out of it, An Chu Sun, I tell you, or your life will be hell. Remember what happened in the west!"

But Father was unmoved.

"You can die even if you hide in the house," he said. "You can choke on water. Life is not about avoiding trouble. It's about making things right. Look, Chairman Mao is wearing the 'Rebels' armband. This is a group for blue-collar workers. I am a blue-collar worker. Why shouldn't I be a Rebel?"

As Father made this speech, he pointed at Chairman Mao's picture on the front page of the *Liberation Daily*. Mother was speechless because Chairman Mao was, indeed, wearing a "Rebels" armband in the picture. She didn't have the power to criticize our great leader, but she wasn't ready to give up, either.

"This revolution attacks too many people—helpless old women, storekeepers, schoolteachers—everyone. If my father were alive, he would be classified as a 'class enemy,' too, just because he used to own a store."

"Storeowners exploit people to enrich themselves. My uncle made me run barefoot in the winter to deliver his charcoal. He treated my family like his slaves."

"But my father did no such things. He was gentle and honest. Why should he be punished like your uncle?"

"That's up to Chairman Mao to decide. He saved us from foreign powers and capitalists. He gives us poor people dignity. He is our protector!"

That afternoon, Father took out Mother's little Bible along with her stage photos of which she was so proud, the only diploma she had ever earned when she graduated from the Shanghai Feature Film School, and other documents and pictures that were not in line with the revolution. He piled them up into a small heap in the yard and lit a match. Mother stood there like a log. She did not move until the fire faded into smoke and the pile of paper was ash.

She did not argue with Father for burning up her past. She saw the trouble that could come from keeping those documents. The Bible and her religion were considered superstitions and anti-revolutionary. Her school principal had just been named as a class enemy in all the newspapers. Her old pictures could be used as evidence of her bourgeois upbringing. The past had turned into smoke long ago, anyway. She might as well let go of those faded memories. Mother turned around, her face as gray as the ash and walked straight into the house. She didn't even notice me as I stood silently in the doorframe and watched.

Around this time, a lot of strange women started to come to the house. They came in groups of fives and sixes, and Mother was scared. Every time they approached her, she walked backwards until she was cornered while they bombarded her with criticism. I didn't understand what they were screaming about, although they repeated one phrase over and over: "family planning." It made me mad. As far as I was concerned, Mother held the highest authority. No one was allowed to push her around. These witches were no exception. However, I felt helpless because Mother would always send me out when these people came, telling me that it was grownups' business.

Years later, I learned that these women came from the Neighborhood Committee. They were in charge of birth control.

In 1966, the Chinese government started to realize that its policy of encouraging women to bear more young patriots was leading to a population explosion, so it began dissuading families from having children. Mother was almost four months pregnant with her fourth child when the neighborhood committee stepped in and wanted her to have an immediate abortion. But Mother would not. So, these women started to make frequent trips to our house. Their visits got louder and more heated until the old biddies were defeated by Mother's stubbornness and it was too late for an abortion. By then, I knew, too, from her protruding stomach that she was carrying a baby. None of her summer clothes could cover her swollen body, so, when she went out, Mother cleverly pulled the cotton cover from her padded winter jacket and wore it as a blouse. She always managed in an impossible situation.

One morning, Father took Mother to the hospital on his bike. She was in such pain we were scared and listened obediently as Father sent the three of us to different places until mother had the baby and could come home.

Those were the two longest days of my life. I stayed with a middle-aged, childless couple. The husband was a co-worker of my father's, and the two of them liked me a lot, but I cried and cried, and wanted to go home. I would have run home if I knew how. I stood by the front door for the entire two days—at least that's how I remember it.

Then Father appeared with my two sisters. He took us home and promised us that Mother would return the next day with our newborn sister.

That night after dinner, Father walked us to the hospital to show us where Mother was staying. Children were not allowed inside so we circled the building. I walked and walked, wishing I could see through the walls and find Mother. I stared until my eyes were dazed and my neck was stiff, but I failed to penetrate the bricks separating us.

Mother came home the next day, just as Father promised. She arrived in a pedicab with a baby in her arms. The child was beautiful with round, dark eyes shining like a pair of black pearls, hair short and smooth as silk, and tiny little hands balled into fists. They named her *Wen*, meaning "Culture" in honor of the Cultural Revolution that was going on. She was the last child Mother would have and the end of my parents' dreams of having a boy. The doctor tied her tubes without her consent before she was released. Just as the leaves began to fall across the city outside the hospital, the Sun family tree stopped putting out branches and ceased to grow.

About the same time, I started first grade. My school was in a narrow alley, a makeshift affair converted from an old French residence. My classroom was small and dark. The floor squeaked and groaned under the stampeding of forty students. To accommodate all the children, the room was crammed from wall to wall with wooden desks and chairs. The first row was only inches away from the blackboard.

My biggest enemy in school was a crumbling, steep wooden staircase, which I had to climb up and down every day. For our morning and afternoon exercises, the school gave us only five minutes to get downstairs and line up in the alleyway or along the sidewalk in front of the school. Twice a day, when the school's loudspeakers suddenly blared to life and barked out orders to assemble downstairs, a frenzied countdown began, prompting a rush for the exits. Hundreds of children swarmed into the small hallway, running headlong down the dark and narrow staircase. With kids of all different sizes and ages hurrying to make sure they were not marked "late," it was a miracle that no child ever tumbled down the stairs. I quickly learned to grab onto the banister to save myself from embarrassment. Or a broken neck.

Every morning, Mother carefully hooked a Mao pin on the front of my green jacket and tied a red triangular scarf around my neck. I had learned that my red triangle signified a corner of our national flag. It was red because of all the blood our ancestral martyrs shed for the birth of our country. We each wore a corner of our flag to honor those who died for us. So, I never complained about this ritual even when it was too hot to wear it around my neck. After all, several kids in my class did not get to wear it. They always got picked on because they were the children of the anti-revolutionaries. Our national symbol would be soiled if they got to wear a corner of the flag.

In addition to my army-green canvas knapsack, I had to carry a special Chairman Mao Quotation Book bag for our daily studies. The very first words I learned to read and write were "Chairman Mao is our red, red sun. Long live Chairman Mao. Long live the Communist Party of China. We love our motherland." The first song I learned to sing was "The East is red. The sun rises. China brought forth Mao Zedong. He works for the happiness of our people. He is our savior." The first dance I learned was called "The Chairman Mao Quotation Dance." For quite a few years, I thought China occupied the center stage of the entire world and everyone looked up to our great leader Chairman Mao.

The school day was short and most of our time was spent studying Marx, Lenin, and Mao. Like the grownups, we often lined up in rows of four, held political slogans and flags, marched around the neighborhood, and sang revolutionary songs until our feet were sore and our voices hoarse.

At other times, we were divided into little study groups, learning about each other's family past. Based on our interviews with our parents and grandparents, we were asked to share every bitter life experience the older generations went through during the first half of the Twentieth Century, before Mao Zedong liberated them. The deeper the sufferings our ancestors had gone through, the more loyal and reliable we were judged to be by our classmates and society.

I had a hard time gathering enough "bitter past" stories from my family. I was not even looking for shocking, extreme examples like the ones broadcasted over the radio, where I heard about people who ate clay to fight against hunger and died with swollen stomachs and bony limbs. Or those who sold their children and wives to pay off their debts. Or the landlord who forced mercury down the throat of a farmer's daughter, placed her in a lotus position, and buried her along with his dead son so he could have a wife in the underworld. I was just looking for some stories to prove that my family came from a solid peasant or worker's background. I wanted my classmates to know that I was also a Chairman Mao defender like the rest of them. But Mother shied away from such topics.

"Go and ask your father," she said.

Father gave me his stories, which were not exactly good enough to meet the revolutionary standard. Father insisted on giving me the truth about his family's past, instead of making up tales of woe, like a lot of other people did.

The truth was that his family was well-to-do until the Japanese came and burned his grandfather's plant. Then, he moved in with an uncle who owned a charcoal store. That uncle was very wicked, greedy, and ruthless. In exchange for food and shelter, he made my grandfather—his own brother—a charcoal presser, my grandmother a house servant, and my father a delivery boy at the age of eight. To escape the oppressor, they fled to a slum, and his parents were forced to become poor vegetable vendors, living off penny profits, and half-rotten leftovers. Finally! A story I could tell with pride!

While my father's family did go through a lot, they unfortunately could not be classified as either peasants or members of the working class. Even vendors were considered to be small-time exploiters. Having a great uncle as a charcoal store owner would only paint my own face black, regardless of whether he was a good or wicked person. I feared I would have to spend the rest of my life staring at the floor if anyone found out that my great grandfather had a factory, not that it mattered if it was burnt to ashes by the Japanese. Chairman Mao only liked workers and peasants.

I thought for a while. "Do you still have any of the clothes you wore when you were a delivery boy?" I asked.

"Of course not. Why?"

"Little Zhu in my class brought an old, broken bowl to the class. He said his grandmother begged with that bowl after the Japanese invaded her village, killed her parents, and burned down her house. The teacher passed it around the class so we could all hold it and feel what it was like to be a homeless beggar. I thought that your old clothes ..."

"I'm sorry, but I don't have them anymore."

I was disappointed.

"The past is the past. We should look forward to the future. Only the future holds hope." Father tried to comfort me, but it didn't work.

Now what can I do to prove my worker-peasant lineage? I thought hard, but in the end, I had to shake my head, call on all the wiles of my seven-year-old brain, and with a little editing, reinvented my father's family history like this:

"My father came from a very poor family. They lived in a slum and barely had shirts on their backs. My grandparents worked very hard from morning till night in a vegetable market, but still didn't have enough to feed their family of nine. My father was forced to be a child laborer at the age of eight, delivering charcoal to help his parents."

Chapter V

To Grandmother's House We Go

ALL THOSE SCHOOLROOM LESSONS about our "Bitter Past and Sweet Present" stirred my curiosity about my mother's mysterious background. The more Mother held back her past from me, the more I wanted to know. Grandpa Ho De and Uncle Chon Gao were the only relatives I knew about. Where was my grandmother? Why wouldn't Mother ever talk about her? I was defeated by Mother's silence.

One day, Mother unexpectedly budged under my tedious and relentless bombardment of questions. It turned out that I did have a maternal grandmother, and she was very much alive! However, she was not Grandpa Ho De's wife. She was my real grandma and a cousin of the woman who raised my mother. I was amazed to learn I had two sets of grandparents through my mom, although this grandmother was the only one still living.

Mother immediately regretted her confession. For the next few weeks, I kept on nagging her every day to help me carry out the next stage of my plan: I wanted to visit my grandmother, and the two uncles and four aunts who lived with her. My father's family never liked us. Maybe we would get lucky this time and my mother's relatives would.

"It's impossible," mother resisted. "I haven't seen, or heard from them in twenty years. As far as I'm concerned, they don't exist. I'm not part of that family anymore."

"Please, Mom, please?!" I kept on begging.

Mother stopped talking, and hugged me tight. It was too painful for her to continue. But I couldn't share her pain, and struggled to free myself from her grip.

"It's not that I don't miss them," she finally said. "I dream about them all the time. But they gave me away, just like an object. They never thought about me. I had to live where they chose. You have to understand my feelings."

Did I understand her feelings?

Not really. I only cared about visiting my new, real grandmother. However, judging by words, I thought Mother would never take me there. I was disappointed.

One Sunday morning, Mother surprised us by cheerfully announcing to all of us, "Get into your best clothes. I am taking you for a trolley ride and a visit to your grandmother!"

I gazed at Mother with such admiration for I knew that she must have gone through a lot of inner struggle to reach this decision.

"I'm finally going to meet my grandma!" I squealed.

Mother was as excited as I was. She changed into a new cotton blouse and a pair of black silk pants she saved for special occasions. Ping and I had matching pale lavender blouses with little duckling prints on them, navy-blue pants, and brand-new black cloth shoes with white trim. Min had a crisp, ivory white blouse with buttons on her back. All of us wore homemade clothes down to our feet, with the exception of baby Wen. She had on a store-bought, bright red corduroy outfit, a present from a neighbor of ours who lived in the apartment building next to us. She was a government cadre on medical leave and adored Wen.

I skipped out of the house. My eyes were especially round that day. I opened them as wide as possible to make sure that I didn't miss anything important.

Mother held baby Wen in her arms, and made Ping, Min, and me hold hands, and walk in front of her. Before we boarded the trolley, she stopped at a fruit store and bought two bamboo boxes filled with apples. A tall clerk with a blank face silently bundled them together one on top of the other with thick, red cotton yarn. Ping and I felt very important carrying the packages and inhaling their precious scent. It was a big deal for us to see and smell apples. Except for summer watermelon and sugar cane, we only saw fruit on New Year's Day.

Bus # 24 was the only trolley line in Shanghai at the time and it was our first streetcar ride. Mother seated us in the very back row. I was too restless to sit straight. Instead, I kneeled on the seat, and craned my neck to get the view out of the rear window. Everything slid backwards as the trolley pulled ahead along its shining track. My ears were ringing with the trolley's bell: "Ding, ding, ding …"

My grandmother lived with my oldest uncle and his family in a crumbling row house. The downstairs was crowded with a lot of old furniture and beds. It was easy to tell which bed belonged to Grandmother. One stood out among all the others, neatly made and surrounded by shelves filled with glass jars. Polished until they glistened and glowed, each jar contained a kind of snack, with an assortment of cookies, sweets, roasted melon seeds, or preserved fruits. It was like a fancy candy shop. I was awed by this impressive sight. Its thoughtful creator, my elder uncle, had dutifully filled his father's position since he was lost at sea and wanted to make sure that everything was within arm's reach for my grandmother.

When we first entered the house, the room was obscured in darkness, even though it was sunny outside. As my eyes adjusted to the dim light, I was captivated by the gleaming jars and their contents, and I realized that the darkness was intentional because all the curtains and blinds were drawn. A group of men and women crowded around a banquet-sized table under a halo of cigarette smoke. They were obviously having a good time and did not notice our intrusion. Little did I know that we had landed in the middle of a hot game of Mahjong.

My grandmother loved Mahjong more than anything else in the whole world. She was drawn even more to it since my grandfather perished at sea. Now that Mahjong was declared illegal, it was too risky for her to round up all her old pals for a game. Many of her partners quit the game for fear of getting themselves into trouble. To satisfy my grandmother's Mahjong cravings, my uncles, aunts, and their spouses started to learn the game. Behind drawn curtains and shut doors on a round table wrapped with thick blankets, they built my grandmother a haven where Mahjong still existed and excited the blood, even if it was family members only. The blankets on the table muffled the clicking noises caused by the ivory rectangles. My grandmother loved the sound of Mahjong more than music.

It was very easy for me to pick my grandmother out of the crowd because she looked just like Mother, except older and smaller. Her silky white hair was pulled back into a bun, the typical hairstyle for an old woman at the time. A Manchurian blouse of black silk and matching pants made her appear even smaller and more delicate. She knew it was Mother the very minute she laid her eyes on her, even after thirty years of separation.

"It's you, Ai Zhu," she said matter-of-factly.

She addressed Mother with her birth name and little emotion. If she felt anything, she certainly hid it well. Mother pulled us closer to her, and introduced us one by one. Everyone was surprised at the sheer number of daughters Mother had and exchanged greetings with us. I met several aunts and their husbands, one uncle and his wife, and some children.

While our visit was cordial and friendly, it was not the intimate family scene I had wished for. I wanted my grandmother to embrace me with all her love. I wanted her to squeeze me tight, like I was her lost and found treasure. I wanted her to hold my hands and touch my cheeks with the tips of her fingers. I wanted all her affection to pour over me and satisfy my many years of hunger and thirst for a real grandmother. But I didn't get any of this. My grandmother never reached out for me. She never reached out for any of us, not even Mother. She spared us only one lingering look before she went back to her Mahjong game. She had enough of her other grandchildren around her already without us. At that point, I almost regretted having pushed Mother to come here. I certainly did not get a sense that we belonged there at all.

My grandmother remained cool to us for the rest of our visit. She kept herself several feet away from Mother as they sat on the same edge of the bed. My mother was quietly choking with emotion, waiting for some personal outpouring, some explanation. But nothing came. They never even touched each other. My uncles and aunts used my grandmother as a barometer and gave us an equally lukewarm reception. I was very disappointed. I felt doomed not to have a grandmother to love me.

What I got most out of the visit was the last living knowledge of a fading phenomenon, found only among the old-world, upper-class Chinese. I was fascinated by my grandmother's feet, which were no bigger than a child's. They were less than five inches long and oddly shaped. My grandmother was the only woman I had ever met who had bound feet. By the time I left, I had memorized every little detail about them. Only after we left my grandmother's house did I dare to ask Mother about her feet.

A few months later, my family and I visited Grandmother for the second, and last, time at her sixtieth birthday party. It was a bittersweet reunion. All of Mother's real brothers and sisters, their spouses, and children were there. She even got to meet her littlest brother who was conceived after she was given away.

I could not believe my luck: I gained four more aunts, two more uncles, and a roomful of cousins. There was plenty of food and laughter. Everything went well, and everybody seemed to be happy together until the end of the day, when I innocently asked a question I should not have asked.

"Mommy, why did you leave in the middle of the party today? Aunty said you were embarrassed by how little you brought for grandmother's birthday, and you went out to buy more. Is that true?"

There was a long silence. Mother stood there like a wooden statue.

She had left in the middle of the party and sneaked back in (not without her sisters noticing) with a large birthday cake—a last-minute attempt to enlarge her modest pile of cheap presents (a box of cookies and two hand towels) sitting humbly next to a mountain of expensive, elaborately packaged gift boxes from her brothers and sisters. She was worried that she would be looked down on as a failure by her long-lost family. Or just as bad, having been cast out some thirty years ago, she feared they would interpret her small gifts as disrespect towards her mother. In either case, it was a disaster. And all her fears came true!

Mother choked on her tears and broke down. She had brought only a few simple presents, but even they were beyond her means, and she had cut into our food money to get them. Realizing what I had done, I was at a loss as to how to change my story to make Mother feel better. Curse presents and parties! I felt miserable.

"I'm sorry, Mom," I mumbled. "I didn't mean to hurt your feelings. I shouldn't have pushed you to visit Grandmother."

"It's not your fault," Mother said as she patted me on the head. I looked up and saw her eyes were red.

I never saw my grandmother again. Mother preferred talking about her family to actually seeing them. It was too painful for her and I stopped asking to see my relatives. Besides, the Cultural Revolution was about to pull my entire family to pieces.

Chapter VI

HONESTY AND PUNISHMENT

ONE DAY FATHER DID not come home. He did not come home the next day, or the day after. Instead, my father's family came to our house. They whispered to Mother in low voices behind closed doors. From Mother's face, I knew that she wasn't yet ready to tell us what was going on. Her face also told me that whatever it was, it was not good.

One morning, Mother called me to her side just as I was leaving for school.

"I'd like you to stay home today," she said. "I need you to go to a place with me."

I returned my army-green school bag to the hook on the back of the bedroom door, wondering what was on Mother's mind.

"What is it?" I asked. "Is it about Father?"

She didn't reply.

Her silence stopped me from asking more questions.

The house was strangely quiet. Ping and Min had gone to school. Wen was sent to a sympathetic neighbor's apartment in the building next to us. I stood watching Mother packing up a quilt, a toothbrush, toothpaste, a comb, two towels, and some of Father's undergarments, shirts, and pants, as if he was going to travel somewhere for a long time.

I waited patiently as Mother darned a few socks and patched some of his undershirts. She even hid a few packs of cigarettes among his things.

Mom always disapproved of Father's smoking habits and now ...

She saw my confused eyes.

"He needs the cigarettes," she said. "What I want doesn't matter. They have detained him ... your father's company. I was just told today and they gave us permission to take some bedding and clothes there. You have good eyesight. I want you to go along with me."

I did not ask Mother any more questions. I figured that she had told me all that she knew, or wanted to tell me. I followed her out of the house to wherever she was going.

We walked in silence.

I wanted to talk but didn't dare for fear I would say the wrong thing. I knew Mother had a lot on her mind and just hoped that Father would be alright.

We stopped in front of a small iron door, set deeply into a long stretch of concrete wall. I looked up and discovered a white-on-blue porcelain plate, which read, "Dong Hu Road #20."

Mother knocked.

"Hello?"

The iron door gave out a low echo but no one answered.

Then we noticed that the door was ajar. Mother peered in as she carefully pushed it open. A small concrete path led toward an elegant Western-style villa.

As I took a closer look at the house, I realized that it was not a friendly place, for all its second-floor windows were barred from the outside with coarsely chopped strips of wood. From the freshness of the splinters, I could tell that someone had just finished this lousy job.

With my heart beating in my throat, I followed Mother into the house. The old wooden parquet floor moaned quietly underneath us as we walked through the halls, looking left and right for

some sign of life. It was so deadly quiet I got scared. The silence
didn't last. A wave of sound approached us, an echoing, maddening
roar, mixed with slapping or stamping of some sort. Mother gave
me a serious look that I had never seen before, grabbed my hand in
hers, and walked toward the noise. We stopped at a doorway and
looked in.

In front of us was a room, large, dark, and bare. In the middle,
under a flood of yellow light, half a dozen angry men formed a circle, yelling and stamping at the same time. They waved their arms
frantically in all directions, creating black shadows which flew all
around the room. I had never seen hysteria before. When they finally
turned toward us, I saw they all wore red Chairman Mao quotation
bags across their shoulders and red bands around their left arms
that read, "Shanghai Municipal Workers' Propaganda Team." Only
then, did I find my father, crouching on the floor in the center.
His red "Rebel" armband had been ripped off. His Chairman Mao
quotation bag wasn't on his shoulder anymore. He looked like a
wild man with a long raggedy beard, protruding cheekbones, and
hair flying in all directions. His shirt sleeves were torn, and his face
was gray with fatigue. It looked as if he had not slept or eaten for
days, which happened to be the truth as we learned much later, for
he had been kept in a tiny, brightly-lit room around the clock for
days on end with only a writing desk and a chair set up to extract
"confessions" from prisoners. He had worn the same clothes for the
past two weeks and washed himself from top to bottom with a thin
cotton handkerchief, the only possession he happened to be carrying at the time of his arrest.

When Father rubbed his bleary eyes and realized that we were
there, he tried to produce a smile, and struggled to get to his feet.
But the men pushed him back down on the floor. He fell helplessly. I wanted to dash into Father's arms, comfort him, and pick
him up. But as if in a nightmare, I could not reach him, for one of
the men there stretched out his arms, and blocked me. His cold
eyes and stone face made me shiver, as he towered over me. He
acted like a leader.

"Confess," he bellowed. "And then you can go home."

Father closed his tired eyes and remained motionless.

With his hands behind his back, the man paced and then circled around Mother, looking her up and down.

"Look at your pretty wife and young child. If you don't cooperate, you'll never see them again. You are an enemy of the people, the enemy of our great Cultural Revolution. Admit it."

The words hit me hard as they echoed through the empty hall, lingering in every corner of the room before they subsided. I could not quite understand what was going on. I did not see the connection between my beloved father and an "enemy of the people." But I knew what they would do to enemies of the people: tall paper hats, public condemnations, house searches, having your name written upside down and crossed out in black to humiliate you in front of your own house! And I would be called the offspring of an anti-revolutionary bastard.

Why, Father?

How could this happen?

What will happen now?

I kept seeing an image of the boy in my class who was not allowed to wear a red tie and be a Little Red Guard and how everybody teased him, abused him, and laughed at him. My mind raced aimlessly as another round of maddening shouting began, accompanied by forceful arm-swinging, and thunder-like stampings. One of the tormentors pushed Father to the ground again and punched him in the face.

Father just lowered his head and waited for their anger to be exhausted. He crouched like an injured bird, helpless, wronged, and hurt. I felt the whole world was against him. These evil men's black magic could suck Father's strength out of him and make him crumple. I had never seen my father so weak. I was frightened, and started to cry. At that moment, I felt my body turning to liquid that poured out of my eyes, my nose, and my mouth. I felt everything was losing shape and color in front of me. And then I heard Father's voice for the first time.

"Don't you worry, my daughter," he said. "I never did any-thing bad against our people or our country. I have always obeyed Chairman Mao. You have to trust me."

Father's voice was as calm, and so strong that his words over-powered the noise in the room.

I trusted my father. I had always trusted him. Even at the age of eight, I could tell a good man from an evil one. Father pos-sessed every virtue of a good man. He was a loving person. He loved Chairman Mao. He respected and helped everyone who needed help. On the contrary, these strangers here were of a nasty breed. They communicated hatred and contempt, not just toward Father and Mother, but also me, a child. What did I do wrong? I had to conclude that these men were the bad ones. Yet Chairman Mao let them represent him. They worked for Chairman Mao!

Does Chairman Mao know that they force people to make confes-sions by yelling and hitting? I wondered.

I felt very sorry for Father. These people would not listen to the truth. They only wanted Father to say what they wanted to hear. I wished I could help Father, but all I could do was sob uncontrolla-bly. Mother finally broke her silence.

"Why are you detaining him without the knowledge of his family?" She sounded like a teacher criticizing her students. "Why are you forcing him to make confessions that are lies? That is not Chairman Mao's teaching. That is not part of this Cultural Revolution."

Mother started to recite some of Chairman Mao's quotations on revolution and solidarity.

These men seemed to be scared by Mother's intellectual reason-ing. They started to swarm toward us. They wanted to push us out of the room before Mother could finish her words. Mother and I put up a fight. But we lost the shoving match. Father's helpless eyes met mine for a brief second before they slammed and barred the door in our faces.

I held onto Mother's right arm and plodded home with my head hung so low that I saw only the concrete pavement moving by the entire way. I felt it was the end of the world.

That night, we rushed through a dinner of stale, watery rice and gathered around our mother trying with our childish sense of justice to think of ways to get Father out of detention. It got late, and the house became pitch black, but no one bothered to turn on the light. The darkness carried our little voices around the room with a strange clearness and Mother sat and listened. When we failed to find a way to save our father, my sisters went back to our visit that morning, asking over and over about everything we went through.

"Did Dad get anything to eat there?" two-year-old Wen asked.

"I don't know," I answered. "But his cheeks were very bony."

"I'll save him my b'nana." I could hear her little nose sniffing the very ripe banana that had been given to her by a kind neighbor. She'd been holding it since she came back home hours ago.

"Just eat it yourself or it'll rot."

"Save it for Daddy. He's hungry," she said, inhaling its luscious smell again and again.

We heard a gentle but clear knock on our front door. Mother told us to stay still while she got up and went outside. She opened the door but saw no one in the thickening darkness. Just as she was closing the door, she heard a voice.

"Open the door, Madam Sun. It's me."

A figure slipped into our yard.

Mother came back into the house, closed all the curtains, turned on the light, and told the man to come in. I recognized him as one of Father's co-workers.

"I'm risking my own life to come here," he said. "But I want you to know what has happened to your husband."

In a low whisper, we finally got Father's story.

The Housing and Land Management Agency my father worked for managed the most exclusive residential real estate properties in the entire city of Shanghai. The ruling politicians and social elites all took advantage of the agency to get the best accommodations in town. Lately, however, in the ever-changing political kaleidoscope, it was very difficult for the company to predict who actually was in power. First, the veteran politicians were tagged as revisionists and purged. Then, a new crowd of fresh political leaders swept in and, of course, wanted to move into the expensive, upscale apartments vacated by their unlucky predecessors.

The problem started a couple of months before, when a family claimed to be friends with one of the members of Mao's inner circle, later known as the "Gang of Four." They took up residence in a luxury building—the only one left in the city that still had working revolving doors, heating, air-conditioning, and electrical elevators.

I knew that building very well. Father had worked in the boiler room there. I passed by it every day on my way to school. A couple of foreigners remained in Shanghai after 1949 and it seemed as if they all lived in that building. One was a tall Russian man with a white turban around his head. For some reason, he always walked around with a pail in his hand and never seemed to notice anyone else around him. Another one was a Jewish woman who walked around with a thick veil so that no one ever saw her face. The rumors were that she had no nose because her husband had cut it off. My friends and I tried several times to approach her and find out if were true and then ran away screaming for fear of seeing her noseless face. We never found out why she would not let anyone see her face, or, indeed, if she really did not have a nose.

When the newest tenants moved in, they refused to pay any rent or utility fees, and demanded that the workers renovate their apartment for free. The angry workers wrote an open letter of criticism against this abuse on a posterboard. Before the letter was to be displayed in the lobby, the workers asked Father for his support by signing the letter. Since he was the local union leader for his company, he gladly complied.

A few days later, the revolutionary leaders of his company called Father and expressed their anger about the poster. They warned him that his signature made him look disloyal to the Party, and told him he was being investigated as the plotter behind the poster.

It might have ended there but a couple of weeks later, someone noticed a thumbtack had been pressed into the wall of the company cafeteria—right on the giant painted head of Chairman Mao. This was clearly an intentional anti-revolutionary crime, whose perpetrator intended to assassinate the great Chinese leader. In a public meeting, the leadership expressed their determination to capture this criminal and have him prosecuted.

The final damning evidence came in the form of a dead cat, which was found outside the boiler room where Father worked. Killing a cat was a serious offense in those days, since "cat" in Chinese was pronounced *mao*. With the leaders still holding a grudge against my father for putting his signature on the poster, the company decided to kill two birds with one stone, whether they were the right birds or not. They would prosecute my father for both the thumbtack and the dead cat, fulfilling their public commitment to catch the anti-revolutionary criminal at large, and punish my father for signing the poster. This is how our lives as enemies of the people began.

Chapter VII

Life without Means

WE WERE NOT ALLOWED to visit Dad after the ruckus Mother caused. We did not know if he was still imprisoned in the same place or if he was even alive. Mother and I went to the prison several times and always found the iron gate locked.

No one brought us any news. When I met Father's co-workers on my way to school, they walked by me as if they had never known me, their eyes focused at some distant object, their faces emptied of any expression. At first, I kept on staring at them, expecting some delayed greeting. I thought the hope in my eyes would soften their hearts and bring back the smiling faces I was used to. But it didn't happen. I was not in their world anymore. They didn't want to have anything to do with me. I kept looking backwards to see if they would turn around and give me some sign that they were the people I knew, the people who used to hold me, tickle me, and give me candies. Gradually, I realized that all those men and women I used to call "uncles" and "aunts" were not my friends anymore.

Now I knew that because of my father, no one wanted to be close to us. I decided that it would be best if I kept myself away from everyone. As soon as school was over, I hurried home. I learned to look at the ground as I walked. The thought of my quiet little home and my mother and sisters comforted me. I knew I would always have them.

One late afternoon, my father's mother surprised us with a visit as my sisters and I sat in the dark kitchen drawing pictures. We watched with crayons in hand as our grandmother squeezed her ample body through our narrow door, and stumbled into our living room.

"Pumpkin with scallions! What kind of dinner is that!?" Her eyes caught the humble meal my mother had prepared for us.

How can she even see the tiny pieces of scallion? I marveled. It was so dark I couldn't even tell the colors of my crayons. My mother seldom turned on the lights these days.

"Two *fen* a kilo isn't cheap enough to lure anyone to buy it," my grandmother kept on. "People are tired of eating pumpkins. They are rotting in piles at our market. Who can eat any more of them?"

We lived on pumpkins that fall: steamed pumpkin, stir-fried pumpkin, roasted pumpkin … pumpkins cooked in every possible way. In fact, pumpkin was the only thing that kept us from starving.

"By the way, I came here to tell you that An Chu's sister Xin Feng has denounced him. She went to the neighborhood meeting and declared that he is no longer her brother."

My grandmother said this very casually, as if it were no big deal.

We all froze in the dark. The air was thick and still. Xin Feng was my father's youngest sister and my grandmother's favorite.

"Xin Feng is graduating and doesn't want to be sent to the countryside because of her anti-revolutionary brother," she went on nervously. "Of course, I know you'll understand."

Mother quietly turned on the light. No one said anything.

My grandmother suddenly felt awkward seeing five pairs of eyes staring at her. She started to back out of the door. Then she got angry.

"Don't act so shocked. You would have done the same thing in her position." And then, she was gone.

On the fifteenth of the month, Mom sent Ping and me to collect Dad's paycheck. She instructed us to check the cash and buy five kilos of rice from the grain shop on the way home. We walked to the accounting office and presented Father's name seal to a clerk. Although she always talked to us, this time she only acknowledged us with a nod before opening a drawer and taking out a stack of paychecks. She went through the entire stack twice and looked puzzled. She went to the back of the office and made a call. Soon, she came back and returned the seal to us. "I've checked with our party secretary," she said. "The company has decided not to pay your father anymore since staying in detention is not work." She walked back to her desk and started to flip through some paper as if nothing had happened.

"Comrade Aunt, Comrade Aunt …" I kept on calling since I didn't know her name. Finally, she rose from her chair and came back to me.

"What do you want?" She grew impatient. "If you want to know more, go and find the party secretary. It's his decision."

"But how can we live without Daddy's paycheck?"

"That's not my business."

Ping and I walked away, shocked. We already knew that Father's paycheck wasn't much, but it was the only thing that put food on the table and coal in our stove. We didn't have to tell Mother what happened. When we went home empty-handed, without the rice or the money, her face went black.

Usually we managed to scrape by, illegally selling some of our rice vouchers to stretch Father's meager salary. Now, with his income gone, Mother started cutting back on everything. The first thing to go was the fuel we used for cooking.

To help, Ping and I combed the streets and parks for sticks and newspapers, but they didn't burn long enough to make a meal. Luckily, we found a local research lab that dumped its used coal near its garbage bins. We went through the ashes and found quite a few half-burned coal nuggets, so we filled our pockets with the black prizes and ran home to show Mother.

Every day after school, Ping and I hurried home, put down our school bags, picked up a basket, and rushed toward the ash heap. The garbage bins gave off terrible smells, but we had to find enough charcoal before dinnertime or starve. It was hard work combing through the burnt-out coal slag and finding a few coal nuggets disguised under a coating of white powdery dust. Ping and I picked up the grayish white lumps, rubbed them with our hands, and scraped them with our nails until we saw the dark charcoal underneath. We soon learned to tell which ones to scrape and which to let go by weighing them with our hands. The good ones were heavy, and we put them into our basket; the light ones we threw back into the pile. We worked until our legs became numb from crouching, our nails hurt from digging, our throats became clogged with dust, and our patience ran out. Then it was time for us to carry the basket home, wash up, and help Mother with the cooking.

The coal bits were too small for a conventional stove so Mother created a homemade one in the backyard. She assembled a few bricks in a half-moon shape with an open front. Then she laid down some rolled-up paper, twigs and branches, and, on the very top, a pyramid of our precious, half-burnt coal nuggets. It was time to cook. She put on our iron wok with rice and water and struck a match. Our proud faces were lit up by the glow of the stove. We twittered in Mother's ears and rubbed tears from our eyes when the wind blew smoke in our faces, patiently waiting to get the first whiff of cooked rice.

With no money coming in, Mother started to sell her memories in exchange for food. Piece by piece, she said goodbye to the keepsakes of her past: jade figurines, silver spoons, lacquer trays, silver necklaces, embroidered silk quilt covers, and a pair of gold spectacle frames that belonged to Grandpa Ho De. Her hands lingered in the air as she held each object and looked at it for the last time before wrapping it in a cloth and going out to the pawnshop.

Mother asked me to come with her whenever she went to the "Exchange Center." People usually went there to sell things that they no longer wanted or needed. Often the man behind the counter would look at our things and then look at Mother, not quite understanding why she wanted to sell such nice things for a fraction of their worth. As soon as the transaction was done, Mother stuffed the money in her little purse without checking the amount, grabbed me under the arm, and ran out of the store, as if we were shoplifters. She became very pale and had to lean against a wall, too weak to continue our walk home. I held her arm, tried to support her with my light frame, and we staggered home together.

After we got back to the house, Mother would have cramps and cold sweats. I often found her curled up in the bathroom with a bucket in front of her, throwing up. I waited by her side until she stopped and asked me to carry her to bed. I sat with her, afraid that she would not get better and that we would lose her.

Every time Mother got sick, Ping and I quietly took over the house and chores. We filled Wen's baby bottle with sugar water and changed her diaper when she cried for mama. She cried a lot when Mother was sick. Sometimes we couldn't figure out why and didn't know how to help her. We made watery rice for lunch by adding last night's hot water from the thermos to yesterday's leftovers. When night came and Mother didn't get out of bed, we mimicked her way of starting the stove so we could make dinner. I blamed myself for being young and useless when the stove disobeyed me, giving out massive amounts of smoke instead of fire. Sometimes, it stuck out a tiny fiery tongue at me to build up false hope—and just as I thought it was going to spread, it turned into a puff of smoke and disappeared. We kept on trying, encouraged by our growling stomachs. By the time the fire started, Ping and I looked like we worked in a coal mine. I thought about how Father looked when he was a charcoal delivery boy. Luckily, we didn't have to parade ourselves around the city the way he did.

The best we could do with the fire was to make a kettle of hot water, a pot of half-cooked rice, and a bowl of half-raw Chinese cabbage, always with either too much or too little salt. Another day passed without Father, but we would go to sleep with something in our stomachs. What would happen tomorrow? No one knew.

Normally, no situation seemed impossible for Mother. Lately, however, I saw her staring blankly. She was getting very low on things to sell. The last time, she sold her best jacket.

"Well, I don't have any occasion to wear it, anyway," she said to me before she surrendered it to the shop attendant.

What could she sell next? I wondered. If Father did not come home soon, I feared for our lives.

One Sunday morning, Mother said she had to go out on her own. She looked strange and didn't take anything with her. We all stood quietly and sent her off with our silent good wishes. Without Mother, the day felt very, very long. The house echoed with only our voices. The floor bore only our steps. I could feel the cold, fall air that had already settled into our concrete walls and floor.

Ten-year-old Ping was our little mommy. On her tiptoes, she divided up the leftover rice and cabbage and made us lunch. Rice in lukewarm water did not taste good. Would Mother be home soon? We felt subdued and had little interest in playing. Minutes dragged into hours until the sun slipped below the horizon and we could barely see in the dark one-room house.

By then, we were aching for Mother to come back, and we feared the long night ahead. If she did not return, who could we turn to? There were too many questions. I could not explain to myself why Mother left and felt hurt that she did not invite me to go along. It was also unlike her not to leave us in the care of a grownup with food and plenty of instructions.

To escape from the darkness inside the house, Ping, Min, Wen, and I held each other's hands and ventured out. As we headed toward the front door, I spotted a strange object in our yard. A closer examination sent waves of fear through me.

"It's a chicken," I screamed, "and it's dead!"

My proclamation sent us instantly retreating backward into the house, our teeth chattering and our hearts beating like drums. We gathered behind the door in the house, and hugged each other tightly to gather enough strength to fight the darkness and fear.

Even in the gloom, I could see the chicken. Its feathered, life-less body and straight legs spoke of death. I closed my eyes to get rid of the image, but it kept coming back, like a nagging premo-nition. For some reason, the feeling of my sisters' quivering hands comforted me, telling me we were not alone, but I could not shake off the feeling of bad luck surrounding us. With our arms curled around each other, we waited in the darkness, hoping only to see the sun and our mama once more.

We were asleep when Mother finally turned on the light. She found us curled up together behind the door and carried us to bed. We did not hear her come home.

Many years later, I asked Mother why she left us that day and where she went. After a long silence, she told me that she had decided to end her life. She wandered aimlessly around the city, searching for an easy, painless exit: A river, a bridge, or a tall building. She did not know how to go on without Father, without money, without a future, without even a past. Then a voice came to her telling her that she was baptized as a Christian, and was not allowed to take her own life. She stopped and dragged herself back home.

After her crisis and unexpected salvation, some good luck came our way. Mother got a temporary job as a candy wrapper in Shanghai Number Two Food Company. She was paid by the number of can-dies she could wrap in a day. Her income was pitifully low, but we would not starve to death.

Chapter VIII

GREAT GRANDMOTHER'S PROPHECY

"I WANT YOU TO GO and visit your grandparents this morning," Mother said to us matter-of-factly as we sat down for breakfast.

We were never close to my father's side of the family, and rarely got invited there even though they lived only a few blocks away. I knew that my grandmother never liked me or my sisters, although no one ever said so. The few times we were there each year, I observed Grandmother spending most of her time around my cousin, Wei, son of my father's brother, the only boy born in our generation. She teased him, tickled him, hugged him, and gave him candies. She gave us lectures. She would not have missed us if we were not there.

Mother could see our thoughts on our faces. As she ladled porridge into our bowls, serving us each some thinly sliced pickled vegetables with toasted sesame seeds, she talked in a slow voice.

"Today is your grandfather's birthday," she said. "Normally, your dad buys some presents and goes there for dinner. But he is not home. He cannot visit his father. Now you are old enough to take the responsibility and help him out."

"But they never invite us when they have parties," I spoke out with my childish sense of justice. "Why should we go there now and give them anything?"

"You can't change how other people behave. But you can make things better by behaving properly yourself. That includes going to see your grandparents today."

Mother made it impossible for us to argue against going. Besides, we were doing this for Father. With that said, Mother sent Ping and me on our way with a small basket of apples.

It was a bright Sunday morning in May. The sun caressed us and a gentle breeze lifted our spirits. It was too pleasant a day to worry about our grandmother's cold stares and aunts' sharp tongues.

"Don't worry, Ping, we'll leave as soon as possible," I said as I skipped along. "Let's just drop off the apples and tell them that we have to go home and help Mother with something."

I was looking forward to leaving my grandmother's house long before I got there.

"We can't do that," Ping said seriously as she struggled with the basket of fruit. "If we are doing this for Father, we have to do it right. We have to stay there for at least fifteen minutes. Or maybe twenty."

"Oh, whatever … "

I was disappointed and gave in, too young to have a precise understanding of time. Ping was two years older than me. Let her decide.

As soon as we got to our grandparents' home, I checked the time on their old-fashioned clock and waited for the fifteen or twenty minutes to pass. I played a waiting game, but the clock got the upper hand. Its needles crept and crawled and the world stood still. I became restless and tried hard to sit still on an oversized wooden armchair facing my grandfather.

My grandfather was a slight, quiet man who had not spoken a word since we came. He simply nodded when he saw us, sitting on the edge of the bed smoking. Every time I saw him, he was smoking. He smoked so much that the top part of his right index and middle fingers had turned yellowish brown. Now, with his head tilted, his chin pointed upward, and his eyes half-closed, he was again puffing happily, his mind carried away by the ascending smoke.

I turned to Ping, but couldn't get her attention. Poor Ping. She was overwhelmed by Grandmother Ya Zhen, who bombarded her with one question after another. I wanted to come to her rescue, but couldn't. No one could answer all her questions.

"Remember the beggar story I told you? I tell you it's that beggar's doing again. You don't believe me? You should if you don't want that beggar to follow you around for the rest of your life—trouble, trouble, nothing but trouble!"

Ping became quiet. I didn't want to respond to her, either.

"So, where is your father now?"

I wish someone had an answer to that question.

"When did you last see him?"

"When will he come back?"

"Is your mother working?"

"How can you live without an income?"

I wonder about that, too, I thought silently. *And I wonder why you never helped us.*

I could hardly keep quiet. I would howl at my grandmother if only I could. But not today. Today, we came here for our father. I jumped down from my chair and headed straight for the window facing the park across the street. Beyond the park, I could see a cluster of blue domes on top of an old Russian Orthodox church. I took a long, deep breath, trying to focus my eyes on the golden, thin rods at the very top. What a meaningless trip! I knew it was time for me to take charge and rescue Ping from this trap or I might explode. But I didn't have to.

Stamp. Stamp. Stamp. The wooden stairs outside the apartment shook so violently I feared they might collapse.

"Is anyone home? Anyone?!" A voice boomed all the way to the top of the staircase, and a stranger appeared. "I have important news ... Is anyone home?"

I turned around, and there was the fattest woman I had ever seen in my life. In the 1960s, everyone lived on rice and cabbage.

No one could afford to get fat. You almost never saw fat people and none as big as this woman. She'd have to squeeze herself through the narrow door, I bet myself. Her face was baby-tender. Her skin was stretched thin by the abundant fat underneath.

The woman was my grandfather's sister-in-law, the wife to his only brother—the one who owned the charcoal store.

My grandfather broke off contact with them twenty years ago when he freed his young family from the servitude of his brother's store. His brother kept their parents and all their remaining wealth—whatever was left after the Japanese burned down my great grandfather's factory. The rumor was that when my great grandmother came to her son's charcoal store, she had so much gold jewelry that she used two silk scarves as parcels to carry them. Obviously, they all did well, except for my grandfather.

"Oh, my dear brother-in-law, your mother is returning to the Heavenly Kingdom." the woman said excitedly. Oddly, she was smiling as she delivered this news.

Does my grandfather have a mother? I wondered as the woman brushed past me and went straight for Grandfather. She wrapped her arms around his neck as if they were very close to each other, even though they had not seen each other for twenty years.

"Don't feel bad," the woman cooed soothingly, looking down at my grandfather's moist eyes and hunched, stiff back. "We have treated her so well over the years. She just had her ninetieth birthday. *Lao Shou Xing,* our Old Longevity Star mother, wants to see her great-grandchildren from your side of the family. I am here trying to fulfill her last wish."

Somehow, tears readily flowed out of her smiling eyes when she mentioned "last wish."

Her eagle vision swept around the room and suddenly fell on Ping and me.

"What!? Whose kids are these?" she asked. "An Chu's? The very ones she wanted to see!"

She looked ready to snatch us up in her greedy claws.

I was scared of this woman. I looked away when she looked at me. But Ping and I had to go with her because our great grandmother wanted to see us—a great grandmother we had never known, who only wanted to see us when she was dying. And this fat woman needed us to fulfill a dying woman's wish—a foolish superstition. If a dying person's wish could not be satisfied, that person could turn into a ghostly spirit and bring trouble.

We followed the waddling woman out of our grandparents' apartment into the alley, onto a main street, and then several side streets, until we stopped in front of a very old, two-story row house. We walked through the front door and were immediately submerged in total darkness. I blinked and tried hard to make my eyes work, but I couldn't see a thing. The smell of cooking oil, garlic, dust, and stale night air floated my way as the big woman led us with the sound of her heavy footsteps up a flight of stairs. I heard the stairs groan and was afraid that the woman would fall backwards onto me or a stair would give way under her. I felt every step with my hands and then climbed up on all fours, making sure that there was wood under me.

Finally, we reached a landing. We stopped there, and waited in the darkness for an unsettling amount of time until the woman found and turned on a light.

A bare bulb suspended on a wire gave out a weak, yellow light, revealing a bed perched on the corner of the landing. A tiny woman lay curled up on the mattress. She looked no bigger than a child. Her hair was white, smooth, and silky. Her feet were as small as mine but with odd lumps on top. She had bound feet! *This must be our great grandmother*, I thought.

The big woman announced what I was thinking: "Bow, children, and pay your respects! This is your *tai zu mu*."

The white-haired child reacted to the sound and opened her eyes. She stared at the ceiling, her face as pale as the walls, and her arms thin as sticks.

"Mother, Mother, I have brought you An Chu's children. They are your great grandchildren … too bad they are all girls," the big woman said in a sickeningly sweet voice with a touch of sarcasm.

She grabbed my great grandmother like a hawk snatching a chicken and sat her up against a pile of pillows.

Great Grandmother's eyes became level with ours. She suddenly came to her senses.

"Move closer, my precious," she whispered in a trembling voice. "Let me have a good look at you."

Ping and I tried to move toward her. She looked us up and down several times. Her lips trembled and her mouth opened, but no words came out. Soon she stopped blinking and slipped back into her dreams.

The big woman abruptly herded us back down the deep, dark stairs.

"Well, now that Great Grandmother has seen you," she said. "I'll take you back to your grandparents."

Ping and I walked quickly down the staircase, helped by the light and mindful of the large, threatening boulder behind, ready to crush us if the rickety stairs gave in.

"The minute … I saw you … I knew exactly … who you were," she wheezed as she fell from step to step, painfully poking me with a fat finger. "You are an exact copy of your father when he was my charcoal boy."

I was glad to get out of that place. As soon as she guided us through the maze of alleys back to the main avenue, we said *zai jian* and hurried home. We had a lot to tell Mother.

When she heard our story, Mother was indignant that anyone would let a ninety-year-old woman live in the dark corridor without sun, air, and windows.

"Your great grandmother is a very gentle woman, too gentle to stand up for herself," Mother sighed. "It's a pity they treat her that way."

The next morning, we received the news that our great grand-mother was, in fact, dying, and had expressed her wish to receive all the members of her family one last time. Mother got us dressed in our best clothes. Instead of sending us to school, she took all four of us to see our great grandmother.

When we got there this time, the stair was lit and the bed in the corridor had been removed. Everything looked neater and the place more spacious. We found Great Grandmother on a comfortable bed in one of the rooms. In front of her, there was a quiet receiving line of relatives, which we joined. Great Grandmother held hands with everyone as she whispered her last words.

"She cannot see anymore," someone in the line explained. "That's why she touches everyone."

I wondered how she lost her sight overnight and how she knew that she was dying, since she did not look any different today than she did yesterday. I had never seen anyone who was dying before. In fact, it had never, ever, occurred to me before yesterday that peo-ple could die. I did not know what happened when someone died. Perhaps, it was the same as when chickens, ducks, or fish died. I thought about the dead chicken in our yard and followed the peo-ple ahead of me until it was my turn.

I was not scared when I touched Great Grandmother's hand. It felt like a bunch of bones under wobbly skin. Just when I was going to withdraw my own hands and step aside, she held them tight and started to feel them with her fingertips.

"This is the softest pair of hands I have ever touched," Great Grandmother exclaimed. "This child has lucky stars over her! This child is blessed!"

I did not know how a dying old lady could talk so loudly. She scared me. I wanted to pull my hands free and run away from her.

Everyone stared at me with awe and jealousy, but Mother came to my rescue. She rushed to my side, hugging me with one arm and extending the other toward Great Grandmother. Great Grandmother only let go of me when Mother touched her. She then took Mother's hands and mumbled: "You are having a hard life. Don't worry. Everything will get better ... better."

Having spent the last bit of her energy, the rest of her "good-byes" were subdued, more like a deathbed scene, with no words of wisdom or exclamations, no whispers, just touches, gentle touches from her waiting relatives, her expressionless face as gray as old white cotton sheets. As I stood in a corner and watched unfamiliar people come and go, my grandmother, Ya Zhen approached me. She had a strange look in her eyes as she stationed her head inches from my face. She squinted and looked me up and down for quite a while. I was very embarrassed by how close we were and couldn't understand what she was doing. "Grandma," I finally managed to say.

"So, you are the one who got your father's good luck," she said in a disappointed voice. "No wonder he is in detention. Now that you've taken his luck away from him, he will never be able to get out of all these troubles!"

I stood in awe.

She was agitated by my silence. "Your father is doomed!"

I still didn't know how to answer.

"And you're not even a boy!" she hissed between her teeth and left.

My face burned as if I were sitting next to a hot stove.

On the way back home, I was unusually quiet and kept my thoughts to myself. Could a dying person see things and tell the future? How did Great Grandmother know Mother was having a hard life? Why did she say I had lucky stars over me? If, indeed, I had all these lucky stars, shouldn't I be able to get Father out of jail? Did I take away my father's lucky stars? If I could, I would trade all my lucky stars to get him back.

Oh, Father, how I missed him.

Chapter IX

EGGS AS MEDICINE

A ND THEN, OUT OF the blue, Father was allowed to come home. It was a complete surprise that started with a loud knock at the front door.

"Is this An Chu Sun's house?" someone shouted. "Open the door!"

I did and just stood there. I could hardly recognize him, my own father: He had lost a lot of weight. His cheekbones held up his face, as pale as death itself. His eyes were closed. He breathed heavily and his chest heaved up and down beneath his torn, inside-out jacket.

Two men held onto his arms so he would not fall down. They dragged him into our house like a sack of vegetables, threw him on one of our beds along with his bundle of belongings, and left.

"Mom, Dad is home! Dad is home!"

Mother dashed into the room, along with my sisters. With her soapy hands, she helped him to sit up. "What happened to you, An Chu?" she asked. "What have they done to you?"

Leaning against a stack of quilts, Father motioned to us children not to get too close to him. In a thin voice, he told us that he had contracted a highly contagious form of something called hepatitis while he was in one of the detention cells only the size of a bathtub.

I did not know what hepatitis was, but I knew it was deadly. It had sucked the life out of my father.

Later, we learned the details: Father's company had been enraged by his "lack of cooperation," or in plain words, unwillingness to confess to their made-up "anti-revolutionary crimes." In his cell, Father read Chairman Mao's quotations, copied the quotations, and wrote humorous essays, but made no confession. He maintained his innocence and held onto his faith in Chairman Mao and his country. Nothing could bend Father's spirit. His captors felt helpless and finally decided to give him a more severe punishment.

When another prisoner who had developed hepatitis was transferred out, Father was put in the infected cell. He became terribly sick. Weak as a child and physically incapable even of getting out of his own bed, he was allowed to go home to recuperate or die.

Mother put all her money together, and called a pedicab to take Father to the hospital, only to find they were tailed by two men. As soon as Father sat down with a doctor, the men approached the doctor, showed their IDs, and whispered something into the doctor's ear. The doctor looked intimidated. He was sympathetic but resolute.

"I am sorry," he said. "You are suffering from a form of political deviation. It's purely psychological. It's beyond my ability to help your condition. I cannot treat you."

Looking at the frightened doctor and the two men standing threateningly with their arms crossed, Mother knew she was wasting her time there. She would never be allowed to buy the medicine that could help him. Struggling to prop him up, she hauled Father back to the house and started her own rescue mission.

Mother went to the farmers' market and traded our rice ration coupons for several hens. We brought them home and put them in our backyard, where they wandered freely and were fed with scraps of anything we had. All Mother wanted from them were eggs with their yolks of liquid gold swimming in glistening, transparent protein. We marked every egg with the date it was laid and stored all of them carefully in an old wooden jar that in better days had been another of Mother's proud family possessions. The mahogany-colored container had a carved imperial lion on its lid and faded golden interior. When our food had run low, she had tried to sell it, along with five others, but even the pawn shop refused to buy it.

"It has a crack," the store clerk said to Mother, pointing to the defect. "We don't take broken things. Do you want me to throw it out?"

"No, no, please don't throw it out. I'm sorry. Please give this one, yes, this broken one, back to me."

On the way home, Mother told me that those jars came from Grandpa Ho De's family estate. She said she didn't see any crack before and maybe the jar just didn't want to leave her. Now this lucky wooden jar took on the most important job in our house, for it stored not just eggs, but our every hope for Father to get better.

No one believed Father could recover without a doctor's care or real medicine. But he did under Mother's unrelenting supervision. Every morning, following her instructions, Ping and I left home with six pennies and came back with a pot of steaming hot soy milk. Mother cracked a couple of our eggs and whisked them into the liquid along with generous amounts of sugar. Father always got a big bowl of it for breakfast every day instead of our normal watery rice. Mother believed that her nutritious soy milk concoction could inject life into even a dying man.

"Soy is protein," she explained to me while she was cracking the eggs. "And a newborn egg contains all the essence of life. If it can bring about birth, why shouldn't it be able to restore health? Your father has to get better."

Smart Mother. I could always count on her. It sounded so convincing, anyway, even though I wasn't exactly sure what she was saying.

Gradually, we started to raise more young hens. We were very tender toward our chicken friends because we counted on them to make Father better. Soon, we named all of them: Black Tail, Dove, Golden Claws, White Wings, Speedy, Sesame, and Bandit. Each name described either a physical feature or the personality of a hen, and we knew all their quirks by heart. We could tell which one had just laid an egg in her nest by the type of "cluck" she made and fought to be the first one to reach the coop, fetch the warm egg, and give it to Mother. She marked the date on it with a pencil and cautiously lowered it into our wooden jar. More liquid gold for Father. We felt very rich and contented. That hen was instantly rewarded with a small, precious handful of raw rice. We kept all the other hens away, watching in envy while our star enjoyed her banquet and triumphantly pecked up every grain. That would give the hen enough energy to produce the next egg.

Ironically, Father started getting paid again during his "sick leave" from detention, so we did not have to scavenge for coal nuggets anymore. Instead, we often spent our time picking grass so our chickens would have enough food.

To gather grass in the city took energy, luck, and vigilance. We watched for any green, young blade curious or foolish enough to stick its head from under the fence of a neighboring yard. We also made visits to the municipal park at the end of the lane but had to do so secretly since it had become a political arena and the public was no longer permitted inside. Ping, Min, and I worked together to get inside. We decided to divide up our roles. One of us stayed outside the entrance, pretending to be playing while watching out for any grownups coming in our direction. The second planted herself inside the garden within earshot of the entrance in order to relay any warnings to the third who was picking the grass. When our covert operation was accomplished, we casually slipped out of the area, carrying a basketful of green treasure secretly hidden under a dirty dish towel.

Little by little, Father started to get better. He got out of bed for short periods of time. His movements were slow, labored, and confined to our one-room house and its small yard. Any desire he might have to go further was quickly killed by the knowledge that right outside our door waited a two-man surveillance team.

For the first time, though, Father seemed happy just to be home not doing anything. He enjoyed watching us tending the chickens, cleaning up after them with a broom, or cuddling with them in the sun.

It was very comforting to have Father around the house. It made up a little for the months he was gone. I enjoyed him so much that I wanted to stay home all day so he wouldn't disappear again before I returned from school. Father saw the fear in my eyes. That was when he held me on his lap and gave me a lecture on life.

"Going to school is the only source of pride for a poor family," he said. "Education gives you the same knowledge and promise of a good life a privileged child has. If, someday, you have a choice of going to a college at the cost of disowning me as your father, I would push you to go. Knowledge stays with you for the rest of your life but I cannot. My love tells me to choose what's best for you and your future. As for me, I will always be part of you. You will always be my daughter in my heart. I will always be your father. You cannot lose me, no matter what happens."

Struck by his gaze and words, I slowly chewed on his words. Father knew I loved school, but I loved him even more. He was worried that I would give up everything because of him. But if he told me to stay in school and learn, he knew I would. Every morning, when I picked up my army-green school bag and headed out, I thought of my father and my silent promise to do well. And I did just that, but not without a struggle.

Of the forty students in my class, I was the shortest one, always at the beginning of the line and always with the shabbiest clothes. My trousers were often patched at both knees and in the back.

My jacket was discolored, bleached by the sun. And I always wore homemade cotton shoes. My modest outer appearance and my silent nature doomed me to be unpopular—someone everyone picked on.

Even during the Cultural Revolution, you could easily tell a child's family background by his or her clothes. There were plenty of other kids dressed like me. But in my neighborhood, kids were mostly dressed in starched shirts, ironed pants, and shining, black patent leather shoes. Though plain, in politically acceptable colors such as navy blue and army green, their clothes were crisp, tailored, and new. Most kids came from families with political connections and lived in the apartments high above my shabby little bathhouse. They had live-in nannies and servants they called *arh yi*—"aunts," who cooked for them, cleaned their apartments, and washed and pressed their clothes. Their parents were attended by *si ji tong zi*—"comrade drivers" in white gloves—who drove their government-issued cars. Even my teachers were afraid of them.

"Hey, The One from the Bathhouse," they often called me in school. "How do you live there? Taking baths while you sleep?"

They had too good a time making fun of me to stop.

"Anyone want to meet a beggar living in a bathhouse? Just see where my finger is pointing!"

"Look at the patches on her pants and elbows and her shoes … she looks like a walking quilt!"

"Can anyone tell the difference between her and a scarecrow? No, because there isn't any!"

I could hear kids laughing behind me, but I wouldn't look back or respond. I pretended that they were talking to someone else. I knew that if I answered, I would make a fool of myself, and they wouldn't be punished anyway. I'd learned that much.

Once during our political science class, I was sitting straight with my hands behind my back, the way we were taught, while the teacher copied Chairman Mao's newest quotation onto the blackboard. A boy sitting behind me suddenly leaned forward, grabbed my pencil-box, and threw it on the floor.

Crash!

The teacher turned around, just in time to see me dropping down and crawling on all fours to retrieve my precious pencils and crayons, which were rolling everywhere, before they disappeared under everyone else's desks.

"Qin Sun! Did I give you permission to get up and do a monkey dance? Get back in your seat! You are disrespectful to our great leader's teachings. If I ever catch you crawling on the floor while I'm writing his quotations, I'll make you stand in the corner for a week!"

I sat on the floor, frozen, my hands still holding onto the few crayons I had salvaged. I bit my lips and held in my tears until I got home. The moment I arrived home and saw Mother, I cried so hard for so long that I could feel my head buzzing.

"I'll take you back to school right now," Mother said. "I want you to tell your teacher everything just the way you told me." She was outraged when she heard my story and saw my empty pencil-box.

My teacher listened impatiently because it was her lunch hour.

"Well," she finally said to Mother, "when I turned around, I saw that boy sitting with his hands behind his back, like the rest of the class. Although I don't believe her story, I'll ask the boy if he threw down your daughter's pencil-box. He is a very good boy and will tell the truth."

She looked at me severely. "Are you sure it was him? You know his father is a very high-ranking official at the city hall and he is very strict with his children." I nodded timidly.

Of course, the boy denied everything and my teacher believed him.

The next day, the teacher told Mother that I must have pushed down my own pencil-box, and that I lied to protect myself. She almost made me believe that I was the guilty one, except that between classes, the boy behind me pushed me down and pressed mud balls into my pigtails for telling on him. He warned me that he would paste mud balls all over my skull if I dared tell on him again.

Mother shook her head, took out two pencils and a few crayons from Ping's pencil-box, and put them in mine.

Over the years, I gradually earned a good reputation because of my grades. Classmates fought to sit near me in case of a test. They visited me at home with their homework and I helped them. Knowing that I could do something well was satisfying. But knowing that no one could take away my thoughts and ideas was better.

Chapter X

SOMEONE WANTED US DEAD

Just as Father started to get better, nourished back to health by the many precious eggs from our chicken friends, our worst fear came true: he was sent back to detention. Since he was in ill health, we were at least allowed to visit him every few days and bring him things, including food.

Since his return, Father had been the focus of our lives. Now, everything felt meaningless. To save rice, Mother even got rid of our chickens.

It was a hot, hot summer with little to do. I sat on my little bamboo chair in our front yard and tried to amuse myself by waiting for clouds to pass across the patch of sky between the apartment buildings and our sycamore tree. Too often, though, it seemed that the sky reflected my life. Nothing was moving. Nothing was happening. One day, I went out to skygaze but the summer sun was blinding. I shifted my eyes to our tiny house. To my surprise, its stucco walls were alive with activity. The normally plain, sandy surfaces were glistening like fields of jewels, every grain of sand a tiny diamond. I harvested them one by one with my eyes, and discovered a new game using the magic of the sun. When I squinted or tilted my head, the stucco wall began creating an endless variety of pictures. Glittering patches of its uneven surface turned into flying horses, cats, dogs, and all sorts of fanciful shapes to make me forget my missing clouds. This helped me pass the time until the late afternoon when I could go and visit Father.

Since it was close to home, Mother sometimes allowed Ping and me to go by ourselves. We often took along newspapers, little treats Mother specially prepared for Father, and packs of cigarettes. Father's cell was not a normal room. It was a tiny living space—a cage, really—formed by wooden boards, not tall enough to stand up in and not long enough for the prisoner to actually lie down, although he was given a pile of hay to sleep on. A battered desk and chair were the only amenities and were crammed in next to the "bed." On the desk were a writing pad, a pen, and a Chairman Mao quotation book. Father was instructed to sit there all day, reading the Chairman's wisdom and writing out his anti-revolutionary confession.

But Father was as hard-headed as ever. He stood firm on his innocence and insisted that he did not drive a thumbtack into Mao's portrait, didn't kill any cats to threaten our great leader, and was never the high-ranking Nationalist Party officer he was accused of being—he had just reached his teens when the Nationalists retreated to Taiwan. He also denied staying in Shanghai to spy on Communist Party members or making any of the anti-revolutionary remarks, of which he had been accused.

"No one knows me better than myself," he said. "Don't tell me that I joined the National Army, handled guns, and gave orders to soldiers in my diapers. If I know I didn't do it, I didn't do it. No one can force me into a confession."

He left his accusers feeling annoyed and angry.

Detained in his little room, he had more free time than he could possibly fill, so he copied out Chairman Mao's quotations on a white pad time and again. But no matter what, he refused to write down any confessions or falsely accuse any of his co-workers of wrongdoing, as his captors suggested he do in return for his release.

I often asked when he would come home again, to which he always replied, "Soon, very soon."

Only after I grew up did I come to the realization that Father must have been exceptionally strong to maintain his sanity under such cruel conditions.

Father did not come home, and the summer dragged on. The days were too long and too hot. The heat just would not break, and our little house felt like a rice steamer.

Mother had already stripped our beds down to the bare wooden boards and covered them with straw mats, which were supposed to make them cooler. Instead, the heat turned the mats annoyingly sticky and left our sweaty bodies with their woven imprints. I flapped my palm-leaf fan left and right all night long, even when I was asleep. The heat turned the pleasure of resting into torture. I tossed and turned.

The heat wasn't the only thing that kept me from sleeping. The nights were long and creepy. Stories of murder and mutilation kept me up at night listening for any unusual noises. It was the height of the Cultural Revolution when factional violence intensified among political groups, when conflicts gave birth to murderous attacks, and executions were conveniently carried out with a kitchen knife under cover of night with haunting stories of tragic, sudden deaths that made people shut their doors and windows even in the summer heat. I heard grownups whispering about the head of one political group who came home late and found his entire family dead. He went mad and never recovered. His group was taken over by his rival. I imagined a wild man with shoulder-length hair, filthy face, bloodshot eyes bigger than bottle caps, and claw-shaped hands tearing at the air, stamping around in a pool of blood. I shivered.

In spite of all the horror stories, I never imagined political violence could reach my own doorstep, but it did.

It started out as an ordinary summer night. Min got an invitation to spend the night at a neighbor's apartment. As a treat, Mother assigned the two family beds to Ping and me while she made herself a temporary cot with two wooden boards in the kitchen. Baby Wen was placed in the old bamboo crib in the middle of the room. We left our bedroom and kitchen doors open to let in any slight breeze, although that night there wasn't any.

It was hopelessly hot. I dozed off under the monotonous flapping sound of my own fan.

Sleeping in such awful heat often caused nightmares: I dreamt I was in a yard littered with dead chickens. A vicious black dog chased me, and I couldn't run. The sky was raining rocks on me. I often woke up in the dead of night in a hallucinatory state, disoriented, and not knowing what was real and what was a dream. That night I awoke in pitch darkness to roaring waves of sound. Sitting up on my stiff bed in my sweat-soaked clothes, I listened as the noise faded away. By then, I was more awake and realized that it was not a dream. I heard Mother get up and walk toward the front door. I saw her anxiously peering through the mail slot. There was nothing out there but the silent night and the usual yellow light flooding in from the street.

Mother could not make sense out of what had just happened. She was a light sleeper and was woken up by unfamiliar sounds, as if someone was hitting something every few seconds at our front door. Before she could figure out what was going on she heard the loud burst of a motorcycle engine racing away. Alarmed by the unusual noises, she kept the lights off and told us all to be quiet. To be safe, Mother moved her bed back into the room with us and locked up all the doors for the rest of the night. We were so tense that we did not feel the heat anymore and nervously waited for daybreak to arrive.

We did not find out until the next morning how close we came to disaster.

The elderly neighbor who kept Min for the night lived in an apartment right above us. In the middle of the night, she happened to go to the bathroom and heard a slight noise in the darkness below. She approached the window and looked down. Two shadows rolled a motorcycle slowly toward our house. After turning it around and parking it in a position for a fast getaway, they started to hit our front door with a six-foot iron rod.

They could have easily knocked open our decaying, wooden front door with just one blow, except that it was pitch black and they could not see. Instead of hitting the door or the fence—easy targets—they were hitting the sturdy wooden doorframe, wrapped by my unconventional father with old rubber tires. Still, they could have been through the door in a few more blows if it were not for the sudden illumination of the streetlamp outside our house, which unexpectedly bathed both men, their weapon, and the motorcycle under a flood of light. They jumped onto their bike and within seconds disappeared into the night.

Early the next morning, Mother examined a dozen deep dents and gashes on our front door as she listened to the neighbor recalling what she had seen and heard.

"Don't stay here anymore," she advised Mother. "Someone wanted your lives, and they will come back again."

That day, we went into exile.

Mother scattered the family, sending us into hiding for the next few months. I was sent to live with my father's parents and had a very unhappy time there. I soon forgot about the danger, and ached to be back home with Mother.

When our family was finally reunited that fall, Mother took me to see an old man at the end of the lane. She was still seeking answers to what had happened the night of the motorcycle incident.

The stooped, wrinkled bachelor poked his head out of his basement apartment and squinted at us. He was in charge of turning on and off a dozen or so streetlights in our lane and Mother wanted to know when he flipped the switches, and why a light would be turned on at midnight. He seemed to be confused why Mother asked such questions, although he admitted that he sometimes forgot to turn the lights on or off when he fell asleep. I guess it was just dumb luck that we survived that night. The old man happened to wake up and flip the switch of life at the very moment two mysterious men hit our home.

Chapter XI

The Americans Are Coming!

OR SEVERAL MORE YEARS, Father went in and out of detention. It became our way of life. Life settled into a three-part routine: from home to school to Dong Hu Road #20. We were happy that we could go and visit him, get patted on the head, and share the treats that Mother had bought him, even under the watchful eyes of a guard or two.

Just when we thought that the Cultural Revolution was going to last forever and Father would never come home for good, a sign of change arrived with the warming spring air of 1972. For the first time since the founding of the People's Republic of China, the Communist Party opened the country's doors to a delegation of American diplomats led by U.S. President Richard Nixon.

Newspaper headlines, radios, and cars with roof speakers all blared the news:

> *Top officials from imperialist America have landed in China!*
> *They are shaking hands with Chairman Mao and Premier Zhou Enlai!*
> *They are heading to Shanghai!*
> *China and America have signed the "Shanghai Communiqué!"*

The minute Mother heard this news, and every morning thereafter, she put a couple of *fen* in my palm and I ran to the post office to get her a newspaper. She wanted to know exactly what was going on and what it meant for the country. And for us. The crowd at the post office told me that the entire city of Shanghai shared her thoughts.

In all the official media, dinner conversations, and neighborhood gossip, attention was suddenly centered on strange-sounding names, such as "Nee Ke Soong" (Nixon), "Hua Shung Dung" (Washington), and "Mei Guo" (America, or literally, "Beautiful Country").

What had happened?

For all those years of revolution—practically my entire life—Chairman Mao had taught us that America was an "imperialistic paper tiger" that exploited the rest of us, explaining perfectly why we were so poor. So why was Chairman Mao hosting our "paper tiger" enemy as state guests and signing an agreement with them? What was Mao up to? We were all puzzled, even though we were taught never to question the wisdom of our great leaders. Mother was more concerned how this visit would affect our lives. She saw every change as a hopeful sign that Father might be freed so we could have a normal family life again. Being twelve years old, I didn't see any connection at all. To me, Nixon was just a useless newspaper image, exotic and mysterious. His rotten imperialist country was as abstract and distant to me as the moon, although I admit I was surprised that he didn't seem that much different from us. As the head of a country that had exploited the rest of the world for decades, he should have been clothed in pure gold. I also half-expected him to have long, sharp teeth and some sort of horns on his head, which would fit his evil "paper tiger" image better.

"Don't forget the newspaper," Mother reminded us every time Ping and I were getting ready to visit Father. "Tell him to read everything. It's vital that he knows what's going on right now, especially something that is happening so close to him."

Mother meant "close" literally. Nixon's motorcade went right past Dong Hu Road when his entourage arrived a couple of days earlier, and the "Shanghai Communiqué," a historic pact to improve relations between the United States and China, was signed in the Jinjiang Hotel, only two blocks away from where Father was detained.

"So the *lao mei* have returned," Father commented calmly, as he stared at the photograph of Premier Zhou Enlai and President Nixon. "I guess they are not so bad after all."

I heard a touch of sarcasm in Father's voice.

"Why did Dad call them the 'Good Old Americans,' as if they were friends?" I asked Mother casually as I swept past her in the kitchen. "It sounded like he knew them before ... and even liked them."

"Watch what you say," Mother said, lowering her voice as she stir-fried some shredded cabbage, her face reddened by the rising steam. "You will get into trouble talking like that in public."

When she covered her wok, lowered the heat, and turned around, I knew she was upset.

"An Chu Sun," she directed her angry voice at Father as if he were there to hear. "Haven't you learned anything in all these years of detention!? Maybe I shouldn't send you any more newspapers."

"But Mom, he only whispered it. No one heard us!" I defended him. "You know I'm big now and would never say the wrong things outside."

Mother stared at me for a while and then nodded her head. She knew she could trust me.

"You know that your father was a charcoal boy when he was little," Mother whispered to me even though there was no one nearby. "He used to make deliveries to foreigners, as well as local people, and that included an old American couple. They were nice to him, used to give him food, and taught him English—phrases like 'thank you' and 'good-bye.' Your father liked Americans. He should be careful with what he says, though. Dong Hu Road #20 is not the place to say whatever you want."

Mother didn't want the Americans to bring Father more political trouble. We had plenty of it already.

"How about you," I decided to ask her. "Do you like the Americans?"

"America is not at all like what they have taught you in school," Mother answered after a moment of hesitation. "Strictly between you and me, my birth father—your real grandfather—sailed to America many times in the 1930s and 40s and brought home wonderful stories and things. He was a first mate on ocean-going freighters. We were very well-off then."

Now, I understood why Mother never contributed her stories to my "bitter-family-past" school reports: She didn't have any!

Soon enough, the American delegation was gone, together with all the excitement it brought to our lives. Father still stayed in detention, though, and Mother was disappointed that the "Shanghai Communiqué" didn't bring the change to our lives that she had hoped. As for me, the Americans' visit helped me uncover some of my family secrets. Now, I knew we were not always poor. The image of my grandfather on a large ocean-going ship brought America a lot closer to me than the moon. America was part of my family history, but of course I couldn't tell this to anyone, not even to my own sisters.

I never thought of America as a "paper tiger" again.

Chapter XII

IF WINTER COMES,
CAN SPRING BE FAR BEHIND?

T HE FOLLOWING YEARS WERE sad ones for the country. Our founding fathers passed away one after another, including Chairman Mao, Zhou Enlai, and General Zhu De. They were the people who built and ran the nation. Every day, they instructed us what to do. We were taught to believe that they were the navigators for the Chinese people without whom life couldn't go on. A popular song at the time captured this feeling:

> *Ocean-sailing depends on navigation*
> *Everything lives because of the sun*
> *After rain, plants grow*
> *Mao Zedong's ideas make our revolution possible.*
> *Fish have to stay in water*
> *Flowers come from plants*
> *People like us rely on the Communist Party …*

Now that our party leaders were gone, we didn't know how to go on.

When Mao died, I saw people, men and women, old and young, weeping with grief as they walked down the streets. I heard that

factories were being closed down so workers could prepare mourning services. Farmers put down their sickles and raised money to
buy train fare to send one lucky villager to Beijing on their behalf
to view our great leader for the last time. Some people even stabbed
their own fingers so they could write mourning posters in blood,
declaring their red loyalty in both word and color.

But with his death, some of the competition over who was a
true Maoist died down also. Political infighting gave way to emotion and nostalgia. We were no longer brave revolutionary soldiers,
but orphaned children, feeling sorry for ourselves and our country.
Our national flag flew at half-mast, and monotonous mourning
music filled every broad avenue and tiny alley. All we heard and
read for weeks were eulogies. Then, came the funeral days when
all of China gathered like a large family and stood still and silent,
sensing the coming changes for the Middle Kingdom.

Even though Mao Zedong was supposed to be "the red, red
sun in our hearts that never sets," we knew his death would bring
change. We were especially worried about who would succeed
him and become the head of our country. When the radio stations
stopped broadcasting all their usual programs to report on Mao's
death, we listened closely to every detail: Who visited and consoled the immediate family members, who made eulogy speeches,
and who held official meetings afterwards at the Great Hall of the
People, for the person who appeared most on the national stage
might become our next leader.

During the mourning period for Chairman Mao, we wore
only the colors black and white. We put on black armbands and
wore white in our hair as if a member of our immediate family had
died. Led by our teachers and surrounded by large portraits draped
in black cloth, we read farewells and staged our own versions of
mourning services in our classrooms. Our school gathered us all in
the playground and held another larger, more formal service, complete with wreaths and banners we had worked on for days.

It was the saddest time I had ever lived through. I didn't know
that grown men could cry. But they did. Where there was mourning

music playing, crowds wept. On my way to and from school, I stopped when I saw local residents gathered around a street corner, watching them cover a wall with black-and-white slogans and posters.

"Cry for our great leader Chairman Mao Zedong!"

"Chairman Mao, you will always be the reddest sun in our heart."

Some calligraphic characters were the size of a window and the air reeked with the acrid smell of fresh ink.

"Chairman Mao, why did you leave us? Now, we're orphans!" an elderly woman wailed, stirring the crowd.

"Chairman Mao, you gave us our country!"

"You gave our nation dignity!"

"Chairman Mao, take us with you!"

People talked and cried at the same time. I stood in awe as tears streamed down my own cheeks.

One day, after a memorial service in a local park, I happened to walk behind two elderly women and overheard them talking about how the "*yin* world" messengers came and collected the leaders of China and those who had served them well. I was terrified and intrigued by the thought that there was a *yin* world (*yin* being a dark, cold, life-draining force), and that it had agents who could carry off even the greatest among us. I followed them, listening with chills running down my spine.

"The *yin* world messengers are invisible and powerful, you know. See how fast they collected all our great leaders?" one white-haired woman said as she limped along and pointed her walking stick at a Mao portrait in the distance. "They can lift us up with a finger and take us away just like that."

"I guess so," the other answered fearfully. "I know they usually carry people away in batches, one master and a lot of little people— all sharing the same boat, as they say. We never know when it's our turn."

"Speaking of that, did you hear Xiao Ma's mother-in-law passed away yesterday?"

"That lucky old woman, she wasn't even sick. But she got picked to serve our great leader in the *yin* world."

"I guess so."

"Why is she better than us? What could she do?"

"I've heard she's a wonderful cook and came from Chairman Mao's hometown."

"Oh."

The limping woman was finally quiet.

"You never know," the other continued. "Chairman Mao may still pick more followers ... the lucky ones, I mean."

From their tone of voice, both of them were extremely envious of that dead woman for her good luck, dying so soon after Chairman Mao.

I was amazed by the special power Chairman Mao still possessed, even after his death. Could he really choose the people to die for him? My great grandmother once said that I had lucky stars over me. Could Chairman Mao pick me this time to die and follow him? Lots of children fought under him during the Japanese War and the War of Liberation. He called them his *hong xiao guei*— Little Red Devils. I, myself, was one of his "Little Red Guards" during the Cultural Revolution ...

Suddenly, my lucky stars didn't seem so lucky anymore. I felt spooked by my own thoughts. I was afraid messengers from the dark world would come and snatch me. Since they were invisible, how could I tell whether or not they were here already to get me? I didn't want to die, even if it meant having the honor of serving Chairman Mao. I wanted to get away from those two old witches, but my feet and curiosity kept me two steps behind.

I always knew what *yin* and *yang* meant, and yet it had never occurred to me until then that we lived in the bright, warm *yang* world, and when we passed away, we would go to the dark *yin* world. In a way, of course, it did mean we could never really die. I liked that idea!

I was anxious to hear more from the two old women. but much to my disappointment, they fell quiet, so I grew impatient and ran past them. My mind kept on exploring the fascinating ideas of *yin* and *yang* for the rest of the trip home.

What is the yin world like? Is it always dark? Does everyone have to go there when they die? Can people see anything if it is eternally dark? Will Chairman Mao be able to use his loyalists to run a country and start another revolution in that "other world?"

I knew one thing for sure: The *yin* world was too dark for its people to use their red revolution flags and banners. I didn't see how color would be of any use in pitch blackness.

When I got home, I bombarded Mother with all my questions.

"Where in the world did you get these ideas?" she asked, alarmed.

I told her but she dismissed them as silly.

"That *yin-yang* stuff is superstitious nonsense," she said bluntly. "It's from the old times. You grew up in the Cultural Revolution. Haven't you read enough of Chairman Mao's quotations to know that our world is about the here and now? Those old stories—fortune-telling, dragons, demons, *fengshui*—they're not only ridiculous, they're forbidden. There are no *yin-yang* worlds!"

I was speechless. I wanted to ask Mother how then my dying great grandmother could predict the future with her last breath and say things that she didn't know, like that Mother was having a hard life, even though she had no knowledge at all that Father was imprisoned. I wanted to back up my argument with a Mao quotation, as my teachers taught me to do, but I couldn't come up with one, for Chairman Mao never believed in ghosts and spirits. The only spirit he believed in was the revolutionary spirit. I suddenly remembered how he told us to sweep "all the ox ghosts and snake gods" into the dustpan. It was useless. Between Mao and Mother, my new-found worlds of *yin* and *yang* crumbled and disappeared like the old China itself.

The old ways were not the only things to change and disappear. The Gang of Four, Chairman Mao's political confidants and close friends, was arrested, and sent to prison for "political crimes." Among them was Mao's own wife! The last ten years of the Cultural Revolution began to be questioned. I was in shock. If Chairman Mao were alive, would he be sent to prison, too? For the first time in my life, I realized that our government, the Communist Party, and even Mao Zedong, were not perfect. They made bad decisions and did wrong, too. I was still too young to connect "the mistakes of the past" everyone was talking about with the persecution of my family, my father's seven-year detention, the inhuman physical torture, and the loss of my sisters' (and my) childhoods.

Now, we cheered our new leader, Deng Xiaoping, an old Communist Party veteran who was himself persecuted for being counter-revolutionary. He returned to the political stage with lots of confidence and energy. His political speeches started to replace Chairman Mao's quotations on the radio waves and in the newspapers. I was even able to catch a glimpse of him talking in a metal box called television.

At the time, well-off families in my neighborhood started to buy their own Japanese-made, 9-inch, black-and-white TV sets and enjoy the luxury of private shows right at home. My sisters and I brought our own stools and chairs and joined the crowd gathered in front of a little television, set up by the neighborhood committee at the end of our lane. The reception was bad even in our central city location. Black and white images were often distorted by trembling, sometimes flying, horizontal lines, and voices were swallowed up by high-pitched static, while the grown-ups tried to maneuver an oversized, spider-like antenna into the right position.

When night fell, we sat and watched "free shows" ranging from serious political newscasts to entertaining dramas, concerts, and TV series that were still a novelty. Children often gathered in the very front with their little stools, savoring their candies, popped rice, and other treats. Women were the loudest spectators: They competed with the TV by cracking roasted melon seeds, exchanging greetings, passing around rumors, and commenting on the shows while the men shared their cigarettes, puffing away quietly in the back. For a while, the whole neighborhood lived harmoniously, like a big family, in front of a communal television set. After years of avoiding each other for fear of saying the wrong thing, sitting, eating, and laughing together with our neighbors felt good. It made us feel as if life was finally getting better.

But the best news by far came to us in its most dreaded form: a frighteningly official knock at the door. I opened it, and there was Father with all his books and belongings, accompanied by two smiling-faced men. They called Father "Comrade Sun" and were eager to help him with his bags. Mother made a big pot of extra-long noodles to celebrate our family reunion. She said those long noodles would bind us together so Father would never be sent away again. Everybody was happy.

The Cultural Revolution was over. The multitudes of flapping red flags—the very symbols of the revolution—dissipated like summer clouds. Stripped of its rosy adornment, Shanghai looked strangely naked. Our eyes were used to the sight of flags. They came in strings of little fluttering triangles or rectangles of all sizes, in plain red or decorated with golden stars and tassels, hammers and sickles, or the names of various political groups. They surrounded our buildings, classrooms, and public buses, and decorated our streets and alleys. At the age of six, we swore allegiance under them to join the Little Red Guards. Afterward, we loyally carried them over our shoulders at parades and faithfully stood by them during public gatherings. They were sacred for almost a decade and now they were gone, just like that, and no one complained about their absence at all.

Mao jackets and caps gradually disappeared, too. The once politically correct colors of red, white, army green, and navy blue lost their popularity. Without fanfare, people quietly put away the

revolutionary wardrobes that had been part of their lives for decades. They eagerly began shopping in the unfamiliar territory of
fashion. Suddenly, frills, bows, ribbons, suits, tank tops, miniskirts,
and high heels became the hottest commodities on the market.

"Clothing stores" sprang up on street corners, boasting the latest fashions directly from Paris and New York. In truth, they were
imitations at best. In those days, no one knew any real foreign fashion labels. Names like "Paris," "New York," "French," or "American"
were tempting bait for ignorant and eager fashion-seekers, although
the clothes were more likely designed and made locally, based on
people's imaginings of what foreign fashions were like. But for
now, everybody felt content with their own idiosyncratic "mix-
and-match" fashion statements: A woman wore a costume-like
blouse with puffy sleeves over a pair of army uniform pants and
sneakers—part of her revolutionary wardrobe that she had not yet
retired. A man wore a tie inside a Mao jacket—he had yet to save
enough money to buy himself a Western suit. In the early morning,
it was even possible to see a second-class Cinderella in glittering
ball gown and wooden slippers, yawning sleepily and heading toward the fish market to do her shopping. Everyone was looking
for novelty. No one knew what the next fashion craze would be.
At one point, folding umbrellas with colorful floral prints became
a hit. Thousands of them were smuggled into the southern coastal
cities and spread all over the country. People began showing their
individuality even when it rained.

As the country began to prosper, the days of ration coupons came
to an end. People were overjoyed to be able to buy whatever they
wanted. After decades of spartan living, everyone craved things,
new things, things they had never seen or tasted before.

As mandatory political meetings disappeared, people started to
use their extra time looking for ways to make money so they could
buy novelties such as television sets, cameras, electric fans, coffee,
chocolate, foreign cigarettes, and better food for their dinner tables.

Father was very excited to see all the changes around him. Change meant hope. He felt he could finally see light at the end of the endless tunnel of ordeals he had endured. Maybe his company would erase the false accusations in his personnel records and give him a public apology. Maybe he would be reimbursed for his lost salary. Father was filled with optimism.

The newspaper became his best friend. Every day, he read Deng Xiaoping's speeches line by line, searching for the new direction of our future. Father admired Deng very much, for he, too, had endured political hardship.

"Look, Chairman Deng said it right here," he said pointing his finger to a headline on the front page. "'Whether it's a black cat, or a white cat, it's a good cat so long as it can catch a rat.' You don't have to worry about my tainted political past anymore. Deng sees who you are based on your own behavior, not your family background."

Father sighed with relief, for indeed, Deng's political direction was a dramatic departure from Mao's. Father did not have to worry about how his past would affect our future anymore, whether his name was cleared or not. He even dared to dream about me getting a four-year university education, as rumors surfaced about the National College Entrance Exams being reopened to the general public for the first time since the fall of Imperial China.

The political tables were finally turning in our favor. Father could actually go and visit doctors, although his health had already declined dangerously. His acute hepatitis had long since turned chronic and he now suffered from diabetes, high blood pressure, heart problems, and rheumatism. He looked like an old man, even though he was only in his early forties. A decade of physical and emotional torture had put many wrinkles on his face, weakened his body, bent his back, and taken most of his black, wavy hair. Still, he was much happier than he'd been in years.

"Let me go and get that," he volunteered when Mother needed a box of matches or a cup of soy sauce.

"No more ration coupons!" he exclaimed with his arms up like a child before he headed out to the store.

Since private detention was no longer allowed, Father's company was forced to put him back to work. In consideration of his health, he was reassigned to a security job at a warehouse, where he could sit with a cup of tea all day in exchange for a meager salary. For companionship, he found himself an old broken radio, had it fixed, and took it to work. Every morning, he always reported to his job early, sitting in the open with his reading glasses and a newspaper. He read carefully and even took notes on the side.

When the younger workers came to fetch their supplies or drop off their tools, they teased him.

"Hey, old man, when did you become a professor?"

"I'm not one," Father answered seriously, "but my daughters will be. They will all go to college soon."

The workers laughed, for the idea of college was so new that it was still reserved for the privileged few. It was hard for them to make the connection with the daughters of a poor, uneducated man with patched clothes and a politically troubled past.

"Hold your laughs, because you'll need them in a couple of years. I may look like an old beggar, but my daughters are like golden phoenixes from a straw nest. They will fly. Oh, yes, they will."

Though they scoffed at the time, my father's prediction came true, and he lived to see his colleagues eventually greet his daughters as the "Little Golden Phoenixes," which gladdened his heart. Life would not turn out to be as easy as An Chu believed it would be, but for the moment, he, my mother, and their four little girls sensed the fluttering wings of a rare feeling called hope.

A Prophecy Ends
(Shanghai, December 1999)

A TAXICAB CREPT SLOWLY THROUGH Jubilee Court, weaving its way through a maze of waiting limousines, fur-clad women with flower bouquets, and young girls walking expensive dogs. It stopped in front of a tiny two-story home on the left side, its old, plain concrete structure out of place next to the stately villas with their fresh green paint and black, ornate iron rails. The passenger side of the door opened, Ping handed the driver some cash and stepped out.

She guided Yan's legs out onto the pavement, gently wrapped her arms around her body, and pulled her out of the car. She grabbed a stack of dried herb packets from the back seat and slammed the door shut. Ping put her hand under her mother's arm, and they walked slowly towards the house.

Yan had third-stage ovarian cancer and was weak from many rounds of chemotherapy. It took Ping a long time to get her upstairs and settled into bed with a small glass of watermelon juice she had prepared earlier.

Ping checked the time. It was one in the afternoon already, way past their lunch time but she needed to get her mother's medicine going first. Since Yan's refusal a month ago to continue the hospital treatments, Ping knew her mother's life depended on the herbs from the Chinese pharmacy. She opened a packet and poured its contents into a blackened earthen pot. Dried roots, insects, snakeskin, and unidentifiable bits of plants created a small pile in the bottom of the pot, on top of which Ping tossed a gauze-wrapped pack of special ingredients the druggist had prepared to activate the herbs. She shook the pot, and poked and examined its contents, making a mental note how this prescription was different from the last one, before she filled it with water and put it on top of the gas stove. She struck a match and watched the flickering blue fire. It would take a couple of hours of simmering before the medicine was ready. Now, she could think about lunch.

The house is awfully quiet. Is Father home? she wondered.

An Chu usually sat in the kitchen with his radio blasting, sipping a mug of black tea and waiting for her when it was time for lunch. But Mother's weekly appointment lasted much longer than they had anticipated.

He probably left for his mother's house already, Ping thought. *I hope he ate something.* Ping opened up the refrigerator in the musty, dark kitchen and noticed that the bowl of black noodles with vegetables and shredded chicken she left for him had not been touched. An Chu never liked those special noodles for diabetics, but Ping bought them anyway. She reached for a bag of frozen dumplings. They would make a quick meal.

Whenever she couldn't find An Chu, Ping always assumed he had gone to his mother's house. Where else would he go? Since his release from Shanghai Prison ten years ago, he seldom went anywhere or spoke to anyone outside his family. The final, unexpected prison sentence, coming after all those long years of detention hit him hard. Besides losing all his hair and teeth, he finally gave up the most important thing within him: his optimism. He avoided talking about his seven years behind bars with real criminals. In fact, he was silent most of the time, except, of course, when he went to see his mother.

Since his father's death two years ago, An Chu loved spending his days with his mother. Sometimes he came back home only for lunch, dinner, and sleep. Ping heard many reports from neighbors and friends that they often spotted them together in local snack shops, feasting on piles of ice-cream bars, cupcakes, and other sweet treats, along with two cans of Coca-Cola each. And both of them were severely diabetic! An Chu's mother, Ya Zhen, who was now in her mid-eighties and a bit senile, may not have known what she was doing, but An Chu's mind was still sound. Diabetes attacked his vision, affected his circulation, and weakened his legs, and now he was killing himself with sweets! Every time Ping confronted him, he shook his head and denied it.

"Must be a mistake ... must be someone else."

But no one could mistake the coat on his back, torn and dirty, the color faded beyond recognition. Even the migrant workers wore better clothes these days. On the streets of Shanghai, An Chu's coat wasn't good enough for a beggar! He had many new coats in the closet, but he only picked his shabby coat to wear.

Sometimes Ping wondered if it was only the ghost of her father lingering in front of her, for he had no resemblance to the father she so fondly remembered before he was sent to Shanghai Prison. Ping missed his laughter and the humorous remarks that always came to him so easily, even when she visited him in his tiny detention cell during the 60s. But who could blame him? When the Cultural Revolution was finally over, his family and friends all expected that he would get a formal apology from the company and be compensated one way or another for all the mental and physical hardships he had endured. True, they were forced to give him a menial job and keep him on for a few years, but he always stayed hopeful that someday they would clear him and admit their mistake.

Everyone was dumbfounded when, instead, he was taken away in handcuffs again and secretly sentenced to a seven-year term to pay for the crimes he had committed *in support of* (!) the Cultural Revolution. How could anyone be punished twice—for being *for* and *against* the same thing? It didn't make any sense, except that my father was a constant reminder of their guilty past and they finally couldn't stand to have him around anymore, so another unprovable charge was trumped up. The lawyer we hired with borrowed money wasn't even told about the trial until after the sentence was passed.

"This is very complicated," he said. "The order came from up above and I don't have the power to help you."

The downstairs bedroom door was closed. Ping pushed it open. It was pitch black inside. She drew the curtains aside and was surprised to find her father still in bed.

"Dad, are you alright?"

An Chu opened his eyes slightly and closed them again, his face gray.

"Should I take you to the hospital?"

He shook his head.

"Help me to get up," he said. "I'll eat something and feel better."

Ping looked around his bed, searching for clothes. She picked up a pair of thermal underwear, stained and filled with holes. "Dad, let me get you a fresh change of clothes. I'll help you get dressed and then make some dumpling soup for lunch, okay?"

She finally got him seated in the kitchen with a large, steaming mug of black tea. "The doctor gave Mom a new prescription to help her sleep better at night," Ping said as she stirred her pots and pans. "Feel warm in your new clothes, Dad?"

An Chu nodded as he sipped his tea. His face showed some uneasiness about the stiff new clothes underneath his worn, shabby coat.

"Qin called last night. She wants to come and visit us in August. She's bringing Halley with her. But the baby is only one, too small for the summer heat and mosquitoes here. Besides, she shouldn't leave her husband and six-year-old son Keaton by themselves for three weeks. I told her to stay in New York and not to bring any more money here, either. Mother doesn't want any more hospital treatments, so we don't need extra money. But I know she's coming anyway. Min also wants to come in October with Angela. I told her to book a hotel room."

Ping stopped her monologue and started to lower the dumplings into the boiling water one at a time. She glanced at her father. He was staring into his mug, but she knew he was listening.

"You're going to meet your two new granddaughters from America! Aren't you excited?"

An Chu was still quiet, staring at his tea.

Ping brought the pot of dumpling soup to the table and put down three bowls and spoons. As she stirred the pot with a ladle, the scent of sweet sesame oil and roasted scallions escaped with the rising steam. An Chu lifted his head, sniffed the air eagerly, and watched as she scooped a dozen dumplings into the first bowl and presented it to him. He held up the bowl with shaky hands, wanting more.

"Dad, you're not a beggar. I'd like to give you more. I would even give you the whole pot of dumplings, but you're diabetic. Remember what the doctors said about limiting starch? Starch turns into sugar and is bad for you!"

An Chu continued to hold up his bowl. Ping shook her head and gave him two more dumplings. She then prepared a small bowl for her mother. As she climbed the stairs to take Yan her lunch, she took in the sight of a very shabby old man at the table, gulping down his dumplings. When he finished, he wiped his face on his sleeve. Glancing left and right to make sure that no one was watching, he got up, ladled himself another bowl and sat down to eat again. Soon after, Ping heard the loud bang of the front door closing and she knew he had left.

An Chu didn't want to go out. He had woken up with the worst pounding headache he had ever had and couldn't move his left arm to reach the lamp next to him. He struggled to flip himself sideways and finally turned on the light. Everything in the room was a blur, with patches of light and strange shapes swimming in front of him. Did a blood vessel break in his eye? He was worried but he didn't want to go to the hospital and have it checked out. No doctors could help him. They only wanted money. He closed his eyes, turned off the light, and remained in bed. He probably would have stayed in bed for the entire day if Ping hadn't come into his room, but he was glad she did. It was time for him to get up and visit his mother. She often forgot to eat her lunch these days, and sometimes she ate twice. He needed to check on her. Besides, he didn't want her to be disappointed since she waited for him every day, rain or shine, in front of her building. His visit was often the highlight of her day.

He limped slowly forward. It took him a long time to cover the thirty feet between his house and the lane. He adjusted his walking stick with his right hand and wobbled on. First, he wanted to stop by a vendor who made delicious, roasted steamed buns that his mother liked.

By the time An Chu got what he had wanted, the winter sun was already making its way toward the horizon. The small package of buns weighed heavily on his wrist as he plodded his way forward. All of a sudden, he saw only darkness in front of his eyes and collapsed onto the sidewalk. As he lay on the frozen ground, he saw himself still walking toward his mother's house.

Hurry, I must hurry. Mother is still waiting for me. She is hungry.

He kept on walking, and walking, but he couldn't get to her. He tried hard to open his eyes and move his arms and legs, but he couldn't. A few passersby saw an old man lying on the sidewalk and came to help.

"Grandpa, Grandpa," they called, but he didn't respond. They decided to carry him into a nearby bank and placed him on a long wooden bench. At least it was warm inside. They tried to wake him up.

Ya Zhen stood outside her building, her arms folded, hands in her sleeves, feet stamping like an anxious little girl, and gleeful eyes full of hope. She was cold and hungry. She didn't know how late it was. Time didn't mean much to her these days, but she knew her son would come soon and bring her food. He always did, and she wanted to look out for him and catch him. A gust of wind howled at her, grabbed her hair willfully and tossed it into her face. She struggled to push it away from her eyes, her hands waving frantically in midair as if to shoo away that naughty natural force.

"Hi, grandmother," a young neighbor greeted her as she was leaving the building. "It's cold. Why don't you step inside?"

"My son is coming," Ya Zhen exclaimed eagerly with a big smile, her stomach growling. "He and his old beggar, they always bring me my lunch."

"Old beggar?" The young woman looked confused. She walked away.

An hour later, she came back to the building with an armload of groceries and found Ya Zhen still standing there, her lips purple and her body shivering.

"Hi, grandmother. It's cold. Let me take you inside." She extended her one available arm.

Ya Zhen moved away from her. She was determined to stay there and wait, her eyes stubbornly surveying the people passing by.

The young woman shook her head and walked into the building.

These days, it was hard for Ya Zhen to tell the beggar apart from her own son. Though she called him "Son," the now elderly man coming to her home daily bearing food looked a lot like the one who had arrived at her door and asked for food almost a lifetime ago. She was young then, barely nineteen, and about to have her first child. He had come to her to be fed and she fed him so he wouldn't die of starvation. He turned out to be not just a poor, homeless man, but a tricky, manipulative wandering soul who took advantage of her vulnerability and sympathy. How could she have known that it was all a trap? Instead of repaying her kindness with gratitude, he decided to ruin her entire family. The punishment she received for having cared for him couldn't have been crueler:

It was heart-wrenching to watch her poor, innocent baby grow up and trudge through his ill-fated life one misstep at a time until he finally became old and turned into an exact copy of the beggar himself!

Others might say that she was confused and crazy, but Ya Zhen knew that her mind was very clear and sane. She was right all along. How else could she have explained the transformation of her son, his resemblance now to the beggar whom he had never met, and the continuous disasters that had taken place in his life: the loss of the Sun family fortune, the endless poverty and hardship, the revolution, the prison sentence and the four granddaughters he had given her to end their family name and put shame on her face? Worse still, there was not a thing that she could have done to avert his fate and had to watch powerlessly until her son and the beggar finally fused into one.

Ya Zhen often wished that An Chu had not been so innocent and hardheaded, like she was when she was young. She wished that he just would have listened to what she had to say and learned to protect himself and his future. Sadly, the revolution had brainwashed him, making him believe all her words were only superstitious nonsense. Her poor boy. He had never lived a decent day in his life and as a mother, she knew that, ultimately, she was responsible for everything that had happened to him. She was now old and helpless. Ironically, they had swapped roles. She was the one who now depended on her old beggar-son to come and feed every day. He brought her food and called her "Mother," which made her uneasy. And yet she was looking forward to his visits and waited eagerly.

It was getting late. Ya Zhen didn't want to leave and seek shelter inside, even though she was no match for the Siberian air. The colder she felt, the harder she stamped her feet. Her hopeful, searching eyes grew dimmer and dimmer. Finally, she couldn't feel her arms and legs anymore. Even her lips were numb. Still, he didn't come. It was time for her to give up. Reluctantly, she turned around and walked back into her apartment. A great weariness came over her as she stumbled into her bed. She lay there in long, utter silence. Her disappointment gradually gave way to a memory that had played and replayed in her head so many times throughout her life. It took her back to the days right before An Chu was born when a beggar came day after day to be fed until one day, he failed to appear. Just like today. And then, he never came back. Her heart constricted, and she panicked at her own premonition: The end of this endless spell had finally arrived. Her son and the beggar were never coming back. The dark spirit had finally taken her son.

Four of Ya Zhen's five daughters gathered around her. The room was dark, and the air was heavy. Their mother had been bedridden for a week now. She wasn't eating or drinking anymore but lay motionless with her eyes closed. Only the gentle rise and fall of her chest showed that she was still there. They waited in silence for their eldest sister to arrive and bring them some news about An Chu.

At some point, they heard muffled footsteps in the hallway and soon after, a key being inserted into the lock of the front door. She had finally arrived. She walked straight toward them, her head hanging low, very low.

"How is Mother?"

"Still the same. We don't think she is conscious anymore."

"How is An Chu?"

"He took his last breath an hour ago," she said mournfully to the startled gasps of her sisters. "You must get to the hospital quickly if you still want to see him."

"*Shh!*" They motioned to keep her voice down.

"Why?" she asked. "Mother can't hear anything anymore." Still, she slightly lowered her voice. "Poor An Chu, his blood sugar was zero by the time he got to the hospital."

As the five of them huddled in the dark and quietly wept, two lines of tears silently streamed down from the corners of Ya Zhen's closed eyes.

An Chu, my son! Where is the beggar taking you? I cannot let him harm you and torment you anymore. I must free you from him so your next life will be a better one ...

She saw herself walking on a gray, murky path. Her pace was brisk, and her mind determined. Suddenly, she made out two, dark familiar figures ahead. Ya Zhen began to run. She had to catch them before it was too late ...

On her bed, shrouded under a darkening evening veil, Ya Zhen quietly released her last breath. No one heard it. No one saw that her final moment had arrived and was gone. All five sisters, blinded by grief, were consumed by the death of their brother. The darkness eased their pain and they stayed surrounded and enveloped by it until they couldn't see each other's faces anymore. One of them finally got up and turned on the small light on Ya Zhen's night table. They all looked toward their mother. The only visible sign of their mother's life was no longer there. Her chest was still, and her heart had stopped.

Ya Zhen had gone to chase after the beggar and her first-born son.

AFTERTHOUGHTS

THE CHANGES AFTER THE Cultural Revolution made it possible for me to attend Shanghai Institute of Foreign Languages and earn a bachelor's degree in English and English literature. I was honored to be the first college graduate from the Sun family. My success boosted my parents' confidence in life, but it did not change my father's beggar's fate.

After being released from detention, he was accused of more crimes that he had never committed—this time, supposedly, on behalf of the Cultural Revolution—by the same political chameleons who first prosecuted him for being a counter-revolutionary. He was convicted in a secret trial without the presence of his own lawyer, family members, or even a jury. His sentence was long and severe: Seven years in Shanghai Prison, where hard-core criminals who committed unspeakable crimes were sent.

It was double jeopardy for Father and our entire family. We did not see it coming and it hit us hard. Now that the revolution was finally over and we could see some light at the end of a very long tunnel, we thought we could finally live in peace. With my younger sister Min and me in college and bound to get good jobs, we would not be poor for much longer. Then, Father had to go to prison for another seven years. How could a person be punished for being for and against the same thing? It defied logic and troubled us.

We went through the next seven long years, not knowing whether my father, with his untreated heart condition, high blood pressure, diabetes, chronic hepatitis, rheumatism, and deflating spirit would ever make it out of prison alive.

Father served the full seven years of his prison term, drawing on all his strength to survive his unjust punishment and reach the end of his life's journey as a free but broken man. In an intriguing twist to his beggar's fate, he and Ya Zhen passed away within hours of each other. While he was a political prisoner, he missed two daughters' weddings, three daughters' university graduation ceremonies, and the birth of his first grandson. He never recovered from his political persecution but remained hopeful up to the very end of his life that his convictions could be overturned.

I love you, Father.

Mother learned to live in the dreams, hopes, and futures of her four daughters. Her religion, which had given her the strength to go on with her life, helped yet again in the absence of her husband. She had learned to accept whatever life unmercifully threw at her, be it political persecution, poverty, or pirates. In her dark, troubled world, there was little hope of a happy ending. She coped by letting the days slip away one at a time until an ordeal, a famine, a seven-year sentence, or a death sentence, was over.

At the age of fifty, Mother was already dwelling on her past. Without Father, she could not live in the present tense. On those endless hot summer days and nights, sitting side by side on a pair of bamboo chairs as we worked on a sewing or knitting project, Mother often retraced her life's journey with me. She invited me into every part of her personal story, which we visited, revisited, examined, and reexamined.

She often wondered what would have happened to her if her mother had never given her away and she had grown up with her real brothers, and sisters, or if her birth father had never perished in the Pacific Ocean, if her life path had never crossed Father's, or if she had never gotten married.

It was through her stories that I learned all about Mother, learned to respect and admire her, learned to share her cherished, yet unfulfilled, young dreams, and her many grievances when life let her down. Most of all, I came to realize that my mother was my heroine and my friend. I could share my hopes and dreams with her, hold her hands, and show her a brighter path where life can be a success story. Indeed, we became, by the truest definition, best friends.

I love you, Mother.

ACKNOWLEDGEMENTS

WHEN I WAS LITTLE, I envied my classmates who didn't go to school wearing patched clothes and worn-out shoes, and never had to worry about their next meal or whether their father was still alive. I often wondered why I had to be born into my family and given such a hard life. When I grew older, I realized that my life was special because it was molded by challenges, hardships, bitterness, and love, all of which made me strong. Now, I would never want to trade it for anyone else's in the world. I'm eternally grateful to my family, especially my mother, Yan, my father, An Chu, and my sisters, Ping, Min, and Wen. You all have made my life's journey a special one.

My deepest thanks to Guernica Editions and its tremendously talented staff and partners for bringing *Once Our Lives* into the world, especially editor-in-chief Michael Mirolla, publisher Connie McParland, and graphic designer Allen Jomoc Jr. for creating my book cover. You are a true artist! I am extraordinarily grateful to my editor, Sonia Di Placido, who worked on my manuscript and provided so many perceptive, sound, and sensitive suggestions to make the book the best it could be. Thank you all.

I am forever indebted to Senator John McCain, who helped secure my visa to the United States, to Uncle Jack Ho and Aunt Wai Kwan Wang, who welcomed me to America and supported my ambitions, and to Barbara and Carl Brown, who generously opened their home and their hearts to me during my years at the University of Arizona.

I want to thank Diane Margolin, the publisher of the *Santa Monica Star*, who for the past fifteen years has provided me a public writing platform in her paper and gave me a place to share my stories and refine my craft. I am grateful to Lisa Hagan and Carolyn Doyle Winter for having given me confidence in *Once Our Lives*. Thank you to Alexandros Plasatis, the editor of *the other side of hope* magazine for believing in my writing and publishing my first short story, "The Proposal." And loving thanks go to Dr. Michael Pisani, as well as Edna and Dr. Lewis Lipsitt, for lending me an ear and supporting my quest to see this work from the heart published. Michael and Lew, I wish you could be here to witness the birth of my book.

To Frank McCourt, Amy Tan, Maxine Hong Kingston, Lisa See, Gish Jen, and Helen Zia: You are my inspirations and my idols! To Zhu Fang Zhen and Jia Ray Liao, my honorary grandparents, I am eternally grateful for the life-changing free English lessons you gave to me when I was sixteen. To Margaret Wang, my professor at the Shanghai Institute of Foreign Languages, you opened my eyes to Shakespeare and the beauty of the written word.

I want to thank the many special people who encouraged and cheered me on over the years from New York, Washington, D.C., California, Maryland, Pennsylvania, China, Hong Kong, Morocco, India and Latvia, my beloved family members Keaton Stubis, Halley Stubis, Yi Dai, Angela Bamfield, Jeanne Fuchs, Ligita Stubis, and Dong Nan Dai, and my dear friends Anthony Taibi, Constance Kovar, Ye Faye, Jim Feldman, Pamela Levinson, Robin Ganzert and everyone at American Humane, Leah Yaw, Heather Heath, Gerry and Lindsey Biel, Kui Hui Wu, Meeta Charturvedi, Margaret Tsang, Christine Crosby, Christine Biddle, Xin Zhang, Rabbi Bruce Lustig, Sinaly Roy, Mary Seibel, and Vivian Wu, to name just a few.

To my readers, thank you all for walking down this very special memory lane with me. I hope you enjoyed the journey.

Last, but not least, thank you to my husband and my love, Mark Stubis, the most literate and literary man I know. I will never forget the many late-night, candle-lit hours we spent together, talking about and shaping this book to reflect the lives we once lived.

About the Author

QIN SUN STUBIS was born in the squalor of a Shanghai shanty-town during the Great Chinese Famine. Growing up during the Cultural Revolution, she quickly learned that words could thrill—and even kill. She saw her defiantly honest father imprisoned and tortured for using the wrong words. Shunned as political pariahs, Qin and her family sustained themselves with books and stories of adventure and past glory. With the help of a borrowed radio, an eccentric British teacher, and a fortuitous assignment as a library assistant, Qin discovered and fell in love with Western literature, committing to memory the strange but beautiful sounds of Keats, Wordsworth, and Lincoln.

But it was in bed late each night, after scouring local parks for enough firewood to cook the family's meal of rice, that Qin and her three small sisters heard the dramatic stories that make up this book. The four girls listened to their mother, an aspiring actress in the early days of Asian cinema, recount colorful tales of pirates, prophesies, fortunes won and lost, babies sold in opium dens, glorious lives and gruesome deaths. Based on actual experiences and family lore from Imperial to Post-Revolutionary times, these stories represent a wealth of colorful but little-known Chinese history.

Eventually, through sheer grit and perseverance, Qin won admission to the famed Shanghai Institute of Foreign Languages and graduated with a bachelor's degree in English and English Literature. With the help of family, friends, and U.S. Senator John

McCain, Qin was granted a visa for study abroad. She arrived in America with two suitcases and not much more. After winning several scholarships, she graduated with a master's degree and a profound love for her new adoptive country.

For the past 15 years, Qin has been a newspaper columnist and writes poems, essays, short stories, and original Chinese tall tales inspired by traditional Asian themes. Her writing is inflected with both Eastern and Western flavors in ways that transcend geography to touch hearts and reveal universal truths.

The only Chinese she knows who never learned to ride a bicycle, Qin now lives in the Washington, D.C. area with her husband, Mark, a classical pianist and media executive, and their children, Keaton and Halley. To learn more about Qin and her work, visit www.QinSunStubis.com.

The amazing true story of four generations of Chinese women and how they struggled to survive war, revolution, famine, and an eerie ancient superstition. The book takes the reader on an exotic journey filled with luxurious banquets, babies sold in opium dens, and kidnappings by pirates – seen through the eyes of a man for whom the truth would spell disaster and a lonely, beautiful girl with three identities.

A moving account of family lore and life, *Once Our Lives* is paradoxically both heartrending and heartening – heartrending in its depiction of this family's suffering and heartening in its depiction of the love that survives it all. I was riveted and moved.
—**Gish Jen**, award-winning author of *Thank you, Mr. Nixon*, featured in *The New Yorker's Best Books of 2022, NPR's Books We Love, Oprah's Favorite Books of 2022,* and *The Best American Short Stories of the Century*

This gripping memoir illuminates the full humanity of real people across four generations as they traverse the tectonics of modern China. A truly haunting tale of resilience, endurance and hope.
—**Helen Zia**, acclaimed author of *Last Boat Out of Shanghai: The Epic Story of the Chinese who Fled Mao's Revolution*

Qin Stubis combines oral traditions of mythologized family lore with the creative non-fiction writing of memoir. The reader experiences firsthand the vacillations of recent Chinese history.
—**Dr. Jennifer Rudolph**, Professor, Asian History, WPI, and co-author of *The China Questions*

A wonderful writer whose extraordinary ability and beautifully descriptive writing allow her to share her unusual experiences with readers in a uniquely powerful way.
—**Diane Margolin**, editor and publisher, the *Santa Monica Star*

Qin Sun Stubis is notable for the warmth of her writing and her ability to touch the hearts and minds of a wide variety of readers – a rare talent.
—**Christine Crosby**, founder and editorial director, *GRAND Magazine*

GUERNICA
World
EDITIONS

$21.95 U.S.A. / $25 CDN / £14.95 UK

ISBN 978-1-77183-796-5

9 781771 837965